Vanity Fare

Vanity Fare

A Novel of Lattes, Literature, and Love

MEGAN CALDWELL

WILLIAM MORROW
An Imprint of HarperCollins*Publishers*

To Scott,
who loves me even though he never says it

VANITY FARE. Copyright © 2013 by Megan Frampton. All rights reserved. Printed in the United States of America. No part of this book may be used or reproduced in any manner whatsoever without written permission except in the case of brief quotations embodied in critical articles and reviews. For information address HarperCollins Publishers, 10 East 53rd Street, New York, NY 10022.

HarperCollins books may be purchased for educational, business, or sales promotional use. For information please write: Special Markets Department, HarperCollins Publishers, 10 East 53rd Street, New York, NY 10022.

FIRST EDITION

Designed by Janet M. Evans

Library of Congress
Cataloging-in-Publication Data
has been applied for.

ISBN 978-0-06-218836-6

13 14 15 16 17 OV/RRD 10 9 8 7 6 5 4 3 2

ACKNOWLEDGMENTS

Thank you to all of these wonderful people who helped me in the course of writing this: my agent, Louise Fury; Myretta Robens; Kwana Minatee-Jackson; Clare Toohey; Robin Bradford; Carolyn Jewel; Emily Isaac from Trois Pommes Patisserie; my editor, Jessica McGrady; and my friends Eva Metalios, Lori Blumenthal, and Liz Maverick.

Also to Rhys, who inspired Aidan's character (even if he's moved on from *Pokémon*).

Extra thanks to Anne Clark, who joined me for wine and *Wuthering Heights,* which is when I first thought of the book.

Vanity Fare

Delicious. Inviting. You can't wait to savor every bite.

Are we talking about a book or a bakery item? At Vanity Fare, you don't have to make the choice. Our baked goods—Tart of Darkness, for example—are classics in their own right. Never stale, never half baked, our offerings are as fulfilling and worthwhile an indulgence as the best in fiction.

Pull up a comfy chair, grab a book from the shelves, and revel in the experience.

1

AIDAN WAS ESPECIALLY MUSHY THAT MORNING, CLINGING to me as I dropped him off at school.

"But, Mom, why can't I stay home with you?"

I sighed and patted his shoulder as we walked. "Because you have to go to school, honey, it's part of knowledge, and knowledge—"

"—is power, I know," he finished. "It's just so boring!"

I waved at another parent who was shepherding an equally sad child—a classmate of Aidan's—into the school building. "So is moving boxes, and that's all you'd be able to do if you quit school now. Besides, if you stayed home with me, all we'd do is drink coffee and read. That's no fun, right?"

He wrinkled his nose. "No, that's boring." He heaved a six-year-old's sigh. "Okay, but can we do something fun after?"

"Yeah, fun after school," I repeated. "I love you." I leaned down and kissed him, and he wrapped his arms around me in a tight squeeze.

He released me, and swung the door open—all by himself!—and headed into the school, turning so I could blow him one last kiss. He returned it, the sweetheart, and my chest felt tight with emotion.

I wore one of those goofy mom smiles on the way home.

That was worth it all. *He* was worth it all. And he was why I had to get over myself. He thought I was pretty great, and I trusted his opinion.

I went up the stairs to the apartment, determined to figure out just what the hell I was doing with my life. Besides planning postschool activities.

It sure didn't help when his father threw spokes in my wheels, a wrench in my works, and some third thing I was just too upset to recall at the moment.

I picked the phone up on the third ring, my hands shaking from what I'd just seen on the news feed scrolling across the bottom of the TV.

The caller ID told me who it was before I even answered, so he didn't get a chance to even say hello.

"So, were you going to tell me about Blumenthal Jackson or did you just think I'd miss it because Aidan was watching the Yu-Gi-Oh marathon or something?"

The bastard didn't reply. I heard him breathing, though.

"I saw it on CNN." I had to keep myself from shrieking into the phone. "Your company? Collapsed? Ring a bell, Hugh?"

"I didn't know myself." Wait. He actually sounded like he didn't. But he was a lawyer, he was used to lying well. "Until today." His voice was worn out. Shredded.

I felt a momentary pang of sympathy, the way I used to when he had a tough day at the office. And then I remembered what he'd done, and how he'd left.

"What, you had no idea? Come on, Hugh." I walked to the window and looked out on the street below: nannies hustling their charges to the local Tot Time at the library, a few delivery trucks double-parked, and a group of Catholic girls in their short, pleated skirts walking slowly up the street.

Normal life in Brooklyn. Which I loved, but would have to leave if I didn't do something about it. Because Hugh sure as hell wasn't going to be able to. Which his next words proved.

"I won't be able to send money next month." His next few sentences sounded as if they were shot out of a cannon. I could barely keep up. "For the rent. Aidan's health insurance is okay for a while, but you'll be dropped from the policy in thirty days. I'll try to get situated as soon as possible. I'm sorry, Molly."

There was a silence, and I heard Hugh swallow.

"What about COBRA? And there must be something that's being done for the employees, right?" Hugh had always left the bookkeeping details to me, since he was too busy. Maybe he'd forgotten.

"Um, well, I didn't tell you, but about four months ago I went freelance for the firm. It was either that or they were going to let me go entirely, and I needed the job."

Oh. He hadn't forgotten. In fact, he'd managed to do some of his own bookkeeping. That was newsworthy in itself.

He continued, "So my benefits were cut, then. I've been paying for your insurance myself."

I swallowed as it hit me.

"So what you're saying is"—I closed my eyes and felt my jaw clamp—"that not only is your company going belly-up, but it's not even your company?"

I didn't think it could get worse than it had six months ago when he'd left.

"Yeah, well, I didn't want to make things any tougher for

you than they were"—he paused, and I heard him take another deep breath—"and I thought the firm would be okay in a few months, but . . ."

"Where the hell does that leave us, Hugh? You know, me and more importantly, your son?"

"I'm sorry." He hung up. Running away from the problem, as usual.

I put the phone down. "Yeah, I'm sorry, too." Sorrier than you'd ever know.

CNN was still on, detailing the fallout: *Top story tonight is the collapse of venerated Wall Street investment group Blumenthal Jackson. According to the New York district attorney's office, the company's chief executives will be charged with violating the RICO Act. Investors stand to lose up to fifty billion dollars. More as the story dev—*

I flipped the channel, not wanting to hear any more of the details.

VH1. Safe choice. I just needed a minute to process it. Then I could figure out what the hell I was going to do.

A commercial. How come my life wasn't like the movies, where an appropriately themed song would just be starting as I turned the channel on? I'd sit down and my expression would soften, and I'd nod my head.

Oh, geez. Be careful what you wish for: "I will survive."

Yeah, thanks for spelling it all out for me.

I'm afraid and petrified right now, Gloria.

If this moment were any more ironic, it'd be a hipster movement, replete with coy T-shirts and rainbowed unicorns. Gaynor herself was wearing more glitter than a drag queen, while a tiny spandex-clad girl spun on roller skates.

I plopped down on the couch. Six months ago, it wouldn't have crossed my mind to notice how so many songs—scratch that, *all* of them—were about love or falling in love or losing a love.

Hugh had never said he loved me.

I was an idiot not to realize that meant something. I sure as hell knew it now.

I had to get a job. Fast. *Now.* Yesterday.

After Aidan went to sleep that night clutching his stuffed Pikachu, I changed into my sweatpants and padded out to the living room in my bare feet. Damn, I needed to give myself a pedicure. I hadn't had one since the fancy wedding Hugh and I had attended the previous summer. Hugh had told a story about his administrative assistant and some Wite-Out that had made everyone howl, me included.

That night, we'd slow-danced under the stars to "Always and Forever," like we were in high school.

It galled me that he had already been cheating on me, even then, and I was too naïve to recognize the signs. At one point, he got a call on his cell phone and dashed to the parking lot to take it. He'd come back about ten minutes later, shrugging apologetically.

I sat down at the dining room table with a notebook and the classified section. I tried very hard to ignore the cover of the latest romance novel I was devouring, a world where husbands didn't leave and insurance didn't run out. I picked up an animal cracker, a hump-less camel, from the leftovers in Aidan's lunch and munched on it to buy some time while I thought.

I was going to make a list of what I could do. And *would*

do, I reminded myself sternly. After all, lists were only good if one actually was able to check off the items on the list. I had plenty of unchecked lists in my life. First one, of course, was the list where I had written "marry someone and stay with them until one or both of you keeled over."

Unchecked.

How about the one that said "establish a career in your thirties so you can be comfortably ensconced in it in your forties and never have to worry about paying the bills again?"

Unchecked.

Mm, how about "have the possibility of ever having sex again?"

Definitely unchecked.

I glared at the notebook as if it were its fault I was so . . . *unchecked*. This whole finding-a-job thing was a pain in the ass. I thought I had more time. A month. Two. I had poked around and sent some résumés out, but between cursing Hugh's name and taking care of Aidan, I honestly hadn't done enough.

I'd never thought I'd have to.

Six years ago when Aidan was born, Hugh had supported my decision to stay home. The prospect of entering the workforce again was terrifying, maybe even more than being a divorced mom. But if we were to recover from Hugh's latest mess, I'd have to.

I wrote at the top of the page: *Find a job.* I leaned back and stared at the paper.

What kind of job could I get?

Before Aidan, I'd done marketing for an online start-up. There were so many problems with having that as your prime résumé skill: First of all, marketing is the most nebulous term imaginable. A guy prancing around the block in a sandwich board could say he did marketing. Second, having worked at an online start-up was practically as bad as admitting you wore culottes back in the 1970s. Which I also did.

And third, I hadn't worked full-time in six years.

And I was forty years old.

Not to mention cranky, tired, stubborn, and mad as hell.

But they would only discover that if they hired me.

Which they wouldn't, because my résumé read like crap.

Okay, Molly, I told myself, *focus.*

I had a degree in English literature. That and experience doing marketing for an online start-up would get me an interview at Starbucks.

Heck, at least I'd never run out of coffee again.

Focus. Caffeine should not be the center of the universe.

I rose and went down the hall to peek on Aidan, whose head was smothered underneath his blue Power Rangers bedspread. I uncovered him, kissed his smooth, sweet-smelling cheek, and padded back to where my doom, er, *list* lay waiting for me. Was it wrong I wished I could set it on fire?

Thank goodness the phone rang.

"Hello?"

"Hi, sweetie." Suddenly it felt like a couple of weights had been lifted off my shoulders.

"Hi, hon."

At least I had chosen my friends wisely. Keisha had moved from Brooklyn a little over a year ago to California, but we still talked as much as we had when we first met in college. Maybe even more.

I tucked the phone up to my ear and grabbed the throw from the floor. "Hold on, I'm tucking in," I said.

I lay down on the couch, feeling the groove where my body had imprinted itself. Apparently, I had lain in this position a lot. I pulled the blanket up to my chin, relishing the cozy warmth of it against my skin.

"Okay. Settled."

"You all right?" Keisha asked, a soft tone to her voice.

She always knew. I sighed. "No, not really. Hugh's company collapsed." I stared up at the ceiling. Funny how widening one's eyes and staring at one spot was what people always did when trying not to cry, and it never worked. I gulped. "Which means he can't send money anymore."

"What about Sylvia?" Her tone dripped with disdain.

I laughed. "I don't think *she's* going to send me money, either."

"Ha, ha. No, I mean, I wonder if she's going to walk if he's not pulling down the big bucks anymore."

Keisha and I had speculated more times than I cared to remember about just what kind of person Hugh's new girlfriend was. Morbid speculation on my part, and rampant curiosity, I guess, on hers. Anyway, we'd decided she was smart enough to suss out Hugh was vulnerable, but not smart enough to realize he usually had to rely on others to help him through the rough spots. I'd had a lawyer friend do a Lexis-Nexis search on her and discovered her age (younger), her address (tonier), and her profession (more professional). Now we were taking bets on when she'd wise up and dump him.

"I dunno," I said. "Hugh can be pretty sweet when he's needy."

Keisha's moment of silence spoke of her derision more than her words would have.

"All right," I admitted, raising my hands in a gesture of defeat. Not that she could see me. "I fell for his 'find my keys' puppy look. Anyway, enough about him. What am I going to do?" I tried to keep my voice steady.

"Is Starbucks hiring?" Keisha replied in a matter-of-fact voice.

"Fuck you," I said in my most outraged tone. I didn't think it would fool her for a moment.

It didn't. She laughed. "Well, you do have that English degree. You could teach."

"Don't you need more than a B.A.?"

"Not to substitute teach, I don't think. It could help you out for a little while. Maybe some tutoring?"

"In what, romance novels?"

"You *could* finally put that English literature degree to good use."

"Like the way you're using your film degree?"

"Ouch, that's cold." Keisha had moved back to Cottonwood, California, to take over managing her father's art cinema when he had gotten too old and tired to do it all by himself. She loved her job, even if it was as much about Goobers as Godard, so my teasing her wasn't nearly as mean as it sounded.

The idea took hold in my brain. "I *was* pretty good at figuring out the leitmotifs and recurrent imagery and all that mumbo. Although teaching probably pays about as much as Starbucks." I began to feel a ribbon of excitement thread through my body.

"You'd probably like the clientele a little more. And the hours would be good for Aidan."

"It's an idea. A damn good idea, actually. Glad I thought of it."

She snorted. "Why do you have to pay that Dr. Lowell anyway? Just send me a wad of cash each week and I'll hear all your problems."

"You already hear them for free."

She gave an exaggerated sigh. "You're right. Good thing I like you so much."

"Bye, hon. Love you."

I hung up and found my latest book—*Love's Scoundrel,* or something like that, and headed to bed, stopping in to check on my son one last time.

And I swore, as I kissed Aidan's fragrant cheek, I would not let anything I wanted go unchecked again.

Green Eggs and Ham Croissant

Food is a fancy a coogle may coggle,
And this snack's no match for the
    zeep-wearing schmoggle,
But if you want taste in,
And a bit of green egg paste in,
This one's the one you'll want to
    partake in.

2

THE NEXT MORNING, I WAS STANDING IN MY BEDROOM IN MY underwear, contemplating the future.

Which right now meant pants. But not jeans. My therapist, Dr. Lowell, was always urging me to take a step forward, and for me that meant no jeans.

Jeans were the go-to pant of the Brooklyn Moms generation. Brooklyn Moms were usually formerly fabulous women who'd given up any semblance of fabulousness to stay at home with their little darlings. Brooklyn Moms read literary fiction, didn't care how bad their asses looked in high-waisted Levi's, and thought putting on makeup was bowing to the cosmetics proletariat.

I was a Brooklyn mom, but I wouldn't be a *Brooklyn Mom*. My ass would thank me later.

If today was the first day of the rest of my life, I wasn't going to do it wearing jeans. Not that I *blamed* the jeans.

I could have tried a little harder to keep Hugh, not accept the role as boring wife and mom. I could have surprised him at the door wearing only Saran Wrap, like I read in that forbidden book at the library back in the 1970s. But I was usually too cold to wear so little, and Saran Wrap was not a good look for my thighs.

And Hugh was at fault, too, even before he cheated on me. *He* certainly didn't try very hard. As soon as he got his JD, he became Mr. Big Lawyer and seemed almost embarrassed to have a Brooklyn Mom as his wife. So instead of talking to me, Mr. Run Away from Problems had gone out and had an affair.

And now there was no money. Not even for jeans.

I was saved from my musings by the phone. I sprawled across the much-too-big-now bed to grab it from the nightstand.

"Hello?"

"Hi, Molly. It's John. I've got something for you."

John was a friend from college who was friends with both me and Hugh. Now he ran a marketing company and hired me to do occasional copyediting on his medical journal clients. A job. Which usually meant cash!

"I've got an assignment for you. Something more involved than what you usually do for me." He continued, "Can you come in today to discuss it? I want to give you some samples of the work, or else I'd just tell you over the phone." I tried to figure out if I could make it in and out by the time I had to pick Aidan up. I checked my watch, hopped off the bed, and walked to the closet, opening the door wide.

"Sure," I replied, pulling my shoulder up to hold the phone so I could start going through the clothes. "Can you give me a clue?"

He laughed. "Let's just say it's one of your favorite things. Is an hour okay? I know you have to be back by three."

"An hour. I'll be there." I hung up and stared at the closet, the phone dangling from my hand. The black pants? Or maybe the black pants? Hm, how about the black pants?

God, there must be at least ten pairs in there, and I hadn't worn one of them in over a year.

I tossed the phone on the bed and pulled one of them out, resolving to wear the remaining nine by this time next year. A woman's got to have goals, after all.

At last I was ready. My black pants were on, my black sweater was on, my makeup (black eyeliner, natch, although my lipstick was red. I had thrown out my black lipstick when I gave up the Mohawk) had even gone on without a fight. I was ready.

I looked at myself in the mirror, checking for obvious damage. Besides the smattering of gray threading through my black hair, I didn't look too bad. I might even be so bold as to say I looked pretty good. I wasn't fat, I wasn't too wrinkly, and my eyebrows were as close to perfect as I could get them, at least without fifty dollars' worth of hair removal help. If I squinted and turned to the side, I really did look like Sela Ward, like Keisha kept telling me, only minus the fame and the acting career. Maybe there was hope for me after all.

Ignoring the seductive raised script of *Love's Scoundrel* beckoning from my nightstand, I grabbed a copy of Henry James's *The Ambassadors* off the bookshelf as I walked out the door. If I wanted to do any teaching at all, I had to refresh my memory of the classics, right?

The wind whipped through my coat as I walked the few blocks to the subway. Although it was midday, there were loads of people walking the streets. What did they do to make money? Were they all independently wealthy? Maybe some of them were writers. Maybe one of them had written

Love's Scoundrel. Maybe she was the Mom-jeans-wearing woman holding an enormous cup of coffee from the super-pricy café up the block.

After I passed her, a man almost bumped into me but hopped the curb right before impact. He wasn't wearing a jacket, but had on a megaheavy fisherman's sweater, a cranberry-red cashmere scarf, and a matching hat perched on top of his dreadlocks. He apologized to me in a lovely Caribbean accent, then walked quickly ahead, stopping to buy a Styrofoam cup full of the mysterious hot liquid the tiny Hispanic women sold on the street. One of these days, I was going to buy some myself and figure out what it was.

I loved Brooklyn.

Once on the subway, I avoided having to delve right into James by reading the subway advertisements ranged along the walls.

There were ads for a series on HBO that was "Compelling. Breathtaking. Beautiful."

If they made a show of my life, it'd be "Boring. Weepy. Forty." Fuck, even *I* wasn't interested in that, and it was my life. Another ad caught my eye: "What would it be like to make a difference in a child's life?"

I got up, ignoring the furtive glances sent my way by my fellow passengers. Ever since 9/11, people—that is, New Yorkers—had been friendlier, but also much more suspicious of out-of-the-ordinary behavior. Giving up your seat in a full subway car was definitely out of the ordinary.

I went over to the ad. Its plain, simple font declared "Become an NYC Teaching Fellow, and teach in a low-performing public school while getting your master's degree.

Applicants receive a full salary as well as subsidies toward your degree."

An answer to my prayers, and I hadn't even been praying. Not for *that,* at least—if Hugh suddenly gouged his own eyes out, *then* I'd know my prayers had been heard.

I pulled out a pen I'd jammed into my purse and scribbled the URL down on the back of a Citibank statement. Twenty-four hours ago I would have been grateful just to have a job with free coffee. Maybe there was actually something I could do that I'd enjoy. That would be a career.

Plus John had an assignment important enough to necessitate an in-person meeting, a deviation from our normal e-mail correspondence.

What kind of job was it? It certainly couldn't be anything remotely like what I had edited for him before: medical equipment journals with meaty (ugh, literally) advertorials on the proper procedure on removing a kidney (so much easier with the Kidney-You-Not 3000!) or the ten best ways to distinguish vaginal warts from herpes with a do-it-yourself kit, no less.

I got off at the Twenty-third Street stop and trudged up the few blocks to John's office, feeling virtuous because I passed Starbucks without stopping for a venti. Or an application.

John was in the reception area, a nicely appointed room in soft, muted colors, the kind with names that would be better in a sandwich: avocado, eggplant, mustard. He looked up as if he had been waiting for me, although I was guessing he might have been motivated by the receptionist. She had dark red hair, which she was tossing with insouciance as I walked in. Her emerald-colored blouse was so low cut I could see a light dusting of freckles on her chest, which was as impressive as her insouciance.

"Ah, there you are, Molly," John said, giving his receptionist one last look. She lowered her lids, then gave me a sidelong glance that said "Yeah, I'm hot, you're not."

Yeah, well, at least I'm not spotted like an overripe banana.

John had always been the most fashionable of Hugh and my college friends, and since his business had taken off, he had allowed himself the luxury of looking good in an expensive, pampered metrosexual kind of way. Today he was wearing jeans—definitely not Levi's—even I knew cost well into the triple digits, and a boldly patterned dress shirt with its tails hanging out. His short brown hair was cut just so, and his five o'clock shadow was perfect for noon.

"Come on in here," John said, propelling himself off the desk and walking farther into the office. He took my coat and hung it up on a silver hook, then tossed a piece of paper onto the desk and poked his head over one of the cubicles. "Hey, Matt, can you fax that agreement back?" He looked at me and jerked his head toward his office. "Make yourself comfortable. I'll get coffee. Milk, one sugar, right?"

I nodded. There was a special place in heaven reserved for people who remembered how you took your coffee. I sat down in the chair on the left, facing John's desk. It was made of glass and tubular steel, the kind of desk fancy male executives had in the movies. In the movies, though, they never had reams of paper spread out all over it, or a fuzzy, waving gremlin wearing an I ♥ MYRTLE BEACH T-shirt. John had kept some of his roots, at least.

"Here you go." John set the coffee cup on the edge of the desk. I picked it up and took a sip. John reached down to the floor and pulled some sort of pastry from a bag. Even from across the desk, I could smell the butter. He tore it in half and handed me the bigger piece.

I took a bite of the pastry. Double mmm. It was light, flavorful, and had just enough cinnamon. I wasn't sure what it was, some sort of Danish muffin hybrid—a Duffin? A Manish?—but I knew I was going to eat every bite. And, if I wasn't careful, I might end up licking the bag, too.

"Well." John leaned back in his chair, still holding on to his uneaten pastry. If he didn't eat it soon, I was going to lunge across the desk and snatch it with my teeth.

"I have a new client. A company that needs something a little different from our usual expertise." John was using his Corporate America voice, a language I had mastered about as well as I had being able to tell my local Chinese restaurant that I did not want green peppers in my hot spicy tofu. Which is to say not at all.

I almost dropped the whatever-it-was in my lap, especially since I had just discovered an escaped crumb resting on my upper lip. Gotcha! No crumbs allowed. Not since the bastard walked out on me, at least.

"So what kind of client is it?" I tried to look as if my most pressing thought wasn't how to wrest the remainder of the pastry away from him.

"The bakery that makes what you're eating is my client."

I was confused. "Is this some sort of pharmaceutical thing?" Because, ugh, if it was I didn't want to know what it cured.

Reading John's usual clients' work was enough. I didn't want to actually ingest it.

He laughed, waving the food around in his hand. My eyes followed it like a tracking device.

"No, a bakery. Just a bakery. It's going to open in a couple of months, and the owner-chef is a new client. I don't know if I told you, but I've got a new partner. She'll be the lead on the project, but she needs help, someone who's clever with words and knows a little bit about how we do things here. So of course I thought of you."

John poked the fuzzy gremlin with a fancy fountain pen, not meeting my eyes. I wondered what his new partner was like.

"Me as the point person? I haven't done copywriting before, not really."

"The rest of my staff just got a huge project thrown on them, so I don't have anyone else who can. I know you can do this—you did press releases at your last job, and you've done some marketing copy on a few of those medical journals." He waved his hand toward his wall. "And I'd like to have someone on the project I can *trust*." He eyed me meaningfully as he popped the remaining piece in his mouth.

"Okay," I said slowly. "But tell me more about your partner. I didn't know you had taken one on."

John ran his finger around the inside of his collar. "Her name is Natalie Duran."

"Like Duran Duran?" *Is she hungry like the wolf?*

He gave an absentminded bobble of his head. "She was at OM." He said the name as if I would recognize it, so I nodded my head in agreement, as if I actually knew. "But she wanted to branch out and do some more interesting work. She brought several clients over with her, we'll be expanding beyond medical marketing, and this project is the first new one we've taken on.

"What I need from you," he continued, fastening me with what I could only surmise was his Businessman's Stare, "is to make sure the work gets done, and done well. Natalie is a hotshot, she hasn't worked in a smaller firm before, and I want to make sure we don't screw this up."

"So . . . ," I said, tracing the curves of the chair with my finger, "you want me to keep an eye on her? And what, report back to you?"

He smiled in relief. "Exactly."

"That's spying, John." I felt myself start to sweat. "And she's your partner. If you don't trust her, why are you working with her?"

"Because," he said, leaning back into his chair and crossing his legs, "she can land the clients I've only dreamed of before. She brought Simon in, for example." He paused. "It pays five thousand dollars."

Oh, well, then. For that kind of money, I'd change my name to Molly Hari.

"Okay," I agreed. "Thank you. I'll take it. So tell me more."

"Simon—that's the owner—is opening a bakery near the New York Public Library, the big one on Forty-second Street. He wants to do something relating to both the library and his store. He needs a *hook*."

"Like, to drag people in?" I was being deliberately obtuse. It gave me time to think.

John grimaced in that "you're being deliberately obtuse" kind of way. "No. To get people talking about his shop. I think you can help Natalie with the copy—you're the worst punster I've ever met, and I mean that in the nicest possible way. She'll do the big-picture concepting, of course, but the fleshing-out stuff will be you."

I sat back, finishing the rest of the coffee. "Sounds do-able," I said in a hesitant voice.

"Great. Look, I'll just buzz Simon and set up a meeting. He's very hands-on, he wants to be intimately involved with the project." He leaned back in his chair. "Simon was the pastry chef at The Modern, he's appeared on some of those cooking shows, too. The buzz is growing on him, and this shop will be so much more than a bakery."

"And what about Natalie? When will I meet her?"

He scowled. Was it just me, or was he not at all pleased with his new partner?

"She's out on calls this afternoon. I'd rather you met Simon alone for the first time. I'll bring Natalie up-to-date later."

No, it wasn't just me. There was something fishy about John's new partner.

I looked around John's office while he punched in the phone number. He had the magazine covers of his various projects framed and hanging on the wall. My favorite had to be "Have a Heart," published by a company that made artificial hearts. Although I also appreciated "Playing Footsie," put out by the National Podiatrists' Association.

John hung up the phone just as I was envisioning what "Intestinal Fortitude" or "Braindead" would cover.

"Great news! I got Simon on his cell, and he's actually right down the block. He'll be here in a few." John checked his watch, an overly large, overly masculine timepiece strapped to his hairy wrist. "You've got at least half an hour before you have to be back on the subway, right?"

I nodded and took a deep breath. Work, of sorts. Money, of green.

John checked his BlackBerry for a few minutes, then sat back in his chair. He looked hesitant. "I want to let you in on what Natalie's done thus far." He scowled. "Not very much, actually. Not that I want either of us to let Simon know that."

I nodded encouragingly. "Of course not."

He sighed and planted his elbows on his desk. "So far she's come up with Books and Bread as a name."

We both frowned. He continued, "But she's good enough that if she really concentrates, she'll be able to nail something."

That sounded unpleasant. As did the name she'd thought of.

A male voice down the hall conjured up much pleasanter visions. He had a British accent, the upper-crust, devil-may-care Hugh Grant kind of accent. The kind that made me a little weak at the knees, so I was glad I was sitting down.

"John, just give me a sec while I flirt with this lovely lady out here." Only when he said it, it sounded as if he had just said something much naughtier. Judging by her husky laugh, the redhead agreed. And that voice came from someone who made those pastries?

There had to be something wrong with him. I held my breath as the door opened.

He walked into the room, and I just about fainted. He was gorgeous.

He had curly chestnut brown hair, the kind that must've trailed romantically in a breeze, green eyes—*green*, not hazel—and a dimple. I was surprised I didn't faint, actually. He was tall and slim with a very British detachment to his walk.

And he was wearing a black turtleneck sweater and black flat-front slacks, and he had on faux Beatles boots: shiny, pointed, and dangerous.

Why *wasn't* I fainting? I was older than I thought.

The God spoke.

"You must be John's secret weapon," he said, making *that* sound much dirtier than it should. It simply was not fair that he looked like that, sounded like that, and apparently could bake like that. He held out his hand and smiled. "I'm Simon."

"Hi," I said, staring up into his face. Green eyes. Brilliant, emerald green eyes. Man, did I love green eyes. Hugh's eyes were brown, a fact I'd always secretly resented.

Another man had apparently walked in while I was gawking but stayed just inside the door, leaning his back against the wall. Simon gestured toward the guy without looking at him.

"This is Nick. He represents our American investors."

Nick nodded. Ah, the quiet, forbidding type.

John rushed into the conversation. "Simon and Nick are in from London, from Simon's home office. Of course, Nick is from here, but Simon—"

"I'm from over there," Simon finished, taking a seat next to me. He swung one long, lean leg over the other. I brought my finger up to my mouth to make sure I wasn't drooling. I wasn't, but I did find another crumb. I stuck my finger in my mouth to lick it off, hoping he wouldn't notice.

He did. He smiled, a knowing, sensual smirk that made his eyes crinkle up at the corners.

"You like my baked goods, then?" Simon's eyes glowed.

He definitely knew what he was saying. A slow heat began to build in my stomach. It wasn't the coffee.

"Yes," John answered, "she was practically licking the bag."

Simon's lids dropped halfway down, and he swept his gaze from my feet to my head. "Was she? I would've liked to see that."

Oh. Dear. He was . . . *flirting* with me. It had been so long, I wasn't sure, but it certainly felt like flirting.

The other man, Nick, chose that moment to speak up. Good thing, since I wasn't quite ready for the flirting thing. "We've only got fifteen minutes," he said, in a brusque voice. He definitely had an American accent, a glaring, flat contrast to Simon's lustrous tone. "So perhaps we can talk about what we came here to talk about?"

Well. That was certainly to the point. The three of us all straightened in our respective chairs, as though he had blown a bugle wake-up call or something.

Simon waved one hand toward Nick. "Go ahead then, killjoy. Tell them." He rolled his eyes at me, and I tried not to giggle. Or imagine him naked.

Nick didn't react to his boss's—it was clear this was a hierarchical relationship—goading. "The store will be near the main library. Diagonally across from the Nat Sherman cigar store. Do you know it?"

Smooth skin covering lean, sinewy muscles. Maybe a matching dimple on Simon's . . . I cleared my throat, hoping my thoughts weren't showing on my face. I glanced over at Nick.

"I've been there, to the library. Not to the Nat Sherman store, though. I don't smoke."

Brilliant, Molly. How about just announcing "Hi, I'm a dork, and I'm not used to speaking to people."

John interrupted before I could further stick my foot in my mouth. "Obviously the area is prime for Simon's business. There are tons of tourists, office workers, loads of people traveling through there every day." Nick snorted somewhere behind me.

Yes, New York City holds a lot of people. In other breaking news, Brad Pitt is rumored to be handsome, and scholars reveal William Faulkner was wordy.

"But I have to have more than just fantastic baked goods, don't I, Molly?" Simon smiled, unleashing the full effect of his dimples on me. Maybe he should just stand outside handing out samples. That'd get at least half of the city's population—the female half—to buy his stuff.

No wonder he was a rising star—I bet few men who looked like this could bake like that.

I reached back into the annals of my brain to try and locate that part that used to know how to do marketing. "Yes, in that high traffic area you have to have something that'll pop, so people will choose your store over anybody else's." That sounded pretty good, if I did say so myself. Thank God for buried memory.

"Precisely," Nick answered in that dry voice. "You want people to buy your products." The way he said it sounded like how I explained things to Aidan. He must really think I was dumb.

I made an attempt to rally. "Of course you do." I almost added "duh!" just so he'd get the point. "And you want to tie the shop into the library in some way?"

Simon waved his hand. "Yes, since my pastries are a work of art. Like a Gauguin or a Picasso."

It probably wasn't the time to point out that those guys painted pictures and didn't write books.

Simon continued. "With you and Natalie on the team, I'm certain we'll have fantastic results."

I heard another snort in the distance. Well, at least Nick's disdain was consistent.

John interposed, his Corporate America voice in full effect. "Molly will need some time to get up to speed. I'll be filling her in on the details. And, of course, Natalie will be the point person. She's already come up with some fabulous ideas. We can guarantee a fantastic presentation."

"We'll need more than your assurances." Nick's expression was as cold as his words.

"Of course they'll come up with something fantastic." Simon's tone allowed for no disagreement. The thought crossed my mind that he was probably accustomed to getting exactly what he wanted, all of the time.

Nick unfurled himself from the wall and walked out without another word. Simon followed, giving me one last saucy look as he left. Beauty and the Beast.

I turned to John, whose face immediately assumed a soothing expression.

"It's nothing you can't do, Molly. It's just writing some lively copy, after Natalie generates the look and feel. You can do that."

I could do this. I just had to let my imagination run un-checked. And not about the interesting positions my new sort-of employer and I could get into. He sure was beautiful. Arrogant, but beautiful.

"Molly?" John's sharp tone pulled me from all sorts of visions that Supposedly Steady Moms should not be having. "I've got some basic marketing copy books I can let you bor-row. You'll be meeting with Natalie as soon as I can find out when she's free. You'll do fine, Molly," he said in a reassuring tone. He rose, and I did, too, smoothing my pants with my sweaty palms.

John handed me a beige canvas bag filled with a menacing-looking three-ring binder. It was so large it bowed the sides of the bag out. I slung it over my shoulder and it landed with a loud *whump!* on my back.

"Thanks, John, really." This money meant Aidan wouldn't be gnawing off his own hand, even if his mother had to pretend to be the marketing Mata Hari for a month.

"Good-bye, Molly. Say hi to Aidan for me," John said as he kissed my cheek.

I wondered just how intimidating Natalie was. Or how long it would be before Simon suspected I was a fraud. I knew Nick had already made up his mind.

I wondered just what I was getting into.

I wondered just what I would get out of it.

I didn't stop to wonder at the possibility I would fail. I couldn't afford to.

A Room of One's Scone

Take a moment—two moments, even—for yourself. Remember how it felt, how it smelled, how it tasted to relax for five minutes with a deliciously creamy pastry just perfect for pairing with a cup of tea. Remember what it was like before you did things like count carbohydrate grams and obsess over a teaspoon of butter?

This scone will bring it all back to you. It's light, flaky, and packed with raisins and cinnamon, dusted with a delicate layer of spun sugar.

Okay, not spun, just regular, but it'll taste like spun sugar. If you knew what that was.

It's a pastry worth locking yourself in your room over. A place to ponder the greatness of life, of you, while you eat every single crumb.

3

"GIVE IT TO ME."

Dr. Lowell held her hand out, offering no chance to refuse. I leaned forward on the sofa, feeling the butter-soft brown leather squish under the weight of my thighs. I thrust the paper toward her, then scooted back to wait as she adjusted her half-moon glasses.

I didn't want to watch her read it, so I looked around her office, noting the framed degrees rising vertically up her bone-colored wall. So many degrees. So many ways to analyze just how screwed up a person was.

She cleared her throat, darted a mischievous glance at me, and began reading. Out loud. Dear God.

THINGS THAT ARE BETTER WITHOUT HUGH

- Being able to watch teen movies like *What a Girl Wants* with Colin Firth without having to change the channel quickly when he comes into the room
- Not having to watch SportsCenter
- Being able to read trashy romance novels without having to see a raised eyebrow

- Not having to watch any *Sports Illustrated* swimsuit issue cover model search

- Getting on the computer when I want to

- Being able to go to sleep when I want

- No wet spot

- No little shaving whiskers in the sink

- All the mess is my mess

- Three words: more closet space

She chuckled, folding the paper and holding it out to me. "Do you mind if I keep this?" Her brown eyes were gleaming behind her glasses. At least someone found me amusing.

I shook my head. "No, of course not."

"It sounds like you're regaining your sense of humor."

"A little bit," I admitted in a cautious tone. "Although Hugh called a couple of nights ago."

Her eyes narrowed. "What did he want?" Her tone was as frosty as the bitter February day outside. Bless her little therapist's heart.

I told her.

Her eyes widened and she shifted forward in her chair. "So what will you do now?"

I gave a rueful laugh. "Isn't that why I pay you the big bucks? To tell me?"

She smirked in reply. "No, Molly, you pay me the big bucks to help *you* figure out what to do." Why did I have to find the one therapist in New York City who was as snarky as I was?

I exhaled. "Well, I don't think I can pay you any size bucks, at least not until I figure this stuff out. My insurance will run out in a month. John called, I'm doing some temporary work for him, thank God. But after that? I'm scared."

She placed her hands in her lap and nodded. "Of course you are. That's natural. What we have to work on is not letting you get overwhelmed." A lump rose in my throat as she spoke—how could she sit there, all New York City Upper East Side comfortable and calmly tell me not to get overwhelmed? I resented her, resented anyone who had figured it out better than me.

"You mean having no visible means of support for me and my six-year-old son are not reason enough to get overwhelmed?" My tone was sharper than I'd intended.

She waved her hand at me. "It is reason. But you're stronger than that, Molly, you just have to believe it yourself."

I rolled my eyes. "Okay. Well, so far I made this list for you, like you asked, and I looked at the classifieds but then this thing with John came up." I paused, and shifted on the couch.

"Yes?" Her tone was hopeful, encouraging, confident.

"I thought I might look into teaching. Substitute teaching at first. And then . . ." My voice trailed off.

"Stop it, Molly." Dr. Lowell leaned forward in her chair and gripped her armrests with her hands. "Do not let yourself do this."

"Do what?" I said in a monotone.

"This." Her voice was dismissive. "Climbing into a hole and pulling everything in on top of you. Break it down. Take one thing at a time."

I placed my hands on my thighs. "I guess I could ask my mother for help. For Aidan's insurance, at least." Dr. Lowell's expression made it look like she had swallowed a bug.

Which is what I bet my face looked like, too. Dr. Lowell was very—*very*—familiar with my mother, at least from the times when I talked about relationships, child rearing, and insecurity. Which was every session.

She leaned back in her chair and tilted her head in an unspoken question.

I sighed and rubbed my palms down the arms of the sofa. "I'll just explain the situation, make sure we both know it's temporary, and go from there."

She nodded. "You are thinking for yourself, Molly." She lifted her chin and met my eyes in a challenging gaze. "Try to do at least one thing in your everyday life each day that is a step forward, no matter how small. That's your assignment for next week."

At least it wasn't another list.

"If there is a next week—I won't be able to pay you, remember?"

She waved her hand. "This is important, Molly. We'll keep meeting and figure it out later."

The chill winds outside Dr. Lowell's office building couldn't be any worse than my mother, I thought optimistically. Could they?

When I got back home, I picked up the phone and punched the numbers as if I were making reservations for the Bataan death march.

She answered on the second ring. So much for hoping I could just leave a message.

"Hello?"

"Hi, Mom. It's me."

"Hi, honey." She always sounded faintly confused, as if I had startled her in the middle of doing something. Possibly something worthwhile, like reading James Joyce, although knowing her, I bet she thought he was a lightweight, even though she named me after one of his characters. My mother was funny like that.

"Did you hear the news? About Hugh's company?"

"Oh, what is it?" Her tone was hopeful. She'd always liked him. I felt a tiny morsel of glee at being able to knock him down a few pegs in her eye.

Nothing like a Pyrrhic victory, right? Even if it meant no health insurance. "Apparently he lost his job a while ago, he's been working freelance for them. And now they've folded."

"Oh, that's a shame." She clearly did not realize the import of what I was saying. I pressed on.

"So that means he won't be able to send me money anymore. Lord only knows what the divorce agreement will say."

"Oh." Her voice changed. She knew what was coming, I could tell. And was dreading it. Nearly as much as I was dreading asking.

Silence for a moment.

"Can you loan me some money? At least until I get a job? Just for Aidan's insurance."

"What are you going to do?" Mom had always doubted my ability to make a living. I had to prove her wrong.

"I'm thinking about substitute teaching. Maybe try to get my teaching certificate. The hours would be good for us, for me and Aidan, and it'd be something I think I'd like."

"That sounds like a great idea, honey." She sounded surprised. Heck, *I* was surprised. She was not known for her supportive qualities.

"So . . ." I trailed off, hoping she would follow my lead so I wouldn't have to ask again.

"I can't lend you the money." Her tone was flat.

My stomach fell.

"I'm sorry, sweetie," she continued, "but I just don't have it."

Not have it? This from the doyenne of Short Hills, New Jersey?

Our silence hung for a moment between us—me wanting to ask what the hell she had done with the money, and her obviously not willing to explain. And then, of course, I felt like a petulant, needy girl for even asking, but to ask and then be turned down was something I hadn't even thought of.

"Oh."

"I wish I had it, honey, but, well, I don't."

"Well, all right, then," I said, infusing my voice with as much of a cheery tone as I could, considering the only person I could possibly ask for financial assistance had just said no.

"I should go take care of the dishes or something," I continued, desperate to get off the phone.

"Okay, honey." My mother's voice was a little wistful, not something I'd ever heard from her before. I felt even worse than before. I wanted to stay on the phone with her, but I needed even more to go drown my sorrows. In a pile of soapy dishwater.

"Bye, Mom."

I walked to the kitchen, my mind buzzing with a bunch of things: my bank balance, Aidan's annoying habit of asking for food when he was hungry, my future, his future, *our* future, and that Ben Folds Five song where Ben Folds demands that the bitch give his money back.

Middlestarch

No regrets about entering a love-
less marriage here . . . you'll adore
this sourdough bread, which delivers exactly what it promises: flavor,
depth, and comfort. It looks deep
and rich, and that is precisely what
it is. It takes a long time to chew,
and an even longer time to digest.
You'll enrich your life with every
bite you take.

4

THERE WERE SOME DAYS WHERE BEING A MOM TO A SON LIKE Aidan was a joyous, wonderful delight.

This was not one of those days.

I took a step forward, for me, at least, and had slicked lipstick on prior to picking Aidan up at school. I hoped that didn't make me too conspicuous among all the other stay-at-home moms.

What was it about dedicating your life to another person that made you give up so thoroughly on yourself? Did having a child mean you lost what made you your own person in the first place?

Of course, who was I to talk? All those unkempt women presumably had husbands at home who actually wanted to have sex with them.

Me, I had some animal crackers and a six-year-old who usually regarded me only as the conduit to get the disc into the DVD player.

"Mommy, can we have fun today after school, too?" Yesterday we'd played three mind-numbing hours of some sort of Pokémon activity. I still wasn't sure what we'd done, but I did know Aidan had won every time.

"Uh, sure." I pushed Aidan's hat down a little lower on

his head and checked that his mittens were still attached to his sleeves, even though he refused to wear them. "We can hang out at home. That's fun, right?"

His face crumpled in disappointment. "I don't want the fun to be just with you, that's no fun," he said in six-year-old contradictory speak.

"We can watch TV and eat popcorn." I upped the stakes. "And I think there's some Christmas candy left over from the package Grammy sent you." Just, please, no Pokémon games.

His face brightened. At least bribery still worked. Even if it was two-month-old stale chocolate.

"Can we watch a movie?"

I sighed. "Yes, we can watch a movie." Was one of Dante's circles of hell reserved for mothers who allowed their kids to watch TV *in the daytime*? Or did it only *feel* like that?

He ran all the way home, his little legs pumping. He'd stop periodically and turn around to give me an impatient look. It took only a few minutes to get from school to our apartment, but apparently to him it seemed like an eternity.

Aidan quickly settled down to watch his daytime movie, *Toy Story,* munching on popcorn, his little feet wiggling off the end of the couch. I sat down, too, and felt the warmth of his body along my leg. I yanked the throw from the floor and pulled it over us. He leaned into me, and I smelled his delicious little-boy smell: popcorn, innocent sweat, and Old Navy cotton. It didn't take Dr. Lowell to point out that this was the most important reason not to get overwhelmed.

And the most important reason to make some money.

I picked up the pad of paper I had left on the sofa the night before. Time to make another list.

The most pressing item was to figure out just what this new freelance job required. I knew I had a week to write copy relating to baked goods. Beyond that, my understanding was a bit fuzzy.

The next would be to figure out how to get involved with the teaching program.

The third would be to figure out how much money I thought I'd need. And round up some babysitting help for when I needed time away from the apartment.

I looked down at Aidan's head. He was so trusting, so certain his parents knew everything.

The fourth would be to focus on what was good about my life, not on what was bad. Aidan was number one on the list. He looked up at me and smiled, snuggling even closer to me.

"Mommy, would you like a piece of chocolate?"

I smiled back and nodded. He stood up, reached into his pocket, and pulled out the bag, handing it to me to tear open. I handed it back to him and he picked out a brown M&M for me, smiling broadly when I chewed exaggeratedly and gave a blissful sigh.

"I know you like chocolate, Mommy. I do, too, but not as much as you do."

"What *do* you like more than I do, honey?" Besides your father.

"Pokémon, pizza, movies, drawing, *Teen Titans*." He rattled them off as if he had been preparing his answer for weeks. *Why haven't you asked me before, Mommy?*

"What do you like?"

Just what I was wondering myself.

"You."

He frowned. "I know that already."

"Um . . ." British men with dimples, not having to worry about the bills, faithful husbands . . . the usual. "Peanut butter, books, coffee, jewelry. Sleeping. I think that's it. Besides you, of course."

He flung the blanket off us and jumped off the couch with a look that made me say *oh, no* in my head. "Then I'm going to make you a special treat."

Images of peanut butter–smeared books wearing earrings swam through my head. I got up off the couch, too, even though I was pretty darn cozy. And my favorite part of *Toy Story* was coming up, the part where the toy dinosaur complained about his short little arms.

I followed him into the kitchen. He was already dragging a chair so he could reach my coffee beans.

"Let me help you with that, honey."

"I can do it," he replied in his best I'm-six-and-totally-competent voice. He tried to open the jar of beans but couldn't figure out the vacuum seal.

"Let me." I opened it, then grabbed a bowl and placed a handful of beans into it. "That should be enough, right?" Before he could respond, I hoisted the beans back up onto their shelf, so he wouldn't waste them. Given a choice between him and the beans, I knew I'd pick him, but I also knew I wouldn't be too nice about it. He'd be scared by my no-caffeine Mommy face.

"Go back and sit down. It's a surprise." He pushed me out of the kitchen and down the hall.

I was snuggled back under the throw when he came back and handed me his special treat with a triumphant grin.

"Oh, Aidan, a peanut butter coffee bean sandwich. Thanks, honey." He pulled a book out from behind his back—that damn *The Ambassadors* again—with another wide smile. "And I brought you a book to read, too."

"Thanks, honey."

"And Mommy?"

"Mm?" Actually, the sandwich wasn't half bad, once I got over the gritty crunch of the beans.

"Can we get a pet? I mean, now that Daddy's moved out?" I bit my tongue before I suggested we replace Daddy with a rat.

Ah, the sandwich had an ulterior motive. "A pet?"

"Yeah. Maybe a tarantula, or a snake, or an elephant."

"An elephant wouldn't fit."

"Or a cat. Grammy has a cat." Grammy's kinda on Mommy's hate list right now, honey.

"Mommy's allergic. Maybe a turtle?"

"Turtles are boring."

I thought for a minute. I sure as hell didn't want a spider or a snake roaming around. "Maybe we can get a special kind of cat." That weird-looking hypoallergenic one. It would be a cat, though. "We'll have to see."

He grinned and hugged me. For that kind of hug, I'd have gladly sneezed my head off.

And the dinosaur had just tried to scare someone with his fearsomeness.

To Infinity . . . And Beyond!

Aidan had finally fallen asleep, after pondering—and discarding—about a hundred possible names for the as-yet-unfound cat. He'd finally decided on Beast, after his favorite

Teen Titans character, Beast Boy, which I thought would be pretty appropriate, given how hideous the cat would probably look.

I turned on the computer and found the teaching fellows' website. The deadline for applications was mid-March, which gave me about a month to prepare. Classes for the master's degree began in June, and my teaching, if I were accepted into the program at all, began the following September. So I would need money to get through the spring and summer to be able to do this. Did I have it?

Even presuming I got the money from John, the answer was a resounding no. And I had just about promised to buy Aidan a pricey, ugly cat. What the hell was I going to do?

I put the list down on the table and walked to the kitchen for coffee. And then I spied the uneaten bit of a chocolate chocolate-chip muffin I'd bought for Aidan in a devil may care bit of spend thriftiness a few days before.

After all these years of hoping, would my problems actually be helped by baked goods? I stuffed the stale muffin into my mouth. It was nothing compared to the deliciousness of whatever Simon had made, but at least it gave me enough renewed vigor to return to my notebook.

Aidan was on his third movie that day when my friend Lissa arrived, agenda in tow. Lissa was a solid friend, someone who'd always been there at the other end of the phone, even though she was a full ten years younger than I. She'd jumped in to babysit Aidan as soon as Hugh left, practically pushing me out the door so I could go get a coffee, or thumb through a magazine, or anything to make me "get back in touch with myself." Lissa was a bit of a granola-head, but she had such a good heart, it didn't bother me. Plus she worked in the fashion industry, so I figured she needed some sort of self-defense mechanism. And I admired her shoes.

She held a copy of the *Village Voice* and pointed toward the computer.

"Lissa, I don't want to," I whined. Oh, my God, I've become my son.

She smiled that sassy grin at me in reply, showing her clean, white teeth. I could see why men fell at her feet so often. Especially dentists. "It'll be good for you, Molly. And who knows, you might meet someone really nice."

We sat at my desk with the computer whirring in anticipation. Of what, I didn't want to guess.

I'd sunk so low as to go online to find a date. Lissa had assured me it was better than living the rest of my life alone and bitter. No, wait, *I* had decided that.

Back when I figured out that this was me, this was my life, and I was going to take charge. Even if it meant revealing myself to any number of strangers on the Internet.

I'd tried to argue to Lissa that I wasn't even divorced yet, but she told me—in no uncertain terms—that the longer I took to dip my toe in the water the longer it was going to be before I got wet. So to speak.

We'd agreed that this was just a toe adventure. Nothing had to happen. But I had to try.

"Mommmmmy!" Aidan's screech sounded like his leg was being amputated or something. Luckily, I knew him well enough to know he just wanted me to see something on the TV.

"Yes, that is disgusting," I said in a suitably revolted voice. Satisfied, his eyes glazed over again as he watched the dinosaur eat the rest of the scientist. I headed back to where Lissa still had that annoying smile on her face.

She gestured toward the screen. "I've already entered the basic information. You just have to be specific about what you want."

Money. Time. Security.

Oh, what I want *in a man*. Oh, well, that's easy: money, time, security.

I sat down in front of the screen and held my fingers above the keyboard for a second. "And if I don't do this, you'll stop babysitting?"

I'd told her about the new freelance job, and my tentative career goals. As I'd known she would be, she'd been very encouraging. And then she had issued her threats.

She poked me in the shoulder. "Stop dawdling, Molly."

I took a deep breath, feeling the air filling my lungs. I peered at the screen. "Lissa, I do not weigh a hundred and thirty pounds. In my wildest dreams, maybe."

She poked me again. "Everyone lies."

I thought of Hugh. "Yeah, I guess you're right."

I looked at the first blank category, then read it aloud: "Name five items you cannot do without."

"That's easy," Lissa said, "coffee, coffee, coffee, books, and coffee." She laughed as she pulled her chair closer with a loud scrape on the wooden floor. I could smell her perfume, a slightly musky scent that smelled like decadent flowers.

"Coffee, books, what else? Hm."

"Jeans?"

I wrinkled my nose. "Let's not go there."

I began typing. *Coffee, books, eyebrow pencil, Stevie Wonder discs, and my son.* "Actually," I said, pulling back from the keyboard, "that is pretty much all I'd need if I were stranded on a desert island. Well, a CD player for the discs. And maybe a mirror to apply the eyebrow pencil. Otherwise I'd end up looking like Groucho Marx."

She peered over my shoulder. "It makes you sound down-to-earth but sophisticated." Sometimes Lissa baffled me with her fashionista doublespeak.

"In other words, an absolute lie."

She punched me. For a tall, skinny chick, she had a lot of strength behind that fist. I rubbed my arm and glared at her. "Look, Lissa, let's face facts. I'm forty. I am an about-to-be-divorcée with a small child."

She punched me again. I waved my index finger in her face.

"And I'm Irish with pale skin, which means all that punching is going to leave bruising. Thanks, Lissa, now any potential man will think I'm into S&M, when all I'm really into are M&M's."

She laughed. "You *are* pretty, Molly, and you know it, if you'd just stop wearing the same clothes every day. Men really go for the sexy librarians, you know."

"And," she continued before I could react to that, "you're shy, but you do have a mouth on you, as you say yourself. You're very smart—and remember how many times you told me to go for something? Now it's your turn. Once someone gets to know you, they'll adore you."

"*If* I let them get to know me."

My own words brought me up short. *Won't let them*? Was I that scared?

I swallowed hard and thought about it. Well, damn. I had to do something about that.

Dr. Lowell's frequent advice rang in my ears: I was a woman, a woman who was occasionally witty, sometimes pretty, always well read. Not to mention well caffeinated. I put my fingers back down on the keyboard determinedly. I could do this. I *could* place a personals ad.

"What kind of music gets you in the mood?" Lissa read out loud, then leaned back and shot me a measured look.

"Mood for what?" I asked, striving to keep an innocent look on my face. "Paying bills? Macramé? Laundry?"

Lissa raised her fist in a menacing gesture. "Okay, okay, I get it," I said, "gets me in the mood." I gave her an exaggerated wink. "I feel like I'm a housewife speaking in code. Why can't they just ask you what kind of music makes you want to have sex?"

Lissa rolled her eyes. "Just fill it in, already."

"Stevie Wonder, Soundgarden, Teddy Pendergrass, disco divas, and Fela."

"Four out of five of those make you sound like you're definitely not Irish. The Soundgarden thing is just bizarre."

I shrugged. "Well, honestly, could you see me wanting to date someone who liked listening to earnest white guys with guitars? Or worse yet, earnest white girls with guitars? And breathy harmonies? My admirers are just going to have to understand I like soul music," I finished in a lofty tone.

"And Soundgarden."

"Not to mention Gilbert and Sullivan, which is totally out of left field. I know. But it's me. Okay, what's next. Books. Cool, I can do this. 'Name five books that touched your life.' Touched your life? What kind of yoga-practicing touchy-feely garbage is that?"

Lissa squinted her blue eyes at me. Even squinted, they were bigger than the ones in those doe-eyed children paintings. "One more word and you get no babysitting from me."

"Okay. Let's see. That's too hard—there are too many out there to name."

"So list the first five that come to mind."

I typed. "Edith Wharton's *House of Mirth,* Jane Austen's *Pride and Prejudice,* Neal Stephenson's *The Diamond Age,* Dashiell Hammett's *The Maltese Falcon,* and Raymond Chandler's *The Big Sleep.*"

Lissa looked impressed.

"I bet you thought I was going to say *Love's Scoundrel* and *Love's Scoundrel Returned.*"

Her expression faltered. "No, I was just thinking how amazing it is that I've actually heard of any of those books. You've read a lot more than me." Her voice was unquestionably mournful. I felt uncomfortable.

"Well, let's face it, *Love's Scoundrel* doesn't stand up to repeated readings." Her expression eased, and she read the next section of the profile out loud.

"Write a brief description of yourself and what kind of person you're looking for."

"Oh, this will be fun. If I don't burst into flames from the embarrassment of it all. Go away, Lissa, this is uncomfortable enough without you watching."

She smirked and grabbed a glossy fashion mag from her bag. I watched as she settled down on the couch, wrapping the throw around her thighs. Even that gesture was elegant. She stuck her tongue out at me, then flipped open the magazine, staring at it in exaggerated concentration. I turned back to the computer.

> Forty-year-old mom with a love of caffeine, her son, and black clothing (not necessarily in that order) seeks a man with the ability to laugh at himself, enjoy a good pun, and not be afraid to dance in public. I like Gilbert & Sullivan operettas, Jorge Luis Borges, caramel, Christmas socks, and sensible shoes. I'm not nearly as obnoxious as I seem in print, and the only thing that is a must is that you like children, or rather, a child. Specifically mine.

There. I took a breath and hit SUBMIT.

> Congratulations, your personal profile has been added to our database!

the computer screen said in a cheery green script. Lissa put the magazine down and walked over to me. "There, it wasn't so bad, was it?" she asked. I looked up at her and shook my head. "No, it wasn't so bad. It's just so . . . single adult of me, and that's hard."

Lissa sat back down in the chair next to me and patted my shoulder. "Ah, honey, it is hard. *This* is hard. All of it. And you're doing great."

I was? Oh, right. I *was*.

"Thanks. You've been great through all this, sorry I've been acting like such a pill."

"What else could I expect from such an old bat?" Lissa said with a grin.

I punched her in the arm.

"Um, Molly?" Lissa had lost her sassy tone.

"Yeah?"

"Do you think—that is, I was wondering—could you recommend some books for me to read? Tony mentioned some, and it sounded like he assumed I'd read them, and I don't want to sound dumb. Fashion majors don't usually read the classics," she finished with a self-deprecating laugh.

Tony was Lissa's new boyfriend, a slick Manhattan type who always had an expression like he had one up on you. I was not fond of Tony. "You're not dumb, Lissa." I checked my watch. "Aidan!" I called. "Time to get ready for bed!"

He scrambled up from the floor and blinked like I had just woken him up. "But the movie—"

"You've seen the movie a zillion times, it's late, and you need your sleep." He shuffled down the hall, his tired little body movements belying his drifting "I'm not tired" wail. "Anyway," I said, turning back to Lissa, "you're not dumb," I repeated.

She wrinkled her pert little nose. "I'm not stupid, but I've never thought of myself as sharp or anything, not like you. So can you lend me something?"

"Sure." I thought about it for a second, the idea of teaching her taking root in my head. "You could be my first student! Hey, have you ever read *Ethan Frome*?" She shook her head. I wondered just what they had taught her in that girls prep school she went to. Besides being well groomed, beautiful, and perfect.

"Boy, do you have a treat in store. I mean, if you like relationships that are doomed to failure." I stopped and smacked myself in the forehead. "No, wait, that's me."

She laughed as I walked over to the bookcase and unearthed the "Wharton" section, which was filed right between Evelyn Waugh and Phyllis A. Whitney. I handed it to her. "It's really good. And it's one of her shortest ones, besides the novellas."

She tucked it into her brightly colored tote bag along with her magazine. "Thanks, Molly. Tony will be impressed."

It made me mad to hear the pathos in her voice. I'd been there, I wanted to tell her, it's not worth it. Don't try to change yourself for a man, it never works. They won't change themselves for you, either.

"Don't forget to tell me about any interesting replies to your ad," Lissa said as she headed to the door, her blue eyes gleaming in anticipation.

"I brushed my teeth, Mommy," Aidan said in a sleepy voice. He'd already climbed into bed.

"Be right there," I replied.

As I closed the door behind her, I grabbed *The House of Mirth* for some light bedtime reading and walked to his bedroom.

I needed to write some more lists:

- Books everyone should read

- Books everyone has read, but won't admit

- Books everyone says they've read, but no one really has (see: Ayn Rand)

- Why friends are better than men (see: do not let them down)

- Why men are sometimes better than friends (see: sex)

And the last one, How Molly will get a job, support her child, and enjoy the rest of her life without her no-good, cheating husband. Nonfiction, natch.

The Bun
Also Rises

There's nothing so wonderful as an item that delivers what it has promised. In this case, it's fresh, fresh, freshly risen bread, so fresh it practically deserves to be slapped. Its buttery-rich crust encases a delicately moist center, swirled with Spanish chocolate.

5

"PLEASED TO MEET YOU, MOLLY." THE WOMAN CLASPING MY hand looked anything but pleased. Her grip was so tight as to be almost painful, and one of her rings was cutting into my hand.

"Likewise." I pulled my hand away and tried to surreptitiously return the flow of blood to my fingers.

It was midday Thursday, and I was in John's office for the second time that week.

Natalie and I stood in John's conference room, which was decorated in various tones of chocolate brown. The massive conference table was sort of a butterscotch color, and I wondered briefly why I was thinking so much about food—unless I had suddenly morphed into Willy Wonka or something. And then I remembered: stress = desire for sugar. And boy, was I stressed.

Natalie was at least a full head taller than me, but even lying at 130 pounds, I bet I outweighed her by twenty pounds. She had that New York City thinness usually caused by being fabulous, successful, and overbusy, probably caused by her fabulous success. Her auburn hair was cut in an artful shag, the kind of haircut that never looks as good in person as it does in the magazines.

On her, it looked great.

She looked down her nose at me and lifted one perfectly plucked eyebrow. "So you're John's college friend?"

If she'd said "so you're John's talentless hanger-on, and I'll be enduring your sorry ass through this entire project," she couldn't have been more clear.

I tried to gaze in her eyes. I managed to look her in the nostril. "Yes. I've had previous copy experience, working for John, and for an Internet company back in the 1990s, you know, back when the Internet was going to save the world."

"Hm," she sniffed, clearly not amused by my lame attempt at wit, "well, there's nothing for it but to get to work." She stalked over to the conference table and plopped an enormous notebook down on it. The sound echoed through the room, and I jumped a little.

"Sit down," she said impatiently, "let's talk. Here, you take notes." She slid a pen across the table to where she'd pointed for me to sit, and I did. She pushed the notebook toward me, too, then settled herself into her chair.

Like me, she was wearing all black, the New York color of choice. Unlike me, she looked as if she'd bought her clothes within the last five years. Her jacket was unbuttoned to reveal a slim sweater, the kind that Barneys sold for well over my monthly therapy bill.

She fluttered her hands on the table, and I saw the ring that had speared me earlier: gold, with an enormous green stone glittering at its center. Green like Simon's eyes.

I exhaled, remembering how encouraging he'd been. Or, maybe not encouraging, but not actively dissuading, as this woman was.

"Well. What is first?" I queried, trying to keep my voice pitched low.

Her lip curled. I had to wonder just what John had gotten himself into, and more importantly, why?

"The bakery is near the New York Public Library, and Simon wants to associate the two so that the bakery is a destination point, just as the library is."

Oh, is that all?

"Okay. Should I write that down?"

She rolled her eyes. I was pleased to see a couple of wrinkles lurking underneath, along with some dark circles. "Write down whatever you think will get the job done."

I wrote *Destination Point.*

"How's it going?" John's head popped into the doorway.

"Fine. Molly and I are just starting to brainstorm. I think we'll work well together, thanks for bringing her in, John." Her tone was completely devoid of derision.

My mouth almost dropped open, but I caught it in time. If this was how she behaved when she approved of the person, imagine how she'd be if she didn't like them. I gave an involuntary shudder.

"Good, great," John said, bobbing his head up and down. What was it about this woman that made him so spineless? I'd never seen this side of him before.

"So——" Natalie let her word dangle there until John spoke again.

"Great, so I'll just leave you two to it. Natalie, the bankers' meeting has been rescheduled for four thirty." She nodded. "Say hi before you leave, Molly, okay?" He withdrew his head and shut the door.

"Where were we? Oh, yes, a destination point." She paused, then looked into the distance and spoke. "Books and Bread." She offered it as though I should be grateful for her brilliance.

I nodded, and bit my tongue. Maybe later I would pat my head and rub my tummy, too. "Books and Bread," I repeated. "Alliteration works."

"Always," she said, giving me a condescending smile. "I considered Socrates and Scones, but then I thought how many people wouldn't know who Socrates was. Books and Bread is far more mainstream."

If by *mainstream,* she meant *stupid,* her tone would make sense. But I wasn't going to say anything; after all, I thought *both* names were stupid.

"Um," I ventured, "do we know if bread is one of Simon's primary products?" I'd gotten the phrase from that book John had given me. I knew she'd like the alliteration. "I think we should get a list of the bakery items and see what pops out at us. Not popovers, ha-ha," I finished with a weak laugh. She gave me a blank stare. She really did *not* think I was funny.

"Certainly. I'll give Simon a call later this afternoon, he should be able to supply whatever I need." Now her voice held the contented just-fed tone of a satisfied kitten. Ah, so Simon was supplying her with something. Something he didn't pull out of an oven.

No wonder John was panicked.

"Meanwhile," she continued, "what else do you think is striking about the bakery? Something we can leverage for maximum memorability?"

This woman was *so* into alliteration. I should keep that in mind as I worked with her. "Likely its library location?" She looked pleased. I felt like I could do this. "Its primary pastry production?" Her smile faltered. Perhaps I was overdoing it. "And, of course, the delicious desserts." She beamed. I had her.

"Excellent!" she said. If I just kept up the Awesome Alliteration, maybe this wouldn't be a debacle after all. "I like how you're thinking, Molly."

If she knew what was in my head, she wouldn't be saying that.

"Anyway," she said, flinging her wrist out so she could check her watch, "I've got another meeting now." Well, that wasn't very long, was it? Hardly worth my trip in. Not that I could say that to her. "How about we meet on Monday, say four?" She picked up a pen and held it poised over an appointment book she'd pulled out from somewhere.

"I can't at four. I pick my son up after school. The latest I can meet is one."

Her lip curled, and she gave me a surveying glance. So much for liking my thinking. "Ah, a mother, I see. One it is, then." She scribbled something down and stood, shoving her chair firmly behind her.

I rose also, wondering if the meeting had gone well or terribly, terribly badly.

"Nice to meet you, Molly," she said, giving me one of those little finger wiggles celebrities did on TV.

"Nice to meet you, too," I echoed. The door slammed shut, leaving me alone in the chocolate conference room. I sat down, unconsciously putting the notebook back to rights.

Why couldn't I be a confident woman? I needed to remind

myself of Dr. Lowell's constant refrain: You are strong, capable, smart, and you can do this.

I think I can, I think I can, I think I can, I thought as I
gathered up my belongings and headed toward the door.
Damn that little engine. John lurked just outside—waiting
for Natalie to go?

"So. Natalie," he pronounced as he gestured toward his
office. "What did you think of her?" He sat down in his Big
Corporate Guy chair and rested his hands on his chest.

I lowered myself into my chair and crossed my ankles.
"She seems . . . quite capable," I said in as noncommittal a
tone as I could manage. His eyes narrowed.

"Capable, yes. Trustworthy, no."

"For goodness' sake, John," I blurted out, "what's the
deal with her? Why did you bring her in if you don't trust
her?"

He spread his hands wide. "She's got clients I could never
get. Sometimes you've got to take chances."

Take chances like not settle for something—or someone—
who is just okay. Take chances like believing in yourself.
Take chances like doing something that seems difficult in
order to keep your family together.

Take a chance, Molly.

"Why did she join you?" I asked.

He frowned. "Fair question. She left her other firm rather
quickly, and wanted to join another company with a fully
operational support staff, but not one that was too big." He
let his words hang for a moment. "She also brought us
Simon." Oh, that explained a lot. "She's a hell of a smart
woman, isn't she?"

"Yes," I agreed. She *was* smart, even if I'd also append snotty, condescending, and far-too-skinny to that description. I stuffed the notebook into my purse. "We're meeting again on Monday; meanwhile she's going to get the bakery menu so we can start fleshing out the concept. I've been reading those books you gave me, just to bone up on the fancy marketing lingo. Natalie seemed to like it when I used it."

He stood up. "Great, I'm really glad to have you on board with this thing, Molly, I think it'll work out great. Have you thought about what you're going to do, now that—?"

Now that Hugh's left? Oh no, not more than once a minute or so. Twice a minute when Aidan's hungry.

"Yes, I'm thinking about doing some substitute teaching, maybe see about getting my teaching certificate." I smiled brightly, as if it were just a pleasant idea to keep me busy.

"Sounds great. Okay, well, I'll see you Monday. Give me a call if you have any questions about those materials. Oh, and Molly?"

"Mm?" I said, pushing my arms through the sleeves of my coat.

"I gave Simon your phone number. He asked for it so he could review some stuff with you."

A sharp sizzle went up my spine. Simon asked for my number. Somehow I didn't think Natalie would be too happy if she knew about that.

"Oh. Sure, no problem. See you Monday."

I headed out the door, my heart lifted slightly by the possibility of Simon calling. Not that it could outweigh the very distinct probability that Aidan and I would be living in a cardboard box by the summer, but at least it was something to look forward to.

And—I chuckled to myself—at least I could still be hopeful about something. It was a start.

"Molly."

My spine sizzled even more when I heard his voice on the other end of the phone. It was Friday, Aidan was safely off at school, and I was in the kitchen contemplating just what I could make out of a bag of navy beans, some elderly mozzarella cheese, and a yam.

I'd have welcomed the interruption even if it weren't the Gorgeous British Guy.

"Yes?" I plunked the yam down on the counter and lifted my cup of coffee instead.

"It's Simon." He said it as if there were no chance I would have forgotten him. Damn, he was right.

"Hello, Simon. How are you?"

"Been better, actually. Look, I know it's short notice, but can you meet me in the city today? Now, or as soon as possible?"

I put my coffee down. "Uh." I looked up at the clock on the microwave: 10:23. "Yeah, sure. I can be there in forty-five minutes." I looked down at my jeans and old T-shirt. "An hour. Where do you want to meet?"

"The Noho Star. It's at the corner of Lafayette and—"

"I know where it is. See you then."

I clicked the phone off, then picked my cup up and drained all the coffee remaining inside. I'd need all the help I could get.

I marched into my bedroom, ruthlessly kicking aside last night's pajamas, which were lying on the floor. My closet door was halfway open, and I flung the door wider so I could survey its contents.

What could I wear that would indicate I was professional, smart, capable, confident and, yeah, totally foxy for a forty-year-old?

Clothing could only do so much, I thought prosaically as I pulled on another pair of black pants and a chocolate brown sweater. I rummaged underneath my bed to locate my brown boots, then found my only pair of gold earrings and a topaz ring.

My hair was pretty much okay, I thought, as I scanned myself in the mirror. I put some makeup on, adjusted the hem of my pants over my boots, then grabbed my purse. I knew I only had three dollars plus a MetroCard; I figured Simon would pay, but just in case, I would only order coffee anyway.

I snagged Henry James from where he was languishing, still unread, on the bedside table and tucked it into my bag.

If nothing else, it made me look smart.

"Over here," he called as I walked into the restaurant. It hadn't changed since the last time I had been there, back when I used to work in the neighborhood. Simon was sitting at one of the circular tables, his arms draped around the back of one of the chairs. I headed for the other chair, but he shook his head, removed his arm, and gestured for me to sit in the chair closest to him.

"Thanks for coming in on such short notice." His accent was even more delicious than I had recalled. So was he, for that matter; he was wearing a dark green V-necked sweater that only served to make his eyes look even more incredible. A purple paisley shirt peeked out from under the sweater, and I could see a few curly brown chest hairs, too.

Color Identification: In this class, students will learn to properly identify colors, despite distractions, inner thoughts, and lustful thoughts. You'll never confuse persimmon with rust again.

"No problem. So what's up?"

The waitress appeared and handed us each a menu. I made a perfunctory scan of the contents, then closed it, as if I hadn't decided back in Brooklyn what I would order.

"I understand you met with Natalie yesterday?"

"Yes, and we're meeting again on Monday. Is that why you've called me here?" *Like, did she say no way would she work with a clearly incompetent friend of John?*

"In a manner of speaking, yes. Natalie's off the project."

"But—but we just started working together." Shit, did that mean I was off the project, too? Why the hell was I here? What was I going to do without that five grand I'd already spent in my mind? Fuck, fuck, fuck.

He blew out a breath that raised one of those curls off his forehead. "I don't wish to discuss it. She's off, and we've got work to do." His voice held that autocratic tone I'd heard the first time we met. I didn't feel like arguing, but I did need to know about my status.

"So where does that leave me?" I asked.

"What do you mean?" He gave me a look like I was stupid. I was really tired of people doing that.

"The project. Me. Am I still working on it? Are you going to hire another firm?" Poor John. He'd been so excited.

Simon shook his head. "It's too late. And I have faith in you." Did he know that when he smiled like that my insides turned to Jell-O? Oh, yeah, he sure did.

"What can I get you?" The waitress had returned.

Simon gave her an easy smile. "I'd like two eggs scrambled, bacon, toast, and coffee. Molly?"

"Just coffee, please."

He scowled and flipped his menu open. "Not just coffee, Molly. Don't be one of those, you need to eat. Here, try the fried chicken salad, it's got Stilton cheese in it, a very good supply of protein."

And fat, my mind added. I nodded in acquiescence. Maybe I wouldn't have to eat dinner.

He took my menu and handed it to the waitress, then leaned on the table after she left. "So. The investors need to see a presentation of our products, and we can't delay any longer."

He spoke as if he were discussing the weather. Not the fact that he'd just dumped something on me for which I was totally unprepared, in so many ways. All I knew was that Simon had some cockamamie idea about a bakery and a library. Great. Reading and food. I liked both, but that was hardly the basis for a marketing plan. *Natalie, I hardly knew you.* "Have you talked to John about this?" I was surprised I could manage a normal tone.

He waved his hand, brushing my arm. It sent a shiver of awareness over me, and I blinked to keep myself focused. "John is not the lead on this thing. I am now."

Oooh, Mr. Corporate was going all Alpha on me. I liked it. I liked it a lot. Was that wrong?

"Ah. So." Stop me before I uttered another noncommittal monosyllable. "What's the next step?" And will I make more money?

He smiled at me, and my stomach flipped. Flipped! "The next step is for you and your lovely self to sit down and write me some killer copy. Something fun, inviting, and sexy."

It was too obvious. But so was he.

"Right, then. Fine. Good." At least the monosyllables were actual words. Now if I could just get myself to ask about the money . . .

"In a week." Aagh! "And I'll make sure you get continual feedback so we don't end up with our asses in a sling. Not that there's anything wrong with that," he said, grinning naughtily. "Of course you'll be making more than we originally agreed to, but I'll leave those details to John," he said in a much more serious tone.

Books and bread. I could work with that as a starting point, right? I could. But before my mind could start to churn there, I had another thought; so technically John was employing me, and only on a freelance basis, but wasn't it a bit . . . *odd* that Simon was being so aggressive? I mean, besides the fact that I'd seen myself and really didn't deserve this kind of attention. And a week. Ouch.

Lissa, Keisha, and Dr. Lowell would tell me to stop selling myself short, but really—I wasn't all that. Did Simon think if he flattered me I'd work harder? Better? Faster?

Okay, now I was getting inappropriate.

I folded my hands in my lap. "I appreciate the confidence you're showing in me. I hope I can live up to your expectations."

That naughty smile came back, only this time it was even naughtier. "Oh, I'm certain you can, Molly. Absolutely certain."

Dorothy Parker House Rolls

You'd bet this has got a bite to it—
and you'd be right. Tangy, dry, and
ever so slightly bitter, this by-no-
means meek breadstuff is something to eat when you're ready to
take a chomp out of the Big Apple.
It's better in short (story) bites, but
one taste of this sage-and-onion
roll and you'll be ready to take your
place at the Algonquin Table (we'd
say the head of the table, but the
table is round, dear, *round*!).

6

"I THINK I MIGHT BE A VAMPIRE." I WAS PROPPED UP IN BED, the phone held to my right ear, a blessedly full cup of coffee in my left hand. I wasn't sure how to talk to Keisha about what had happened that morning without totally freaking out, so I was avoiding the problem.

"What makes you say that? Have you had a sudden urge to drink people's blood or something? Because if so, I'm sure glad I don't live next door to you anymore."

"No, it's that I can drink coffee at—let me check—eleven o'clock at night and *still* be asleep by eleven thirty. And I'm cold all the time. And I'm very, very pale. Plus I want to nap frequently."

"All that means," Keisha replied with a gusty sigh, "is that you're a mom. An Irish, sleep-deprived, coffee-obsessed mom. And besides, vampires are up all night chasing blood, not coffee."

"Dunno why. Coffee tastes better." I sniffed in disdain. "Maybe I'm just dead."

"Now *there's* a happy thought. So how's the assignment going?"

I put the cup down on the headboard and rolled over onto

my stomach, wishing I could bury my head in the pillow. "I don't even know where to start."

"At the beginning?"

"Oh, you're funny."

"Ah, shucks, you're just saying that. But really, Molly, it's not so hard. Break it down, piece by piece."

"Have you been talking to Dr. Lowell again?" I said with a suspicious tone. "Because you know, I've never seen both of you at the same time. Maybe you're really her."

She uttered a disgusted sigh. "If I were her, would I be spending my free time talking to you?"

"Good point. Okay. Piece by piece." I reached over to the side of the bed, drawing out a gray folder from the big bag John had given me. "Here's one of the files. It's a PowerPoint nightmare, and it's totally boring and I don't want to read it anymore—"

"You're whining. Speaking of which, how's Aidan?"

"Fine. Completely unaware his mother is . . . *me,* and his father is, well . . ."

"A fuck. Look, Molly," Keisha said, in the serious tone she usually reserved for telling me how much she valued our friendship (after a few cocktails, of course), "you are totally competent. You are beautiful in a regal Irish kind of way. You can do this. You *will* do this, or I will come to Brooklyn and kick your ass."

"Promise?"

"Yup. Now, what's your first step?"

"Get my ass kicked?" I asked hopefully.

"No. Go to where the store is being set up—Midtown, right? Scout it out, bring a notebook, have some coffee. Like I had to tell you that part. Then get to work with that big brain of yours. Remember, that English literature major brain?"

Midtown Manhattan. The library. I started to get excited just thinking about it.

"And by then I'm sure you'll have figured out some ideas," she said in her best "I've just solved the problem" voice. "Listen, I've got to go, *The Lion in Winter* is about to start, and I can't miss the first meeting between Peter O'Toole and Katharine Hepburn, you know, on the boat."

"Bye, hon."

"Bye."

I hung up, a little grin on my face. At least I was smiling more lately. I downed the rest of the coffee, then looked a little sadly at the bottom of the cup. If I wanted more, I'd have to make it, which meant grinding the beans and cleaning that little gold filter thingy, and really, I should be going to sleep because Aidan was going to get up at seven.

Sometimes I wished I *were* a coffee vampire. Instead of blood, coffee would swirl through my veins, bringing life to my body and breath to my lungs. Maybe I'd have coffee beans instead of red blood cells, little puffs of steamed milk instead of white blood cells. I'd never need to worry about needing a caffeine fix again. It would be coffee heaven.

It was a chilly February day, the kind of day that reminds you why people get so rhapsodic about spring anyway. I emerged from the subway and blinked as my eyes adjusted to the light. The library was a couple of blocks away, so I started walking, keeping a mental note of the retail shops right nearby:

- A clothing store for women who clearly had very different lives than I did. I mean, plaid short shorts?

- A video game store with graphics so violent I wouldn't even wish them on Hugh.

- The Stationary Shop: my auto-editor noticed *stationary* was spelled wrong. I bet they sold lots of *papar*.

- A shoe store.

- An odd-lot store with a window full of teakettles, plastic storage boxes, stuffed animals, canned goods, and other random things you'd never want to own but somehow felt compelled to buy.

And then I saw the bakery storefront. It didn't have a name or anything, but it was diagonally across from the Nat Sherman store, and the windows were covered over with newspaper, a sure sign of construction within. It looked big. It looked official. It looked as if someone who might even know what the hell they were doing should be working on it.

I took a deep breath. And then held it, because Nick the Unfriendly walked out the door.

"Good morning." I tried to keep my voice from trilling upward.

He looked even more forbidding in natural sunlight. His brows snapped together, and he appeared to be gritting his teeth. I wondered just why he seemed to dislike me so much. And why Simon couldn't have been there instead.

"Hello, Miss . . . ?" His tone was almost rudely disinterested.

"Hagan. Molly Hagan. And it's Ms."

Dark blue eyes raked me up and down.

"Ms. Hagan. So, you're here scouting the territory?"

I took my notebook out from my right hand and clasped it to my chest, hoping to obscure the Pokémon stickers Aidan had insisted on decorating it with. I took a quick peek down and realized Pikachu was smack dab on the back, facing him. Darn. Nick's lips curled in an almost smile as he looked at the sticker.

"Yes. The store looks impressive."

This time his lips did curl in a smile, revealing ultrawhite, ultrastraight teeth. "You're impressed by newspaper-covered windows? Remind me to invite you over next time I paint my window moldings."

A joke! Mr. Forbidding made a joke!

"Would you like to go inside?" He gestured toward the door. A lock of straight black hair fell over his forehead.

"Mm, yes."

I walked in just ahead of him and felt his solid warmth behind me. The door swung shut, and we were definitely alone. Me and Mr. Scary. I wished I'd gotten a bit more sleep the night before, I was going to need it to deal with him.

"This is the main retail space," he said, waving toward the open space we had entered, "and back there is the kitchen. We'll be making all the goods on-site rather than trucking them in, and the emphasis will be on the artisanal qualities of our goods."

"So Simon, that is, Mr.—?"

His lips thinned. "Baxter."

"Mr. Baxter will actually be cooking back there?"

He gave me a look of utter disdain. "No, of course not. Simon is an artist. He creates the pastries, he doesn't actually cook them. Did you actually think he was going to make the product?"

Put that way, of course not. But . . . "Yeah, I did," I admitted. It wasn't as if he had a good opinion of me anyway.

His tone grew gruffer, if that was even possible. "Simon won the James Beard award for Outstanding Pastry Chef two years running, he was named Best New Pastry Chef in *Bon Appétit*, he—"

"I get it. Simon is a star. He won't be measuring flour." I really didn't need for him to make me feel any stupider. I could do that on my own. Man, I was old—shouldn't I have Googled him or something?

He exhaled, as though my dumbness had taken his breath away. "Ms. Hagan, let's go get some coffee and talk about just what Simon requires."

We stepped out in the sunshine together and I dared to glance over at him. He was tall, a lot taller than Hugh. I guessed he was about six foot three. As though being verbally intimidating wasn't enough, he had to throw physical height intimidation into the mix.

He lifted his chin toward a coffee shop halfway down the block. "There. I'm hungry, too. Do you have time to eat?"

"Yes, I have to be back on the subway no later than two. But that gives us at least an hour."

We slid into a booth in the surprisingly deserted restaurant. I took a few deep, calming breaths from behind the enormous, laminated menu. When I lowered it, I discovered his intent gaze on me.

"What would you like?" he asked, his voice low and rumbly.

And, just like that, I wanted to spill it all: my anxiety about this assignment, my worry about paying the bills, my fear that I would never figure out what the hell I was going to do with my life.

Foolish. This guy didn't even like me. And I sure as hell didn't like him. Why did I suddenly feel the need to share? "Er . . . yes, I think, well, yes, I think the Greek salad. And coffee, of course."

The waitress stepped over, a wide grin on her face as she looked at my companion. It faltered a little when she saw me. "What can I get for you?"

"I'll have—"

"She'll have the Greek salad and a coffee, and I'd like a piece of cherry pie and coffee also."

"How do you want your coffee?"

He regarded me, raising one brow. I was hoping Mr. Autocratic would just guess. "Light, one sugar, please."

"Black for me."

The waitress took one last look, then walked toward the kitchen.

He really *was* a hard-ass. "Taking your coffee black in a place like this is living on the edge, Mr.—"

"Harrison."

A solid, dependable name. Not the least bit intimidating. Names sure were deceptive.

"And I like a little danger—don't you?"

Danger like taking on an assignment for which I was completely unqualified? Uh, no.

"Not really, unless you count fighting my son for the remote control."

"A son—how old?" His blue eyes were focused closely on me, and I felt myself wanting to fidget, because that scrutiny made me nervous. I sat on my hands instead.

"Six. He's in first grade."

"What's his name?"

"Aidan."

"Aidan Hagan?" His brow climbed high in disbelief.

"Hagan is my name. His is McLaughlin."

"Ah."

"Do you have any kids?" I darted a quick glance at his left hand. Nothing there.

His voice was soft, almost wistful. "No. I like kids, though. My sister has two, one of each. Seven and four. They're in Minnesota."

"Is that where you're from?"

He reverted to his normal hard tone. "No." Well, all right then.

The coffee arrived, just in time to avoid an incredibly awkward silence caused by my indefatigable curiosity. So what if this man kept looking at me as if I were something he'd like to scrape off his shoe? I was taking one of those steps Dr. Lowell talked about: Make conversation with someone who patently despises you. Or something like that.

I took a sip of coffee. Not truly awful, just mildly awful. "What else can you tell me about Simon's concept?"

"What do you know?"

I shrugged. "Obviously not enough. What do you think I need to know?"

The food arrived just as he opened his mouth. He gave the waitress an impatient scowl as she set our plates down. I surveyed the salad. There were only three olives, maybe four, tops. And the iceberg lettuce was almost paler than me. The feta cheese looked good, though.

I chewed on a forkful of cheese and gave him a surreptitious glance. He had cut off a piece of pie and was lifting it to his mouth. Pop, it went in. And a little bit lingered on his lower lip, which he licked off quickly, giving me an abashed, little-boy grin as he did so.

If he loathed me less, I might have to admire the view. Because, objectively speaking, he sure was easy on the eyes. Good thing his moments of charm were few and far between—limited to one, in fact, thus far.

"Basically," he said, spearing another piece of pie, "Simon is hoping his bakery will cement his place among the cooking elite. He's made good progress, but working at someone else's restaurant naturally means he has to share the limelight."

"Naturally," I murmured, surreptitiously picking an olive pit from my mouth.

"The bakery—provided it's successful—will be the springboard upon which we can build Simon's empire. The bakery is only a piece of the pie, so to speak," he said, his mouth twisting up at the corners. Another joke! He'd doubled his moments of charm to two in under ten minutes!

"How are you involved?"

Nick shrugged. "I'll handle the paperwork, the finances, basically everything that isn't the actual baking. We've got start-up capital, and it all has to be managed properly. So even though this is a start-up, it's not as though Simon and I aren't qualified."

Unlike me, his tone implied.

He leaned back and placed his hands in his lap. "I have to tell you, Ms. Hagan, I am not at all sanguine about Simon's putting you in charge. In fact, I believe it's a mistake. A big one that we cannot afford. But Simon is in charge."

Okay, forget *implied,* and substitute *said.*

He gave me another intent gaze, as if to see that his words had the proper impact. My eyes dropped to my plate. I drew a deep breath and thought of Aidan.

"Well," I said, looking up and giving him a bright, totally artificial smile, "I'll just have to dream up something totally original to knock your socks off." Oh my God, had I just used that phrase?

"I'm looking forward to it," he replied, in a voice that indicated he was doing anything but. "My socks are getting complacent," he added in a dry aside.

Another joke! Mr. Forbidding might have to change his name to Mr. Fun-Loving!

He finished the piece of pie and regarded the plate as if he wanted to lick it clean.

He might be ruthless and nerve-racking, but he liked dessert. There had to be some good in him.

"When *are* you starting to work on this?" he asked, raising an eyebrow. It sounded as if he thought I was already slacking off.

"Um . . . now?" I had that raised question tone in my voice.

He nodded in approval. "Good. What times are good for you?" He took a sip of his coffee.

"Huh?" I was too startled to sound anything but dopey.

His voice held a distinct note of irritation. "When can you meet? To work on the concept?"

"You mean . . . with you?"

He pushed an impatient hand through his hair. "Yes, with me. With Ms. Duran off the project, we need someone to work with you to ensure the mission statement is upheld."

Mission statement? I was guessing that wasn't something you'd find in a Franciscan church.

"And," he continued, giving me a drop-them-to-their-knees-on-the-trading-room-floor stare, "Simon is on his way to Salon du Chocolat."

As though I knew what the hell that was. "Oh, of course. Well, how much time do you think we need?"

I added it up in my head: one hour for him to defrost, about twenty-seven minutes for me to stop staring at my shoes, and another eight minutes of updates.

"Not more than two hours a week, I'd say." He frowned, as if even that was too much time with me.

"Tuesdays at noon, then?" Tuesdays with Scary. Fun!

He pulled out some man-gadget and looked down at the little display. "That should be fine. Can I have your phone number?"

"My phone number?"

"Yes, Ms. Hagan, just in case I need to reach you." He spoke as if he were talking to someone not so swift. Which, actually, he was.

"Oh. Okay." I gave it to him, and checked my watch. 1:42. Rats, not time to leave yet.

He gestured toward the waitress, who came bustling over as if he were asking her to bear his first child. "You all set here?" she said, giving him the once-over. Twice.

He didn't seem to notice. I guess if you were that determinedly handsome, and that autocratic, you took it for granted people found you attractive. At least until they got to know you.

He slapped a credit card down on the table as I was scrabbling in my bag for some cash. He frowned at me. "I'll take care of it. It's business."

Nope, sure wasn't anything personal here.

"Thanks."

I rose to go as he signed the credit card receipt. We walked back out into the street, where the sun had managed to fight its way through the clouds. The sky was a bright blue and I blinked as my eyes adjusted. Nick, of course, just pulled out some super-sleek shades and put them on, making him look even more threatening. His lips pulled down at the edges as he looked down the street. I saw why when the Glory of Simon appeared.

"Afternoon Nick, Molly." Simon stood in front of us, curls waving in the breeze, his green eyes squinted against the sunlight. He really was a vision.

"Good afternoon, Simon," Nick said in a curt voice. He sounded so—flatly and solidly American. As opposed to Simon's patrician British accent. "I thought you were on your way already. Ms. Hagan and I were discussing the project."

Simon winked. "I didn't think you were indulging in anything illicit, Nick, not you, buddy." He looked at me, frowning a little. "Nick's explained he'll be working with you?"

"Yes, he has, Mr. Baxter." Keep it professional, Molly. Never mind his laughing green eyes made me think about all kinds of things. Simon smiled, like he knew what I was thinking. Hey, he could read minds, too!

"It's a shame we won't be working together, but Nick in-
sists," Simon said, spreading his hands wide in a helpless gesture. Which fooled no one—helpless he wasn't.

Nick's arm stiffened on my elbow. "If it were what I
wanted, Simon, we wouldn't be in this situation," Nick shot
back. What the heck was going on? I felt like I had gotten
stuck in the middle of a kung fu movie, and I was the wooden
board.

"Uh, I'd love to stay," *and watch you two scrap over territory like wild dogs,* "but I've got to get back. Mr. Harrison,
thanks for the information and the coffee. I'll see you next
week. Simon, I mean, Mr. Baxter, it was nice to see you
again."

As I walked toward the subway, I couldn't shake the feeling that both of them were watching me. Why? What the hell
was going on?

And why did I feel as if I were stuck in the middle of a
rock (that'd be Simon) and a hard place (that'd be Nick)?

Tom Jonesing for Cookies

Rich, sensual, unabashedly luscious . . .
this cookie of undetermined origin will
bring keeping-up-with-the-Joneses to a
whole new level. English cream, country butter, hand-milled flour, and an excess of chocolate makes this cookie the
most rambunctious lot in the bunch.

7

"MOMMY?"

"Mm?" I was poring over my cookbooks on the floor of the kitchen, searching for inspiration within the seldom-cracked pages. Aidan's hand tugged at my sleeve.

"Mommy." His tone was peremptory now.

"Yes, honey?" I lifted my eyes from Betty Crocker's words of wisdom. Aidan was regarding me with a serious look in his brown eyes. I put the book down and gathered him into my arms. "What is it?"

"Mommy?"

I nuzzled his head. He had lost that baby smell a few years ago, but he still smelled delicious. It took concentrated effort not to bite him.

"Yes, honey, what is it?"

"Is Daddy ever coming back?"

My throat closed over. Hugh and I had sat down with Aidan when I felt I could without blubbering, and explained the situation, but six-year-olds being what they are, we knew he'd eventually need a refresher course on Why Mommy and Daddy Are Not Living in the Same Place Anymore.

I brushed my lips over the top of his head. "No, honey, he won't be living with us again, but you'll see him as much as you ever did." More, now that Mr. Billable Hours had lost his job.

He twisted his head to look up at me, a sad little look on his face. "I don't like going to his new house without you."

Oh, boy.

"Why not, honey?"

"Daddy's not fun. He just sits and watches TV. And not kids' shows, either. Football," he announced in a scornful voice.

Believe me, I had the same complaint when he was plopped down on the couch every Sunday afternoon.

"What do you do when you're there?"

"That lady gives me cookies. That's nice." Ah, bribery. She hadn't even borne a child—at least, not that I knew of— and she had already learned the sugar secret. What was a smart woman like her doing with a dumbass like Hugh?

"And what else?"

He shrugged. "Daddy takes me shopping sometimes. She always comes, too."

I hope she pays, I thought. "Do you want me to talk to Daddy about it?" I'd rather eat fried lima beans, or engage in some exploratory dental surgery, but if it'd take that worried little look off his face, I'd do it.

"I want you to come next time. It'd be fun, then."

He gave me a big, winsome smile, and I couldn't help but smile back. My hero.

"I can't come, honey. But I'll talk to Daddy, promise." I kissed him again. He snuggled more into my arms.

"Okay. And Mommy?"

"Yeah, honey?"

"When are we going to get Beast?"

"Maybe next weekend." *Hi, I'm Molly, and I lie through my teeth to my son.*

"Goody. 'Cause no one at school believed we were going to get a hairless cat, and I wanna bring him to show-and-tell."

"I'm not sure— Oh, never mind. Okay. We'll start looking for him next weekend."

"I'm hungry."

That I could handle.

I rose from my position on the kitchen floor, tossed Ms. Crocker aside, and headed for the cupboard.

"Aidan, what do you think about Yam and Mozzarella Surprise?"

She took the paper from me with a look of surprise. "I didn't ask you for a list this time, Molly, did I?"

I grinned at her. I liked ruffling Dr. Lowell's feathers. "No, let's just say I was inspired."

She smiled back and unfolded the paper. She adjusted her glasses lower on the bridge of her nose, then cleared her throat.

THINGS EVERY NEWLY SINGLE WOMAN MUST DO

1. Take out a personals ad. One where you lie about your weight, your age, and your desperation.

2. Fantasize about having sex with every inappropriate man possible. Throw in a few appropriate ones just to prove you're not completely hopeless.

3. Purchase inappropriate clothing (not necessarily just to wear during sex). Preferably in pastels. And florals. Hopefully both.

4. Scour the obituaries, counting how many single women died, and how old they were. Obsess about oncoming death. Wonder if they were wearing pastels when they croaked.

5. Make lists justifying why the single life is okay.

"Very nice." She folded the paper back up and smoothed out the edges, schoolteacher-style. "May I keep this?"

"Sure." I shrugged.

"Am I to presume you've done some of these items?"

"The personals ad. And the obituary thing, but that was only for a couple of days. Then I got skeeved out, so I stopped."

"And . . . ?"

"Nothing yet. I don't think I'm being too picky, but I don't want to rush into anything. I'm still married, after all."

"Of course, but it is a good thing to dive back into the dating pool. You don't know how long the divorce process is going to take."

Did everyone have to associate dating with water? Because I felt like I was going to drown.

"And the fantasizing?"

Was now the time to mention Simon, the Beauteous Brit? "Um . . . a little bit."

She gave me an approving smile. "Excellent. Did you speak to your mother?"

"Yes. She said she couldn't lend me anything," I bit out.

Dr. Lowell frowned. "Couldn't or wouldn't?"

I rolled my eyes. "I didn't ask her to clarify when she turned me down. Although I would've liked to ask her why she said no."

"You didn't." It was a statement. Dr. Lowell knew me—and my issues with my mother—well.

"Nope."

"So what are your other options?"

Suddenly I was mad. "Why do there always have to be other options? What if there aren't any? What if Aidan and I have to move to Idaho or somewhere and grow potatoes? What if I can't do it?"

"Why are you so angry, Molly? Not that it's bad to be angry," she continued in her mellifluous therapist tone.

I flung my arms up in frustration. "I'm angry because Hugh's a fuck who left me, and now he's taking away my means of support, and I have no money, and Aidan wants a freaking cat, and the only cat we can get is that hairless hypoallergenic kind, which are expensive. And I can't let Aidan down. Not that I can afford to do anything." My words came out in a rush, running together toward the end. I gave a little hiccupy cry.

"So what are your other options?" she repeated, handing me a tissue. I blew my nose and glared at her. She smiled back.

"I found out a little more about the teaching thing. I've got to get my paperwork together."

"That shouldn't be too hard."

"Easy for you to say," I replied with a sniff.

"Yes, it is," she returned in a complacent tone. Sometimes I wanted her to explode in a mystical spontaneous combustion thing. Sometimes I wanted to pull her up off her leather-padded chair and do the samba with her. Guess which time this was.

"Your assignment for next week is to find out exactly what you need to apply to this program. And, just for fun, how about doing something . . . *inappropriate*?"

Who knew my therapist could be so naughty?

"I've had worse homework," I replied grudgingly, getting up off the couch.

"This is like homework," I wailed into the phone later that night.

"That's because it is," Keisha replied. She was clearly not putting up with any of my crap.

"You're right," I admitted. "And I should just do what I used to do when I had a big assignment in college—"

"Eat a bag of cookies and whine?"

Ouch. "No," I replied in an exaggeratedly patient tone, "break it down, piece by piece. Which is, actually, what Dr. Lowell is always pushing me to do."

"And me, too! I tell you, honey, you should just send me the money you pay her."

"What money? If I don't figure out something soon, I'm going to have to stop seeing her. And paying for electricity, cable, eyebrow pencil, books—" I heard my voice escalate in a rising panic.

"Calm down. You'll figure it out. You're smart."

"Yeah, that and three dollars and seventy-nine cents gets me a small cup of coffee at Starbucks."

"And it's that kind of attitude that will defeat you."

I plucked at the throw on top of me, pulling out a piece of yarn. "I know that, I do, it's just that it's so hard for me to get over it. To get over myself."

The truth of it hit me like a slammed door. My hand stilled.

She knew it, too. Her voice was softer when she spoke. "You can do it. I have confidence in you."

I paused a second, then continued. "I am sorry to be so lame."

"Don't forget whiny."

"Yeah, thanks for reminding me." I knew she could hear the smile in my voice. "And maybe I'll have this all figured out by the time Aidan has traded in his Pokémon comics for *The Catcher in the Rye*." I contemplated the thought of a grown-up Aidan, at least one old enough to read Salinger.

And then it hit me.

"Bread."

"Okay, now you've lost me," Keisha replied. "Are you talking 1960s hippie talk again? Because you know I can't hang with that."

"Catcher in the Rye Bread! It's genius!"

"What is? Your ability to make weird puns?"

"The bakery assignment. The bakery's right near the New York Public Library. Simon wants something that will tie the bakery and the library together. And what ties things together better than bad puns?"

Keisha giggled. "Isn't it just like you. In the pit of despair, completely insecure, and you come up with exactly what you need."

"Yeast of Eden!" I shouted. She laughed again, that big belly laugh I loved hearing.

"How about 'To Have and Have Donut'?" Keisha asked.

"Flour Mill on the Floss."

"Bread Badge of Courage."

"Buns and Lovers."

By now, we were both laughing so hard our words came out in little gasping puffs.

"Okay, I've got to go write these down. Thanks, Keisha. I love you."

"Me, too, honey."

Once I'd replaced the receiver on the hook and drunk my now-cold coffee, I found my notebook and started scribbling. Boy, was Simon the Stunning going to be impressed with me. I wasn't so sure about Nick the Unnerving, otherwise known as Mr. Supercilious, but I was damn sure going to try to—what was it I said?—knock his socks off. And then I would try to do something . . . *inappropriate*.

It was my homework, after all.

A Raisin in the Bun

It's the quintessential American conundrum: what to do when unexpected riches arise. Here, supersucculent whiskey-soaked raisins are embedded within the framework of a traditional sticky bun, a gastronomic largesse that surprises and delights. Cinnamon, brown sugar, honey, pecans, and butter. And raisins. Amazing.

8

WHAT WAS THE MOST INAPPROPRIATE THING I'D EVER DONE, anyway? It was hard to think of anything. Did that make me a good person, or just unbelievably boring?

I sorta thought it might be the latter. But this was my moment, right? I mean, if not now, when? I wouldn't do anything dangerous, nothing that would risk my self-esteem—the amount I'd managed to build back up since Hugh left. That meant getting crazy-drunk and tearing down the street naked wasn't an option. Not that it sounded appealing anyway—I was likely to be cold and worry what parts were jiggling too much.

But inappropriate could be exploring things I'd been too scared of, not to mention too *married,* to do before. Maybe I could—and should—flirt back with Simon. I mean, it wasn't like he was permanent material or anything; even I could tell his suave persona was just one aspect of his general arrogance.

Of course, if I had his looks and his baking ability, I'd be pretty damned arrogant, too.

But I could, perhaps, bask in that arrogance, have fun with it. With him. It wasn't the worst idea I'd ever had.

I was wrapping my head around possible other inappropriate measures when the phone rang.

"Hello?"

"Molly. It's John."

"John, what the hell is going on? What happened to Natalie?"

There was a brief pause, and I thought I heard him exhale. "Just what I wanted to talk to you about. Can you come in today?"

I checked my watch. "Just barely. I'm not likely to meet anyone there, am I? I don't have time to change."

He chuckled. "No, just me. As long as you're not wearing pajamas, you should be okay."

Good thing I'd changed. "See you in forty-five minutes."

I grabbed my purse and threw *Wuthering Heights* into a side pocket. That, I knew, at least had a romance, albeit a twisted one.

The subway came blessedly quickly, and within moments I was engrossed in Emily Brontë's obsessively bleak story. Dr. Lowell would have a field day with her.

"Hey, John." I poked my head into his office. He was on the phone but gestured for me to come in. I sat in the chair Simon had been in before. It gave me a prepubescent kind of thrill to park my ass in the same spot his had occupied. That was inappropriate, for sure.

"Right. Wednesday morning. We'll be there. I'll make sure Molly is free."

He looked at me and nodded, as if to confirm the appointment. I nodded back.

"Okay. See you then. Bye."

He hung up the phone, then rose and walked to the front of the desk, perching on it with one ultracasual leg swinging back and forth. "Thanks for coming in on such short notice, Molly."

I laughed. Probably more ruefully than I liked. "It's not like I had a lot of other things to do. I'm all done sticking pins in my Hugh voodoo doll."

John gave an uncomfortable chuckle. "Right. Well. You've spoken to Simon? And Nick?"

"Yes, both of them. What happened?"

He waved his hand. "Something between Natalie and Simon. The good news is, he's agreed to keep his account here."

I knew that already, I wanted to say, but I wasn't sure how John would feel about me meeting Simon off the clock, so to speak. "And Natalie?" I had to ask. I wanted to know what happened, just in case she reappeared in all her Prada glory.

He cleared his throat. "She's setting up her own firm. It'll probably take her a month or so to get going, and Simon just didn't have the time to wait—not that he wanted to wait for her anyway."

"Were they an item or something?" I knew they were, Natalie had said as much, I just wanted John's confirmation. Why, I couldn't answer.

"Mm. Which never mixes," he said, almost dashing my hopes of boinking my new boss. Almost.

"Men always leave, don't they?" I asked John with a wry grin. Hey, I *was* recovering if I could joke about it. Wait'll I tell Dr. Lowell!

"I never thought you and Hugh were a good couple, actually. I always thought you were too good for him. Too smart. And I was right."

I had a hard time meeting his eyes. Compliments always threw me, made me feel as though I was undeserving, or afraid. "Thanks for the nice words, and all, but remember, he left me. It's not like he up and left because he suddenly realized he was stupider than I was."

John cleared his throat. "Yes, well, I've met Sylvia, his . . . well, you know"—he gave a helpless gesture—"and she can't hold a candle to you."

Part of my brain wanted to pump him for information about her: Was she nice? Was she funny? What kind of shoes did she wear?

And part of me wanted to clasp my hands over my ears so I wouldn't have to hear anything about her.

And the other part of me—how many parts did that make, anyway?—wanted to ask John why he was telling me this in the first place.

All my parts united to keep my mouth shut. "Thank you," I said, folding my hands and placing them in my lap. *Could we please make that the end of the discussion?*

"Anyway," he said, hoisting himself off the desk and sitting in the chair next to mine, "I was just on the phone with Simon, and he wanted to make sure we were ready to go for next Wednesday. Do you think you'll have a presentation by then?"

"Yes, I do. I've come up with the most am—"

He held up his hand. "Save it for Wednesday. That's not why I asked you to come in today. I've got some more work for you, if you're interested."

"Sure." All thoughts of Simon, and Natalie, and Hugh, and his Better Model vanished from my head. This was *money.* "That's great. More copywriting, or copyediting?"

He leaned forward and picked up a stack of rubber band–bound papers on his desk. "Copyediting. It's a new client, and I wanted to turn this around quickly, and my usual guy is up to his eyeballs in work, so—"

I reached for the papers.

He kept talking. "And, this might sound weird, and all, but I really need a date for Friday night."

"I don't think I know anyone, John."

He did one of those eye rolls I'd seen far too much of from Aidan. "Not a friend, Molly, you. I want to take you. I know you can't tell me now, until you've got babysitting lined up, but there's this cocktail party for Yale business school alums, and I really need someone to go with me."

My face must have registered my confusion. He exhaled in an exasperated sigh. "It's not a date, Molly. We're going as friends, okay? I just would really like to have someone there I'm comfortable with."

I released a breath I didn't know I'd been holding. That would have really been inappropriate, and not in a good way. Being friends with the opposite sex did have its potential pitfalls. "Okay, I'll give you a call later today. Sound good?"

"Great," he replied, sliding the papers into my hand. "Thanks for doing this. It pays the usual rate. And if you could turn it around by Monday morning, that'd be even greater."

I could see why *he* wasn't doing the copywriting. *Great and greater.*

"You're going out . . . with John?" Lissa's tone was, if possible, even more disbelieving than Keisha's had been. She stared at me over Aidan's head as he wrapped his arms around her waist. Man, he had fallen hard.

"Um, yeah." I was modeling my outfit for her, a sleek black cocktail dress that miraculously looked like it was still in fashion. "It's not a real date," I said, parroting his earlier words. "He said he wanted someone there he felt okay with. It's kinda sweet, actually."

"Yale business school? That sounds fancy."

I shrugged, poking one of my dress-up earrings through the hole in my ear. "I'm guessing it'll be people my age sitting around drinking white wine spritzers and talking about their 401(k)s." I looked up and grinned at Lissa. "I should fit right in."

"You will." Her tone was reassuring. "Just walk in wearing that dress and open your mouth to drop one of those fancy words you use. Maybe mention an obscure eighteenth-century novel or something. Just don't talk about romance novels, Pokémon, or how"—her voice dropped into a whisper—"husbands suck."

Aidan raised his head at the mention of Pokémon. She smiled and tapped him on the nose.

"Got it. By the way, are you liking *Ethan Frome*?"

"I'm loving it," she exclaimed, sounding surprised. "It's such a great story, and I almost missed my stop the other day 'cause I was just where it seemed like he might say something . . . but he didn't." Her face fell.

"Get used to that feeling. Literary fiction has a lot of those near-miss moments."

"What time will you be back?" she asked, helping me to adjust my coat just so.

"Not too late. Bye, honey." I waved at Aidan, who immediately went and latched onto Lissa's leg.

"Lissa, what are Captain America's superpowers?" I heard him ask as I locked the front door.

It was already crowded by the time we got there. A sea of blond hair bobbed and floated through the genteel cacophony. Most of the other women had opted for wearing black also, although I spied a few brave floral souls brightening the crowd.

The room was decorated in a pre–Valentine's Day theme, red velvet hearts hanging from the ceiling, darker red velvet curtains swagged back from the windows. There was a three-piece orchestra playing in the far corner of the room, their music a delicately rich undertone to the general hubbub of conversation. The decoration underscored what the perfectly coiffed blondes and well-tailored suits were already making crystal clear: This place was meant for people who had money, who were comfortable with money, and who planned to make a lot more of it in the future.

In other words, not meant for the likes of me. I envied them as much as I had ever envied anyone, even Mary Cobb in the fifth grade, who got breasts a lot earlier than the rest of us girls.

John placed his hand at the small of my back and began to steer me through the crowd toward the bar. I was glad he was there to help me navigate the Room of Intimidation.

As we reached the bar, John removed his hand and came to stand beside me. "A Manhattan, please, and the lady would like . . . ?"

"A white wine spritzer."

"Hey, buddy!" A masculine voice boomed over the crowd. John whipped his head around so fast I had to swivel my neck so he didn't hit me.

"Mikey!" John shouted, lifting his glass in a mock toast. The man barreled through the crowd to reach us, a huge grin on his already wide face. He was tall, too, taller than almost every blond head in there. And, of course, he was blond. I noticed he was wearing a double-breasted David Letterman suit with an exceedingly ugly tie. He looked loaded with largesse, both physical and financial.

John gestured to me. "Molly, I'd like you to meet Michael, my partner-in-crime for most of business school."

The man stuck out his large hand and enfolded mine within. "Nice to meet you, Molly. John, haven't seen you since Vegas." He winked broadly.

John turned a little pink. "Yeah, Vegas."

The man gave a knowing grin. "C'mon, there's nothing to be embarrassed about. I'm sure your friend here"—he emphasized the word *friend* with a knowing leer—"knows what you're capable of."

There was an awkward silence as I pondered what John might have been up to in Vegas, and Michael kept watching my expression. What, did he think I was going to demand John tell me right there? No wonder John wanted a friend if this was the type of conversation he could expect to have.

Michael seemed to figure out he wasn't going to get a rise out of me, so he took another attack, planting his elbow on the bar next to me. "So how's business, John?" There was an undercurrent of aggression in Michael's tone. Ah, the ego of the MBA.

"Fine. Great, actually. We just signed a deal with a Fortune 500 company to do all their marketing and promotion."

"Very impressive."

"And you? Still working for your father?"

The man squirmed a little bit. He pushed his arms forward and twitched his shirtsleeves back a little so his watch was showing. It practically reeked of a five-figure price tag.

"Yes, well, the old man's not doing as well as he had been—"

"Sorry to hear that." John took a long pull on his drink.

"And I've been taking on some of his responsibilities—"

"Good for you, helping your father out like that." I noticed every time John said "your father" he imbued it with a sharp edge. His face bore a somewhat aloof expression, also, which made me wonder, since it was so unlike John's normal openness. Plus I'd never even heard of this Michael guy before.

"Yes, well, the company's doing about thirty million annual sales," Michael finished, gulping the dark brown liquid in his glass as if it were water.

John did the same, upending the glass until it was empty. "Pretty good."

God, I felt as if I were in some financial western: "Draw your accounts receivable, pardner." Or maybe a Dirty Harry movie: "So, do you feel wealthy, punk? Huh, do you?"

"Another drink, Molly?" Michael asked, taking my empty glass from me and setting it on the bar.

"Uh, no thanks. Maybe in a little bit." I spied a waiter with a tray of hors d'oeuvres and tried to make some "I'm peckish" eye contact with him. He made a beeline for me, probably because my dark brown hair made a good target in the sea of blond.

"What are these?" I asked, pointing at a little dumpling thing.

"Portobello mushroom, crab, and brie pot stickers." He held the tray aloft just under my nose, which caught and savored the aroma of rich, aged cheese.

"Yes, thank you," I said, grabbing one and popping it in my mouth. It was almost too big to fit, and I felt my cheeks bulge out.

And then I saw him. And her.

Which meant, basically, *them.*

Just as my mouth was stuffed with snooty mushrooms and runny cheese.

This was not how I had pictured our first meeting.

"Molly?" Hugh walked toward me, a surprised expression on his face. She, because it had to be *her,* walked slightly behind him. I held his eyes for just a beat longer than I really wanted to, mostly because I didn't want to have to look at her.

And then I saw her, really saw her. Blond, leggy, thin, fashionably dressed in a Schiaparelli pink cocktail dress that looked as if it cost more than my entire wardrobe. She smiled, flashing flawlessly white teeth. Worser and worser.

She looked like Lissa, only more polished, more confident, and definitely more well read. I bet she even considered *The Ambassadors* fluffy reading.

And John thought she couldn't hold a candle to me? His candle standards must be pretty high.

"Hi, Hugh," I replied, finally forcing the last lump of dumpling down my throat.

"This is Molly?" the vixen said in a low, husky voice. Even her vocal cords were sexier than me. She held out her hand, slender, slightly tanned, and waited for me to reach up to clasp it. "I should have known, Aidan looks just like you," she continued in a pleasant tone. I had to give her points for trying.

"Yes. You must be Sylvia," I said in as noncommittal a tone as I could muster.

Hugh gave a little nervous yelp and looked anxiously back to Sylvia, as if he were concerned I would leap over him to throttle her. As if I blamed her.

No, I blamed *him*. It wasn't her fault he was a faithless bastard.

"Hi, Hugh, Sylvia." John moved closer to me. "I didn't realize you guys would be here, I thought Mike had you out of town."

John knew her *schedule*? I hoped to God my mouth wasn't literally hanging open because there were probably weird sticky bits of Brie dangling from the roof of it. Why did he know her schedule?

Mike clapped a bearlike paw around Sylvia's waist. "This one wrapped up a big project even earlier than we expected, so she was able to make it tonight. I felt bad making her miss the opportunity to show off her new boyfriend."

Hugh smiled weakly.

As he did most things. Meow!

Sylvia turned to me. Was it my imagination, or was her look just a little bit condescending? "I'm sure neither Molly nor John needs to hear about all that, Mike," she said in a honeyed tone. Not my imagination, then. "John, how's your little company doing? I heard Natalie has joined you?" Her eyebrows arched in surprise.

I could have sworn I heard John's jaw snap. "My company is doing well, thank you, Sylvia," he said through gritted teeth. "We got the Simon Baxter account. Natalie was working on it, but she and Simon didn't quite get along." He made it sound as if she couldn't take the pressure or something. Funny how a savvy businessman could spin anything he wanted.

Sylvia's smile grew more brilliant. White teeth flashed in a face filled with antipathy. "Simon is usually an excellent judge of character. A shame about Natalie. She and Simon, well, they . . ." Her voice trailed off.

Hugh turned to Sylvia, muttering something into her ear. Her eyes flashed blue fire, then she turned back toward us. "Hugh and I are going to get something to drink. Excuse us," she said, grabbing Hugh by the wrist and practically dragging him to the other side of the room.

"Sylvia's a ball breaker, that's for sure," Mike said proudly. John shot me a quick glance, then cleared his throat.

"Molly, would you like to go watch the orchestra play for a while?"

Will it drown out the voices in my head?

"Sure. Sounds great. Nice to meet you," I said to Michael, watching him down another glass of straight liquor.

"See you in a bit, Molly," he replied, looking me up and down like he was inspecting me for defects.

We walked toward the corner of the room where the band was playing. As soon as we were out of earshot I spun around and stared at John. "You never said you knew her. You said you had met her, but not that you knew her. I mean, there is a difference. Why didn't you tell me?"

"I didn't know they'd be here, Molly, honestly I didn't," John said, holding his hands out in an apologetic gesture.

"That's not what I asked, John." Damn it, he was supposed to be my friend. I was tired of being so darn nice all the time. "I asked why you didn't tell me that you knew her. Have known her, I'm guessing, since graduate school."

He bit his lip. Funny, I thought only romance heroines did that. "I didn't tell you because I didn't want you to be upset. I'm Hugh's friend, too, Molly."

"Are you how they met?" I demanded.

He drew himself up to his full height and locked eyes with me. "Yes." He cleared his throat. "I'm the one who introduced Hugh and Sylvia." I think my mouth must've dropped open again, because he was looking at me in concern. "Are you okay?" He shook his head and stared at the floor. "Look," he mumbled, "I had no idea she was—that they were—that." He looked back at me. "Are you okay?"

"Yeah, of course. Why wouldn't I be?" I smiled the widest, fakest smile I could. I knew he'd know it was pretend, but I was betting he would want to drop the subject. Like every man I'd ever known.

He gave me a relieved look. "Good, because I've been feeling so guilty, and that I should have told you about everything—that I'm the reason they met."

My mind went there, right away. "Did you know they were seeing each other? I mean, before he left?"

His look said it all. He opened his mouth to speak, but I

stopped him by putting my hand up. "Look," I said, "let's just not talk about it anymore. Still a bit painful."

"Of course." He sounded relieved. Perhaps because I wasn't going to unleash the Horrific Hagan Hissy Fit. Hey, I was learning! "Mmm," I murmured.

"Anyway," he continued, stuffing his hands into the pockets of his slacks, "thanks for coming tonight. You're a good friend."

It was on the tip of my tongue to say something that would sound suspiciously like an accusation that he was anything but a good friend if he was withholding all this info from me. But I wasn't that mean. Definitely not that inappropriate. Was I?

I couldn't do that, though. He was a good friend, even if he made some poor choices. He had given me work and he was on my side, sort of, in the Hugh versus Molly showdown. So what if he wasn't perfect? I sure as hell wasn't. And besides, friends—the kind of people like Lissa or Keisha—were precious enough. Were rare enough.

So I held my tongue on that, at least. I rested my head against his shoulder. "Would you mind if we left soon? I'm really tired."

Tired of feeling inadequate. Tired of Hugh, and the specter of our relationship. Tired of worrying about the future and how Aidan would eat and if I'd ever be with anyone again.

"Sure, I totally understand," John replied.

We did our best to dodge Hugh and the Perfect Woman as we exited and then headed out to a diner, since that one pot sticker hadn't really helped with my "haven't had dinner since I had to fit into that dress" problem.

It was kinda cool, actually; now that I'd seen more of John's own insecurities, his clear feelings of inadequacy around his buddy Mike, and gotten more of a glimpse into his past, I felt less awful about my own self.

Perspective did that for a person. And good friends.

Tart of Darkness

Obscure, faintly dangerous ingredients—Belgian chocolate, white rum, African groundnuts—combine in a swirl of flavor, topped off with a heady adventure of whipped cream. Delicious, delectable, and almost completely inscrutable, this tart reveals your most secret desires. And if Kurtz had been able to savor this, who knows how the story would have ended?

9

"HAPPY VALENTINE'S DAY, MOMMY," AIDAN SAID, BEAMING. He held out a piece of paper with hearts scrawled all over it. It was barely 8:00 A.M., and I was already crying. But good tears. Definitely an improvement.

I'd spent the weekend on John's last-minute emergency project, and it had taken both days, which meant Aidan got to watch a lot of TV. No wonder he thought I was great. It had been hard work, but it was satisfyingly hard—plus that money would really come in handy.

"Thank you, sweetie," I replied, putting my coffee cup down on the dining room table and taking it from him. I reached for him, and gathered him up in a big hug. I was glad he was still young enough not to mind when I hugged him.

We were in the living room getting ready for school—he watching TV while I tried to cajole him to eat and put clothes on all at the same time. It was a continual miracle he wasn't starving and naked.

"So will you be my valentine?" I asked him, peering into his little face as I held him.

He made a face. "No, you're my *mom,* not my valentine." I unwrapped my arms from him and glared back at him with an exaggerated expression.

"No? Well, if I'm not your valentine, who is?" I demanded in mock outrage.

"Lissa." He smiled up at me, and it wrenched my heart. He was still my baby, but he wouldn't be forever. And he was already falling in love with a blonde. Taking after his dad.

"She's coming over tomorrow night, do you want to make something special for her?"

His face brightened even more. "Yeah! I'll make her a picture with all her favorite Pokémon." He scampered to his little desk and sat down, his face already screwed up in concentration.

"You can start on that now, but we'll have to stop in about fifteen minutes to go to school," I warned. No reply. "Did you hear me?"

He looked up, clearly annoyed. "Yes. Fifteen minutes. I'll finish it up after school."

I nodded at him, then ran down the hall to do a last check of my outfit.

Today was Tuesday. And Tuesday was Meet with Mr. Harsh day.

I had chosen my clothing with an eye toward projecting an air of sleek professionalism: black pants, black suit jacket, black camisole underneath. Either I was a New York urbanite or a really enthusiastic undertaker.

My hair was a little too long, so I pulled it back into a low ponytail, careful to choose a black hair tie. I looked . . . fine. Polished, almost. As long as I didn't forget and stuff an action figure into my pocket, I'd be okay.

Taking a deep breath, I stalked in unfamiliar heels to the bathroom where my makeup awaited me. Eyebrows, foundation, eyeliner, mascara. No lipstick, that seemed too coquettish.

"Ready, honey?" Aidan looked up at me and his eyes widened. "Are you going to a special dinner, Mommy? You look . . . funny." I took that as a compliment.

"No, no special dinner, just a meeting while you're in school. Let's go, okay?"

I met Nick outside the store. He nodded at me as I walked up the street, checked his watch, and nodded toward the coffee shop we'd been to before.

Nice to see you again, too, Mr. Close-Mouthed.

The coffee shop's windows were decorated with cardboard hearts and heart-shaped doilies. A bulbous Cupid shot an arrow just under the BEST GYROS IN TOWN sign. A man was selling roses on the corner, ten dollars a rose.

He pushed the door open for me and I stepped in, the odor of coffee and hamburger grease greeting my nose. It was empty except for a single man sitting at the counter, so I directed a questioning look at Nick, who gestured toward the booth farthest from the door. I walked toward it, slipping my coat off—it was too warm inside—and trying to surreptitiously shake out the wrinkles in my suit jacket. I slid onto the padded bench and placed my bag next to me. Nick sat down and nodded again. I withdrew my notebook as the waitress—the same one from last time—bustled over and handed us menus. For once, I was too anxious to even think about eating.

I pushed the menu aside as I opened my notebook to my page of notes and handed it across the table. Nick put his menu aside and began reading.

There was a long silence.

Just when I was about to confess to being an idiot, he spoke.

"You think this is a sustainable marketing approach?"

Nick raised his eyes and gave me a skeptical look. I immediately started to sweat.

"What can I get you?" It was the waitress, her pencil poised at the ready.

"Coffee. Black. Oh, and a piece of pie, too," he said.

"Cherry, lemon meringue, or chocolate cream?"

"Chocolate cream, definitely," he said, smiling at her.

Apparently it was a deadly smile, judging by the waitress's reaction. She looked at me, her mouth turned down a little. Guess I didn't have such a nice smile. Whatever. "You?"

"Coffee, light with one sugar."

"That it?"

"Yes." She took our menus and left us. Alone.

"Hm." He frowned, looking down at the list of names I'd presented. Then he chortled, which made me jump in my seat.

"I like this one: Bread Badge of Courage. I'm not sure how you'd be able to do Fry the Beloved Country, though." He continued scanning the page, his blue eyes narrowed in concentration. I took the opportunity to stare at him while he was directing his lasered focus on something besides me and my perceived inadequacies.

His harsh, angular features made him look dangerous, raffish almost. Like the hero of a romance novel where the heroine isn't quite sure if the hero is a hero or a villain. At least not until he saves her from some horrid situation and gets all noble and stuff. The jury was still out in real life what he'd end up being.

He raised his head and trapped my eyes with his. "So. Sustainability? Clearly you're creative and clever. Think about it."

It should have been a compliment, but he delivered it as if it were an order.

"Oh, sure." I let my mind wander. "Um . . ."

"Yes?" he said, raking a hand through his hair. It made him look vulnerable, at least more vulnerable than I had seen him before. Which was Not Vulnerable at All.

I shrugged. "I think as long as there are books and puns, you can keep the concept going forever. I mean, the star of the bakery isn't going to be the marketing and clever catch-phrases anyway; that's just the gimmick to get people into the store. The real draw is, of course, Simon's baking, right?"

He nodded, as though surprised I'd had a good idea. Heck, *I* was surprised. "You're right. And this"—he tapped the notebook with his hand—"is really a unique approach. Good work, Ms. Hagan."

Hey, Mr. Frosty thaws!

I blinked at him again. He was going to think I had a twitch. "Thank you."

He looked back down at the list, then let out another bark of laughter.

"Far from the Fattening Crowd. For the Atkins crowd? Have you read Thomas Hardy?"

Blink, blink. Now *I* was beginning to think I had a twitch. "Yes, but honestly, I find him a little depressing."

He caught my eye and frowned, as if he were lecturing me. "Aren't most literary classics depressing? I mean, other than Dickens or Shakespeare or someone. And even in those, someone usually gets their just deserts."

"Just Desserts would be a good name if the store were planning on selling . . ." I stopped for a dramatic pause.

"Just desserts," he finished, chuckling. His expression returned to its normal stoic lines. "But unfortunately, it's not."

The waitress returned with our coffee, placing his gently in front of him and slapping mine down as if she'd like to slap me.

I took a sip and settled the cup back on the saucer. "*Jane Eyre*?" I offered. "That has a happy ending."

He took a bite of pie. "Even in that, the hero has to go blind before they can be together again."

He read Dickens? Shakespeare? *Brontë*? Be still, my heart. Next he'd be telling me he read Jane Austen. I would've guessed he'd only read Machiavelli's *The Prince,* at least when he wasn't perusing *The Arrogant Guy's Guide to Total Intimidation*. Funny how impressions could change. At least a little bit.

"Did you major in English?" I asked him, stirring my coffee. I took a sip and leaned back in my seat.

"No. Philosophy," he answered tersely, as if he regretted his brief moment of openness. Then he surprised me by continuing. "People just aren't hiring philosophers these days," he said with a wry smile, "so I ended up going to grad school for my MBA."

He passed the notebook back to me. "I assume you'll be fleshing these out for tomorrow's meeting?" Again, it was not a suggestion.

"Of course." I tucked the notebook back into my bag.

"And then, if Simon approves, we can work on the next stage of the work. We'll have to coordinate the marketing with the actual design of the shop. So I'll need you on retainer for a bit longer to make sure everything is as it should be."

"Of course," I repeated, trying hard not to bounce up and down in my chair. Maybe Aidan could get Beast after all. *And* we could afford food. Huzzah!

He lifted his fork to his mouth, then paused to meet my eyes. "This pie is amazing. You wouldn't think so, because the coffee is awful—"

I took another sip from my cup. I felt guilty because I hadn't noticed the coffee was kind of bitter. Oh, the irony.

"But you have to have a bite of this. Here—"

He hoisted his fork, a lumpy, gooey mess of pie balanced precariously on its tines. He held it toward me, nodding his head in an impatient way. I had no choice.

I leaned forward, opening my mouth as he slid the fork in. I closed my lips and savored the flavor. Deep, rich chocolate matched with equally rich whipped cream. Did I taste vanilla? I closed my eyes for a moment to concentrate on what I was tasting. I opened them only to see his intense gaze focused on my mouth.

He started, then pulled the fork back and rested it on his plate. He cleared his throat, as if he were unsure of what had happened, and I smiled a little. Inside. I didn't want to make him bark at me or anything.

"You're right," I said, running my tongue over my lips, "delicious."

Now that was inappropriate. Hee. It felt good.

His eyes widened a little, then his face got a hard, closed look to it.

Another customer came into the store, holding a big bouquet of flowers. Not roses, but pink geraniums. They were still pretty, though.

He spotted our waitress and headed to her, holding the bouquet out with a big grin on his face.

Wow, and she was smiling back! She was actually nice-looking when she wasn't despising my entire self.

And it struck me with a wash of what I had come to recognize was incredibly unhelpful self-pity: It was Valentine's Day, and I was drinking crappy coffee in a Midtown coffee shop with a guy who probably didn't register it was a romantic day, and would likely be appalled he was with me if he did. I tried to ignore the lump in my throat.

But incredibly unhelpful self-pity wasn't going to do anything but make me sad.

"For the meeting tomorrow," I said, trying hard to focus on what I was supposed to be doing as opposed to what I wanted to be doing, "is there anything else I should know or be doing besides just presenting?"

He gestured to the waitress to bring our check. "Just make sure you stress the connection to the community. Simon loves that. And make sure to present some of the titles you know won't work—"

"—Like The Bread and the Black or The Sword and the Scone?"

He nodded. "Just so Simon can shoot them down and feel superior. He loves that, too."

The check came and the waitress had apparently been softened up enough by her Valentine's bouquet not to glare at me. Yay.

Nick pulled a wad of cash held by a silver money clip from his pocket. I was impressed all over again. I'd never met anyone who actually used a money clip.

I gathered my bag and started to drag my coat from the pile in the corner of the seat. He stood up and took the coat from me, waiting as I turned around to help me into it.

"Thanks for the coffee," I said, wishing it hadn't felt so right to tease him, not to mention taking a bite of his pie. "And thanks for the tip about the presentation."

He strode ahead of me and pushed the door open, waiting as I went through it. I caught a whiff of a strong, masculine scent, the kind that probably advertised it smelled of rustic oaks, leather, and . . . manliness. It did. *He* did. Good thing he'd made it clear what he thought about me, or my mind would be venturing into very dangerous territory. Inappropriate, even.

"Mom?"

She stood on my stoop, fumbling through her pocketbook, as if looking for keys. Keys she did not have. She looked up, and I was startled to see just how old she looked. Tired, too. Her hair was scraped back into a haphazard ponytail, and her coat was unbuttoned, revealing a sweatshirt I knew she had painted the deck in.

"Hi, honey."

"Mom, what are you doing here?" I grabbed my keys from my bag and opened the first door wide, holding it as she

stepped in with a very un–Mom-like hesitancy. I hadn't noticed it before, but she was dragging a large duffel bag that
looked stuffed to the gills.

"Would it be totally disingenuous of me to say I was in
the neighborhood?" I relaxed a little when she gave a display
of her normal wit.

"Yes, it would, especially since your neighborhood is a
couple of hours from mine. Come on over, I don't have to pick
up Aidan for another half an hour."

We started up the stairs to my apartment, me leading the
way, her following.

"You look nice, dear," she said in surprise. "Did you have
a meeting or something?"

"Yes." I didn't want to tell her about the copywriting,
not yet.

"What kind of meeting?" She was panting a little from
the exertion of the stairs, but that didn't dissuade her from
asking prying questions.

"A meeting for work. For money, Mom," I said pointedly.
I didn't want to be nasty, but she was the one who hadn't
explained why she couldn't lend me any.

"Oh. I thought you might've had a date." Her voice was
disappointed, almost lost.

"No, no date." I exhaled. "I did see Hugh and his girlfriend
the other night, though." We'd arrived at my front door, and I
unlocked it, holding my breath as I saw the apartment
through my mother's eyes. Messy. I dumped my bag on the
chair near the door and headed for the dining room table,
beginning to make neat piles of all the clutter I'd allowed to
accumulate while I went through my mourning period.

Which was over, goddamnit, even though I was still wearing black.

Mom walked in behind me, dumping her bag with a loud thump on the floor. She pulled out one of the dining room chairs and sat down, sighing a little. "Don't worry about that, dear, I just want to sit for a moment. It is cold outside."

"Especially if you don't button your coat," I said pointedly, feeling like I had suddenly become the mother.

"I was distracted."

I sat down in another chair after turning it to face her. "Why, Mom? What's going on?"

She leaned forward and buried her face in her hands. Oh, God, it was worse than I'd even imagined.

"I'm in trouble, Molly."

"What kind of trouble, Mom? You're not pregnant, are you?" She looked up and giggled a little.

"No, honey, not pregnant. That's not trouble, *that* would be a miracle."

"So? What is it?"

She placed her hands on her knees, as if to brace herself. She leaned against the back of the chair and exhaled a long, gusty sigh.

"I'm broke, Molly." She closed her eyes. "I might lose the house, my credit cards are maxed out, and I'm just barely affording to feed myself. God, Molly, how did I get into this mess?"

My question exactly.

"And?" I asked, almost not wanting to hear her answer.

"I . . . I've been investing. Day-trading. Me, self-appointed moral critic of Wayshorn Lane has disregarded her own best advice and taken risks on the stock market. And I thought I was being so smart."

I breathed. "How bad is it?"

"I've lost everything." Her voice was devoid of hope. Like mine six months ago.

The thought invigorated me. If I could get through it—and I was—my mother could, too. She'd raised me, after all.

"Not everything, surely, Mom. You've got your health, right?" She nodded. "Your books, your opinions, your daughter, your grandson, a full head of hair—we'll figure it out. And a whole bunch of useless stocks, right?" I exhaled again, another deep, cleansing breath. "Do you need a place to stay?"

She nodded again.

"Tonight?" I asked, gesturing toward the bag.

Nod.

"Okay. Well, we can borrow my friend Mary's car to bring your stuff over this weekend; tonight you can sleep on the Aerobed in the living room. Aidan will love having you here."

"Dante's over to Mrs. Simpkins's house. She said she'd watch him." Right, Dante, the mean-spirited cat. She began to cry, softly, rocking back and forth in her chair.

"Mom." I went over to her and knelt on the floor, gathering her into my arms.

She leaned her head against my shoulder. "God, Molly, I'm such a fool. Such a failure."

"Ssshh. No, you're not. You produced me, didn't you?" She lifted her tear-stained face and looked me in the eyes.

"And look at me: a poor, sarcastic, undereducated about-to-be-divorced mother. Couldn't be better."

She laughed, as I'd hoped she would. "You're very well educated, dear, a degree from Brown is nothing to sneeze at." She didn't say it, but I knew by the expression on her face what she was thinking: *but not as good as Harvard.* My mother the snob. Even broke, the woman was an education wonk.

I uncurled myself from around her, then checked my watch. Five minutes to pick-up time. "I've got to go get Aidan. Will you be all right here until I get home?" I grabbed *The Ambassadors* from the shortest pile on the table. "If you get bored, read this and tell me what you think." Her face brightened as she took it from me.

"I didn't know you liked Henry James, dear," she said in approval. As I locked the door behind me, leaving my broke-ass parent reading about nineteenth-century dilettantes wasting their lives, I reflected that at last I had been able to impress my mother.

After I'd found something for dinner and seen Aidan through his homework and bath, I went to the bedroom and changed into what I liked to think of as my *real* working clothes: sweatpants and a thousand-year-old Soundgarden tour T-shirt. I found my notebook and walked back to the living room, where Aidan was serenading Mom with his rendition of the Pokémon theme song. His hair was damp, and he was wearing his camouflage pajamas. My little rock star.

"Gotta catch 'em all!" he finished, giving a triumphant wave of his hand. She clapped with an enthusiasm I hadn't seen since I walked down the aisle with Hugh.

"Aidan? Time for bed, sweet pea." He groaned.

"Mommy, just five more minutes? Pleeeeaaaaassseee?"

Mom looked at me and smiled. "He promised he'd sing the *Teen Titans* theme next, Molly," she said.

I knew when I was beaten. "Okay. Five minutes. Then night-night books and bed. Deal?"

"Deal."

I went to the table and cleared off a space for my notebook and computer. I stacked a bunch of bills in the corner to deal with later. Much later. I wondered, briefly, when John would be able to give me a check for the most recent batch of copyediting. For our rent's sake, I hoped it was soon.

"Molly, Aidan wants *me* to read his books tonight." My mother preened a little.

"Sure, no problem. I just need a smooch before you go to bed, sweetheart."

Aidan turned his little cheek up to my face. I kissed it lightly, relishing his soft skin, still warm from the bath. Man, did I love him. I patted him on the back, then gestured toward his bedroom.

"Okay, honey, two books, then bathroom and teeth."

They trooped off, Aidan reaching up to take my mother's hand.

Now I had another mouth to feed. Another body to house. Responsibility, thy name is Molly.

At least it was better than "loser."

"What are you working on, dear?" Mom was done from night-time duty and had come into the living room to peer over my shoulder at the notebook. To my surprise, she giggled.

"Buns and Lovers, how clever! And what's that one?" she asked, pointing at my scrawl.

"Flours for Algernon," I muttered.

"Ha! Is this for fun, or is this part of your mysterious job?"

I drew the chair next to me out for her to sit on. "Job. I'm writing copy for a new bakery. John gave me the assignment. You know, more of that freelance stuff I do for him." I didn't want to tell her I was in charge of the whole thing. The last thing I wanted to see was that Doubting Molly look on her face.

"Oh, how is John?" Mom liked him only slightly less than she liked Hugh.

"Great. His company seems to be doing really well. And he took me to a Yale thing last Friday, too."

"So you're dating him?" My mother moved way too fast.

"No, John is just a friend," I replied, as tersely as I could. I screwed up my face in concentration and bent over the paper so as to signal this line of questioning was finished.

"Can I help? This looks like fun." She reached over my arm and fingered the paper. I succumbed to the inevitable and ripped off a sheet for her. She gave me an inquiring look, and I handed her a pen, too.

"Pear Goriot!" she exclaimed, scribbling it down on her paper. I had to laugh.

"The Crepes of Wrath?" she said in a quizzical tone.

"Wouldn't work unless everyone said *crepes* the same, and they don't. But Nick said to throw in a few duds just for target practice. So I'll include it."

"Nick?" My mother was impossible. I could be on fire and she'd still be querying me on potential boyfriends.

"The extremely"—*handsome, arrogant, dismissive*—"professional man with whom I'm working on this. Nothing going on there, Mom, I promise."

Her face fell. "Oh, well, you'll find someone. Mrs. Simpkins, the lady down the street from me, her daughter met her fiancé on the Internet."

Yeah, been there, gotten loads of wacky replies. Nuh-uh. "Really?" I replied, as if I didn't know anything about it. My mother warmed to the task of educating me. A frequent task, in her case.

"Yes, all you have to do is get on the web"—she said it as if it were a foreign language—"and type in what you want, and voilà!"

If only it were that easy.

"Hmm, I'll have to try that sometime." And when did *you* stop lying to your mother?

"Does the bakery have a name?"

I smiled to myself. "Yes, it does."

Catcher in the Rye Bread

Youthful angst and wry (rye?) observations will change when the teenager in question takes a bite of this mature, well-composed bread. Chock-full of rye, baked into a hearty, rich loaf, this bread satisfies even the most cynical of palates.

10

"VANITY FARE."

I stood in front of them—all of them, including John's assistant, even—in John's conference room. It was the day of the initial presentation, and I was as anxious as I'd ever been. A trickle of sweat was making its leisurely way down the back of my leg, all the way down to my fancy black shoes.

I hoped to God the Chanel No. 5 I'd squirted on myself would mask any odors. At least Hugh hadn't stinted on Christmas gifts. I tried to straighten myself up to be worthy of the perfume, and the presentation, and the whole corporate atmosphere.

Like the rest of John's office, the conference room was tastefully appointed with furniture I would've sworn was plucked from a television stage set—something where the characters were laboring for their art while living in $4,000-a-month apartments. I picked up the dry erase marker and wrote on the whiteboard in capital letters. Then I swung back around to face them.

"Vanity Fare is the name I'd suggest for the store, and the copy I've written for the specific products carry out the literary theme as well. I've made copies of my suggested titles, as well as the blurbs." John's assistant, I could not remember his name, hopped up to start passing out the papers. He looked like a mini-John, from the top of his artful brush cut to the soles of his sleek loafers. I waited until he was finished, then cleared my throat.

"Before you start worrying about the specifics of the copy, however, I'd like to get your initial feedback." I stood and looked at them expectantly. The silence was excruciating.

Simon was the first to reply. It was hard not to stare at him, so I was glad I had an excuse. "Fabulous, Molly, just fabulous." I melted a little inside as he spoke. That accent! Those chestnut curls! That freaking dimple!

"Thank you." I tried not to blush. By the way Nick's lips were thinning, I gathered I was failing in my efforts.

Simon glanced at the paper in front of him. "Although I'm not so sure I like 'The Sword and the Scone.'"

Nick winked at me. I almost fell over.

"Yes, well, as I said, these are certainly subject to change, and if you want to go with the general concept, I'll tweak the initial presentation and we can come up with final, vetted versions," I said, channeling my best inner corporate marketer.

"What do you think, Nick?" Simon spun in his black, padded leather chair to look at Nick, who met his gaze with, I thought, a tinge of disgust.

"I think Ms. Hagan is very clever, and she's come up with an exciting concept." From the tone of his voice, one would think he was commenting on the weather. Very dull weather.

Simon turned to look at me, that devil-may-care grin on his face. "Excellent! Well, thank you, Molly."

John fidgeted in his chair. "Yes, good work, Molly." His triumphant grin was beamed directly at Nick. "I knew she could do something great." *Great*.

Nick stood up, an annoyed frown curling his lips down. "There's much more work to be done here." His tone was almost curt. "Yes, the concept is good, but it needs to be fully fleshed out. We need to make sure the concept works with the product. If the product doesn't match, no amount of brilliant copy is going to work."

Simon leaned forward in his chair to address Nick. "And you have doubts that I can create something that will match Molly's brilliance?"

Uh-oh. I wanted to back away. Yes, Ms. Conflict-Averse to the rescue! Or not, actually.

But while they were staring at each other in some sort of Alpha Male Showdown, I could try to figure out which one I liked to look at more. For purely aesthetic reasons, of course.

Simon's dashingly romantic good looks contrasted with Nick's harsh, commanding features. Both were dressed in corporate urban chic, black flat-front pants with slightly outré button-down shirts. Hugh had always worn those, too, as if to prove being a lawyer didn't mean he was a putz.

No, leaving your wife and child, now *that* made you a putz.

I noticed the dark blue paisley shapes on Nick's shirt matched his eyes. His pants? Well, they matched his personal feelings toward me.

Simon, no slouch in the "match shirt to eyes" department, was wearing a pale green shirt with alternating dark green and fuchsia stripes. I'd forgotten just how intensely green his eyes were. Or, I'd remembered, but I knew how wrong it was to be pondering what they'd look like in the throes of passion when I was supposed to be writing about . . . sticky buns.

I shuddered.

John rose, as if to assert his dominance in the room. Fat chance. Simon and Nick were still glaring at each other.

"Molly and I," he said, waving his arm to include me, "can work on the presentation and have it to you by . . . Is mid next-week good with you, Molly?"

"She'll be working on it with me." Nick's voice was soft, understated, and totally implacable. Simon almost bared his teeth.

John frowned, then smoothed his features as he remembered Nick was, technically, one of his clients. "Oh. Certainly. I just thought—"

"Working on it with me," Nick repeated with all the emotion of an automaton. I felt like he was arguing over a pencil or something. *No. 2 Ticonderoga. Now.*

Simon crossed his arms over his chest. Was he giving up so soon?

"Now remember, Nick, we must keep everything on the up and up," Simon said in what could only be described as a cheeky way. Not giving in, just using different tactics. I wondered if he was thinking of Natalie when he said that. He smirked at me, then deepened his smile into something much more meaningful. Or maybe he was just thinking of interpersonal employee relations in general. I felt my insides melt a little. It had been a long time since anyone smiled at me like that. It felt good, but as I glanced over at Nick, I felt guilty.

Screw it. I was going to have fun. For once, couldn't I just be irresponsible and have fun? I smiled back at Simon. Who knew why he was flirting with me? And why wasn't I just going along for the ride?

"Simon, I know you and Nick have to get back to the office," John said, interrupting my mute tête-à-tête (or would
that be *oeil-à-oeil*?), "and Molly, I've got some other stuff to
go over with you for just a minute. Talk to you soon, gentle-
men." John's voice implied dismissal in no uncertain terms. I
wondered how the two alphas would take it.

Willingly, it seemed. Nick plucked his black Jack Spade
bag from the ground and slung it over his shoulder. Simon, as
befitted the artisan of the company, carried nothing. Probably just a mirror tucked inside some pocket so he could check
if he was still devastating. He was.

I followed John back into his office, wishing I could follow Simon to wherever he was going. As meaningless flirta-
tions went, this one made me feel really good.

John gestured for me to sit. I crossed my legs at the ankle,
the way I'd seen those TV lawyer ladies do.

"Molly, good work. I'm proud of you." He cleared his
throat and twisted his neck, as though his collar were choking
him. "And, I just wanted to say"—he paused, moving some
papers around on his desk—"to apologize about the Sylvia
situation."

"No problem," I said, proud of him that he'd actually
brought something up on his own. He was an exception to
the general male species.

He nodded, and I knew that topic was done. It was fine
with me, I'd rather not think about Sylvia anyway.

"And," he continued, steepling his fingers in a gesture
that indicated he was going to say Something Meaningful,
"since I know you're not seeing someone—" I wondered if

my SolitudeMeter was showing on my forehead. "I wonder if you'd do me a favor. It's not so much spying, as—" He stopped, as if stuck for words.

"As what?"

"Well, Simon asked me about you, and I told him a little, and he said he wants to get together with you, to discuss the project, sometime. At night. Without Nick."

Oh, wow. The last time he'd asked me to pull a Mata Hari it had been with Natalie. This would be so much more fun. "Mm," I replied, folding my hands in my lap.

"So—will you?" John sounded downright nervous. I guess having Simon as his client was pretty important, what with sacrificing his friend in the interests of the company and all. Not that it seemed like a sacrifice from my end, but he didn't know how I might feel about his little proposition.

"Sure." I shrugged, as if being asked out by handsome, younger, richer men was something that happened every day. "Why not?"

"And," he said, clearing his throat again, "if you'd rather not mention it to Nick, that'd be good. I mean, Nick is already a little . . . biased against you, because you don't have the experience. Although," he continued, "he did say he liked your presentation. Will you be all right working with him on the rest of it?"

What would he do if I said no? Hire someone else, probably, and Aidan wouldn't be fed, or housed, much less have a bald feline.

"Of course I will," I replied in as assured a voice as I could.

"Great."

• • •

"Molly!"

I heard the urgent whisper somewhere over the top of the left side of my head. I turned and stared into the shadowed stairwell, just past the elevator banks. It was Simon.

"Mr. Baxter?"

Even in the dark, I knew he smiled. "Simon, please. Come over here."

I walked with a hesitant gait over to the darkness. A lean arm emerged and pulled me into the stairwell. He kept hold of my hand as I steadied myself, and I liked the way that felt. A lot.

"I didn't want John to start pissing for territory again," he said with a chuckle. "So I waited here for you."

"Why?" I mean, really. I could honestly say I am an attractive woman, but please, despite what John implied, this British wealthy magnate hunk could certainly do better than me. Angelina Jolie was taken, but wasn't Halle Berry free?

"You don't know?" I felt his seductive tone all the way down to my shoes. I was now kinda glad Halle had some other fish to fry.

"Umm . . ." So much for articulate. All I could manage was a modified mumble.

"I was hoping we could get together to celebrate your successful presentation. Maybe tonight?" Was this how he started things with Natalie?

And see how well that turned out. But still, John had asked, and he was a good friend, so . . . "Tonight? Um . . . I can't tonight, I don't have a babysitter."

"Ah, you have a child. A girl?"

"A boy. Tomorrow?"

"Can't tomorrow. Friday?"

I mentally penciled my mother down for babysitting. I knew she'd do it, I'd just have to say the word *man* and she'd be cooking chicken nuggets and pushing me out the door.

"Friday."

"How about we meet on the steps of the library? The one near the shop, I mean."

"Okay. What time?" Oh my God, I was actually going to go on a date with the God of Gorgeous. Who died and made me queen of the world?

"Eight. And come hungry."

His tone implied more than just food. Seriously. Was I exuding some pheromone I didn't know about?

Before I could make another incoherent noise, the elevator bell rang. "Better get on that," he said, finally releasing my hand. I stumbled over to it, still wondering what the hell was happening to me.

"Molly!" Her voice pierced the whoosh in my ears.

"Natalie." She stood just outside John's building with one of those corporate cardboard moving boxes. A book with Simon's face on it was on top of the whole stack.

"Um, I was sorry to hear we wouldn't be working together," I said, lying through my teeth.

She smiled in a shark-prey kind of way. "Yes, it is too bad. You're here for the first presentation?"

I remembered what John had asked me, about spying. Did that still apply, even though she wasn't working with his company any longer?

Did that mean I shouldn't talk to her? I was so out of my depth here. The only political machinations I was familiar with were the ones played out in Aidan's classroom.

"Yes," I answered. "The first presentation."

"So what did you come up with?" she said, resting the box on one nonexistent hip.

"Um, you know, food-related copy."

Her smile widened. Sort of. "Of course food related. I was just curious what you're thinking of. I had just barely begun to work on it when . . . well, when things happened, and I hope you had enough time to come up with something Simon would like." Her voice made it clear she didn't think I did, not for a second.

"Yes, well, the concept is— Oh, shoot," I said, glancing at my watch, "my son gets out of school soon, I have to get back."

Even though it was at least three hours until then. She didn't know that, she didn't have kids. And if she did call me on it, well, then I'd have to come up with something. Until then, I was going to play the kid card.

"Of course," she replied. She looked annoyed. Did she really think I was going to tell her about something she was no longer involved in? When she'd made it clear she thought I was less valuable than the Hermès scarf wrapped around her throat? "Another time, then. I'd really like to hear all about it."

This was starting to feel all kinds of weird. And, I was guessing, not at all ethical for her to be grilling me about something she no longer worked on involving people she no longer worked for. What was up?

• • •

"And?"

Dr. Lowell looked at me with an expectant air, a complacent smile on her face. I hated it when she was right.

"And I did really well," I admitted. I'd latched back onto the feeling I had before Natalie, and was floating from the morning's successes, both professional and personal.

She smiled even broader. "Wonderful. I knew you could do it. And did you do that other assignment?"

I blushed. I actually blushed. "I made a dinner date with my sort of boss."

A quick frown passed over her face before she cleared it away. "Sort of boss? Do you mean John?"

"No. Simon. He's British, gorgeous, and incredibly rich. Honestly, I have no idea why he wants to go out with me. Did I mention he's gorgeous?"

She wrinkled her nose at me. "Maybe it's because you're intelligent, witty, attractive, and single?"

"I think it's because he thinks I'll be easy."

"Is he wrong?"

The question made me get all sick inside. I hadn't had sex with anyone, hell, hadn't *kissed* anyone but Hugh in twenty years. Could I really go there? With Simon? It would be the most inappropriate thing I could do without breaking any laws.

"I guess I'll have to think about it. I don't want to sound vain, but it sure seems like he's interested."

Dr. Lowell nodded. "You know you're not good with surprises, so you should anticipate and plan for any of the possible scenarios. Otherwise you might——"

"Might end up a crumpled heap on the floor."

"Exactly."

Oops. I hadn't told her the most important news. Too busy thinking about Simon's Dimples of Death.

"And my mother's staying with me for a little while."

I'd never seen Dr. Lowell surprised. Until now. "What? Why?"

"For a little while. She's got—" I almost didn't want to say it, it felt disloyal somehow. "She's got some money problems, and she thinks she's going to lose the house. She asked . . ."

"You're a good daughter."

I tried not to think of the hours I'd spent complaining to Dr. Lowell about the Woman Who Gave Birth to Me and Almost Died in the Process.

"Yeah, maybe, but isn't it bizarre that just as I'm totally on the edge of fiscal disaster my mother is there, too? At least she's got Medicare," I said, envy tingeing my voice.

Dr. Lowell chuckled a little, then glanced at the clock on the table between us and edged forward on her seat. "Your assignment for next week is twofold: figure out your limits for your date, and figure out how to solve your mother's problems so she can get out of your house. She'll make you crazy, and I should know." She smiled, as if to take the sting out of her words.

I rose from the couch. "Good thing you don't make me do anything difficult, huh?"

She chuckled again. I liked making her laugh.

"See you next week, Molly."

Tender Is the Bite

You don't have to go insane searching for the best taste in the world. It's not in Paris, not in Minnesota, definitely not at Princeton. It's right here in New York City, and it is the best example of jazzy baking you'll find: a luscious swirl of chocolate croissant, drizzled with French butter and American bourbon.

Maddening.

11

"MOMMY?"

"Yes, honey?"

"Will Grandma live here all the time?" Aidan fiddled with the zipper on my sweatshirt. We were sprawled in the living room, superheroes scattered all around. It'd been a tough day at school for Aidan—some controversy involving a girl who'd refused to sit next to him during meeting time—and I felt bad I'd been away from the house so much.

Not that he seemed to mind. My mother and Lissa were way more fun than me, a fact he'd not been shy about pointing out.

"No, honey, she won't." Because if she did, either I would go insane or have to move out myself. "You like having her here, right?"

Aidan slid the zipper up and down the track. "Yeah, but she can't play as long as you can."

"I think that's because Grandma is a little older, honey."

"Is she going to die?" Aidan had stopped fussing with the zipper and had turned his head up to stare me in the eyes, a look of anxiety on his face.

Open mouth, insert foot. "No, honey, not for a long, long, long, long, long—"

"Long, long, long, long, long time," he finished. "Good, because she promised to watch that Scooby-Doo movie you don't like next time you go out at night. When are you going out again, anyway?" he asked, an impatient tone in his voice.

"Tonight, actually." Tonight was the night of the Big Date.

"Good." He began rearranging the Flash and the Green Lantern on the floor, humming as he did.

"Aidan?"

He looked up, clearly irritated at being disturbed. "What?"

How should I ask this? Should I even ask this? "You know how Daddy spends time with Sylvia?" He nodded, still holding tight to Captain America. "Well, Mommy might have someone she spends time with—sometime, not for a long while," I added hastily, "and we should talk about that."

"Will he play baseball with me?"

I sat back on my heels. "Good question." I doubted cricket would be an adequate substitute. "How about I make sure he is willing to try, okay?"

That was assuming a lot—that Simon and I would have a relationship, one where it made sense for him to meet my son. So the idea of a sex-fueled fling might have to be relegated to the back of my mind with the rest of my fantasies, like Hugh being forced to actually apologize for what he did to me, and that incident in high school with Mr. Callahan.

He shrugged, then looked back down at the floor. "Sure." He picked up a couple of the plastic men that were lying on the ground and handed them to me. "Mommy, you be Martian Manhunter and I'll be Batman and Superman and Flash and Green Lantern. You can be Robin, too."

I took the figures from his outstretched hand. Thanks, Aidan. A sidekick and a fire-fearing hairless green guy from Mars. I guess there were worse fates.

"Okay, honey. 'Uh, earthlings, could someone else throw another log on the fire?'"

"Mommy. You can't be silly. This is *serious*."

Before I left the house, I grabbed my notebook and spent my subway time making notes on the essay I had to write for the teachers' program application. It was hard not to be completely negative, and by the time the train got into Manhattan, I was really mad at myself. There was a lot I was doing right, and I had to stop being drawn to the negative. It wasn't productive.

I crumpled up the paper and began a list:

1. Making plans for the future

2. Raising Aidan on my own

3. I haven't cried for at least a week

4. Still have health insurance

5. Money coming in, with more promised

6. Great friends

7. About to go on date with British hottie

Not bad. I got off at Forty-second Street, walking with a confidence I *did* feel. That was cool. Simon was already there, and his white teeth gleamed in the darkness as he saw me.

When I saw him, I simply could not believe my luck. He was just spectacular. *And* he was going to buy me dinner.

"Thai's good for you, right?" It wasn't really a question. Which he proved by talking more right away. "I like slumming it with ethnic food on my own time, there's only so much Le Bernardin you can take. Plus the pastry chef there despises me." Simon took my arm, and we walked in silence to a brightly lit storefront down the block. He strode ahead of me and pushed the restaurant door open.

Even without Lissa's help, I was able to find something to wear. I'd settled on wearing a brown scoop-neck sweater with black embroidered flowers near the bottom. I'd actually worn a skirt, too, which had a little flare to it. Black, of course. I'd thought about wearing the ridiculous heeled shoes I'd bought in a mad frenzy at the last Barneys warehouse sale, but then immediately had visions of toppling off the heels onto the sidewalk while Simon looked at me, aghast and mortified such a clumsy, oxlike creature was his date. I settled on some black pumps I'd bought for a wedding. They had heels, at least.

My mother didn't care a damn about my choice of footwear, she was just thrilled I was going out with someone with a penis. Not that she'd used that precise wording.

Aidan was waxing rhapsodic on the various powers of Pokémon when I left. He barely noticed when I said I was going, he was too busy explaining the differences between poison and psychic types. Mom noticed, and replied to my "good-bye" by crossing her fingers. "Good luck, honey!"

With what? Enticing some man to my bed? Not falling on my face? Making it through one conversation without revealing I was an idiot?

I bet my mother was mulling over all three. Always nice to know your mother is on your side.

The hostess sat us at the far end of the restaurant, farthest from the door. I plopped my purse on the floor next to me, then took the menu from her outstretched hand.

"Singhas for both of us, please," Simon ordered, taking the menu. She nodded, then left.

Thanks for asking what I wanted, bucko. At least when Nick had done it, he'd found out what I wanted first.

I unfolded my napkin and placed it on my lap. He leaned back in his chair and laid his menu on the table. "What a week," he said.

I took a sip of water. "Why?"

He grimaced, then picked up the menu and opened it, shielding his face from my view. "Nothing, really. Complications, mostly." Did that explain what had happened with Natalie?

"Ah."

He flashed me that killer smile. "So what do you feel like?"

Um, I wouldn't want to say right now. "Why don't you just order? I'll eat anything but a whole fish. I hate having those eyes staring at me." I knew he wouldn't listen to what I wanted anyway, might as well save time.

He chuckled from behind the menu. "No whole fish. Fine with me."

The waiter came over, two big brown bottles of beer on his tray, which he poured into the two tall glasses on our table. Mmm, beer. Almost as good as coffee.

The waiter looked inquiringly at Simon, who folded his menu closed.

"Yes, we're ready to order. Tom yam gai, beef Massaman curry, pad thai." The waiter took our menus and nodded in approval.

Simon picked up his glass and lifted it toward me. "Cheers." He took a sip, and I watched his throat move as he swallowed. He noticed me looking, gave me a sly grin, then gestured toward my glass. "It's customary to drink to a toast, my love."

I scrambled to grab the glass. God, five minutes on the date and I'd already screwed it up. I drank a tiny sip of the beer. Yum.

"So, tell me about you." Again, it wasn't a request, but an order. I guess being a culinary superstar did that to you.

I shrugged. I saw his eyes track the movement of my breasts underneath my sweater. I shrugged again, just for the powerful thrill of it. "Not much to tell. I live in Brooklyn with my son, I am between careers right now, I do freelance work for John, I am addicted to coffee and romance novels."

"Where is your ex-husband?"

"Still husband. Divorce is in the works," I admitted. "He's here, lives in the Financial District. He's a lawyer."

"Ah. He was too boring for you, then?"

I picked up my glass. "Look, I really don't want to spend time discussing my marriage. I mean, it's just a little recent to talk about." I took another sip, a bigger one this time. "Tell me about you. How did you get into baking?"

"Luck, I guess. My mum was a good cook, but a god-awful baker. I have an awful sweet tooth"—here he gave me a glance that was this close to a leer—"so I started playing around in the kitchen."

I bet he did. Bet he still did, too. He splayed his fingers out in a wide gesture. "Not much else to tell. Never married, live in London, travel a lot, work hard, play harder, and have developed a fascination for smart women of a certain age." He gave me a meaningful look. I'd seen more subtlety on Saturday morning cartoons.

The waiter arrived with the soup, thank goodness, before I had to think of a reply that didn't ask him what he meant by "certain age." I wasn't a goddamned cheese.

I glanced at him in between slurps. He even dazzled on close inspection. He was wearing an emerald green turtleneck sweater that was cut slim so as to hug his lean form. And, of course, the sweater matched his eyes. I'd noticed he was wearing black pants again and those pointy boots.

So why wasn't I slavering at the prospect of getting cozy with him, as was clear he wanted? Lust aside, it just didn't feel . . . right.

I felt like his motivations weren't right, either. "How long are you in New York?" I asked.

He pushed the bowl away and took a long swallow of beer. "A few more months, at least, until we get the shop open. I really like the ideas you've generated, by the way."

"Thanks. I've done a lot of work on them, and I'm excited to work with Nick on integrating the concept with the design."

"But I don't want to talk about work tonight."

"Ah." Molly Hagan, Mistress of the Interjection. "Well, tell me what you like about New York."

"What's not to like? Bars that are open all night, the restaurants, the diversity, the women." He leered again, only on him it was honestly pretty sexy.

I felt myself weakening a little. Would it be so bad to be easy? At the very least, I'd be able to discover if he was just as suave in bed. Certain parts of my anatomy insisted he had to be, and were equally insistent we all find out for sure.

"I wish I could take advantage of more of what New York City has to offer," I replied. "Until recently, I didn't have any child-care options, and my son is not so fond of staying up all night drinking at some Lower East Side bar. Much as his mom would like to."

"Where do you live?"

"Brooklyn. Park Slope, specifically. It's like the Village, only without the tourists and as many tattoo parlors."

"I've never been to Brooklyn. But I'd like to, sometime."

"Mmm. You should visit." Was that too vague? Not vague enough?

The waiter set the steaming plates of food down in front of us. It had been so long since I had eaten out at a restaurant—diner time with Nick notwithstanding—that I focused on the food, savoring the spicy, sweet pad thai and the rich flavor of the curry. Simon was equally engrossed, spearing bits of beef on the end of his fork and sliding them into his mouth. He caught my eye and licked his lips.

There really oughta be a law against that kind of behavior.

"This is excellent, Simon, thank you." I sounded like a schoolteacher. A prim, missish schoolteacher.

"You're welcome. I like giving stay-at-home moms a reason to get out." He signaled for the waiter, who came right over. "Two more Singhas, please."

I looked at my glass, startled to discover I'd somehow drunk almost the whole beer. I shrugged, lifted the glass, and drained it. Might as well have fun while I was wrestling with my sense of self-esteem.

• • •

"I have got to say, you have the most gorgeous eyes." It was several hours, and several beers, later. Simon and I had gone from the Thai restaurant to a nearby bar, a place with suitably illicit dark corners. We'd discussed movies, politics, the differences between American and British culture, and how successful he was.

Conversation slowed as the drinks flowed. Now he had his hand on my knee and I knew he wanted to kiss me. My conscience and I had decided we'd go to first base. I leaned forward.

There is nothing quite like that first kiss.

Simon's mouth tasted like beer, and desire, and confidence. He didn't waste any time using his tongue, either, and I found myself responding. With alacrity. His hand moved from my knee to my waist, and his other hand clutched my back, kneading it in rhythm to his tongue.

This was nothing like Hugh, thank God.

Thank goodness my conscience and I had an agreement, or I would've found myself draped on the table underneath him.

I eased back slowly, lifting his hand from my waist and holding it in mine. He gave me a long, lazy smile. "I've been wanting to do that all night," he said.

"Me, too."

"Shall we go somewhere?"

I put my hand against his chest. *Do not get distracted by imagining how his skin would feel.* "I think that's moving a little fast."

He grasped my hand, the one against his chest, and moved

it so it was over his nipple. Which was hard, probably as hard as mine. I closed my eyes, willing myself to stay strong.

"I'll move as slowly as you want to, love," he said. His words brought all kinds of images to mind, and I swallowed. I pulled my hand away from his chest, hoping he wouldn't see just how much regret tinged my actions.

"Thanks. Listen, I should get going. I've got my son at home, and—"

"I'll take you home."

"No, don't bother, I'll get a taxi, it's not that—"

He stopped me with another kiss. This one was softer, gentler, the perfect "good night" kiss.

Maybe my instincts were wrong. Maybe he did like me for me.

"Thanks for coming out tonight." He handed me a twenty-dollar bill. "For the fare. When are you free again?"

Not "I'd like to see you again," or "What night is convenient for you?" or even "Can we see each other again?" He really was that confident. Of course, given those eyes and those curls and that body, not to mention incredible pastry skills and that much money, why shouldn't he be?

My instincts were right, damn it, and it all just felt . . . odd. And I don't mean his tongue in my mouth.

Which left me musing, as I held my hand in the air to flag a cab, why was he so damn interested?

And why couldn't I just enjoy it?

Gravity's Rainbow Cookies

Is it possible for a cookie, a mere dessert, to achieve an altered state of consciousness? Pynch yourself. It is. Marzipan, food coloring, almond extract, raspberry jam, and chocolate chips blend into a splendid mishmash of flavors, very confusing but ultimately completely satisfying. Rainbow nonpareils top the cookie, which is a nonpareil in itself.

12

THE CABDRIVER INSISTED ON PLAYING BILLY JOEL'S
The Stranger album all the way through traffic on the Brooklyn Bridge to my apartment. I was too keyed up to sleep when
I got home, but I sure as hell didn't want to talk to my mother,
who was thankfully asleep on the living room sofa.

I crept down the hallway to my own room, took off my
shoes, and flopped on the bed. The very big bed. Where I
slept alone. For now.

I reached across my chest to grab the phone from the
nightstand and dialed the numbers I knew almost as well as
Dr. Lowell's address.

Hm. I wonder why. Thankfully, she was there.

"A *kiss* kiss or just a kiss?"

Leave it to Keisha to ask the question I felt most embarrassed about answering. "A kiss kiss. Tongues and stuff."

"Ooh, sounds fun. Was he a good kisser?"

"Yeah."

"You don't sound so sure."

"No, he was. It wasn't that. It's just . . . I have to keep asking myself 'why me?' I mean, honestly, Keish, the man is totally hot, he's got an accent, he wears those cute pointy-toe
shoes, he's loaded. And I bet he's younger than me, too."

Her tone was that of a staunchly supportive friend. "You're hot, too. You've got those great swooping eyebrows, and your eyes are beautiful and your lips—"

"So maybe Max Factor will want to date me. I don't have anything special, Keisha, I'm not just being self-deprecating."

"So what do you think it is?"

"Dunno." I really was stumped. Unless he had some sort of fetish for older, pathetic women, which I just couldn't envision.

"So you're going to stop seeing him?"

I thought about it for a minute. No, I didn't trust him, certainly didn't trust his attraction to me, but damn, he was gorgeous, and he could buy me a lot of pad thai. "No, I think I'll still see him. I mean, I *could* have a meaningless fling, right?"

Keisha cheered. "Atta girl! You use him like men have been using women for centuries!"

"Put that way, I feel kinda . . . dishonest."

"It ain't dishonest to get what you want without giving yourself away."

My friend the homespun philosopher. "I guess you're right."

"At the very least, you'll get some, right?"

"It's not all about the sex, Keisha. I don't think I'm ready for that, strange though it sounds."

I heard her exhale through the phone. "Doesn't sound strange." Her voice sounded kind of forlorn. Not like Keisha at all. Suddenly, I realized we had spent hours discussing me and my problems, and almost no time on her.

"Keish?"

"Yeah, man problems," she answered without me having to ask the question.

"Tell me." I settled back into the pillows, easing my socks off, and wiggling my toes.

"I met someone. He's . . . well, he's almost perfect. He's smart, and funny, and handsome, and he likes old movies, he's got a job, he's a carpenter, and he likes my dad—"

"And?"

"He's white."

"Oh." I swallowed, not quite sure what to say. I knew Keisha was determined to fall in love with someone like her. Someone who shared her experiences, her views on life, her history. Someone who knew what prejudice was like first-hand. Someone who was not a Caucasian male.

"God, Molly, it's so hypocritical of me. I shouldn't have even said yes when he asked me out, but damn, he's fine." Her voice sounded rueful.

"How fine?"

She sighed. "He's tall, taller than my brother, even, and he was a swimmer in college, so he's got those broad shoulders and that six-pack—"

"So you've seen his stomach," I teased.

She made an inarticulate noise in assent. "Dark red hair, not orangey at all, big brown eyes, straight white teeth—"

"Sounds amazing."

"He *is* amazing. I really like him, Molly." Keisha's voice was almost a wail.

"Honey, you can't help who you fall in love with." Or even who you *thought* you were in love with, but were just fooling yourself because you weren't sure you could do better.

"No, but you can sure as hell try to steer yourself to another port."

"If you were a ship."

She giggled. "He asked me to move in with him."

"He's got his own housing, too? Maybe I should send my mother out there."

"Only he's only got a high school diploma, and she would *so* not be able to deal with that. She's even more set on a good education than I am on finding a guy who's the right color."

I almost didn't say it, but I had to. "Is there a wrong color, Keisha?"

Because if this was the one, the guy, I would do everything I could to push her toward him. She deserved to be happy, she deserved not to make stupid decisions because of what she thought she ought to do.

I heard her start to cry. Softly, almost imperceptibly, but I could hear her tiny sniffles through the phone. It made my heart ache.

I continued speaking when her sobs had abated. "You have to decide what's more important, Keisha. Only you can decide. And once you've decided, you've got to stick with it and don't look back."

And, by the way, since I was so good at dispensing advice, why hadn't I taken my own? Like when I wasn't sure Hugh was right for me, and my gut told me to wait? Thanks a lot, gut.

"I love you, you know that, Molly?"

Yeah. I did. "Me, too, hon. Call me anytime you need to talk."

"And Molly?"

"Yeah?"

"If you do the nasty with the Brit, you have to tell me every last detail. Promise?"

"Promise."

"But, Mommy, you promised!" Aidan's keen could probably be heard all the way into Manhattan. I felt guilty, angry, grumpy, and very, very tired.

"I know, honey, but I have to go to a meeting, and I can't cancel—"

It was Tuesday, and I was about to be late to meet Nick. I'd forgotten that it was some sort of Teachers Get the Day Off holiday from school, and I'd promised to take Aidan to an afternoon appearance of Pikachu at the Times Square Toys "R" Us. We had been planning it for weeks: We'd get Chinese food for lunch, then head into the city and shake hands with a guy dressed up as a cute yellow monster.

I was the lowest kind of parent. The kind who forgot a promise to her son. Suddenly I had a flash of inspiration. That, or I was committing freelancer suicide.

"Honey?"

He was still crying a little, wiping his runny nose on the stuffed armadillo my mother had gotten him for Christmas.

"Yeah?"

"If you promise to be superquiet and do some coloring or something, I'll bring you to my meeting, and we can go see Pikachu right after. We won't be able to have Chinese food, but my meeting is at a coffee shop." He looked confused, as if wondering why he would want to go there. "They have burgers and fries," I explained.

His little face brightened. "Okay."

"So you promise to be as good as you can be while Mommy has her meeting?"

He nodded slowly. "I promise."

The subway ride into the city was agonizingly slow—would Nick be okay with this? I thought his reserved professionalism might mean he wouldn't say anything in front of Aidan. At least I hoped so. Aidan was completely unaware that his mother was feeling the agonies of the carelessly disorganized, and was busy pestering me to do Mad Libs with him.

It was hard not to blurt out *irresponsible, lame,* and *intimidated* every time he asked for an adjective.

We walked out of the subway into the cold air, and I braced myself as I spotted Nick's back. He turned around, and I caught my breath.

He smiled, a genuine smile, when he saw Aidan. I was so relieved he hadn't told me to take my unprofessional self and my child home as soon as he saw me that I smiled back at him, as genuinely as I ever had, too.

He walked toward us, those dark blue eyes focused entirely on Aidan. "You're Molly's boy?"

Aidan nodded shyly. Nick squatted down next to him. "What's your name? I'm Nick."

"Aidan."

They shook hands, solemnly. Nick rose up to his full height and patted Aidan on the head. "Let's go inside and see how good this place's fries are," he said, opening the door to the coffee shop.

Aidan looked up at him and beamed. As he looked back down again, I mouthed "thank you" to Nick. He made a dismissive gesture, as if it weren't a big deal at all.

As we sat down I wondered what Simon would have done if I'd brought Aidan along to a meeting. Probably compete with him for my attention.

That same hardworking, bitchy waitress came over, menus in hand. She smiled at Nick, glowered at me, and softened the tiniest bit when she saw Aidan.

Aidan opened the menu with determination, indicating he could read more than *cat* and *Pokémon*. He looked like such a little man sitting there next to me, his brown eyes narrowed in concentration.

Nick leaned forward. "Aidan, what do you think you want? Are you hungry?"

Aidan gazed up from underneath his lashes. "Yes."

"And after, if your mom says it's okay, you can have pie. They have great chocolate pie. You like chocolate, right?"

Aidan nodded, a little less shyly. "Yeah, only my mom only lets me have it once a day." He said this in outrage, like I made him sleep outside in December or wear pink or something. Nick chuckled.

"She sounds like a good mom."

Aidan frowned. "Yeah, I guess, only my dad says—"

"Ms. Hagan, Aidan and I are going to get burgers and fries, but what are you having?"

Guilt on a plate. "Ah, same thing for me, I guess." Thank goodness Nick interrupted Aidan. There was a heart buried underneath that Thomas Pink shirt after all.

Which snuck back under Mr. All-Business's chest when he spoke again.

"Ms. Hagan, do you have the most recent copy?"

I reached over Aidan and foraged in my bag for the papers. I found two superheroes, some goldfish crumbs, and a couple of used tissues, but no papers.

I looked up, aghast. "Not here." I felt myself start to babble. "I could've sworn I had it, Aidan put his juice down on it, and I told him not to, it'd leave a mark—"

"Did not," Aidan interjected.

"Yes, you did, but that's not the point. Anyway, I can e-mail it to you this afternoon, after we get home from Toys "R" Us. I am so sorry about this." Nick lifted his hand, and I stopped talking.

"It's fine, Ms. Hagan. Really. Aidan and I wanted to talk about the Justice League anyway, right?" His eyes darted to the Captain America superhero clutched in my hand. Aidan's eyes widened. Mine might've, too.

"You like Justice League, too? A *grown-up*?" Nick nodded while Aidan practically bounced out of his seat.

"And Pokémon? Do you like Pokémon, too?"

"I don't know that much about Pokémon, honestly," he replied. "Maybe you can tell me about it while we wait for our burgers."

For the next half hour, Nick and Aidan talked as if they were old friends, Aidan letting him in on the Pokémon secrets and Nick asking questions like he was really interested. My heart melted as I saw Aidan opening up to a new adult. It didn't hurt that Nick was so . . . *open,* which is something I would have never thought he'd be if I weren't seeing it with my own eyes.

When the food came, Aidan ate his burger without comment, still chattering in between bites. Nick winked at me as Aidan finished the last piece.

"Nick," Aidan said, picking up a fry from his plate, "Mommy and I are going to meet Pikachu for real after lunch. Want to come?"

I winced inside.

And then Nick surprised me. "I'd love to. As long as it's all right with your mom?" Two pairs of eyes looked at me. One pleading, the other amused.

"As long as Mr. Harrison doesn't have to be anywhere else," I replied, trying to give Nick an out if he needed it.

"Oh, he doesn't," Aidan said with confidence, eating another fry.

"Well." I placed my hands in my lap, perfect mother style. "That's fine, then."

Nick grinned at me again, and I wondered just what my son had gotten me into.

No fewer than four pieces of chocolate pie later (two for Nick, one and a half for Aidan, a half for me), we headed to Toys "R" Us. I whispered in Nick's ear as Aidan guided us through the crowd on the sidewalk, "Look, you really don't have to do this."

He patted me on the arm, then looped his arm through mine. "I know I don't. I want to. Aidan's a good kid."

"He is, isn't he?" Thinking about Aidan reminded me of home, which reminded me of something I might as well ask Nick about as anybody. The MBA and all.

"Mr. Harrison?"

"Call me Nick. Your son does." Ah, the Iceman Melteth.

"Nick, then. If you'll call me Molly."

"What, Molly?" He darted a look at me, and I felt the impact of those blue, blue eyes. Somewhere, Paul Newman was saying, "Boy, that guy's eyes are really blue."

"Uh . . . do you know anything about gambling? On stocks, I mean?" I blurted it out all at once, and he started a bit, then laughed. I guess it must have sounded like a strange question.

"We're not starting a bakery on Wall Street, if that's what you're wondering."

"No." I grasped his arm, the one holding mine. "My mother. She's . . . she's in over her head, and I'm wondering if you know anything about investments."

I didn't think Simon knew anything about the American stock market, and I really didn't want to ask John. After that, my options were Keisha and Lissa, and I didn't think either one of them could help me.

"Yes, of course." His face had regained that forbidding "don't talk to me" look. I forged on.

"Well, then, if you do know something—do you think you could review what she's got and give me your opinion? Maybe help salvage something out of this mess?" Maybe someone's mess could be saved.

"Certainly. I'd be happy to." He looked anything but. But he had said yes, so I could breathe a little easier.

I knew he wasn't a friend, much less a close friend, but I felt as if I could trust him to help. His arm felt solid against me, and we walked without speaking for a few minutes. It felt comfortable. Nice. And I didn't wonder at all just why he was being nice to Aidan, or helpful to me. Just knowing he was that kind of guy felt good.

Portrait of a Ladyfinger

What happens when a classically brash young American, in this case a dessert, encounters the staid tradition of Europe, in this case classic French baking? At least this story has a happy ending. Egg whites, granulated sugar, and flour are combined to make the usual—and delicious—ladyfinger. Then fresh Maine blueberries, Washington apples, Jersey peaches, and California grapes are heaped on top, all lavishly adorned with fresh whipped cream, straight from Iowan cows.

13

"ITALIAN TONIGHT," SIMON ANNOUNCED AS HE LED ME down East Fourth Street. I bit my tongue before I told him I was allergic to tomatoes. I liked Italian, what carb-loving woman wouldn't? But I didn't like being told what cuisine I was eating for dinner. Even my mother had never done that.

It was Wednesday night, and Simon had called the night before to ask me out. Really, *telling* me out. My mother had overheard and almost jumped through the phone in her eagerness to get me out of the house and on a date. I had no choice, especially when Aidan chimed in.

Apparently Grandma had promised some sort of ice cream fiesta, but only if Mom was away. So Mom *had* to go out. Clever, clever Grandma.

We met at St. Mark's Bookshop in the Village. It was raining, a slow, damp drizzle I felt all the way down to my bones. Simon arrived about ten minutes late, carrying a plaid Burberry umbrella. Because of the rain, his curls were even curlier, which made him look that much more adorable.

I exhaled when I saw him. I really should take this for what it was, and stop fussing. Not that I knew what this was. I felt my breath catch again.

I just knew it was likely to end up in something inappropriate.

We walked onto the wet sidewalk, and Simon held his umbrella over us. I pulled the hood of my sweater up over my head, too. The streets were fairly quiet, for the Village at least. I looked around, remembering hanging out when I was young, punk and oh-so-cool. How things had changed. I knew I had.

We stepped down into the restaurant he had chosen and were assailed with the clash of silverware, clinking glasses, and a noisy hubbub of conversation. It seemed as if a lot of people had the same idea as Simon. There was only one empty table, the one closest to the door, and we sat while Simon frowned and glared at the other diners, as if he blamed them for his poor positioning.

The waiter came and deposited the menus. I wondered for a moment if I should even bother to open mine, since I was willing to bet Simon would order for me.

"I was thinking we'd start with the mussels, then a salad, and then whatever pasta you want," he said, snapping his menu shut.

Who said I wasn't psychic?

"I don't like mussels," I replied.

"You don't? They're great, especially the way they make them here. We'll order them, you'll try one, and if you don't like it, I'll let you order something for me to try next time we're out."

"Sure, but— Oh, never mind." It was easier to agree than to argue. Pretty much described my marriage.

The waiter came just as I had decided on my pasta. "What can I get you?"

"Mussels in Pernod, two house salads, I'll have the fettuccine *con due salmoni,* and the lady would like—"

"Penne with endives, please," I said, handing the menu to the waiter. At least he let me choose my entrée. Thank you, Mr. Prix Fixe.

"Excellent. And wine?"

"Pinot grigio," Simon answered.

"Water too, please," I said as the waiter started to walk away.

"So is the pastry chef here all right, then?" I'd seen they had tiramisu; they had to have someone making it.

Simon shrugged. "I've never been here before. I just wanted a place where I wouldn't be recognized." Well, didn't that make me feel special.

Simon reached across the table and took my left hand. He began to stroke my fingers in a very determined way. My body, traitor that it was, reacted immediately. How long had it been since someone had touched me this way? I mean, someone other than Simon, who had touched me not even a week ago.

"I missed you," he said, lowering his mouth to kiss my palm. "It was a lonely weekend."

I hadn't seen him on Saturday because I was too busy schlepping my mother's essential items from Short Hills to Brooklyn. We put most of her stuff in storage while she sorted out whether or not she would actually lose her house, but my apartment was now a sea of books, I LOVE CATS sweatshirts, and tiny Swarovski crystal figurines.

Plus I had thrown my back out, and had to force myself not to hobble or wince every time a spasm hit. I'd called my doctor, but he couldn't see me until next month and my insurance ran out at the end of *this* month.

So, once again, I was fucked. Or not.

I tried not to look uncomfortable as he stroked my hand. Why was I so determined to question it all? He met my gaze, and I felt my insides wobble.

Stop questioning, Molly. Just start doing, and see what happens.

"Your mussels." The waiter placed the bowl on the table. My nose smelled the Pernod, garlic, butter, and the distinct odor of the shellfish. Except for the mussels, I liked every ingredient.

Simon let go of my hand and reached into the bowl, pulling out the biggest shell and holding it toward me. "Here, try it," he coaxed, gesturing toward my mouth.

I reached my hand to take it, and he shook his head, motioning for me to eat it from his hand. I felt exquisitely self-conscious as I leaned forward.

The mussel was just as I had remembered: awful. I forced it down my throat and reached for my glass of water, which the busboy had thankfully brought when the mussels arrived.

"Delicious, right?" Simon said, reaching into the bowl and downing a mussel with a big smile on his face.

"Mmm," I murmured noncommittally.

"You liked it, right?" he said, an aggressive tone in his voice. I bet this was how he sounded when he ordered his kitchen staff around.

"No, actually. I like the sauce, though," I offered with a placating smile.

He frowned. "Mussels are one of the best foods in the world," he stated.

Okay, Simon the Objective. Since you say so.

I took another sip of water. The waiter brought the wine over and presented it to Simon, who nodded in approval.

"To us," he said, raising his glass.

"To us," I echoed, clinking my glass cautiously against his.

The wine slid down my throat all too easily, and I had to force myself to place the glass back down on the table to avoid downing it all in one nervous swallow.

Simon leaned forward. "So. How are you doing, Molly?"

He extended the *l*'s in my name, adding an almost imperceptible break in between the two syllables in his refined accent. It was deliberately, ridiculously alluring, and I felt a warmth start to spread from my belly to my breasts. So what if he ordered me around? Made me eat nasty seafood? He was interested in me, *me*, Molly Hagan.

Wasn't he?

"Fine, thank you," I said. I tossed my head to prove his complete and utter sexiness hadn't unnerved me. A complete and utter lie.

He chuckled, then placed his fingers on my arm and began to stroke my skin. Up. Down. Up. Down.

Forget it, I was going to throw caution to the winds and have this guy on the white linen tablecloth if he wasn't careful. The waiter came with our salads just as I was assessing how much room there was between the saltshaker and the breadbasket. Simon pulled his hand away and smiled at me like he knew just what I was thinking.

"I've roughed out more of the copy, I'll be giving it to you—" *oh, God, had I just said that?*—"within the next few days."

He speared a piece of lettuce. "No work discussion, love," he said in a dismissive tone. I felt the warmth of my insides turn a little fiery. I was proud of the work I had done for him, and I didn't want to be scolded, as if I were a little kid talking about boogers at the dinner table.

"Right. Sorry," I said, spearing my own piece of lettuce and chewing vigorously. I wanted to bite *his* head off for chastising me, but maybe I was being thoughtless. Maybe he worked hard. I could tell he played hard, that was for sure.

"What are your plans for this weekend?" he asked, pushing an olive to the side of his plate with a moue of disdain.

"My son has two birthday parties, my mother needs help with—well, she needs some help this weekend, and I have to finish the presentation I'm not supposed to discuss," I replied.

He pursed his lips. "Couldn't someone take your child to those parties? I mean, I was hoping we could get away this weekend, my friend has a little cottage in upstate New York."

"No, sorry, I can't," I said, a lot more apologetically than I would have liked.

"Well, can we do dinner Saturday night?"

Why were we discussing the next date when we had barely begun this one? Which, except for the whole "throw me on the table and ravish me" thing was not going so well. And even though I knew I didn't really, it still felt like I could taste that mussel. Ugh.

"No, but if you want to get brunch while my son is at a birthday party on Saturday, we can do that. You'll have to come to Brooklyn, though."

"Brooklyn, hm? Do I need to bring my passport?"

Gee, that was original. Not. I gave him a weak smile. "No, not necessary."

"Great, then. We'll figure out the details later." He hauled his napkin off his lap and wiped his mouth. "I've been reading the most amazing book," he said.

"Fiction?"

He nodded.

"What's it about?" I asked.

"This fantastic tale about two business adversaries who create a world defined only by logic and reasoning."

"A romance, then."

"What?" He gave me a puzzled, slightly annoyed, look. "No, not a romance."

"Who's it written by?"

He waved his hand in dismissal. "No idea. I picked this up at the airport because *Fortune* was sold out. The last time I read a book was at university," he said proudly. "I'll lend it to you when I've finished."

"I'm not really big on logic and reasoning books," I said, smiling. "I read a lot of romance, and of course, the classics, although lately my reading taste is more Jane Airhead than *Jane Eyre*."

"What?" he said, this time clearly annoyed I was making another joke he didn't get.

"Never mind."

"Well, I'll lend it to you nonetheless, and you can tell me what you think."

I think I don't want to read books recommended by someone who never reads, I thought. *I think I would prefer to make my own decisions, thank you, whether about food or my weekend plans or books.*

The waiter returned, bearing our salad plates away with him. There were fewer customers than before, so a few empty tables dotted the landscape and the noise was less obtrusive. I looked around at the walls, which were done in an Italian fresco style, with deliberately faded paint and paintings of Renaissance women wearing gold clothing. It was very homey, and if it weren't quite so loud, very comfortable.

I sighed and leaned back in my chair. The wine definitely made my back feel better. Simon had pulled his BlackBerry out and was scrutinizing it, so I didn't have to drum up conversation. I looked at some of the other couples, wondering if any of them were on dates, or were married, or, God forbid, about to get divorced.

I spotted her first. Her blond hair was pulled back into one of those low chignons *Vogue* had always raved about when I had a subscription. I could see the long curve of her neck where it rose from a column of dark rose silk. My stomach tightened. I looked past her, past her graceful hands making a point, past her aquiline nose I could just see in profile to him. He was wearing a sparklingly crisp white shirt, an equally white T-shirt just showing underneath. His face looked tan, as if he had spent some time in the sun recently.

They looked like a fabulous, successful couple. I wanted to throw up.

Just then, he caught my eye, then gave me a tentative wave. I exhaled and waved back. Simon noticed the motion, then followed the direction of my eyes and saw them also. He turned back toward me. "Who's that with Sylvia?"

"My husband," I said, then quickly grabbed the glass of wine and downed it in one gulp. Then registered he knew Sylvia, too. Of course he did. The woman sure got around.

"Oh. What does he do again?"

"Lawyer."

"Sylvia does like a successful man," he said in a dry tone of voice. I wondered if he had dated her, too. She turned and waved, a light flit of her fingers, as if she were a queen and we her subjects. She gave Simon a raised, knowing eyebrow, then smirked at me.

I felt like I was thirteen again and the prettiest senior girl had just told me I was wearing high-water pants and I was too fat.

Hugh said something to Sylvia and stood up, beginning to move toward us. She just clutched the back of her chair and continued staring. I smoothed my sweaty palms on my pants and swallowed.

"Nice to see you, Molly," Hugh said. He gave Simon an inquiring look.

"Hugh, this is Simon Baxter. Simon, Hugh." They shook hands and gave each other appraising stares. I knew I was biased, but I thought Simon fared better in the stare department than Hugh did. Maybe it was because I'd seen Hugh naked.

"You're with Sylvia, then?" Simon asked, leaning back in his chair and tilting his head up to talk to Hugh.

"Yes, how do you know her?"

Simon chuckled, threw her a quick glance, and looked back at Hugh. "Let's just say I've known Sylvia for a while."

There was so much left unspoken; did he mean *Let's just say we've slept together and we're both more beautiful than you*? or was it more like *She tried, but wasn't able to make anything happen*? or what?

I was guessing that maybe the "or what" was me being paranoid. I mean, just because Sylvia knew John and knew Simon before didn't necessarily mean they'd all slept together.

Oh, ugh, not at the same time.

I needed to stop thinking about all this. When had I started living in *Peyton Place*?

"So, Hugh," I said, grateful for once to have highly developed conflict-aversion skills, "are you taking Aidan to that movie he wants to see? He said he had asked you about it, but if you don't want to take him, my mother said she would." Maybe she'd have to pawn that crystal swan that kept almost slipping off the table to afford the tickets. Hey, a bright side!

"Yeah, I'll take him." Hugh barely glanced in my direction, though, probably too busy wondering just how Simon knew Sylvia.

Simon leaned back in his chair. "Well, Hugh, Sylvia looks as if she's been alone quite long enough," Simon said, arching an eyebrow in Sylvia's direction.

Hugh nodded. "Molly, talk to you later. Simon, a pleasure."

He scooted back to their table as though Sylvia were holding an invisible leash. Simon gave me an inquiring look. "Molly, I would have to say your taste in men was not always as exceptional as it is now." He chuckled a little at his own wit.

I stabbed a piece of pasta instead of replying. He was gorgeous, but did he have to be so darn smug?

Even the cappuccino didn't improve my mood. There I was, Molly Hagan, having dinner with possibly the most beautiful man I'd ever seen outside of a movie screen and I was annoyed. With him. With me for being with him. With him for knowing her, no matter how he'd known her. With the other him for being with her now.

Gah, it was enough to make me wish I were better at geometry, there were so many triangles flying around.

When we left the restaurant, I was full, but not satisfied. It wasn't raining anymore, so we strolled along Fourth Street for a bit in silence, me wondering if I should try to go home and sulk by myself, Simon probably wondering if every passerby was as aware of his beauty as he was. Chances were good they were.

He stopped in front of an imposing door with a lizard on it. There was no sign or anything, just dark red velvet curtains covering the windows. It had been a *très* trendy bar back in the day, and I was surprised to see it was still in business. Most trendy places ultimately ended their life cycle, giving way to another, equally glamorous spot. Kind of like recycling a wife, come to think of it. Sylvia was obviously the new improved model.

I was the Edsel. The Pinto. The Corvair, although I was definitely safe at any speed.

We walked into the darkened room. The requisite stunning hostess sat us at one of the small, round tables in the very farthest corner of the room. I was betting Simon was a lot happier at his positioning here than at the restaurant. You had to lean the menu close to the tiny flickering candle to read the small print, it was that dark, and I had to stop myself from exclaiming about the prices, like some rube. Or a mom from Brooklyn.

The waitress came over, another model-thin beauty with cocoa-colored skin and a dress cut so low as to be R-rated. When she leaned over our table to place the napkins, she was definitely in X-territory. Simon grinned, while I couldn't help but stare. You wouldn't have thought such a thin woman would be so . . . *ample*.

"What can I get you?" she asked. Simon didn't even bother with the menu. And he definitely didn't bother asking me what I wanted, either. At least he was consistent.

"Two sidecars, please." She nodded and took our menus.

"It's got brandy and Cointreau," he explained as she left.

"I've had it before," I said tersely. Did he think I was a rube from Brooklyn, too?

He slid his chair closer to me so our knees were touching. I could feel his breath on my cheek. He moved even closer and kissed my ear. It tingled. Traitor.

"I'm very glad I met you, Molly," he whispered, just before licking my ear. My body started to sizzle. He *was* less annoying when he wasn't talking.

I turned my head and gave him a quick kiss. He leaned forward and captured my mouth, pressing his lips against mine with a sure intensity. I felt my bones melt a little. He put his right hand on my rib cage and began to rub my side, moving his fingers in circles. His hand was perilously close to my breast, but not yet on it. My breasts began to throb, as they seemed to want nothing more than for him to put his hands right there.

His mouth tasted like wine and those chalky white mints that he'd tossed in his mouth when leaving the restaurant. I felt his stubble against my cheek while a few strands of hair tickled my nose.

Simon was a lot better-looking than Hugh. I spent a few seconds imagining Hugh kissing Sylvia, giving her that wide-open mouth treatment I'd secretly thought was kind of drooly, and not in a good way. I hoped Hugh and Sylvia were both thinking how much better-looking Simon was.

I snapped my thoughts back to what was happening here and now. I hadn't made out in a bar since college. He sucked my tongue and bit my lip and my body reacted as though he'd set it on fire.

God, this was fun. And naughty. And fun. I was grateful for the trendy darkness. I doubted anyone else could see us, that is, until I heard the clink of glasses. The waitress! I pulled away from Simon, jerked his hand from my body, and pulled myself up primly in my chair. She bent over our table and placed the drinks down. They were in squat low-balls, and I could smell the liquor even from where I was sitting.

Before I could take it, Simon took my glass and handed it to me, holding his as well. "To the start of something wonderful," he said softly. He clinked his glass against mine, then raised his eyebrow and took a sip. I did, too. The chilled sweetness slid down my throat, a marked contrast to how heated my body was. It tasted decadent and sensuous.

I put my drink down and regarded Simon. How could anyone get tired of looking at him? Even in the dark, his eyes were almost glowing, like a cat's, and as I looked at him, he darted the tip of his tongue across his lips to capture an errant bit of moisture.

I thought of Dr. Lowell as I leaned forward again and lowered my eyelids. I kissed him this time, deliberately licking his lips with my tongue. I trailed my fingers down his arm and placed my other hand on his knee and squeezed, gently. He groaned in the back of his throat. Dr. Lowell would be so pleased at my . . . *inappropriateness.*

It felt good to be so in control. To do something that was for me, with no ultimate goal beyond pleasure. I had no illusions about me and Simon; even if he weren't just here for business, he and I were clearly too different to forge a real relationship together. As for forging a casual lust? I thought we were doing just fine.

"You're someone to take home to Mum, you know that, don't you?" he murmured, starting to nibble my ear again. I froze.

Take home to Mum was not casual lust. Take home to Mum intimated I was a safe, solid choice, not a dangerous obsession. Damn it, I wanted *dangerous,* not parent-approved.

"Too bad your mum's across the Atlantic, then, hm?" I said, trying to gloss over the subject without saying just how execrable an idea I thought it.

He removed his mouth from my earlobe and gave me that wicked grin. I felt a slow burn slide all the way down to my toes. "She's here, actually," he said.

Oh. Here. Oops, so much for casual glossing. "Ah. Just for a visit, then?" I said, hopefully.

"No, she lives here. On Park Avenue and Eighty-sixth Street, with her third husband. He's American. I'm staying with her."

"Ah."

"She hasn't liked many of my past—the women I've dated, but I just know she'll love you."

I had to ask. "Why didn't she like them?"

He shrugged. "They always end up butting heads about something or another."

And I would do the opposite, because I'm a spineless, conflict-averse coward. Oh, Simon, you do know how to sweet-talk a girl.

He moved toward my lips again, but I held my hand up between us. "I think I've got to get home, actually," I said.

"You're doing it again," he said with a scowl.

"Doing what?" I said with a disingenuous smile.

"Running away before things can get . . . interesting."

Did that make me a cock tease? Because honestly, I'd never even come close to being accused of being one, and if I were, that'd be kinda cool in a coldhearted female kind of way.

"Yes, well, I'm not sure I'm comfortable with things moving so fast."

"Why not? You're over age—aren't you? You're free, or almost free, and Molly, you are the most amazing kisser, and my imagination is going wild thinking what you'll be like in my bed." He said that last part in a lowered, husky tone that almost made me toss my scruples to the wind and go home with him. Almost.

I let out a deep breath. "Simon, thank you. I just can't." I reached beside my chair and picked up my purse. I drained my glass and placed it carefully back on the coaster.

I kissed him on the cheek, gave his knee a last, regretful pat, and stood up. Whoa, that cocktail was lethal. I held on to the back of my chair for a little support. He stood, too, but I waved him back down into his seat. "No, please, stay a while. I'll grab a cab just outside."

"I cannot let my date walk out of here alone. Hold on a sec." He flagged the waitress, who model-walked over. She dropped the check down on our table as if she had been expecting it. And gave me a wry look that I couldn't decipher. Oh—I bet he brought all his dates here. Hm.

He pulled out his wallet and dropped a ten and a twenty down on the table. The wallet gaped open, and I could see he had a wad of cash. I stifled the quick flash of envy that almost overtook my lust. Hey, only five more sins and I'd have a complete set!

We walked outside into the brisk February air. He kissed me quickly, then stepped into the street and waved a cab down. As I got in, he took a twenty out of his pants pocket and handed it to me. "I was hoping to send you home in the morning, but since you're so bloody moral—" he said, grinning a little, as if to take the sting out of his words.

I felt abashed. "Thanks, Simon. I appreciate it."

"See you Saturday. And work on those scruples, hm?"

That wasn't all I had to work on, I thought, as the cab sped away.

A Clockwork Orange Chiffon Cake

It's not a futuristic fantasy, but a deliciously whimsical piece of reality that could shock you into behaving badly. Almost so dense and packed with orange zest as to be allegorical, this dessert seems as if it's innocent until it hits you with its flavor, wallops you with the overpowering aroma of power. And orange.

14

"AND YOU JUST . . . LEFT? MAN, YOU ARE GIVING THIS MAN
the worst case of blue balls."

"Well, thanks for making me feel bad. And as if I'm back
in high school. Do you think he'll still ask me to the prom?"

I sighed and rolled onto my back on the bed. It was late,
way later than I should be up, but Keisha had started the last
showing—I think it was *Quadrophenia*—and she couldn't
talk until now. Not that I could sleep anyway. My mind was
roiling with all sorts of things: Simon's kisses, my hesitancy,
my lack of money, self-confidence, health insurance. The
minor stuff.

Keisha snorted. "I think he'll ask you what the fuck is
wrong with you. Oh, wait, that's me. And forgive my memory, but didn't we have this conversation last time? And you
decided to go for it?"

"It just didn't feel right."

"Then he must be doing something wrong."

"Not that. *That* feels great."

"Then what's the problem? You've got the urge, he's got
the dick. Insert tab A into slot B. Works like a charm."

"My friend the pottymouth. Look, Keisha, it's more than
that."

Her tone got serious. "What is it then, hon?"

"I dunno. It's just that—well, since Hugh left, I've been thinking about what I want from my life. From a relationship. And I don't think it's this."

"A few weeks of incredible passion with a gorgeous British guy who's only here for a short time? That's a romance book right there."

"I know. I think I read it. And it ends well, but it's not for me. Not for Aidan, not now."

"You can't deny yourself because of your son," she said in a forceful tone.

I felt myself start to get angry. "I'm not, Keisha. Anytime someone says they don't want something that seems to be good on the surface, someone accuses them of doing it as some sort of self-sacrifice. It's not. It's not a good fit, not for either one of us."

"Okay," she said, abashed. Then her voice got a bit wheedling. "But wouldn't it be fun, just for one night?"

My mind drifted back to Simon, his kisses, how his hands felt on my body. Oh, God yes, it would be fun. My body could handle it, but could I?

"He said he wanted to introduce me to his mother."

"Really?" She sounded almost as amazed as I was. "That sounds so serious. He didn't strike me as a get-serious-right-away kind of guy."

"No, I know. I didn't think so, either. I have no idea what's up with that at all."

"Does that mean he'll buy you dinner and maybe pay the utility bill?"

"If only." I sighed. "He does flash a lot of cash." I sighed in my now-familiar fiscal envy and moved on to what I'd been dying to tell her since I saw the brown-haired pinhead. "I saw Hugh again, too," I admitted. "With her."

"No way. Did she have a big zit?" Her voice was hopeful.

"Not unless you count Hugh."

She laughed, that big belly laugh that always cheered me up. "Were you with Simon the Sexpot? Ooh, I bet Hugh felt all kinds of insecure."

"I think so, actually. It was fun for a minute in a very vengeful way. But then Simon began to crow—"

"Cock of the walk, huh?" Keisha joked.

"And Sylvia was all that and a side of fries, and I just felt—"

"Like your poor pitiful self. Can it, Molly, you deserve better than that."

I bit my tongue before I said something totally defensive and pitiful. Hey, at least I was learning.

"I'm sorry," she said, after a moment. "I shouldn't say shit like that to you. It's just that I know—"

"You know it's true," I said, a little dispiritedly. "It's so goddamned hard, Keisha, and then even when I get the prime stallion, I need to check his teeth."

And why, the question lay unanswered, hadn't I checked Hugh out more thoroughly?

To be fair to the prick, he had been charming at first. And he had cared for me, as much as he could. It was only after we'd been together for a while that his selfish streak started to emerge, overwhelming whatever niceness he'd shown me.

And if I hadn't been with him, I wouldn't have Aidan. Okay, point taken.

"It's okay, hon. If it doesn't feel right, you shouldn't do it. Although I wish you'd say that to yourself when it comes to your tired analogies."

"Screw you."

"Right back at you. And your mama, too. Speaking of which, how is she?"

"Driving me insane. Those goddamned figurines all over the place, her eyes getting all wide every time I even *mention* a man, making a face when she sees what I'm reading. Or saying. Or doing."

"Really? You'd think she'd be over that after forty years." Both of us knew she didn't really believe that.

"She's here. She's hovering. She practically jumped through the phone when Simon called."

"Is she going to lose her house? How does that work, anyway? I thought if you lost money on investments, you just . . . lost it."

I sighed. "I have no clue. I guess she gambled that the stocks she invested in would pay off, so she took out another mortgage. I don't know who the hell gave her that advice. She's not sure what'll happen if she defaults on the loan. And the deadline is at the end of the month, so she's contacting her lawyer, thankfully an old friend, to see what she can do."

"That's rough. I'm sorry. Tell her I said hello, okay?"

"Sure." I waited a heartbeat, then asked what was uppermost in my mind. "What's up with you and the Great White Hope?"

I could almost see her squirming at the other end of the phone. "I'm moving in next month."

"Did you tell him about your . . . ?"

"Issues?"

"I *was* going to say concerns. But call them issues, if you want."

"Yeah, he knows. He said he promises to talk about his ashy skin and take up smoking Newports if it'll make me more comfortable."

"Well, at least he knows his stereotypes. And what does your dad think?"

"Dad's over the moon about it. He can't believe I'm even worried about the whole race thing because Mike is such a great guy. You should've seen him last Sunday watching football with my dad, even though I know for a fact Mike's never watched an entire game in his life."

"He sounds really great, Keisha. I can't wait to meet him."

"Yeah. It's just that, I've always been so aware of my skin. My dad doesn't talk about it much, but things were hard for them here. People always looked at them like "couldn't you find someone your own color?" Never mind no one could figure out if me and my brothers were black or white. I'd always vowed I'd choose a black man, like my mom did. I wish Mike weren't so great, this would be easier." Her tone sounded mournful.

Not for the first time, and for sure not for the last, I thought about the choices I'd made. Hugh's background was as similar to mine as possible, but that didn't seem to matter for the long term. If Keisha loved this guy, and he loved her— and what's more *told* her he loved her—she stood a lot better chance of being happy than I had been, matching Caucasian couple or not.

"Honey, did someone accidentally tell you love was easy? Because, you know, it's not."

"Isn't that a bitch?"

"Yeah, but would it be so rewarding if it were easy?"

"They say that about reading Proust, and did you ever finish that thing?"

"No. You?"

"No, me neither."

"Bye, hon. Gotta read Proust. Or go to sleep. One or the other."

"Bye. Sleep well."

The papers came the next day. They were in a long, official-looking envelope. The return address sported a company name about five inches long. I stuck my thumb in the flap and began to rip.

Dear Ms. McLaughlin:

Enclosed please find the details of the final settlement negotiated between you and Mr. McLaughlin. Please sign, date, and return in the enclosed envelope. If the settlement is accepted, you will receive notification of final divorce within eight weeks.

If you have any questions, please contact Mr. Bradford.

Sincerely,
Lawrence K. Bradford, Esq.
lkb/dw

Enclosures

My copy editor's mind immediately noticed they'd used *enclosed* twice in two sentences. My woman's mind realized this was it.

Divorce.

Final.

I stood there, clutching the papers to my chest as I thought about how it all came down to a few sheets of fancy vellum and a pen. Me and Hugh, watching *Star Trek* in the dorm lounge. Hugh sweating over his final exams with me coaching him so he could pass Ethics and Morals in the Twentieth Century. Graduating an hour before Hugh because Hagan came before McLaughlin, and lording it over him that entire night for being done with college first. Our wedding song, Joy Division's "Love Will Tear Us Apart"; our first apartment together, and its grotesque hallway carpeting; Aidan's birth.

The night he came home and told me he was leaving.

I looked down at the envelope again, my eyes blinded by tears. I remember watching my mother cry when my father left. Funny how the more things changed, the more they stayed the same. Another Hagan woman, another departing man.

And now Hugh wasn't even going to support us. As I found a pen to sign the documents, I hesitated a moment.

Why should I let him get away with failing us again? Why should I accept the agreement, made when Hugh and I had been working on an amicable—and generous financial—divorce? Back when Hugh *had* generous finances.

I dropped the pen on the table and shoved the papers away. Standing up, I strode to the window, looking out at the usual assortment of midday Brooklyn life: Caribbean nannies meandering slowly down the sidewalk pushing their charges, a Fresh Direct truck double-parked a few doors down, a young woman walking an enormous black dog. This was life. *My* life. And I loved it, and deserved not to have to change it because my husband was a cheating asshole. I spun on my heel and headed back to the table.

I stuffed the papers into an envelope and scribbled a quick note to my lawyer. He'd be surprised, but he'd been urging me to be more aggressive with the settlements anyway. I sealed the whole package with a decisive press of my fingers. I wanted them out of the house as soon as possible before I regretted being the strong woman I should have been all along.

Hugh would probably resent me, maybe even grow to hate me, but I couldn't care about that. I had more important things to worry about. Like Aidan. And now my mother.

I dropped the envelope in the mailbox on the way to pick Aidan up from school. I walked away quickly, knowing that was the last time I'd be crying over Hugh.

Aidan was already looking for me when I arrived, and my stomach tensed at what I saw in his face: hope, anxiety, toy lust.

"Mommy, can we go to the toy store before we go home? Jason told me about a new Power Rangers toy he got yesterday."

I had a mental image of Aidan holding my wallet upside down and shaking it. "We can look, honey, but we can't buy anything. Maybe we can put it on the list for your birthday."

His lower lip stuck out almost immediately. How come I can say "get dressed" about a thousand times in the morning and he doesn't hear me, but when I say no he understands right away?

"But, Mommy, my birthday is so far away from now." He drew out the last part of the sentence in a long screechy wail. I saw a couple nearby mothers give me understanding looks.

"Not that far away, honey. Only two months." I thought about the joys of eating, and paying rent, and watching cable. I didn't think Aidan would like being homeless, hungry, and relying on network TV. I hardened my heart a little. "And besides, you've got loads of toys at home you probably don't even remember."

"But Jason said his birthday party was a Power Rangers party, and he said I'd need to bring one to come."

"You've got plenty of Power Rangers, honey."

He glared at me in disbelief. "Not Power Rangers Alien Planet," he said, as if I should know the difference.

"I'm sorry, honey, but Mommy just can't afford it right now. You'll just have to go to the party with one of your other Power Rangers."

"Then I won't go," he said with all the certainty of a piqued six-year-old.

"We'll talk about it later. Look, let's go home, Grandma is out"—*evading the creditors*—"on an errand, you and I can watch Scooby-Doo or something. Lissa's coming over tomorrow night, too."

"You're going out again?" he asked hopefully.

"No. We're just going to hang out at home, all together tonight."

"You'll let Lissa play with me, though, right?"

"Sure I will. After she plays with me for a little."

Once we were home, cookies and juice in stomach and Shaggy doing his beatnik thing on the television, I made myself a cup of coffee and sorted through the papers I'd jammed in Aidan's backpack. Sure enough, there was an invite to Jason's birthday party among the notices for bake sales, special art projects, and infectious disease notices.

Please bring an agile grown-up it read at the bottom. Whatever happened to drop-off parties? Not touchy-feely enough for Park Slope, I guessed. "Agile grown-up" was definitely not me, not with the way the muscle spasms were tap-dancing on my lumbar. And I sure as hell wasn't going to admit to Hugh I couldn't handle something. I tapped the invite against my teeth. I had time to think of something.

Saturday was a nasty, rainy day, the kind of day that made me just want to sit inside, drink tea, and read lurid romance novels. Which, if pressed, I'd have to admit was just about every day.

Simon called at nine in the morning, his voice lowered a few octaves, still groggy from sleep. "Be there in an hour and a half," he mumbled. I, of course, had been up since seven, but I still wasn't very functional. Some days there was just not enough coffee in the world.

"Who was that, Molly?" my mother asked, trying to appear nonchalant. I could tell she was jumping out of her skin to get a glimpse of my new boyfriend, as she called him.

"The Library of Congress, Mom. It seems they've just discovered those books I read are actually well written, and they wanted to invite me to do a seminar on Romance Novels and the Women Who Love Them."

She scowled. Apparently she didn't think I was as funny as I did. "Molly. It's bad enough you read that trash, do you have to make jokes about it, too?"

"I'd rather read that trash, as you call it, than plod through another hundred pages of Hardy's morose prose. Hey, can we call it morprose? Think of all the authors who'd qualify . . . James, Trollope, Richardson . . ."

She held her hand up, steam almost coming out of her ears. "Enough, Molly."

I knew when to stop teasing her. "Sorry, Mom. Yes, that was Simon on the phone. He's still coming out here, and I'll drop Aidan off at his party and then we'll be going out to brunch." At least, I thought, with Simon I got fed well. Given my economic status, I'd take whatever I could get. Unless it meant I had to put out. I wasn't that hard up. I hoped.

The phone rang again, and Mom's face fell. I could tell she assumed it was Simon calling to cancel.

"Hello?"

"Hi, Molly, this is Stephanie, Nicky's mother?"

"Hi, Stephanie. What's up?"

"Well, it seems Nicky's got himself a bad cold, so we have to cancel the party today. We're rescheduling for next week. Can Aidan make it?"

I thought. "Um, no, actually, he's at his dad's that weekend. But I'll drop Nicky's gift into school this week. I hope he feels better."

"Thanks, sorry about that."

"No problem, thanks for calling."

You're sorry. I'm the one who has to figure out what to do with my date and my son. Together.

• • •

I hung up the phone. Mom had a midday meeting with a credit counselor, and she was already dying to cancel. I knew she'd volunteer to sit with Aidan while I went out on my big brunch date, but I really wanted her to see the counselor. Maybe he'd be able to figure out a way for her to keep her house and move back into it. Which, in addition to saving her house, would save my sanity.

"That was Stephanie, Nicky's mom," I said before she could ask. "Aidan, can you come in here?" I yelled.

Aidan trotted in, a big smear of chocolate Pop-Tart on his face. Thank goodness the Maternal Nutrition Police weren't anywhere around. "What?"

"Nicky's sick, so there's no party today."

His face fell. Or maybe didn't fall so much as topple.

"But I wanted to see his house, and get a party bag, and eat ice cream and help him open his presents . . . this is the worst day *ever*!"

My son, the hyperbolic six-year-old. "Honey, we'll do something fun. Mommy's friend is coming over, he's got a funny accent, and he likes to eat pancakes almost as much as you do." God, I hoped that was true. His first time visiting my apartment and he'd be going out on a date with me and my son. "Now go get some toys to take to the restaurant."

He left, still grumbling about the unfairness of it all. Hey, buddy, I feel your pain.

"Are you sure you don't want me to stay here while you go out with Simon?" my mother said in an anxious tone. I knew she was thinking I'd screwed this up already, and he hadn't even gotten here yet.

"No, Mom, you've got to keep this appointment. I'll have another date, you might not ever get another house." Her face paled. Maybe I had gone too far.

"Who knows, honey? This might be it, and you and I will be spinsters together for the rest of our lives." Maybe I hadn't gone far enough. Would it be wrong to tell her exactly how the thought of us sharing a residence until one of us croaked made me feel?

Yes. Yes, it would.

"No, Mom. We'll be fine," I said, gritting my teeth.

The buzzer went off only fifteen minutes later than Simon had said. I couldn't really complain, since I was about to tell him our romantic brunch *à deux* was going to be a ménage à trois.

"Hello, love," he said, bending down to kiss me on the cheek as I opened the door. Aidan ran and hid in the living room.

"Change of plans," I announced in a nervous tone. "Aidan's party was canceled, so I told him we'd take him out to breakfast. Pancakes always help when someone's sad."

His eyebrows rose. "Hm. So where is the little urchin?"

I tried not to let his epithet bother me. To no avail. "In here. He's a bit shy at first, so be patient," I warned. I wondered how Simon the SuperEgo would get along with Aidan the Only Child.

Same thing, different name.

"Aidan?" Simon called. He spied Aidan's head from behind the couch and winked at me. "Guess he's not here."

Aidan giggled. "Maybe we'll just have to go on our own," Simon continued.

Aidan leapt out from behind the couch and launched himself at Simon's chest, knocking them both flat on the floor. "I'm here, don't leave me," he yelped, beginning to punch Simon's sternum.

Simon looked at me, an appalled expression on his face. "Aidan, honey, Simon was just kidding," I said, hauling my son toward me. "We're all going together."

Aidan crouched against my chest, his head buried against me. "Just don't leave me alone, Mommy," he said softly. I shot a quick glance at Simon, who was busy smoothing his shirt.

I squeezed him tight. "I'd never leave you, honey." It shook me to see how upset Aidan was. He hadn't reacted like this before, and I had to wonder if it was Simon in particular, or if it had been brewing since his father left.

I smoothed his hair. "Say hi to Simon, please, honey," I whispered. He shook his head. "Please? Simon said he wasn't sure if you would be able to eat all of your pancakes. Do you want to tell him how many you had last weekend?" *With Daddy and Simon's ex-girlfriend?*

Aidan lifted his head proudly. "Eight. With syrup, too."

"Eight," Simon echoed. "I've been known to eat as many as ten. I'm Simon, sorry for making you feel bad. You're very strong, do you know that?" he asked, rubbing his chest.

Aidan preened. "Yup. Daddy practices wrestling with me, and I win every time."

"I bet you do," Simon said, almost ruefully. He looked at me. "Ready?"

"Almost. Aidan, do you have your bag ready?"

His eyes widened. "No. Where is it, Mommy?"

"It's prob—"

"Aidan, why are you asking your mother to find something you probably put down somewhere?"

Uh-oh. Not good. Simon was already scolding my son,
and neither Aidan nor I liked that at all.

"It's probably in your bedroom, honey," I said, patting
his head. "Why don't you check there?"

He ran out of the room. I looked at Simon, feeling my
forehead furrow. "Are you sure you want to do this? I could
just take Aidan myself."

"Just because I chastised him? Of course not. I am looking forward to this," he said, his face looking anything but
happy.

"Okay. I promise to make it up to you."

He moved close to me and breathed in my ear. "Promise?"

Why didn't that move me? I moved away as I heard Aidan's
footsteps running back into the room. "I'm ready, Mommy,
let's go. Oh, and you, too," he said, including Simon with a
wave of his hand.

"Very generous of you, especially since I'm paying,"
Simon drawled in his best Lord of the Manor accent. I gave
him a sharp look, and he shrugged.

"Is Nick coming, too?" Aidan asked as we descended the
staircase. Bad to worse to pancakes. It was going to be a long
date.

I was lucky Lissa didn't mind leftovers, because that's all I had
in the house Saturday night, and I was in no mood—or finan-

cial shape—to go grocery shopping. We were in the kitchen, waiting for Aidan's chicken nuggets to heat up, and I was venting. I was also lucky Lissa was such a good listener.

"And then Aidan asked him if he was going to take me away, and Simon said 'only if she lets me,' and Aidan gave me this totally betrayed look. I tell you, Lissa, it was awful."

She sighed in sympathy and patted my hand. Lissa was the best pair of ears a complaining person could have.

I took the baking sheet out of the oven and laid it on the top of the stove. "And then Simon didn't like his breakfast, so it just sat there on his plate while he sniffed in chefly disdain. And they forgot to refill my coffee, and Aidan spilled syrup all over his Pikachu Beanie Baby." I grabbed Aidan's Sponge-Bob plate and tossed the nuggets onto it. Then I took a single-serving applesauce container from the cupboard and turned to face Lissa again, waving the container for emphasis. "And when it was all over, and we were back in the house, Aidan told me he didn't like Simon because he was going to take his daddy's place. So I had to spend another hour reassuring him."

"I'm sorry. That sounds really bad. Almost as bad as what happened to me last night at Tony's house." The last part of her sentence was muffled by a tiny sob. I'd never seen Lissa cry, barely seen her out of sorts, so I knew this was something big.

"Wait a minute, let me bring this out to Aidan. Then you can tell me what happened."

I scurried down the hall to deliver dinner; Aidan was already engrossed in his movie, and my mom was sitting on the couch reading. "Back in a sec," I said to her, "Lissa and I are talking in the kitchen."

She nodded, barely lifting her head from her book. It was a good thing my relatives could get so involved in media. I mean, if they actually needed me to talk *and* pay attention, they'd be in trouble.

When I got back to the kitchen, Lissa had pulled up a stool to the butcher's cart and had her head in her hands. I leaned on the cart and took her hand.

She sniffed. "I was at his house for dinner, and he had a bunch of friends over. I was really excited because he hadn't introduced them to me before. And they were all sitting around talking about books, and saying all these authors I didn't know, and I mentioned Edith Wharton, and Tony, he—he said Wharton was for sophomoric females with unfulfilled lives. And this was right after how much I said I liked *Ethan Frome*."

"That's horrible. Why would he do that?"

"And then he told everyone it was the only book I've read in six months. Which is true, I told him that, but I've been so busy with the shows and everything . . ."

"You shouldn't have to justify that to him. And he sure as hell shouldn't be telling everyone at his party. What was he thinking?"

She grabbed a tissue and wiped her eyes. Even crying, she was beautiful. "I asked him that, after everyone left, why he said that. He said it wasn't anything to be ashamed of, it was okay I wasn't as literate as other people."

I was so mad I wanted to go knock his pretentious head off.

"I don't think he knew how much what he said hurt me," she sniffled. Yeah, right.

"Maybe not," I replied. "But maybe you could ask him not to say that kind of stuff anymore."

"I did. He said I shouldn't be silly, his friends liked me anyway."

Talk about damning someone with faint praise. I wondered just how much longer she'd put up with him, then realized I'd done the same thing with Hugh for at least a few years. Only he'd always been after me to be less of an egghead so I could fit in with the Legal Crowd, and the wives who didn't show just how learned they were. I hoped Lissa wouldn't waste her time like I did.

"I brought zucchini muffins," Lissa said, waving her tissue toward the shoe box she'd stuck on the table. "I don't think Aidan will like them, but they're really good."

"Great, thanks, Lissa. And I bet if you tell him you made them, Aidan will give them a try."

I pulled down a fancy plate from one of the never-used shelves, one of the overlarge party platters Hugh and I had gotten as a wedding present.

"So . . . have you gotten any decent responses from the online dating stuff?" she asked, unwrapping one of the greenish brown muffins. She took a bite and closed her eyes in bliss.

I picked one up myself and eyed it skeptically. At least it would be good for me, even if it looked funny. "No. I've gotten some e-mails back, but none of them have seemed appealing. I mean, one guy sent an e-mail telling me how fond he was of his cats, and he sounded really, *really* fond of them, and another guy asked me if I was into role-playing, and he was at least fifteen years older than me. And kinda creepy-looking, to be honest. There was a guy who was a college professor, but he wrote everything in haiku. That was just too weird."

She gave a puzzled frown. "But all the girls at work who've tried it have had at least a few good replies. I'm so surprised you haven't."

"Maybe it's me."

"Oh, shush. It's not. Unless you think you're too picky?"

"No, I don't think so. I mean, I'm open to this, it's just I don't want to completely waste my time. Partially, sure. Completely, no."

We chewed in a moment of companionable silence. I finished my muffin and reached for another one. "Hey," I said, "these muffins are really good. I'm surprised."

"See what can lurk underneath an unpleasant exterior?" she replied in a schoolmarm voice.

"I get it, Lissa, I won't judge a book by its cover. Unless the cover has a naked guy with rippling abs."

Lord of the Tea Rings

It's a world far removed from ours. A world where magical creatures hunt for the ultimate dessert ring, the dessert that will bestow power on whoever eats it. Our hunt has culminated in this rich, vanilla-scented cake, perfect for long days and nights on the road to Middle Earth.

15

"SO TELL ME ABOUT YOUR MOTHER."

I shot back before thinking who I was talking to. "You sound like my therapist." And then gasped and held my hand up to my mouth.

Nick and I were at the bakery this Tuesday; a couple of flimsy metal chairs next to a stack of brushed metal tables. We were here to start working on integrating the marketing into the actual design. I had no real clue what that meant in terms of what I was expected to contribute, but I was game to try.

Thankfully, he chuckled. Whew.

The chairs proved surprisingly comfortable, even with my back still twitchy. Nick arrived with a huge cup of Starbucks coffee, made exactly the way I like it. There *was* a special place in ~~my bed~~ heaven reserved for people who remembered how you took your coffee.

He took a sip and gazed at me over the edge of the cup. The wafts of steam interfered with my view of his blue, blue eyes. What the hell was wrong with me?

Except for a few passing moments, and only with Aidan, this guy had done nothing to alter the impression I had that he disliked me. He definitely didn't approve of the way I was hired, and I was betting he would definitely not approve of Simon seeing me.

I realized he was waiting for me to answer. "Oh, well, somebody gave her some advice on stocks, and she invested, and then she started going online to check how her stocks were doing, and then she got into day-trading, so now—"

He arched his brows. "Now she's in over her head," he finished.

I took a medicinal sip of coffee. "So anyway, things went well for a while, and then they started to turn bad. My mom kept thinking she'd rebound, and she just didn't. She got herself another mortgage on her house and spent that money, too. Now her house is mortgaged, she ran through all her savings, and she's living with me. She hasn't lost the house yet, but she thinks she will."

He stroked his chin. I saw a tiny patch of black bristles where he must've missed when he shaved. The rest of his face was smooth, the strong planes of his face defined by the sun streaming in the large plate-glass window we were sitting near. The light hit his hair, revealing the blue-black highlights in his ink black hair.

"Does she have an accountant? One she can trust?"

"I don't know."

"How about a lawyer?"

"I think so, an old friend, only I don't know if he . . ." My voice trailed off and I made a helpless gesture.

He gave me an impatient glance, then grabbed the notebook I had placed on the table, pulled a fancy black and gold pen from the leather portfolio lying on the table, and began to write.

"First thing would be to get a lawyer to review the mortgage agreement and see if there is anything she can do to
stave off the bank. She's a senior citizen, right?"

I nodded. "Yes, that much I know."

"That could help. Has she consulted with anyone about
her finances? Anyone official, I mean?"

I nodded again. She'd come home last Saturday as dispir-
ited as I had seen her, clutching pamphlets that promised rescue from uncompromising financial situations if she would
just Make a Few Sacrifices.

Mom did not like sacrificing, I could testify to that firsthand.

"Good. At least she's done something. She's not trading
anymore, is she?"

"No, she doesn't have any money. Unless she and Aidan
are investing with Monopoly money."

He grinned at me. "I wouldn't put it past him. He's a
smart kid."

My heart warmed at the compliment. "Thanks, he
thought you were pretty great, too."

A tantalizing thought shot through my mind. "Do you
think—that is, would it be possible—?"

He looked up from his notebook. "Yes?" he said, pausing
his writing to stare at me. I was caught for a moment by the
intensity of his gaze.

"Um, if you are free on Saturday, maybe you could come
out to Brooklyn and meet my mom, stress how important all
this financial organization stuff is. That is what you're writing, right?"

He looked back down at the notebook as if he'd forgotten
what he was doing. "Yes. I've got a few guide—"

I cut him off before he could say no. "But if you explain things to her, not me, she doesn't listen to me, never has, she might actually do what she needs to, and she might not lose the house. And Aidan has this thing—" I twisted my fingers together, not even daring to look at him. I stared at my feet, instead, which were doing a weird twisty thing, too, almost mirroring my fingers.

"What kind of thing?" he asked, in as gentle a tone as I'd heard from him. It gave me the nerve I needed to finish asking him.

"It's a birthday party in a couple weeks. The invite says to bring an agile adult, and while I think I am the latter, I am definitely not the former. I've been having this back pain—and my husb—, that is, his father is not available. So I know it's a huge imposition and everything, but I was hoping, because otherwise Aidan will have to settle for me, and I can't seem to move that well, and—"

"Yes." The word stopped me dead in my tracks.

"Yes?"

"Yes." He ripped the sheet of paper from the notebook and handed it to me. "Now give this to your mother, tell her to assemble the documents I've listed there, and we'll go over everything on Saturday."

"Oh, wow," I said, folding the paper up without looking at it and stuffing it in my pocket. "Wow, thank you. Thank you, Aidan will be so hap—"

"I know, Molly. I'm happy to do it." His ears were a little pink, as if he were embarrassed, and I tried to stop gushing.

He handed me the notebook, and I flipped open to where I'd begun working on the blurbs for the bakery.

It was actually getting comfortable working with him; he had a sharp wit, a quick mind, and he wasn't afraid to tell me if he didn't like the direction I was heading. But he never said it as if I was dumb or anything. I got the feeling he respected me, maybe even thought we were friends. And sometimes, when I caught him staring at my mouth, I almost imagined there was something more there.

Unlike Simon's complete largesse of handsomery, Nick was streamlined. Basic. Utterly and completely sexy, with no extraneous curls, dimples, or suave manner. He must have gotten a haircut recently, since his hair was clipped closer to his head, leaving only a few long bits on the top. He was a wearing a V-necked long-sleeve T-shirt, the most casual thing I'd seen him in yet. It was dark burgundy and clung lovingly to his rugged build. His shoulders were surprisingly broad, and nipped in to a trim waist. His chest, what I could see peeking out from the V of his shirt, was smooth and hairless.

If he were a baked good, he'd be Irish soda bread. Not that I knew he was Irish; but I imagined he'd be delicious, filling, and packed with a few surprises. In the bread's case, it was raisins, and I wondered what his would be: a shoe fetishist? Nah, he'd probably dismiss something like that as foolishness. A closet romance reader? Ditto.

An incredibly good lover? Now that I could see. He'd be thoughtful, unselfish, and get the job done—and done well—in as businesslike a manner as possible.

A far cry from Whimpering Hugh or Seductively Selfish Simon.

Nick tapped his pen against his thigh, and the movement startled me out of my reverie. Good thing, too, because I was starting to wonder just what was under that T-shirt. And jeans.

He gestured around the shop. "So to work. The basic framework of the shop is already decided, of course, and we won't need you to weigh in on anything as out of your area as paint schemes or counter placement or anything." He glanced at my notebook. "What we do want is something that is as visually clever as what you've written. A way to get across the whole literary-food-is-delicious schematic you've laid out in your prose."

Those were a lot of fifty-cent words.

I drew a deep breath and hoped I could say enough of the right things to impress him. "Right. Well, the most obvious thing would be to make sure there were books, actual books, around—kind of the way Barnes and Noble has a café where you can eat and read, you're turning it on its head by bringing the books into the café, and you don't have to buy them."

He drew his eyebrows together. "That'd be hard to maintain, wouldn't it?"

I nodded. "It would be, it's just one thought. I mean, if we could work out a deal with the library to take the books they've weeded out from the collection. That might be one way to keep a constant flow of books in."

"Hm. Interesting thought. Maybe. And what else?"

This brainstorming thing was hard.

"Uh, well, we could also use pages from books as wallpaper. Print famous quotes on the shop's bags."

"Mm hm. Not bad."

"So what is this place going to look like?" I surveyed the room, which in addition to the few tables and chairs was filled with construction materials of some sort.

It was already inviting, with big glass windows and high ceilings. I felt kind of a thrill to be in on something that had the potential to be so cool. Because, *hello,* a bookstore-bakery was my idea of heaven.

He followed my gaze. "From what I've seen, it'll be a fairly basic design, just small tables, a big wooden counter, and a kitchen that the customers can see into."

"That sounds perfect. As long as the lighting is good— nothing ruins a good design aesthetic more than bad lighting," I said, thinking of the restaurants I'd gone to with Hugh for various corporate events.

He nodded and made a note on his Moleskine pad. "Good point. I'll make sure to stress that to the designer."

He glanced at his watch and frowned. "It's later than I thought," he said, getting up out of the chair.

I looked at my watch and jumped up also, spilling my notebook and pen. The notebook splayed out on the floor, and we both reached down for it, bumping heads in the process.

He handed me the notebook and smiled, his eyes getting all crinkly in the corners. "I didn't think we'd be butting heads so soon in our working relationship."

I smiled back at him, and our eyes caught. For a moment, I felt his warmth surround me, hold me, respect me. I sucked my breath in and broke the gaze. It was painful, but necessary. Sort of like a root canal.

"Well." I stuffed my notebook into my bag. "I have to go, Aidan doesn't like it when I'm even five minutes late."

"You'd better go, then," he echoed, a dazed look in his eye.

I hopped off the chair and began to pull my coat on. "Okay. Well, see you Saturday. I'll e-mail you the address and directions." My left arm got stuck in the ripped lining. Damn vintage coat.

One corner of his mouth lifted in a dangerous grin as he rose from his chair. "Allow me," he said, guiding my arm through the sleeve. He was so close I could smell his scent—a woodsy, masculine aroma I'd smelled before—and a very faint odor of toothpaste. Clean and sexy, that's how I liked them.

I fumbled for my bag and threw it over one shoulder. A piece of hair had fallen in my face and I blew at it, but it merely lifted, then fell back on my nose again. He put his hand up and smoothed it back, resting his hand on my head for just a moment. I wanted to lean into him, to see if he tasted as good as he smelled, but I knew that would be a bad idea.

Not just because it would be unprofessional and far too forward, but also because I knew it would make him uncomfortable. He had made it clear we were to have a professional working relationship, no matter how blue his eyes were and how he looked at me every so often and how he made my heart race.

"Okay, thanks, well, good-bye then," I stammered, heading for the door. I stifled a moan when the door stuck. In seconds, he was behind me, pulling it open. His arm slid alongside mine, and I had a mad urge to turn around so I'd be pressed against his chest.

Thankfully, the door opened, and I hurried outside before my id could do something my superego would regret. I turned to look at him. "Okay. Thanks. Okay, see you a week from Saturday."

"Saturday."

I felt his stare all the way down the street to the subway.

• • •

I'd dreamt of him that night. So I was almost ready for her question as I was seated in her big leather patient's chair. "So you like this guy then, this Nick?" Dr. Lowell would have done well in the Spanish Inquisition.

"Yeah, I guess I do," I admitted.

"What about Simon? You still seeing him?"

I shrugged. "Sort of? It's complicated." Great. Reducing my life to a Facebook status.

"And you think a relationship with Nick would mean something?"

I felt my ears turn red. "God, no, he doesn't want to have anything to do with me, it's just so . . . refreshing to be able to be with a man who's honest and forthright and basic." Not to mention handsome, smart, and nice to my son. And arrogant, intimidating, and totally determined to keep everything professional.

"So what are you going to do?"

"Do? I can't do anything."

She frowned in that "you've regressed" way. "You most certainly can, Molly Hagan." I'd have said she was talking to me as if she were my mother, but my mother never talked to me that way. "If you like this Nick, then you should tell him. If you want to just have a sexual relationship with this Simon, do it. And Aidan—"

"I don't suppose I could just tell him I want to sleep late on Saturdays, could I?" I asked.

"No, but you will have to talk more to him about his father and you and the changes in your relationship."

I thought about how upset he got when Simon mentioned leaving without him. "I will. More, at least, I mean. He has noticed Hugh isn't living there any longer."

She regarded me over the tops of her glasses. "Of course, Molly, but Aidan is young. You forget that sometimes because his vocabulary is so large. But his emotional age is still six, and it's important to keep his concerns in mind and try to address them before they become an issue."

I heaved a breath of exhaustion. "But what if I just want to crawl into a hole and pull the covers over my head? What then?"

"Why then, my dear," she replied drily, "you will miss out on the joy of watching your son grow and thrive, seeing yourself grow and thrive, and completing next week's assignment."

"Which is?"

"Do something you would never do in a million years."

"Fly a plane, try out for American Idol, *wear* white after Labor Day—"

"Or before," I muttered.

"—read Proust, perm your hair, get a suntan—there are any number of things you could do," Keisha chirped.

"Right. How about 'wipe the memory of Hugh from my mind' while you're listing impossible things?" I asked in a whine.

"Ah, Molly?"

"Mmm?"

"Take me off the invitation list to your pity party, I'm not coming."

I laughed despite myself. "Well, I do have to admit I looked pretty good today."

"What'd you do?"

"Met with Nick."

"Nick—Tall, Dark, and Intimidating?"

"That's the one."

"So what did you wear?"

"Those black tailored pants, a scoop-neck black long-sleeve, and a black beaded sweater."

"Did you have a meeting with the Future Nuns of America or something? Geez, how about a little color sometime?"

"I had my cherry earrings on, the ones that look almost real? And by the way, Ms. Pot, aren't you usually dressed in black, too?"

"Not since moving back here, Mrs. Kettle. You would not believe what I am wearing today."

"Try me."

"A pink Old Navy T-shirt and khakis."

"You are kidding me."

"I said you wouldn't believe me."

"Is that because of the new guy? Because if it is, I take back every nice thing I've said about him."

"No, it started when I got back. People in California just don't wear black like New Yorkers."

"More fools them."

"You say that now, but do you know what people pay for rent out here?"

I groaned. "You people always play the rent card."

"All right, I gotta go. Let me know when you do something completely unlike you."

"Maybe dress in pink and tan?"

"Ha-ha."

"Love you, too, honey. Bye."

I hung up the phone and padded into the kitchen to see if there was any coffee left in the pot from the morning. Armed with half a cup of coffee and about as much milk, I wandered into the living room, where Aidan was building some sort of menagerie with Lincoln Logs and Mom was watching.

It was a nice, cozy, domestic scene. It was also as fragile as my finances. I pulled out the stack of bills and began sorting through them: must pay now, pay in a few days, wait another billing cycle. The first pile was way larger than the other two, and I sighed, thinking of how much money Hugh and I had wasted when he had gotten his first cushy legal job. Dinners at Union Square Café, Betsey Johnson sample sales, Chinese takeout, trade paperbacks at retail prices.

We had lived a good life, full of lovely clothes and good food. At least until Aidan arrived.

I knew Hugh adored Aidan, and he definitely loved him, but I had to wonder if Aidan's arrival meant Hugh had to face being an adult. And he wasn't very good at being an adult. Is that why he ran?

I just wish we'd been more responsible with our finances back when it didn't matter so much. I'd still have to figure out What to Do with My Life, but the looming decision wouldn't be fraught with so much worry.

And my mother's finances were now my burden, too. She'd always had more than enough money, the benefit of being the descendant of some clever investors back at the turn of the twentieth century. Now over a hundred years of careful financial planning was residing on Wall Street's trading floor.

I knew I wouldn't hear from the Teaching Fellows until at least early summer, so I pulled out the *New York Times*'s classified section and headed for the marketing section. The freelance work would help, but I should probably try to find something full-time. Let's see. I could:

- Market for an MRI facility in Queens
- Become the Marketing Director of Wealth Management
- Market to take the company "to the next level"
- Manage a supermarket's marketing efforts

How could everything be both boring and intimidating? I was too picky, and also way too underqualified. If I could find a job where it was important to be able to juggle appointments (playdates, doctors' visits, afterschool activities), utilize diplomatic skills (getting someone to eat peanut butter and jelly when they really, really wanted to go to McDonald's), multitask (play superheroes while doing the dishes/cooking dinner/putting on makeup), balance budgets (allowances are not elastic), and operate on a very small amount of sleep, I'd be set. Of course, I already had that job, and it paid nothing. In fact, it cost me money to work there.

Not that I'd trade it for anything in the world. I looked over at Aidan's head, bent over the floor. Just as I did, he looked up and gave me one of his sweet smiles. To paraphrase a refrigerator magnet I saw once, A BAD DAY BEING A MOTHER IS BETTER THAN A GOOD DAY AT WORK. I waved at him as he bent his head down to the important task of building a log cabin for some plastic frogs.

I just had to figure out how to be a mom *and* afford to feed us. I hadn't gotten a check from John yet. The next thing I knew, Dr. Lowell's voice rang in my head as clearly as if she were speaking to me. "Yeah, yeah, something I would never do," I muttered, getting up and reaching for the phone.

"Corning and Associates. How may I direct your call?" John's Redhead Receptionist, I was pleased to hear, had a nasal tone to her voice. There was some justice in the world.

"Hi, this is Molly Hagan. Is John in?"

"Let me check. Hold on, please."

I straightened a pile of books my mom must've gotten into while I waited for John. If I concentrated hard enough on them, maybe I wouldn't have this panicky "going-to-ask-for-money" feeling in my stomach.

"Molly?"

Rats. Even Voltaire couldn't save me. "Hi, John."

"I was just going to call you. How's it going?"

"Fine." Especially since I hadn't worked on anything since the last time we talked.

"Great, because the Cooking Channel wants to get a taste—ha-ha, get it?—a taste of what Simon's new venture will be like."

"Uh . . . when is this presentation scheduled for?" I asked. My voice rose at least an octave. A television network?

"Probably in a week and a half," John replied, not realizing he was making my heart jump out of my throat.

"Oh."

"What were you calling about, anyway?"

"Right. Um, I was wondering when you'd be sending—"

"The consulting fees. Of course, I totally forgot. I'll have Ida send the first payment out tomorrow."

"Okay, thanks. And—do I have to be there for the presentation?"

There was a moment of silence.

"Of course, Molly. You're presenting the concept," John replied, sounding as if he were gritting his teeth. "Simon will field questions afterward, but you're the details person."

I imitated his Big Corporate Guy tone. "Right, of course, I knew that, I was just checking."

"We'll have time to go over the presentation—say next Tuesday?"

"I'm busy on Tuesday." Tuesdays With Scary were, sadly, the brightest part of my week.

"Wednesday, then." Now he sounded annoyed. I refused to allow his Business Male Voice to intimidate me.

"Right. Wednesday. Will Simon and Nick be there also?"

"No, just us."

"Okay, see you then. Good-bye."

"Bye, Molly."

I hung up, a little bit in shock, but also ridiculously pleased with myself: I had called John, something I did not want to do, to ask about my money, something I really did not want to do. And I had done it. Dr. Lowell would be proud.

I stuck my head out the doorway to make sure Aidan and Mom were still busy, then I did a little end zone victory dance. Midshimmy, I thought about things I would never do.

And I got a really good, really scary idea.

Bite in August

Mere words—no matter how many you use—cannot describe this rich, dense masterpiece. A chocolate truffle for the plebeian; a drama in white and dark chocolate for the cognoscenti. Don't wait for Christmas to celebrate.

16

"I STILL DON'T HAVE A POWER RANGER FOR JASON'S PARTY," Aidan wailed. I kneeled in front of him, struggling to get his sneakers on. He was too busy bemoaning our lack of finances to help.

"Aidan, could you just push a little?" I asked, brushing my hair out of my eyes. He glared at me and jammed down hard, smashing my finger. I stifled a word Aidan should not hear. "Not that hard. Look, Aidan, I'm sorry I can't get you a Power Ranger Alien Thingie—"

"Alien Planet," Aidan replied in a sullen voice.

"But we just don't have the money. Right now," I added, so he wouldn't start thinking we had no money whatsoever. Only one of us needed to have that worry.

He gave me a hurt puppy look, pushing his lip as far out as it could go.

I sighed, straightened the hem of his shirt, and looked in his eyes, resting my hands on his legs. "Honey, I promise, if I could afford to get you the toy, I would. But I just can't."

His lower lip receded, just a bit. "Okay, Mommy. I can ask Jason if he has any extra." He stuck his finger in his nose, and I just as quickly removed it. "Are you coming with me?"

I glanced around, making sure Mom wasn't hiding behind the enormous log cabin/judo stadium/Dipsy Doodles theme park Aidan had completed last night. I lowered my voice, just in case. "I'll be there, but do you remember that man Nick we saw at the coffee shop that day?"

He nodded. "The one who liked the Justice League?"

"Yeah. Well, he said he'd go to the party, too, and he said he'd help you with some of the contests."

His face brightened. Maybe almost as much as if he were clutching a brand-new Power Ranger Alien Thingie. Sorry, *Planet.* "Cool!"

"I hope so," I muttered. Aidan leapt off the chair and ate the judo players' dressing room.

My mother bustled in, her coat tucked under her arm. "Well, I'm going out for a bit," she said cheerily like she wasn't facing financial disaster.

My mouth gaped. "Mom, did you forget?"

"Forget what, sweetie?"

"Forget," I said in an exaggeratedly patient tone, "that my . . . friend is coming here this morning to talk to you about the financial stuff? Remember?"

"Oh, honey, I can't," she said, drawing her arm through her sleeve. "I promised Mrs. Simpkins I'd go over for the day to visit with Dante. He's been moping a bit, it seems."

I stood up and held her arm. "No, Mom, Dante has to wait. You've got your own circle of hell to go through"—*and so do I*— "and you're staying here, at least until Nick leaves."

"Nick? You haven't mentioned him before." She took her coat off and draped it on the couch. Of course, a potential

Molly-Man was able to get her coat off faster than reminding her of her commitments.

"He's one of the guys I'm working with on that copywriting job, you know, the bakery one you helped me with?"

She gave me a puzzled look. "I thought his name was Simon. I know it's not John, I know John."

"This is another one."

Now her face was positively ecstatic. "*Three* men? You're working with *three* men? Molly, even you should be able to find someone with that many to choose from."

Thanks for the vote of confidence. "Mom, I don't want another man in my life right now." I shot her a quick look to see if she bought it. Her eyes narrowed. "I'm working to pay the rent, remember?"

She waved a hand in dismissal. "Of course, dear, but a boyfriend couldn't hurt, could it?"

"Paying the rent couldn't hurt, either. It's not a date, he's coming over to talk to you about your financial planning, and he's going to be Aidan's 'agile grown-up' at this birthday party we're going to later." I checked around to make sure Aidan wasn't *just* having Dipsy Doodles for breakfast. Oh, good, a stale Pop-Tart. The nominating committee for Mother of the Year probably wasn't going to be calling me anytime soon.

She plopped down in the chair, picking up *The Ambassadors,* which she had left splayed open on the table. "Well, I'll stick around, then," she said, as if she were the queen granting an audience or something. Not an impoverished snob.

"Good, Mom. Thank you," I said through gritted teeth as I went to my bedroom to get dressed.

What did you wear when you wanted to look casual but nice? Not jeans and a sweatshirt, which was my usual Saturday garb. I grabbed a black turtleneck sweater and black wool pants. I slipped on some silver hoop earrings and slid a chunky silver ring on my right hand. My left hand remained unadorned.

Aidan was on his third episode of the *Power Rangers' Marathon* when the buzzer rang. I leapt up to get it, my heart in my throat. What if Nick changed his mind and realized the prospect of spending his Saturday with me, my son, and my mother was going to be miserable? What if it *was* miserable?

As I waited at the top of the stairs for him to ascend, I felt a mixture of dread and anticipation settle in the pit of my stomach. The anticipation won out as I saw the top of his head. Even his mass of black hair looked solid. Reassuring. I knew he wouldn't let Aidan down.

Whether he would let *me* down depended on my ability to get over myself and do something I would never do in a million years.

"In a minute, sport." Nick ruffled Aidan's hair, realigned a Lincoln Log, then sat down at the dining room table. Mom held a small plate with baby carrots, some stale Wheat Thins, and plain yogurt toward him like it was caviar. My mother may have lacked funds, but she certainly had finesse.

Nick shook his head no, and she lowered the plate slowly onto the table. One of the carrots had that old mushy carrot look to it, so I grabbed it and held it in my closed fist.

"Mrs. Hagan, I understand you don't want to lose your house. Of course not. The goal here is for you to do what you need to do to save your financial situation."

Nick looked at me over my mother's head and winked. I was really getting to like that wink.

"But, Mr. Harrison—what you say here is unless I give up all my habits, all the necessities of life, I will lose my house. That I cannot tolerate."

I stood up and walked over to observe Aidan's progress so I wouldn't bite my mother's head off. I couldn't take her supercilious attitude—never had been able to, actually—and it took all of my strength not to yell at her.

Something I definitely wouldn't do in a million years. And never would, my temper and her finances willing.

Nick leaned back in his chair and folded his hands behind his head. "Well, then, Mrs. Hagan, you will lose your house. And your necessities of life. It's that simple. Sometimes you have to make short-term sacrifices for long-term gains."

Welcome to the club, Mom. "Spoken like a true money man," my mother said, wrinkling her nose. Apparently successful men who tried to tell her how to live her life were not nearly as attractive as successful men she wanted to date her daughter.

"Yes, ma'am," Nick said politely. It sounded like he'd had experience dealing with people like my mom. "I can run the numbers for you, if you like, and show you what I'm talking about."

Mom shoved the papers away from in front of her and rested her elbows on the table, ignoring his comment entirely. "Now where did you grow up? And where did you get your degree from?"

He unfolded his hands and crossed his arms across his chest. "I grew up in Manhattan, and went to school in Boston."

"Harvard?" my mother asked in an arch tone of voice.

"B.U.," he said. Before my mother could lower her eyebrows, he continued. "And an MBA from NYU." She brightened considerably. "But discussing my past does not solve the problem of your future, Mrs. Hagan. And," he said, looking at Aidan, "Aidan and I have a party to go to in about fifteen minutes. Right, sport?"

Aidan grinned. "Right."

"Well." My mother sniffed. "It's clear nobody is going to give a woman a break for making an honest mistake."

I couldn't hold back any longer.

"Mother, investing what you could not afford is not an honest mistake. Mixing darks with colors is an honest mistake. Asking for white rice instead of brown when ordering Chinese takeout is an honest mistake. I would say this, *this* was a dishonest mistake. A terrible, awful, misguided mistake. And the fact that Mr. Harrison—"

"Nick," he inserted. So it's Nick now. Oh. Well, then.

"—Nick is kind enough to give you the benefit of his advice does not mean it is his fault you have behaved recklessly, irresponsibly, and foolishly." I stopped speaking, feeling my heart racing and my armpits begin to well with perspiration. Was it because he'd been friendly, or because I'd told my mother what I really thought?

"Well, Molly Moira Hagan, I guess you have done well enough yourself that you can cast a few stones at your mother."

I gave a weary sigh. "That's not the point, Mom. I'm not saying I've done a fantastic job of this, either—" I looked to see if Aidan was listening, but he wasn't. "I married a man who dumped me, and is now not able to support us; I stopped working so I could be a mom; I hope to start a new career, but I won't know about that for a while; and I've generally made a mess of my life, but that doesn't mean I'm not right."

She looked at me—hurt, anger, and remorse flashing in her eyes. She held my gaze for a few seconds more, then dropped her eyes to the table.

She looked as old as she ever had, and my heart ached with seeing her that way. My mom. My judgmental, intellectually snobbish, condescending, Swarovski crystal–collecting mom laid low by her obsessive need to beat the market.

"Mrs. Hagan," Nick said, pulling the papers she'd pushed away back to him. "I promise, it's not as bad as all that." He looked up at her. "What is as bad as all that is refusing to deal with the effects of poor fiscal management. You're an intelligent woman," he said, and I saw her preen, "and you know as well as I do that you have to do something. Or you'll lose everything."

She bit her lip, then nodded slowly.

"And," he continued, bending toward the table and picking up a pen, "I have a fantastic financial guy who, as it happens, owes me a favor. He and I were at NYU together. Here's his number," he said, scribbling on the margins of the paper, "and you will call him on Monday. Or I won't be able to come hang out with Aidan and Molly anymore." There was that wink again.

"Blackmail?" She sounded almost . . . flirtatious. Who knew my mother had it in her, even in the pit of her financial despair?

Oh, I guess I did. Especially when there was a man and Molly in the same sentence.

"I'm serious, Mrs. Hagan." He tapped the papers with his index finger. "This is serious. This isn't something to be glossed over. I can tell that, just by reviewing your numbers for a few minutes. So—you'll do it?"

She nodded again. And looked at me, asking for something she had never asked for, not in all my years of knowing her: comfort. I went over to her and wrapped her in my arms. She laid her head on my shoulder, gave a little sob, and pulled away. "Don't you have a party to go to?" she asked, peering at Aidan over my shoulder.

"Sure do," Nick replied, patting her on the arm. "Listen, call me whenever you want if you have any questions about this stuff."

"What was your undergrad degree in, anyway?" Mom asked, apparently bouncing back enough to quiz him further about his college career.

He rolled his eyes at me before he replied. "Philosophy."

"Interesting," she said, quirking her lip. "I didn't know philosophers were financial planners."

"Didn't you ever hear of John Stuart Mill, Mrs. Hagan? David Hume, Karl Marx?"

"Hm."

Ha. Hoisted on her own snotty petard.

"Sorry my mother is so difficult." Nick, Aidan, and I had left the apartment and were heading the few blocks over to the local chichi children's gym for the birthday party.

"She's not, really. It's hard to have to adjust to a new life-style—"

"Even if the adjustment is caused by your own idiocy," I said, more bitterly than I meant.

"She seems like she's trying, though," he replied in a soft voice. Every hard-ass had his soft spots—Nick seemed to go for the standard children-and-old-ladies option.

"I was actually thinking more of myself." I gave a humor-less laugh.

He clutched my arm as we strode down the street, Aidan holding his hand on the other side. "You can't beat yourself up for your mistakes, Molly. People do things for reasons, and sometimes the original reasons change. It's okay."

Right. He'd heard what I told my mom about Hugh and my life. I relaxed into his grip, feeling his warm strength. "Thanks."

As we walked I couldn't help but think about the last time Aidan and I had walked this sidewalk with an adult male. It'd been early last summer, right before Aidan and I had gone to visit my mother. The day had just been fading into night, and we were headed for the pizza/gourmet place that catered to families just like ours.

Aidan was running ahead, and Hugh and I were watch-ing him do his little skip-jump down the sidewalk. "He's such a sweetheart." I sighed.

"Yes, he is," Hugh had replied, sounding unusually seri-ous. I remember glancing over at him, and he caught my eye, then shook his head, as if to say it was nothing.

But it was something. It was blond, beautiful, and named Sylvia.

I must've done something, maybe tensed up when I thought of Hugh, because Nick nudged me with his arm. "What?" he asked, keeping an eye on Aidan, who was bounding ahead of us.

I shook my head. "Nothing," I said. But it was something. What it was, I wasn't sure yet.

We arrived at the play place a few minutes later, Aidan practically speechless in his excitement. Whenever we'd been to parties there before, the kids had gone into an enormous padded play area, emerging sweaty, tired, and happy forty-five minutes later. I usually hovered in the corner, idly conversing with whichever parents deigned to stay, drinking flat soda and wishing I had brought a book.

This time, though, the parents shepherded the child and adult of choice into the room, providing both with weird sock/slipper hybrids to put on their feet. Nick slipped his sneakers off without question, then helped Aidan with his. They walked into the gym area, both of them stopping to wave before joining the group already assembled in the middle of the floor. I didn't see a Power Ranger anywhere. Hmph.

How could Mr. Intimidating suddenly turn into Mr. Nice? He and Aidan shared a smile, and I saw something in his eyes that told me. Oh. He really does like kids that much. Wow.

"Is that your husband?" one of the other moms asked. I'd seen her around the playground; she was one of those who hadn't completely given up on being attractive. Her long, blond hair was pulled back into a low ponytail, tiny studs— diamond, I guessed—in her ears, and she had on an argyle sweater I'd seen in the J.Crew catalog, but had passed over in favor of being able to afford dinner that week.

"Uh, no, just a"—what was he, exactly?—"a family friend."

"Oh, that is so nice of him to do, then. I had to promise my husband he could watch football all day tomorrow."

"Football's over, I think; wasn't it the Super Bowl a few weeks ago?"

She rolled her mascaraed eyes. "Football, hockey, I don't know. Anyway, I had to promise I'd take the kids—I have a younger one, too, she's at a friend's house—to the movies while he sat on his duff and watched sports. All because I am forcing him to play with his son." Her tone was almost as bitter as mine had been a little while earlier. At least I didn't have that kind of bargain to make anymore.

She gestured to one of the plastic folding chairs in front of the big plate-glass window that opened into the gym. "Would you like to sit? It's not like there's anything we can go do in the half hour or so, might as well rest a little. My name is Caroline," she added, holding out her hand.

"Molly." I clasped her hand and perched myself on the chair, nervously smoothing my sweater. Caroline crossed her legs and swung to face me. "So where is your husband? Off watching sports or something?"

"Um, we're in the middle of getting a divorce, actually," I said, surprised I could admit as much to a stranger without crying.

She gave me a sympathetic smile. "Sorry to hear that."

"Actually," I said, realizing it was true, "it's much better for us this way. He's happier, I'm happier . . . Aidan's working on it."

"That's good, then. It must be hard, though."

"Mm," I replied. Changing the subject seemed like a darn good idea. "What do you do?"

She shrugged. "My husband is a lawyer, he works crazy hours, so it made more sense for me to stay at home and take care of the kids. I was the IT director of a financial services company."

She probably had a better résumé than I did. She definitely had better mom-style.

"So is that your boyfriend?" she asked. She raised her eyebrow at me, as if to imply I had gone out of my league. Or maybe I was just projecting.

"No, just a family friend," I repeated. Maybe if I said it enough times it'd be true. "Actually, someone I'm working for right now."

"Oh, what do you do?" She sounded surprised, as if she couldn't believe I actually did anything. Besides trot my son around to birthday parties, of course.

"Copywriting. Freelance." I stopped myself before I started talking about the Teaching Fellows' program. She was just a little too inquisitive, and I felt like I should be more reserved. I glanced over into the gym, where Nick was heaving Aidan onto his shoulders. His shirt raised up, revealing a taut abdomen with a trail of dark hair leading down . . .

"What kind of copywriting?" Ms. Nosy asked. I had to force myself to look away and into her sparkling eyes.

"For a bakery. Not a regular one, it's being opened by one of those celebrity chefs." I knew that because of course I had Googled Simon a few dozen times.

But now, if you wouldn't mind, I'd like to return to watching Mr. Not-As-Intimidating's Tummy.

"That sounds fattening," she said in a coy tone. "It's hard to stay away from forbidden treats, isn't it?"

Was she reading my mind? There was nothing I wanted more than to get closer to one of those forbidden treats. The one wearing the jeans and the sexy smile. But I wouldn't do that in a million years . . . would I?

"Mommy, Nick says we can do that again sometime, just us. Can we? Mommy, can we?"

We were walking home, Aidan clutching tightly onto Nick's hand, me holding the party paraphernalia—a goodie bag; a doubtlessly smooshed piece of birthday cake Aidan had insisted on taking home for Grandma; and a Power Rangers party hat with a ripped antenna.

It had gotten colder, and I shivered a little in my coat. Nick tucked my hand into his arm and pulled me toward his body.

Oh, I liked the way that felt. Aidan stopped to gaze in a toy window, and Nick and I stood back a little on the sidewalk, watching him literally press his nose against the glass.

"Aidan, honey, back up a little, please. The store doesn't want your breath on its glass." He moved about half an inch, then stared at a Batmobile with purple and green tires. I turned to look at Nick.

"Thanks again. Aidan loved it, and he definitely had a much better time than if I had done it. I would've spent the whole time complaining about my sore back and having to crawl around on the floor."

He laughed. "I doubt you would've spoiled Aidan's time like that. The way he talks about you, you're not the type to put yourself ahead of your kid. Although he did say not to get between you and your coffee, but I think I guessed that already."

"What did he say?" Usually Aidan's comments about me were reserved for times when I didn't let him have what he wanted.

"That you always let him have dessert, no matter how late it is. That your favorite Justice League character is Martian Manhunter—good choice, by the way; that you like to read, and you can be very silly. He likes that a lot."

"Mommy?" Aidan's attention was back on us. "Mommy, now that Grandma's staying with us, does that mean Dante will, too?"

I heaved a sigh. "Um, no, honey." Because if I had to live with my mother and my mother's cat my head would explode. I tried to get him distracted from thoughts of that hideous beast. And for once I didn't mean my mother. "Aidan, what movie did you want to watch when we get home?"

He took off down the block without even answering, and Nick and I started walking quickly to keep up with him. "When in trouble," I whispered, "dangle the possibility of mindless hours of viewing in front of them. Works every time."

"Works for Simon, too," Nick whispered. I choked back a surprised laugh. "Who's Dante?" he asked.

"My mother's cat. Hates everybody but my mother, and barely tolerates her. He has a tendency to mark his territory everywhere."

"Ah, sounds . . ."

"Horrid, I know."

"I was going to say it sounds like Simon."

I let out a surprised bark of laughter and leaned into him. Boy, did that feel good. Oops. "Here we are."

Aidan was waiting for us on the front stoop, an impatient look on his face. I turned to Nick, noticing how he still looked totally handsome, even though I was sure the brisk air had turned my face to a beet. Well, the air and other things.

"You don't have to come up if you don't have the time. I mean, I'm guessing you probably have plans or something . . . ?" I couldn't believe what a wimp I was.

He gave me an incredulous look. "And miss out on whatever Aidan's planning on picking for his movie tonight? You won't get rid of me that easily."

Okay, Molly, you're up. Time to get brave.

I opened the door and we went upstairs, Aidan having latched onto Nick's hand again and talking about superheroes, Pokémon, dragons, and the other creatures that inhabited his imagination. Mom was still out, and the house was blessedly calm. She had made a stab at straightening up, too, so the table was almost clean. I shucked my shoes off in the hallway; Nick and Aidan were having a lively debate about which movie to choose.

"Mommy? I picked *Tarzan*." He waved the cartoon jungle hunk in my face.

"Okay, honey, let me put it in." *Tarzan* was my favorite kids movie. After all, it was secretly a romance, and I always felt that little goo moment when Jane decided to stay with her muscle-bound ape-man. Plus even in the cartoon, Tarzan was hot.

I headed to the kitchen to make coffee. At least I knew he liked *that*. I tried not to notice how much my hands were shaking as I tipped the ground coffee into the filter. When it was ready, I walked to the living room and said his name, then shook my head when he couldn't hear me and gestured for him to follow me back to the kitchen.

"What did you say? Tarzan was yelling something," he said with a smile.

"I made coffee, would you like some?"

"Sure. Nothing in it, please." As if I didn't know that.

"Hard-ass," I replied with a smirk, ducking back into the kitchen. I heard him behind me, and smelled his distinctive scent. I could feel him two feet in back of me. This was the time. Now or never, million years, etc., etc. I turned around abruptly, almost bumping into him.

"Nick, can I ask you a question?" My voice was high, strained.

He backed up a little, putting his hand on the counter and meeting my eyes. "Sure. What's up? Got another birthday party to go to?" His smile was easy, relaxed.

"Uh, no, not exactly. I was wondering. That is, I was—" I turned to look at him. His face had frozen. I wondered if he suspected what I was going to ask him. I wondered what I'd do if he said no.

"I wanted to know if you would be able to go out with me. On a date sort of thing."

His eyes closed for a minute, as if he were in pain. Then he opened them slowly, gazing deep into my eyes as he opened his mouth. "I'm sorry, Molly. No."

"Oh."

He stepped into the kitchen, brushing my arm. I jumped back, away from the contact. He reached into my cabinet and took out two mugs, then poured coffee into them. He met my eyes, a pained look in his.

I opened the cabinet doors with a sudden mad craving for cookies. Rats. Somehow I had turned into Mother Hubbard.

He raised the mugs. "I'll carry these in, then."

His footsteps echoed down the hallway as I slammed the cabinet door shut. Rejected. And just for a date. What was wrong with me?

Nothing, Molly. Nothing is wrong with you. I was beginning to *like* my inner voice. *You don't know how long he's here for. You don't know where he lives. You don't know anything about him.*

And whose fault is that? my inner voice said querulously. *He's not very forthcoming, is he, and you wanted to go out with him why?*

Because he's kind, good with Aidan, and smart. Oh, and totally, amazingly sexy, too.

Well, as long as your own motivations are clear.

And even though he said no, I did do something I wouldn't have done in a million years.

Which was more than I had a few minutes ago.

The rest of my life didn't seem so scary anymore.

Yeast of Eden

In this American classic, Iowan corn-meal vies with its more dramatic, seductive sibling—the Illinois-grown pumpkin—for the favors of the alluring California walnut. Chewy, delicious, and filling, you'll remember this bread long after the romantic triangle has played out its inevitable drama.

17

"WHERE'S YOUR MOM TONIGHT?" LISSA ASKED, REMOVING
her too-cute-for-words shoes. She'd come over right after
work, and it looked like she could use a hug.

"Mom's visiting her devil cat. I think that's who was giving her the stock tips—*more Purina stock, Kathleen.*"

She laughed, then sat down on the sofa with an audible
sigh. "Oh, my, that feels good. It's been such a day."

"What's up?" I said, sitting down next to her. Her skirt
was full and pleated, with a desert scene played out in shades
of green and blue across its folds. I leaned against her shoulder and smelled her soft, springlike perfume. It suited her.

"Work. It sucks. And Tony. He sucks, too."

"Which one is worse? Let's prioritize."

"Tony. He's worse."

Tony was quickly moving toward the top of the "People I
Am Not Fond Of" List. Topping the list, of course, was Hugh;
second was probably Tony. Sylvia probably rounded out the
top five, following the guy at the deli who glared at me when
I asked for more milk in my coffee and the Park Slope mom
who scolded Aidan when he'd accidentally bumped her precious offspring. Oh, and Natalie. But I barely knew her, so
why did I put her on the list? And then I remembered her

snotty smirk when I first met her. *That's* why she was on the list.

"What's going on with Tony?"

"I like him so much, he's exactly what I've always wanted in a boyfriend: smart, successful, cultured. But it seems like I'm not exactly what he's always wanted. I'm trying, I really am, but he's always pushing me to do more. He says it'll make me grow as a person."

"Do you think he's right?" I asked, trying to keep my tone neutral. I'd received that "make me grow as a person" line myself. Fuck them both.

"I do think he's right." I could tell she was trying hard not to be defensive. It wasn't working. "I'm not as smart as he—"

"Now stop it right there." I wished someone had said this to me, I thought as I heard my vehement tone. "Lissa, you cannot possibly believe you're dumb." *Or not ambitious, or social, or what I need in a wife.* "You've done all sorts of amazing things, you're doing well in your job, you're friends with me, even . . . fer Chrissakes, you're not *dumb*."

"Thanks, Molly. I just wish I didn't feel so stupid when I was with Tony and his friends. He knows about wine, and food, and the best nightclubs—"

"All that means," I replied through gritted teeth, "is that he has a subscription to *Time Out* and does stuff at night."

She was too far gone to listen to me. "And when he and his friends talk about movies and art—" She wrung her hands. "I'm hopeless."

I grabbed her and shook her. "Lissa. Listen to me. You are not dumb. You cannot walk around defining yourself by the man in your life."

A little voice mocked me in my head. *Like you did?* Hugh had always pushed me to be a Domestic Goddess, not understanding that boiling water was an accomplishment for me. He'd gotten frustrated when I'd forgotten to pay the bills, or pick up his dry-cleaning, or put my coffee mug in the sink.

Never mind that I was playing with our son, taking care of the household as best I could, and playing therapist whenever he felt insecure.

Never mind that kids were kids only once, but laundry was forever.

Never mind that he never asked me how I was doing, or if I had had a good day.

Never mind all that. *I* couldn't anymore.

Lissa's voice jerked me from my memories. "Can you help me?"

"Of course I can." I patted her hand. "You're my friend, I won't pass judgment. Unless you want me to."

We started our crash course in culture by watching *Pride and Prejudice,* the good version, the one where Colin Firth takes a dip in a pond. White shirts haven't been the same since.

Right when Lizzy was freaking out about her sister running off with Wickham, the phone rang.

"Hello?"

"You're there." It was Simon.

"Yes," I said, turning my back away from the screen so I wouldn't get distracted by another hot Brit. "I live here."

He did not appear to appreciate my sense of humor. "Well,

I need you to get dressed in your classiest clothes and head up to my mum's on the Upper East Side right away."

"What? Why? Is there a problem with the copy or something?"

He snorted. "No, of course not, I just need you up here. You see, Mother is throwing a party, and I got the dates wrong, and I need you up here."

"What? No!"

His voice got a steely edge. "I need you up here, Molly." He lowered his voice to a quieter, but still kinda nasty, tone. "My mother hopes to set me up with one of her friends' daughters, and I need to prove I'm seeing someone."

"I can't, Simon."

His voice got almost whiny. "Please, Molly? You don't have to stay long, just long enough to prove I'm not see— That is, just to introduce you to Mum and her husband."

"Not seeing Natalie? Is that what you were going to say?" I felt my temper—that thing I'd just begun to meet—start to rise. "Thanks for making me feel like a weak substitute."

"That was uncalled for." He sounded icy.

"You called me, buddy," I said. "And I can't shoot up to the Upper East Side just so you can dangle me in front of your mother. We've had two dates, Simon, that doesn't mean I'm obliged to you for this kind of thing. Certainly not at the last minute."

I could not believe I was saying this. Talk about not in a million years!

"Fine." He sounded really pissed off. "I'll speak to you about this later, Molly."

And he hung up without even saying good-bye.

I shook my head as I replaced the phone back in the cradle.

"Something wrong?" Lissa asked. She'd paused the DVD, thank goodness. I needed to wallow in some romantic Austen-ness.

"No. Just a man thinking he can order me around like I was his property."

She gave me a surprised look. "Wow. You sure are teaching me a lot, Molly. Tonight's lesson is: Don't be at his beck and call." She nodded, a satisfied expression on her face. "That's a good one to know."

I felt embarrassed she'd heard me get snippy, but also happy she'd heard a woman talk back to a guy. "Want some ice cream?" I asked, heading to the kitchen. "Colin Firth's hotness demands some icy cool yumminess, don't you think?"

"Uh-huh. And Molly?"

"What?"

"Thanks."

After she left, I peeked into Aidan's room. Mom still wasn't back yet, and the house was as still and silent as my love life. Or as still as it would be after I had another talk with Simon. Aidan was wearing his astronaut jammies and had thrown the covers off in his sleep. He was sprawled across the bed, one arm above his head, the other just touching one of his coiled plastic snakes.

His breathing was deep and regular, as free of care as I could hope for. I bent down and kissed his cheek, and he swatted idly at my face, still sleeping.

When the man in my life was this cute, how could I possibly bemoan my fate? I was luckier than I knew, and being Aidan's mom was worth it.

I closed his door as I walked back into the hall, thinking of what I'd say. And that I was about to do something I never thought I'd do in a million years: Tell a gorgeous man I didn't want to date him.

Much Ado About Muffins

Are the chocolate chips paired with the flour here? Or maybe they're with the dried cranberries? And what about the walnuts? They seem to have an eye toward overthrowing the pecans. There's a superfluity of ingredients here, all changing partners as quickly as you change your mind.

But once you taste this muffin, you'll never switch again.

18

"WHAT ARE YOU ON ABOUT?" SIMON'S VOICE WAS PISSILY British, very clipped and clearly angry. And I hadn't even slept with him. Sheesh.

"I'm just saying that it's probably a bad idea for us to see each other." *Because I don't need to be ordered around, and ordered for, and besides, I get the feeling you're scared of your mother.*

"Is this about Natalie?"

I tried not to huff in frustration too loudly. "No. It is not about Natalie. I barely know the woman." Even though she made my Most Hated list.

"Then why? I deserve an explanation."

I was guessing "because you're an entitled brat" wasn't a good response. It was all I had, however.

He continued without waiting for whatever whitewashed lie I was going to come up with. "Did Nick talk to you?" I could tell Simon was close to yelling. My stomach tightened. I took an extra few seconds to reply so I could ensure my voice was at its normal timbre, not a tremulous squeak.

"Not about you, if that's what you're asking. Why, should he have?"

I heard him exhale. "I just wanted to make sure he didn't poison your mind against me or anything."

Was that why Simon was so interested in me? To piss Nick off? And here I thought it was because he thought I was easy. Heck, so did I.

"Look, Simon, I'll see you at the presentation. Good-bye."

I replaced the receiver as calmly as I could, Simon still sputtering on the other end. Part of me couldn't believe I was turning down sex with a gorgeous guy; another part of me wanted to jump up and down because I was turning down sex with a gorgeous guy. And, almost, kind of, sort of, because I had let him know I was mad.

I hadn't done that since . . . ever. That's what always annoyed Hugh the most: Whenever we argued, I'd keep everything bottled up and not let him know what I was thinking. He'd beg me to say something, anything, but I couldn't handle the pressure of saying I wasn't happy with something.

If I had just spoken up . . . but I couldn't blame it on me, any more than I could blame it on my wearing jeans. Hugh and I weren't suited for each other, and maybe he was stronger than I was for recognizing it. Although the way he figured that out was just as wimpy as I was—cheating on your spouse was unforgivable in my book. Even if my book usually featured a half-naked man on the cover.

I'd made the right decision, I knew that. I kept going over it, like touching a sore tooth, wondering if there was something there I wasn't understanding. Likely as not, I was always surprised by the endings in movies that everyone else had predicted. *The Sixth Sense*? Totally didn't see that coming. *The Crying Game*? No way. So why should my own drama be any different?

I stopped my rumination long enough to make sure my mom and Aidan weren't getting in people's way. We were taking advantage of a special admission offer to the American Museum of Natural History, and my mom and Aidan were in pig heaven wandering around the dinosaurs exhibit.

I jumped when someone touched me on the arm. And wanted to run away when I saw who it was: Natalie.

"Oh, Natalie," I exclaimed. "How nice to run into you here." I was such an incredible liar.

"Hello, Molly. Lovely to see you as well." Oh, she was a liar, too!

"So," I said, shifting on my feet from side to side, "how is setting up your own company going? Have you gotten office space yet?"

She made a moue of annoyance. "It always takes longer than it should, of course, but I expect we will be up and running soon. Speaking of which," she said, "are you available to take on any work?"

What? "Um, well, I don't know." If I'd been any more incoherent I would have been speaking Esperanto.

"And who's this?" Natalie turned as Aidan returned, my mom right behind him.

"Oh, this is my son, Aidan, and my mother. This is Natalie, she used to work at John's company."

"With John," she corrected as she bent down toward Aidan. "Nice to meet you, sir," she said in that tone of voice people who'd never been parents used when talking to adults.

"Hi," Aidan said back. "Mom, can we go to the gift store?"

I met my mother's eyes as she gestured helplessly.

"Sorry, hon, we can't . . ."

"Let me." Natalie opened her purse and pulled out a red patent-leather wallet. She withdrew a twenty-dollar bill and held it out to Aidan.

"Wow, thanks!" he said, taking it from her.

"Um, Aidan, I'm not sure we should—"

"Of course he should, Molly." Did she have to sound so condescending? "Consider it an advance, if you want."

"Oh, you're hiring Molly? Well, isn't that nice."

My mom was so desperate for me to get noticed by anyone she'd sell out her own grandchild. But what could I do? It wasn't as though I could get Aidan to give it back, not without causing him a whole lot of grief, and for what? For somebody who didn't like me but inexplicably wanted to hire me?

Whatever. I couldn't think about it now, not with Natalie and my mother both staring at me, and Aidan already pulling my arm in the direction of the gift shop.

Molly placed a business card in my hand as I was led away. "Give me a call soon, Molly, okay? I have work that'd be perfect for you, and I could use a hand." She leaned in and said in a confidential tone that set my spine on edge, "One of my clients is testing a new line of breakfast treats aimed at busy moms. Plus I'd really like to hear what you've done with Simon's shop." Thankfully, she didn't mention whatever I might—or didn't—do with Simon.

"Sure," I replied, knowing that calling her was one thing I was definitely not going to do—ever—in a million years.

But at least Aidan got himself a stuffed lizard I didn't have to pay for. So maybe the day wasn't a complete loss.

• • •

Seeing Nick that Tuesday wasn't nearly as uncomfortable as I'd anticipated. Given that I'd anticipated his turning into Mr. Ice World again, that didn't mean much. But still. His blue eyes lit up when he saw me, and he led me into the bakery, that omnipresent arm once again holding mine to guide me through the doorway.

The bakery still had the under-construction newspapers on the windows, but the floors were freshly varnished, there was a lovely cream-colored paint on the wall, and the tables and chairs had been set up.

"Would you like to see the kitchen?" Nick asked, gesturing toward a huge plate-glass window.

"I'd love to," I answered, stepping forward.

Wow. No wonder Simon felt so special if he got to cook with this kind of equipment—those huge stainless steel fixtures that TV show chefs had positively gleamed. Pots and bowls were artistically placed on silver shelves lining the spotless white walls, and an overhead rack held measuring spoons, measuring cups, and other cooking devices I couldn't identify.

It was gorgeous. *I* wanted to go in and cook there, and I never had that impulse.

I looked around and gave an approving nod. I had to stop myself from giving that same nod of approval when I looked at Nick. I cleared my throat instead.

"This is all so lovely. It really looks like a thing, you know?" Did I just utter something so moronic? Oh, yeah, I did. I cleared my throat. "So John mentioned doing a presentation to the Cooking Channel. Were you trying to keep it from me, or did you just not know?"

He twisted his lips in what looked like disgust. "It's Simon's idea. He wants to get as much advance PR as he can, so he's flying a bunch in and giving them the full dog and pony show. I told him we weren't ready yet, but John said we were."

"Why would John say that?"

He darted a quick glance at me. "I assumed you'd told him we were ready."

"Me? No, why would I?" I gave a rueful laugh. "You've met me, Nick, do you think I'd actually be that bold?"

"If there were something you wanted badly enough, yes, I think you would."

His reply brought a sharp recall of the last time I had wanted something badly enough. *Not in a million years . . .*

He walked over to one of the low tables, pulling a chair out and gesturing for me to sit. He met my eyes. "Anyway, there's no avoiding it."

I felt like a chastened schoolgirl as I walked over to the chair and sat down. I pulled out my notebook, and felt myself draw a deep breath. "Well, then, let's get started." I opened my binder and pulled out the pages where I'd been making notes.

He bent his head over the pages, and I caught his scent: leathery, musky, masculine.

"I've added several since last week," I said, hearing the strain in my voice. "I'm not sure they'll all work. Lady Windermere's Flan, for example, since I wasn't sure the store would offer flan."

"Mansfield Pork," he read with a chuckle.

"Obviously that won't work, I was just brainstorming," I said nervously.

He looked at me, a warm smile lighting his features. "You are way too clever for this. I wouldn't have expected to have so much fun working on this project. Normally it's number crunching and dealing with marketing executives. They're not exactly a barrel of laughs."

"Thanks. I'm having fun, too."

He kept looking at me for a few seconds longer. "Anyway," he said, returning his gaze to the notebook, "send me the blurbs, I can input them into a PowerPoint presentation. Simon really goes for the bells and whistles." He had a weary tone in his voice.

"How many of these types of presentations have you done?"

"More than I can count. Even before I went to college, I . . . well, anyway, a lot."

I wondered what he had been about to say. And why he was so mysterious about his life.

"So you can tell me what to expect."

He shrugged. "Nothing exciting, really. You'll get up, explain the general theme, throw in some high-concept works like *amortize* and *scalable,* and they'll ask questions, which Simon and I will answer."

"Put that way, it sounds much less frightening than what I had imagined."

"It's not like they're even close to being as smart as you, Molly. Certainly not as sharp. And definitely not as intriguing." He clamped his mouth shut, as if to stop himself from saying anything else. I wanted to pry his mouth open so he could say even more. I grinned.

"Thanks, Nick. I doubt the network execs are as intriguing as you, either."

He gave a half-smile. "I shouldn't have said that, it was"—
He paused for a moment. Complimentary? Charming?
Seductive?—"inappropriate."

"I won't argue the point." But if I have to stare at you any
longer, I'm going to turn into a blithering idiot. I forced myself to
look down at my papers again. *Definitely* not nearly as attractive.

"How's Aidan?"

I smiled. "He's great. He's bugging me about when you'll
be coming to take him back to that place again. I told him
you had a lot of work to do, and he had to be patient. Patience
is not really part of a six-year-old's repertoire."

"I could come out this weekend, actually."

I paused a moment before replying. "Aidan's with his
dad. And my mom's spending the weekend with her friend in
New Jersey. I'll have the whole apartment to myself." Oh,
shoot, that sounded like a proposition.

Judging by the color his ears turned, he thought it was,
too. "Well, the next weekend, then," he said stiffly.

"Great. Aidan will be thrilled." Me, I'll be hoping I won't
accidentally stuff my foot into my mouth again.

"*So what are you going to* do this weekend?" Keisha asked. I
was lying on my bed, the ubiquitous cup of coffee on my bedside table. Aidan was asleep, Mom was reading, and I hadn't
had to pawn my engagement ring yet. It was a good day.

"I hadn't really thought of it until Nick offered to come
over. I guess I'll do some cleaning, maybe take a pile of old
toys to the Salvation Army."

"Ooh, girl, you are going to be one crazy party animal."

"Well, what would you suggest, Ms. Smarty-pants?"

"Let's see. What wouldn't you do in a million years? Maybe go ice-skating in Prospect Park?"

"Yeah, and freeze my ass off. No thanks."

"How about take yourself to the movies?"

"Can't afford it. Next?"

"Drink yourself into a stupor and do some drunk-dialing?"

"It'd be a good idea if I actually wanted to talk to any-one."

"Bonk Simon silly?"

"That's over. At least, according to me."

"Darn. I wanted you to spill all the juicy details."

"Speaking of which, how's the Great White Hope?"

"The first time you made that joke, it was mildly funny. Now? Not so much. But he's fine. I'm fine. We're fine to-gether."

"Okay, so you're making me a little nauseated with all the fine stuff." I paused.

"I love him, Molly."

I swallowed. "That is so great to hear. I am really happy for you."

"Thanks. Me, too."

"And now," I said, glancing at the clock, "I've gotta go before I turn into a pumpkin. Or an incredibly grumpy mom."

"Bye, hon."

"Bye."

As I hung up I realized I still had a goofy smile pinned to my face. Keisha's happiness did that to me.

Lightning—and love—really did strike in the oddest places. Who would've thought Keisha would find the love of her life in Cottonwood, California? Where, according to Keisha, the most exciting things happened one hundred years ago when it was an Old West frontier town?

I was still smiling when I went to sleep that night.

You Pecan't Go Home Again

Setting off for far-off places, places as exotic and far-flung as your dreams. But your reality can—or pecan—be as good, too. Taste this delicious pecan burrata, filled with dough and nuts and warmth.

Bet if they served this at home you wouldn't have left in the first place.

19

THE NEXT MORNING, REALITY HIT. HARD.

I heard the phone as I was starting the first of the break-fast dishes. Thank goodness Aidan liked oatmeal, I couldn't afford those gold-bricked kids' cereals anymore.

"Hello?"

"Hi, Mol."

"Hugh."

"So how are you?"

Was this a social call? "Fine," I answered slowly.

"Good, good. Look, there's something I need to ask you."

I carried the cordless into my bedroom and sat down on the bed, which was still unmade. "Okay. Ask." I balled the top sheet up and threw it into the hamper. Don't tell me I can't multitask.

"I need to get my grandmother's ring back."

I fell back onto the bed and stared at the light fixture. "Ring back," I repeated dully.

"Yes. Look, I know this is hard, but it was my grand-mother's ring, and since—"

—since you left me and we're going to get a divorce, I'm not family anymore. "Of course." I swallowed everything I wanted

to scream at him. It'd be different if he'd actually bought it for me, but since it was his family's heritage—I shut up.

He seemed almost too relieved at my easy capitulation. Why did I always have to make it so damn easy for him: *sure, Hugh, I'll work so you can get your JD; of course, Hugh, I'd love to wait to get pregnant; oh, now?; okay, Hugh, I'll quit my job. It is best for Aidan.*

"I know it's none of my business, but does this mean you and Sylvia—?"

He cleared his throat. "I just want the ring back, Molly."

Oh, so Mr. Indiscreet was finally trying to change his oversharing ways. His discretion didn't make the lump in my throat any smaller.

His voice cut through my memories of when he had given me the ring: Christmastime, about a block away from the Rockefeller Center tree. We hadn't been able to get any closer, and it was freezing, and all I could think about was getting something hot to drink when he pulled it out of his pocket and stood there, grinning sheepishly at me.

I hadn't been cold the rest of the night. I was making up for it now.

"You can just pack it with Aidan's stuff next time he comes for the weekend."

"And have him throw it out by accident because it's not one of his toys? No, Hugh, you'd better get it from me in person. I don't want you thinking I hocked it—" *to pay the rent or something frivolous like that.*

"Oh, good point," he said. "When should I come get it? Or are you going to be in the city anytime soon?"

"You can come get it later this week while Aidan's in school, if you want. You're not working, right, so you have the time?"

I heard him take in a breath. Zing! Molly scores a hit!

"Sure. Morning okay? I've got some work to do later in the day."

Like fun you do. "After 11:30 is fine with me. Just call first, okay?"

"Sure. See you tomorrow."

After I hung up, I just stood for a moment. It was really over. I mean, I knew it was over, but this meant it was really *over* over. I strode to the bureau where I kept my jewelry and found the small black velvet box I'd tucked the ring in right after Hugh left.

It was a beautiful ring. The diamond was square cut and rested on a plain gold band with a small diamond on either side. Hugh was lucky—if it hadn't been a family heirloom, I'd have sold it long before this.

I put it back in the box and wiped my eyes with the back of my hand. The dishes were still waiting, there was no time for me to indulge myself in a good cry. And actually, I didn't even want to cry.

I wanted to rip Hugh's throat out, I wanted to stomp so hard my downstairs neighbors thought I'd taken up clogging, I wanted to do a tequila shot, but I did *not* want to cry.

"Is this Molly?"

I wiped my hands on the dish towel so I could hold the phone better. I didn't recall ever getting two phone calls so close together. If the first call hadn't been Hugh, I might have almost said I was popular. "Yes?"

"Molly, this is Caroline. Jimmy's mom? We met at the birthday party last week."

"Oh, of course." The fabulous blonde.

"Well, I know it's last-minute and everything, but a group of moms are getting together on Saturday for a little get-together, and I was wondering if you'd like to come."

Hey, someone was asking me out! "Uh, sure . . . I'm free, actually, 'cause Aidan will be with his dad anyway."

"Oh, good. It's just something we do every month—we call it Scrapbook Saturday, and we just hang out and work on our scrapbooks."

Oh. God. The only thing I knew about scrapbooking was that I had no interest in doing it. Was it too late to plead illness? Death? Morbid fear of cute captions?

"Great. What time?"

"One o'clock. It's at my house this month, I'm on Third Street, the closest house to the park. Last name's Kostov. Come hungry, I'm making lunch, too."

At least I'd be fed. "Thanks. See you Saturday."

And now I had something else besides the ring return and the investor presentation to dread: a group of Park Slope moms sitting around cutting out scraps of paper to pin into their own precious moments scrapbook.

Wednesday morning, I woke up with a familiar ache in my lower abdomen. Cramps. Ugh. And me about to head into the city to work with John on my presentation.

I popped twice the suggested number of menstrual pain tablets and made a big pot of tea. I could feel the bloat in my stomach. The cramps were exacerbating my back pain—my lower back ached like a really pissed-off mule had kicked it. I got Aidan off to school, just barely, then came home and ran a bath. The hot water eased my discomfort, but the pain returned as soon as I toweled off.

Damn. Cramps, John, and the presentation.

As usual, my wardrobe matched my mood: black. I pulled out my loosest pair of black pants and a long black suit jacket. I grabbed a gray sweater to wear underneath so at least I wasn't completely funereal. In my current state, I knew I could use the extra warmth. I wore my most comfortable nice shoes, not sneakers, but flat and wide to fit my puffy feet.

I made a face at Henry James as I grabbed another romance from my towering stack of luridity. I was not going to suffer for my brain today.

The subway ride wasn't long enough. I felt in a little less pain, but now I felt a little loopy. I walked up to John's office, noticing the trees on the sidewalk were daring to get a few buds on them. I could not wait for spring.

"There's no need to be intimidated, Molly," John pronounced as he led me into the conference room, the place where I'd originally pitched the concept to Nick and Simon. Perched to the left of where I sat was a wicker basket filled with what I presumed were Simon's bakery samples. I grabbed one of the croissants and stuffed it in my mouth.

And remembered, again, what made him a genius. That croissant was absolutely light, and flaky, and even smelled like butter. It was the most fabulous thing I had eaten since the first time I'd eaten his food, and it was almost worth it, though the starch was heading straight for my thighs.

He opened my notebook and leafed through the pages until he found my outline. He paused, thrust his lower lip out, and nodded. I waited at least five minutes before I spoke.

"I'm sorry, does that lip thing mean you approve or disapprove?"

He looked up, a confused look in his eye. "Lip thing? No, this is fine, Molly, I'm just wondering how the network people will react. I mean, you're pretty . . . esoteric here."

"My mother will be so proud," I said drily.

"Not that it's bad, but the blurbs—I mean, I assume they refer to books?"

Yes, Mr. Communications Major. "Well, we could tone those down a bit." I allowed a tone of superiority to creep into my voice. "They're for the concept; we might not end up with these as the actual blurbs. If we have to dumb them down or something. Anyway," I continued, "didn't you once tell me you could sell ice to Eskimos?"

He preened a little. It was an obvious ruse, but it worked. "Of course I can. No problem. Let's get Matt in here to take notes."

John's assistant trotted in, bearing two Starbucks coffee containers. He set one down in front of me, saying, "Milk and sugar, right?" then placed the other in front of John, who took a sip right away, then scowled. "It's black. I wanted sugar." Matt leaped to his feet and returned a few seconds later with a sugar packet. He watched as John dumped the packet into his coffee. John took a sip and nodded, and Matt eased into the chair closest to the door.

"Matt, Molly and I have a presentation next Monday—I told you the date, right, Molly?—and we need to have you take notes then input into a PowerPoint file."

"Actually," I said in a hesitant voice, realizing just how close Monday was, "Nick said he'd do that."

John scowled again in a duplication of his "no sugar" face. "Nick?" His tone was accusatory.

"Yes, Nick." I bet if I'd have said Simon, John would have started tap-dancing on top of the fancy Lucite conference table. Now his expression was that of someone who'd just stolen his puppy.

"Does Simon know about your working with Nick?" If I were younger and more beautiful, maybe with some dark secret, this would be a romance novel come to life. And if I could figure out who was the hero, I could work on that younger and more beautiful thing, too.

"I assume so. Not that we ever talked about it."

"Well, I guess we don't have to worry about the materials, then. Nick can certainly handle that." John took a big swallow of his coffee.

"So . . . what should we work on?" I asked, a lot more brightly than I felt.

"The presentation itself, of course," John bit out. "First thing will be to work on your speech. The intro of the inspiration for the idea, why you think it will work in New York City, how the concept is unique among foodstuffs shops."

I didn't think they wanted to hear all about my and Keisha's brainstorming. I'd have to come up with something else.

"Okay, no problem. What else?"

John drummed his fingers on the table. "Molly, I'd like to actually hear what you're going to say."

"Oh. Well. Let me see . . ." I launched into a story involving Midtown Manhattan, Dorothy Parker, *Sex and the City,* Woody Allen, and a dozen chocolate egg creams. After a while, Matt just laid his pen down and stared at me. John didn't even give me the courtesy of waiting to hear what happened to the plucky little pigeon whose leg had been smooshed by a copy of Proust. I reminded myself to only take two Pamprin at a time from now on.

"Molly. This is not going to work. Try this—"

After rehearsing his version a few times, I felt more comfortable with it, although I still didn't think it was as interesting as my story. Although it was just about as true.

John visibly relaxed as I grew more comfortable with the material, and he clasped my arm as I got up to go. "You'll be great, Molly. You *are* great. Remember that." I was starting to. That felt good.

"What the hell is scrapbooking, anyway?" Keisha sounded as incredulous as I felt. I was wearing my favorite flannel pajamas, the ones with the fancy shoes all over them, drinking a cup of hot chocolate. Aidan was sleeping, and Mom was off somewhere trying to stay out of my hair. I hoped.

"Um, I looked on the Internet, and it seems to be a fancy way to preserve your pictures. Sorry, *photo memories*."

"Besides sticking them into a photo album?"

I sighed, leafing through the piles of pictures I'd stuck in a shoe box underneath my bed. "Yes. Way more than just sticking them into a photo album, not that I've even dragged my lazy ass to do that."

"And people like to do this?"

"Apparently so. I don't understand it, either. I mean, it's hard enough to get the photos organized and into albums"—I dropped a pile of pictures on the bed listlessly—"but to add a whole other dimension of difficulty just boggles the mind."

"So why did you say yes?"

"I didn't realize what it was until it was too late. And what was I going to say: 'Oh, thanks for the invitation, but I think I would rather go hang myself than sit around and cut up lace doilies to decorate pictures of my son? And my lame, soon-to-be ex-husband?' Oh, did I mention these people write cute captions underneath?"

"What, like, 'my husband was a loser'?"

I bit my tongue before I told her about the engagement ring. "As if you needed a cute caption to know that."

"No, really, though. What do they say?"

"From what I saw—and by the way, there are like a million sites devoted to people who scrapbook—it's stuff like 'First grade rocks!' and 'Lola does a pirouette.'"

"Wouldn't it be funny if people had captions for their everyday lives? Like 'Jan endures her mother-in-law's cooking' and 'Francis picks his nose in his car.'"

"Or 'woman tries to fit in with people with clearly different priorities.'"

"Well," Keisha said slowly, "it would be something you would never do in a million years, right? So think of it as an exercise."

"In futility?"

"Ha-ha. No, really. Try to be open-minded about it. Try to have fun with it."

"Okay. I'll try."

"Love you, hon, gotta go. Bye."

I hung up the phone, then regarded the photos strewn on the bed. There were pictures from much happier times: vacations, school barbecues, Thanksgiving, Christmas. Times when Hugh, Aidan, and I were a family, and my mother hadn't yet morphed into Mrs. Schwab.

A million years was coming a lot faster than I would've thought.

By Thursday, my cramps had abated, but now my stomach was experiencing soon-to-be-ex-husband cramps. I dropped Aidan off at school and returned home to wait. I'd sent Mom off to an early matinee—I figured it was worth the five bucks not to have her there when her darling Hugh arrived.

I had just finished scrubbing dried-up grape jelly off the floor when the door buzzed. I heaved myself up, brushed off my knees, and hit the buzzer. I'd tried not to worry about what I was going to wear, but I did put an almost inconspicuous amount of makeup on so I wouldn't look too haggard. You know, from worrying about the little things like the gas and electric bills.

The top of his head came bobbing up the stairs and he was whistling, *whistling,* as if everything was just grand. My fingers itched with the urge to grab one of Aidan's *Star Wars* light sabers and bash him on the head.

His pace slowed as he reached the top of the stairs where I was waiting. "Molly." He gave me a look I'd seen him practice many nights before an important deposition.

"Hugh. Come on in." I waited for him to enter, then slammed the door extra hard just to watch him jump.

He walked into the living room and stood, shifting his weight from side to side. His eyes swept over the table's surface, darting away from the big stack of bills I'd left right in the middle.

"How you doing, Molly?" he asked, widening his eyes like he was really concerned.

"Fine, thanks," I replied. "How's not working going for you?"

He clamped his lips together, and I saw his jaw clench.

"By the way," I continued artlessly, "if Sylvia says yes, do you think you could get her to work out a child-support agreement? Since it seems like she'll be making the money in the family. Unless you got a job?" I made my voice sound extra-sweet. I paused, letting it sink in. "You can answer that later, let me just go get the ring."

It was hard to find the ring through the mist that was clouding my eyes. It was not tears, it was *not*, and I'd be damned if I let Hugh see how he affected me. I blinked, hard, then peeked at myself in the bathroom mirror. Not too bad. I looked as if I hadn't gotten enough sleep, but then I always looked like that.

"Here you go," I said, holding the ring out in its little box. "Let me know when I can expect child support again." Hugh hesitated for just a moment, then took it from my outstretched hand. He opened it for a minute, and the overhead light made a radiant sparkle on the floor. I peeked at it again. Probably the last time I'd ever see it. I swallowed and looked away.

"Thanks, Molly. I know this is a tough time, I . . ." He

spread his hands out, as if he couldn't control anything that had happened to us.

"Sure. Right. Look, I know you've got to be going," I said, starting to walk to the front door again. He followed, his head bowed like a teenage boy who'd just been busted by the principal.

"Thanks. See you," he said, giving me a little wave.

I closed the door quietly this time and leaned against it, gazing up at the ceiling.

As usual, Dr. Lowell got to the tough question right away. "How did it feel?"

I drew my eyebrows together in thought. Screw the wrinkles. "It felt like closure, actually. It didn't hurt to see him. It did hurt to give the ring back because that means it truly is over. Not that I want to be married to him anymore, but that part of my identity is finished."

"Is he going to marry her?"

"He wouldn't say. I did ask, I couldn't *not* ask. He might marry her as soon as he's gotten his divorce. That would be weird."

I stopped speaking for a moment and reached for a tissue from the family-size box on Dr. Lowell's side table. Hugh. Married to someone else. Someone taller, blonder, sharper.

Someone not as funny, not as kind, not as clever with a pun. Someone who didn't have Aidan as a kid. Someone who probably couldn't talk about romance novels as easily as she could talk about the latest in literary fiction.

Someone who wasn't me. I scrunched that tissue in my hand. I didn't need it after all.

"But," I said, "that all doesn't hurt that much. Not like it would have six months ago. Aidan and I are better off without him, actually. Aidan gets a mom who's not resentful all the time, and I get to try to be happy."

Dr. Lowell nodded in a satisfied-therapist kind of way. "That sounds fantastic, Molly." She brought her fingers together and ticked off each point as she made it: "You are over Hugh. You are discovering your own personality. You have realized you can make it on your own. You are taking risks and chances in ways you never would have before. Good for you," she said, finishing her words with a few claps of her hands.

I inclined my head in a modest bow. "I'd like to thank the Academy, my therapist, my son, not my mother, and Keisha. But really," I continued in a serious tone, "this morning was hard, but I didn't fall apart." I shook my head slowly. "Weird. I would have thought I would always fall apart."

She assumed her pondering expression, and I knew she was going to say something pointed and salient. "Funny how our idea of our own personality is quite, quite different from the reality. Keep that in mind, Molly."

"I will," I said in an assured tone. "I will."

"And this is the study," Caroline said, opening the heavy wood door. I'd had my mouth open since I entered her apartment. It was easily twice the size of mine, with dark wood wainscoting and magnificently imposing Victorian furniture. Not that I liked Victorian furniture, but the place just reeked of money, and I had to keep squashing enormous pangs of envy. Caroline's husband, the lawyer, had taken their kids out to a

movie, so there were only women in the room, and you could hear the thrum of conversation even from the front entryway.

"This is an amazing apartment, Caroline," I said, knowing it was better to sound gushing than jealous. She shrugged, like it didn't matter.

"This was Alex's parents' apartment, and they moved to Florida. I'm not a big fan of all that dark wood, myself," she said, gesturing me toward where I presumed the scrapbooking was to take place.

"Ladies, I'd like to introduce you to Molly. I met her at one of our kid's—oh, yours, Nancy—birthday parties. Molly lives over on Fourth Street, and she's never scrapbooked before, have you?" Caroline looked to me for confirmation. I nodded slowly.

"Virgin!" the group shouted. There were about six of them, all seated around an enormous dining room table, the kind you might've expected Miss Havisham to preside over. I saw a few familiar faces from the playground, and sat down in the nearest chair. There were materials strewn all over the table: cloth, construction paper, pinking shears, glue sticks, sequins, cardboard photo frames, markers, and, blessedly, wineglasses with some alluring ruby-colored liquid inside.

Caroline must have been reading my mind. "Can I get you something to drink? I've got soda, water, juice, chocolate milk, and wine."

"Wine, please." Maybe if I got tipsy I wouldn't feel so uncomfortable. That, or I wouldn't care anymore.

The woman closest to me took a sip from her glass and gave me a warm smile. She had dreadlocks down her back and was wearing one of those African kente cloth skirts. "My name's Tamsin, nice to have you here, Molly. What made you interested in scrapbooking?"

I'm not. "Um, well, Caroline called and invited me." I tried not to stammer, but it was hard. All of the women were giving me a look I'd seen on the faces of people looking in the cages at the zoo, that slightly condescending *Homo sapiens* way. Regarding the lesser, nonscrapbooking species.

"Don't bother her, Tam," Caroline chided, placing a glass in front of me. I gulped a big swallow down before I could think, then leaned back in my chair so I wouldn't chug the whole thing.

The problem was, this felt like high school again. When I'd somehow get in a room with the popular girls and they'd be talking about stuff I had no clue about: makeup, dates, blow jobs, Long Island iced teas, long phone calls with boys. I'd sit there, with a wan smile pasted on my face, trying to blend into the woodwork. Some of the nicer girls would try to include me, but I would invariably say something that was hilarious, even though I'd been serious when I'd said it. And I'd skulk out, hearing the guffaws of laughter behind me.

"Molly, where on Fourth Street do you live?" It was the woman farthest from my chair, a silver-haired woman with purple eye shadow. "Oh, I'm Sharon, by the way," she said, shaking her bob a little as she spoke.

"Between Seventh and Eighth avenues."

"Near the catering place?" she asked, tilting her head quizzically.

"Opposite side of the street and up a little. Just next to the other apartment buildings."

"Ah, I see." She nodded, as if she had discovered something very important. "And what do you do?"

"Um . . . I'm in the middle of getting a divorce, so I'm also in the middle of figuring out what I want to do. That English degree I got twenty years ago isn't much of a help now," I replied with a dry chuckle. There was a round of answering laughter around the table. "Meanwhile, I'm doing some freelance copywriting."

"You brought some photos, right?" Caroline asked as she sat herself down in the chair next to me. I couldn't help admiring her preppy mom style: immaculately pressed khakis, a pink short-sleeve sweater with the matching cardigan tied around her shoulders. She wore little pearls in her ears, and her makeup was perfect. I grimaced as I looked down at my jeans and thrift-store sweater. But I had managed to apply some makeup, and I'd even worn my favorite pair of earrings, silver hoops that swung whenever I moved my head.

I reached down to my bag and pulled out a plastic shopping bag. Caroline gestured to the table in front of me, and I turned the bag upside down and dumped the contents.

When Caroline had invited me earlier that week, my only idea about scrapbooking was ladies writing cute comments and pasting precious borders around their family photographs.

But I realized it didn't have to be all pink ribbons and pinking shears. I could make something that was a scrapbook of my life, something to memorialize important events in my life. Right now, the most important event besides Aidan was my marriage, which was soon to become my divorce.

I pulled out of my back pocket the list I'd made of everything I'd brought.

THE DETRITUS OF MCLAUGHLIN AND HAGAN

1. Wedding invitation.

2. Pictures from our honeymoon in Jamaica. A red bikini was not the best choice for me.

3. Pictures from our first Christmas. Red bikini underwear (even with a Santa hat) was not the best choice for Hugh.

4. A photocopy of his law degree.

5. Dry-cleaning slips for Hugh's fancy Donna Karan shirts.

6. The picture of my first sonogram.

7. Aidan's birth announcement.

8. Pictures of Aidan's first day home, his first nap home, his first burp home, his first poop home, his first morning home, his first smile, his first laugh, his first step, his first fall, his first day of preschool. I couldn't believe we had been so diligent about recording his life.

9. The announcement of Hugh winning his first big case.

10. Pictures of Hugh in Hawaii on a corporate retreat. Pictures of Hugh skiing in Tahoe with the partners from his firm. Pictures of Hugh in Atlantic City.

11. The separation agreement.

12. The Amazon.com order for all the books I'd ordered the day after he left: *Making It on Your Own, Who Needed Him Anyway?, Survival of the Fittest, Welcome to the Lonelyhearts Club, Raising Children in a One-Parent Home, D-I-V-O-R-C-E, Sex and the Single Mom.*

13. The paper confirming my name change.

14. The slip for the last forgotten batch of Hugh's shirts at the dry-cleaners.

It was a helluva lot of material. I hoped, when I was done, I'd have something that would have real meaning for me, some physical manifestation of the emotional upheaval I'd been through in the past six months. Plus it'd be fun to write snide comments underneath Hugh's pictures.

Caroline peered over my shoulder, picking up one of the photos. "Which one was yours?" she asked.

I pointed to him. He had one of those green eyeshade visors on, the kind gamblers wear in old movies. His companions were all holding dollar bills in the air.

"He looks normal. Kind of like a frat boy," she said in surprise. I looked at the picture a little more closely. Besides the visor, Hugh had on a light blue three-button polo shirt, dark blue Dockers shorts, and sneakers without socks.

"He does, doesn't he?" I replied in wonder. When had we grown apart? Probably when he was attempting to climb the corporate ladder in the big city while I was playing Chutes and Ladders with Aidan at home.

"I'm guessing your project will be a little different from the rest of ours. But Sandy over there"—she pointed at a dramatic-looking woman with raven black hair and scarlet lipstick—"did a tribute when her cat passed away." The woman nodded, her regal features set in a sympathetic look.

"But no matter, the principle is the same. Did you bring a photo album, too?" I reached back into the bag and drew out the book, which was covered in black. She gave me a wry glance. "I can see where you're going with this. This will be fun."

She took the album from me, then opened up the pages. "First thing is to define your goal." She gave me another amused look. "Judging by your materials, I'd say you already have. Next is to lay out the order of your items." She picked up the list. "Is this how you'd like it to go?" I nodded. "Then all that's left is to put it together."

She stood up and leaned over the table, pulling a tablet of construction paper over to me.

"So how long were you married?" Tamsin asked, taking a sip of her wine.

"Ten years. We were together ten years before that." There was a murmur of sympathy from the women around the table.

I flipped through the construction paper and found the black section. I ripped out one of the sheets and set it in front of me. I opened the album to the first page, and peeled back the plastic covering.

I laid the wedding invitation in the middle, then stared hard at the black paper, hoping to get inspired.

"More wine, Molly?" I gave a start as I saw I'd somehow managed to finish the first glass.

"No, thanks, not just yet," I said as Caroline gave my pages an approving look. "Seems like you're getting the hang of it," she said, touching me on the shoulder. "I know you were skeptical, but this is fun, isn't it?"

It was. It was also something I'd never do in a million years.

• • •

"Ladies, time for a break." Caroline stood to my right, waving her hands to get our attention. Her bracelets clinked pleasantly as she waved. The last hour had been spent in almost total silence, all of us working on our projects, with only an occasional murmured "pass the scissors" or "can I have your glue?" I looked up and blinked, pulled out of my trancelike state.

I stood up, feeling my legs protest a little at having been still for so long. Caroline held her arm out to a room farther in the apartment. I followed her pointing, and found myself in a huge room with a long table on one side and an entire windowed wall. It was cloudy outside, but even so, the view was spectacular.

"Wow." I stood there for a moment, allowing the pangs of envy to envelop me. If only Hugh hadn't been so lazy. If only I'd continued working, kept my résumé current, not had Aidan . . . but then I wouldn't be happy. I'd have a nicer apartment, sure, but I wouldn't be happy.

And I felt . . . almost happy. Molly Hagan, no engagement ring, dicey financial future, and scrapbooking. And almost happy. Would wonders never cease?

After I piled a plate full of warm, nummy things, I headed toward the unoccupied couch and settled myself in. I surveyed my food, hoping I hadn't been gauche enough to take way more than everyone else. Tamsin came and sat next to me, and I was relieved to see she had even more of the Chinese noodle salad than I did. She speared a piece of tofu, then turned toward me.

"Sorry about your divorce. How is your son taking it? He's how old?"

I twirled a noodle on my fork. "Six. He's doing okay, I guess, although he clings a little more. Not that I mind. I kind of need that right now."

She nodded, attacking a cherry tomato with enthusiasm. "Kids are smarter than we think. He probably knows you need that, too. Is he getting along with your ex?"

I shrugged. "I think so—it's hard to tell, he mentioned not wanting to spend as much time with him anymore. But it's because his dad is doing the same things he always did: watching sports, hanging around the house, napping. Aidan just didn't notice before because I was always there."

"I know what that's like," Tamsin said. "My husband thinks bonding with our kids is when they all cheer for the Knicks. But they adore each other, so I guess that's okay."

"How old are yours?" I asked, moving my fork to investigate what I thought might be curry beef. Mm.

"Nine and seven. One of each, Sidone is the oldest, Vashon is my baby."

"And where do you live?"

She gestured with her fork. "On Fifteenth Street. Vashon and Caroline's oldest son play T-ball together."

"How long have you been scrapbooking?"

She gave a mock grimace. "Six months now. I know, I sure don't look like I like to cut borders and write cute phrases, but it's really . . . relaxing. It's a good thing to do, just for me, and it makes me happy."

"It is very zenlike. I am totally surprised at how engrossed I got. So," I said, spearing another piece of beef, "what do you do?"

"I do fund-raising for a nonprofit. It's part-time so I can be with the kids."

I sighed. "I know, that's the most important part, isn't it? Being with your kids. Unfortunately, you need money to do that."

"What does your ex do?"

"He's a lawyer. But he's an unemployed lawyer right now. I have no idea if he'll be able to help us as much as we'd need for me to stay home with Aidan. So I've applied to the Teaching Fellows' program to become a teacher. It'll mean a change of life, but not as drastic as a traditional nine-to-five. That is, if I get in."

She waved her fork. "You'll get in. You're smart."

"You know that because . . . ?"

"Because you're smart." She said it so confidently I couldn't argue. "When do you hear?"

"Well, I sent in the application materials, and then I made the first cut, which meant I had to go in for an interview. It was awful. I felt so self-conscious, and stupid, and I know I sweat and stammered and all those things I used to do during Speech and Presentations Class in college. But at least I answered all the questions, even if I looked like I'd been doused in water several times."

Thinking of being able to provide for Aidan was what made me get through it and not run out crying from the room. Then I realized I hadn't answered her question. "Um—a few months, I think?"

"Good luck." She laughed. "That self-conscious part sounds like me when my mother-in-law questions my child-rearing habits." She took another bite and smiled at me. "So—what kind of stuff would you be teaching?"

I shrugged. "They place you where you think you can do the most good. I have that English degree, so either high school English or elementary or middle school. I'm not picky, I just want to be able to do something useful that also pays the rent." And how.

She nodded. "That sounds like a good goal."

I twirled a noodle around my fork, then lifted it to my mouth. If I kept eating, maybe I wouldn't have to worry about dinner that night. Mom was off at a meeting, so she wouldn't be home anyway, and without Aidan in the house, it was so . . . lonely. Better for me not to rattle around the apartment too much.

Caroline came over just as I was considering whether I should get thirds. Most of the other women were onto their dessert and coffee, but there were still a fair amount of noodles left. I felt extra pathetic when I realized I was contemplating asking for some to take home so I didn't have to worry about lunch the next day, either.

"Are you having fun?" She still wore that perky J.Crew smile, but I knew there was more there than just pastels and the perfect life.

"Mm, yes, thank you. Thanks so much for inviting me."

She smiled. "I could hear you were skeptical when I asked, but admit it: It's fun."

It was fun. I never would have thought I'd be the kind of person who liked scrapbooking, but I could still surprise myself after forty years. Go me.

I'd just about finished when Sandy, the Goth-looking deceased cat owner, lifted her head, swept back her Bettie Page bangs, and addressed me. "Molly, tell me, what kind of copy-writing do you do?"

"Actually, before this project, I just did copyediting for medical journals. Boring stuff. But the guy I work for hired me to write copy for a new chain of bakeries that's opening. It's been a lot of fun, actually."

"I own an ad agency," she said in a smug voice. "Which company is it?"

Oh, dear, someone who actually knows what they're doing. "Corning and Associates, working with Simon Baxter."

Her eyes widened. "Oh, then you must know Natalie Duran. She was with them briefly."

"I met her, yes." And now she's bribing my son. "We actually were working together on the bakery project, but now it's just me."

She lifted her perfectly arched eyebrow and said, "Hm," then swept her supercilious eyes down my body. I dug my nails into my legs so I wouldn't duck my head like I used to in high school. "Natalie has big shoes to fill. She's quite talented." The implication being, of course, that I was not.

Tamsin's mellifluous voice cut through the frosty air left by Sandy's obvious disdain. "Molly's smart, I bet she's doing a great job. Aren't you?"

I gave her a relieved smile. My hero. "We'll see. I have a presentation next week."

"Really? Well, you have to practice with us. Right, ladies?" Caroline looked around the room, nodding approvingly as the other ladies nodded their heads.

Suddenly I wished Caroline weren't quite so friendly. "Uh . . ."

"Oh, come on, Molly," Tamsin chimed in. "It'll be good practice. We won't be nearly as tough an audience as those corporate geeks."

I shot a look at Sandy, whose eyebrow was still raised. Only now she was regarding me with an amused stare. *Yeah, well, I always thought Siouxsie and the Banshees were over-rated anyhow, lady.*

"Please, do show us." She sounded as if listening to me was the last thing she wanted to do . . . probably almost as much as I didn't want to do it. Stand up in front of a crowd of strangers and give a presentation off the top of my head? I wouldn't do it in a mill—

"Okay, sure," I heard myself saying. I put my half-finished scrapbook project to the side, stood up, and straightened my pants with a nervous gesture.

*After the women—with the notable omission of Sandy—*had given me their applause and plenty of confidence-boosting feedback, I'd made plans with Tamsin and Caroline for lunch while our kids were at school. I'd also committed myself to attending the next scrapbook day and was ridiculously proud of the Post-Mortem Marriage Book I'd started. I wished Keisha could see it.

I ambled down the street from Caroline's apartment, thinking of how the day had surprised me. How I had surprised myself. I glanced at my watch, and realized there were at least six hours left of the day before I could reasonably put myself to bed and not feel pathetic. Suddenly, I didn't want to go home. At least not yet.

I walked onto Seventh Avenue, Park Slope's main retail

drag, and looked longingly at the window of the local arti-sanal jewelry shop. Was it wrong that I briefly debated the merits of rent versus a bracelet?

I walked past one of the oldest bars on the avenue, a place where you could still get a steak and fried onions for $15.95. Hugh and I had never been there—he'd turned his nose up at its placidly middle-class demeanor—but it looked cozy and nice. The windows were all fogged up against the cold, and the people inside looked as if they were enjoying themselves. Without allowing myself to have any second thoughts, I pushed the door open and went inside.

A few people glanced up as I came in, but there weren't any of the looks I'd feared of "hey, you don't belong here." I walked over to the bar, shrugged off my coat, and draped it over the barstool. As I sat down, the bartender came up.

"What can I get you?" she asked, blowing a piece of gray hair away from her face. She looked to be about fifty-five, with a nice, lived-in look to her face.

"Guinness, please."

She nodded in approval and grabbed a pint glass, holding it under the tap. The beer was as thick and brown as I'd re-membered. She placed it in front of me and waited for me to take a sip.

I gave a satisfied sigh. "That good, huh?" she said with a smile. I smiled back, feeling as if there was no one more con-tent than I at that moment.

"Mm. It's been a while since I've had a beer. I gave it up for rent."

She threw her head back and laughed. "Very funny."

"I only wish I was kidding."

Her name was Lois, she told me, and she'd worked there for twenty years. She knew most of the people who walked in, grabbing a glass and pouring their drink of choice without even waiting for their order. She asked questions without being too nosy, and I found myself telling her all about Aidan and a little bit about Hugh.

"Have you been dating at all?" she asked, refilling my glass.

I took a sip and rolled my eyes. "Kind of. Not really," I continued, thinking that I'd just broken things off with the only guy who seemed remotely interested in me.

She nodded sagely, as though she could read my mind. "Dating is probably good experience for you. You don't strike me as someone who spent a lot of time dating, even before you were married."

"Really? How can you tell?"

"The way you walked in here, sort of hesitantly. As if we'd ask you to leave."

I gave her a wry look. "That just means I don't have much self-confidence."

She nodded again in agreement. "Exactly. And people who date a lot, and know how to date, are self-confident. So probably in about six months you'll be striding in here like you own the place."

I took a big swallow and wiped my mouth with the back of my hand. "I sure hope so. I mean, about the self-confidence thing."

"All you need in this world, Molly, is self-confidence. Everything's gravy after that."

I thought about what Lois had said as I walked home. It

was remarkably similar to what Dr. Lowell was always saying. And Keisha, too, come to think of it.

When I got home, I pulled out my notebook and made a
list. This time, it was all about me.

THINGS I AM GOOD AT

- Being a mom.
- Being a daughter. Sometimes.
- Being a friend.
- Talking on the phone.
- Reading.
- Eating. Especially pastries.
- Drinking coffee.
- Loving Stevie Wonder.
- Making puns.
- Dressing in black.
- Making fun of myself.
- Liking myself.
- Loving myself.

The last one was the hardest to write. I took the paper,
folded it twice, and stuck it in my lingerie and sock drawer,
where I kept all of Aidan's cards from birthdays and Mother's
Day over the years. I'd show Dr. Lowell—and probably Keisha, too—when I could look in the mirror and say it all to
myself without hesitation. Especially the last one.

That was something I would do in a million years. Or less,
if I just gave myself a chance.

The Adventures of Huckleberry Pie

This pie might seem to be one thing at first bite, but as you dive deeper, you'll find it is so much more. It's blended with all-American berries, not just the huckleberry—an elusive fruit that takes many forms—but also blueberries and cranberries. It takes a trip down the Mississippi of your taste buds, so delicious it almost makes you want to craft a new word to describe its taste. It's more nuanced than it seems, and it flips the idea of the average pie on its head.

Go beyond what you see on the outside—a plain, average piece of pie—and come to love this new American classic.

20

THAT MORNING, AIDAN DECIDED HE WANTED TO WEAR shorts. In thirty-seven-degree weather. With a slow, steady drizzle of cold rain outside. It took an extra ten minutes to talk him out of it. He succumbed to the combined bribe of Jiffy Pop popcorn for breakfast and a half hour of extra SpongeBob SquarePants after school.

Meanwhile, Mom was wandering around the house picking things up and putting them down again. My book? Up, then down. Aidan's last school picture? Up, down.

"Mom, are you testing gravity, or do you think you could stop that?" My words came out sharper than I meant. She jerked away from the candy cane Christmas candlestick I'd forgotten to put away.

"Sorry, dear. Just . . ." Her voice trailed off. I felt horribly guilty for snapping at her.

"Never mind. Just help me get Aidan's shoes on, okay?"

After Aidan was suitably dressed, Mom walked him to school so I could get ready. I wore a pair of black pants and a crisp white cotton shirt with a black blazer over top. I wrapped a double strand of jet beads around my neck and made sure my hair was smooth, not fuzzy.

I took an extra few minutes with my makeup, too. I

viewed myself in the mirror, almost satisfied with the result. If I turned my head just right, I looked like one of those career women who were always being featured in *O, The Oprah Magazine.*

I dumped the contents of my vintage carpetbag purse on the table and extricated my MetroCard, my wallet, a pack of Kleenex, and my lip salve. I placed them into a slim black clutch I'd bought for Hugh's high school reunion. It was a little fancy for daytime, but it was fairly inconspicuous, and way more professional-looking than my usual purse.

Dressed for success, that was me. And my interior almost matched the exterior.

On the way to John's office, I stopped off at Starbucks and indulged in a tall skim latte. I sipped it as I walked down Twenty-fifth Street. Maybe it would be easy. Maybe the Cooking Channel folks would love my ideas and give me a standing ovation.

And maybe I'd sprout wings and fly around the room.

The first person I saw when I stepped off the elevator was Nick. I smiled, then felt it falter as I caught sight of his face.

"Ms. Hagan." Gone was any hint of friendliness. Nick's eyes shone a frozen blue, his lips creased in a thin line.

"Ni—, Mr. Harrison," I replied. "Am I late?"

He frowned. Or scowled, really, and glanced at his watch. "No. Five minutes early, in fact." He said it as if it were an accusation.

"Oh. Well, then." I straightened the hem of my coat. "Should we go into the conference room?"

"Not yet. Take a seat, please." He gestured toward the reception area sofa. I perched on the edge, feeling myself start to sweat.

"Thank you." He sat down as well and leaned forward, placing his hands on his knees. "Moll— That is, Ms. Hagan. We have a problem."

Ms. Hagan. I looked at him stupidly. "A problem?"

"Yes, and it's a serious one. It seems one of John's competitors knows of our potential marketing plans."

"Is that bad?"

I saw his jaw clench. He cleared his throat. "Yes. Since only you and I know the specifics of the campaign, and I didn't tell anyone . . ."

My throat closed over. "You think I—?" My voice came out in a tiny little squeak, as if Minnie Mouse were on the witness stand.

He looked at me, not saying a word. Ouch, blue ice.

"No. No, I didn't tell anyone about it." Then I got a sick feeling. "Except—oh, God, except I did the presentation in front of these women, these scrapbookers—"

He flipped his hand out in an impatient gesture. "And?"

"And one of them is in advertising, and said she knew Natalie." Fuck. And I'd already known Natalie was trying to get something from me, I just didn't know what. How dumb was I anyway?

His lips tightened even more, if possible. I couldn't be any dumber than what Nick obviously thought of me. Fuck again. "And you thought it would be all right to demonstrate your presentation to a group of people, at least one of whom works in the same field? When you knew how crucial this was?"

Put that way, I'd screwed up bad. Really bad.

"God, I'm sorry."

He leaned back, pulling his hands up his thighs. "Yeah. Well. I wish you had thought before you spoke."

Me, too. "I'm sorry," I repeated.

"Well." He checked his watch. "We might be able to salvage this." His tone was still frosty. He got up and watched me without holding his hand out to help, like he normally would have done.

Totally professional. *I would not cry, I would not cry, I would not cry.* I swung my chin up and stared him in the eye. "Right. I'm going to go knock their socks off."

His lips lifted in what was almost a smile. "You are."

Would he ever trust me again? Worse, would he ever call me Molly?

Still reeling from the encounter with Nick, I slipped into the conference room and clutched my presentation so hard my knuckles turned white. I was determined not to let that slipup make me slip up even more now.

"Thanks to all of you for coming today." John had come to stand next to me, so close I could feel the breeze stir when he waved his hand.

There was a platter full of Simon's products on the conference table. Everything smelled delicious, and all I wanted to do was crawl into the nearest cupcake and dissolve into tears.

But I knew for both my and Aidan's sake I couldn't. I couldn't help, however, taking an extra deep sniff as the sugary, buttery aroma permeated the air.

John waited until he had everyone's attention before he started to speak. "Corning and Associates is embarking on a new direction, one that will bring the company's expertise to the forefront of the consumer experience. And, we hope, revolutionize it." He gestured toward me before I could try to decipher just what he'd said. "I'd like to introduce our creative marketing consultant, Molly Hagan. Molly will be explaining the initial concept of Simon Baxter's exciting new venture. And, we hope, intrigue you so much you'll be interested in featuring Simon's bakery on the appropriate programs. We are"—he leaned forward as though he were confiding in them—"offering you an exclusive look at this ahead of your competitors." He gestured toward me. "Molly?"

There were half a dozen of them, men and women, a range of ages, all with at least ten pounds too many. I guess cooking network execs probably had to eat more than regular people.

John sat down in the chair next to me while Simon was on the other side. Nick leaned against the wall near the door. My eyes kept flicking toward him. No change in his hard, cold expression. I had really done it. Shoot. It hurt way more than it should have.

I dropped my eyes down to the folder John had made to accompany Nick's PowerPoint demonstration. I flipped it open to the first page, drew a deep breath, and started speaking.

There was a full thirty seconds of silence after I stopped. I was really proud of myself that I didn't automatically think they hated it.

The oldest of the execs sat forward. He tilted his head as he spoke. "Food and entertainment. A delightful mix."

It was as if his approval had unleashed some sort of floodgates—the other people in the room all began to smile and talk among themselves. I heard "Anthony Bourdain," "throwdown," and "special" all exclaimed from them at one point or another.

Simon had joined the group, and I heard his accent weaving in and among the other voices: "Yes, this is scalable, and we will be looking to expand, once Vanity Fare is established as the premiere pastry destination in New York City."

Wow. That sounded pretty neat, once I actually thought about it.

Nick remained where he was, near the door, his sharp eyes taking in the scene. I tried not to look at him, I really did, but that still-pathetic part of me wanted to know we were okay. That he thought I'd done okay, and that he knew I hadn't betrayed him. The company.

I wondered if Simon had told him about us, and that we weren't us anymore. I highly doubted it. Simon wasn't the sort to reveal anything that might possibly make him look bad.

"You did great," John said, walking over and placing a hand on my arm. "I think they're gonna bite."

"Thanks." I darted another glance at Nick. "Um, John, did you hear anything about a competitive agency finding out about the marketing plans?"

His face blanched. "No. Why?"

"It's probably nothing, just that Nick said there'd been some talk, and that it seems like it's something I did. That Natalie found out what we were planning."

He frowned and drew me to the far corner of the room. Simon was still going strong, now declaiming a variety of bon mots to the group of enthralled executives.

"How would she have found out? Have you been in touch with her?"

I jerked out of his hold. "I wouldn't do that, even if I liked her. Which I don't," I added, just in case he wasn't clear on that. I sure as hell wasn't going to tell him about my encounters with her—they sounded fishy, even to me, and I knew exactly what had happened during them.

"So what happened?"

"Yes, Ms. Hagan, tell us. What happened?" Nick had uncoiled himself from the wall to join us, the snake.

I felt myself turning red. "It's that I was with this group of ladies, women from my neighborhood, and we got to talking, and they asked me what I was working on, and then they asked me to show them what I was going to present, you know, just for feedback and to see and everything"—boy did I sound lame—"and it turns out that this one woman knows Natalie, and she must've told her the gist of what I'd done." I held my hands out to both of them. "You have to know, I had no idea it was going to cause a problem."

John rushed in before Nick could condemn me with some more coldly spoken words. "I'm sure it'll be fine, Molly, Natalie can't do anything at this point." He gestured toward the still-chatting group of people clustered around Simon. "The presentation is done, the secret is spilled."

"The point isn't whether we are in jeopardy," Nick said, his voice tight and clipped. "The point is why Natalie appears so hell-bent on interfering."

At which point John and Nick both turned and looked at Simon.

And I felt sick.

"I'll speak to him after this," Nick said. It sounded more like a threat than a promise, and I was glad I wasn't Simon.

Eventually the Simon Show ended, and the crowd dispersed. John led them out of the room, and I could tell he was pleased by the response.

And I was able to grab a cookie, something with macadamia nuts and white chocolate. So the day wasn't entirely shot.

Simon came over to me, an intimate gleam in his eyes. Uh-oh.

"I knew you could do it," he said, placing his hand on my arm. "You came through magnificently. I have to admit I was a bit concerned about your ability to make the presentation. Of course there was never any doubt about your fantastic wit." He lowered his eyes to my chest.

"My wit's up here, Simon," I said, tapping my head with my finger.

"Right." He didn't even have the grace to blush. He leaned in closer. "Are you free tonight?" he whispered.

What would it take to make him understand? I had images of pelting him in the head with his own pastries until he finally got it. I shook my head no, then looked up and met Nick's eyes. Something in them made my stomach tighten.

I stared at him for a long moment, drinking in the want I read in his eyes. Want and . . . sadness?

I edged a little farther back from Simon, and met his gaze. "I meant what I said, Simon," I whispered back.

"What about Nick?" he snapped, still in that quiet whisper. I wondered if I should just tell Simon to skip the middleman—me—and date Nick instead.

"What about him? I'm not dating him, either." I glared at him.

"What about that birthday party?" His voice had a self-righteous tone that set my back up.

I began to put my papers into my bag. "See," I said in as calm a voice as I could muster, "this is exactly why it's not appropriate. We can talk when this is all over."

He put his hand on my arm again. "When?"

I turned and looked at him, and was startled by his expression. It was possessive, sulky, and . . . mean. I didn't like it. And I was quickly coming to realize I didn't like him. And I didn't want to go out with him, even when the project was over.

Had I really gotten that strong? I drew my hand away, put the last of my papers into my bag, and walked out, not answering him or myself.

Far from the Fattening Crowd

In a new, carb-obsessed world, it's hard to imagine the old ways, where people ate bread, pasta, and rice without guilt. And enjoyed plenty of flavor. At Vanity Fare, we try to integrate the old, tasty ways with the new diet-conscious ways. Taste our fruit mélange of strawberries, kiwis, bananas, and blueberries melded together with a low-fat custard. Low carbs, low sugar, loads of taste. Eating right to stay fit never tasted so good.

21

"HELLO?"

It was around 10:00 P.M., Aidan had gone to sleep a while ago, and Mom was fussing in the kitchen. It pleased me that she'd taken on some of our domestic tasks—she'd always turned her nose up at mastering any kind of culinary skill as something ordinary women did. I had grabbed a book and was hiding out in the bedroom, waiting for Keisha to call.

My mind, however, refused to concentrate on the feisty heroine and the noble, dangerous hero. Instead I kept replaying that afternoon's conversation with Nick. It kinda broke a bit of my heart that he would even think me capable of that kind of duplicity. And I had to figure out what to say to that scrapbooking she-devil when I saw her again.

"Hi, Molly." Not Keisha. A man's voice. Not John. Definitely not Simon.

"Nick?"

"Yes," he replied in his pompous voice. Then his tone changed. "Listen, sorry to call so late, but I just got back from a dinner meeting. Is it too late?"

I rolled onto my back on my bed, wishing my heart weren't pounding so fast. "No, not too late at all. I stay up later than I should, actually. I always mean to go . . ." I was babbling. "Anyway. What's up?"

"I just wanted to call and say I thought you did a terrific presentation today." His voice was more than professional. Thank goodness. "The network is very excited about the opening. It was a few of their staff I had dinner with tonight, actually."

How high school crush-ish of me was it that I was happy he hadn't just had a date?

"Thanks for calling. I'm really sorry about practicing in front of those women, I had no idea—I was nervous as hell, actually." Even more when I thought you didn't trust me.

"Natalie's a bitch," he said bluntly. "It's over, you told me what happened, and it's fine." Men. Always able to move on while women chewed discontent like a bone. "I knew you were nervous, which is why I wanted to call and let you know how well you did. And—"

He stopped. I waited a heartbeat, two, then spoke. "What?"

I heard him take a deep breath. "I just wanted to explain about before. About saying no. It's just . . . well, it wouldn't be right right now."

I assumed my cheeriest, doesn't-bother-me-at-all voice. "No problem. Really."

He gave a dry chuckle devoid of humor. "No, it is a problem. But I just wanted to tell you, it's not you. It's not that I don't— That is, I wish things were different."

"Oh. Okay. Thanks." Different? Different how? Like I was taller? He wasn't so picky about who he dated? He didn't want to mix business with pleasure?

He exhaled so hard I could almost feel the breeze in my ear. "Is Aidan free this weekend? I want to take him to that place again."

"Are you sure?"

"Of course. I promised. Plus I like him, he's a cool kid."

I tried to swallow the lump in my throat. "Thanks. Yeah, he's free anytime. No birthday parties this weekend, thank goodness."

"Okay. How's Saturday? Around one? I figured we could grab some pizza and then I could take him over."

"Saturday's great."

"Okay. I'll see you then. Bye."

"Bye."

I hung up, then stared at the phone for a while. He had called me. At home. At ten o'clock at night. To tell me I did well. After I'd screwed up royally. And that he wished things were different.

And that he wanted to hang out with my son.

I was all gooey inside. I mean, I knew the end result was the same, but he thought well enough of me to make the effort to reach me. That meant something, at least. My quick success with Simon might have made me a little cocky, if such a thing were possible. Maybe it was enough that Nick was my friend, had my back, liked Aidan. Maybe he even trusted me. Heck, he'd gotten my mother to listen to advice, and that was something I had never been able to do.

It wasn't that bad being turned down. Although I wished I could've kissed him, just once, to see if his lips felt as good as they looked.

Ah, but what would an about-to-be divorced romance reader be without an unattainable fantasy?

Luckily, the phone rang again before I could answer that question.

"Hello?"

"Hey, babe. How'd it go?" It was Keisha. She'd been my cheerleader throughout the preparations, so I knew she'd want to hear all about it.

"Good. Actually," I said, trying to sound casual, "Nick just called to tell me the network is really excited. Seems like they might do something on the shop."

"Nick, huh?" Leave it to Keisha to find the crucial nugget of information in there. "So what else did *Nick* say, hm?"

"That he wished things were different."

"Different how?"

"He said he had to say no to my asking him out, not because of me, but because things aren't different, somehow."

"Well, that's fairly cryptic. What do you think he means?"

I shrugged, then realized she couldn't see me. "I don't know. I'm guessing it has something to do with the whole church and state thing—a while ago, John mentioned I shouldn't say anything to Nick about Simon."

"Whoa, slow down. I feel like I need a diagram."

"Well, basically, I think Nick is the watchdog for the finances and all that—"

"And the dog better not be sniffing around any other bitch's butt, right?"

"Oh, I love your way with a metaphor. Yeah, that's it in a nutshell."

"Or a kibble."

"You'd better stop or I'm going to have to smack your nose with a newspaper."

"Only if you leash me first, Mistress. Hey, that's an idea: phone sex!"

"Um . . . I love you, Keisha, but not that way."

She giggled. "No, silly, I mean you. To make extra money."

"Oh, yeah, that'd be great: *Are you sure I don't look fat like this? Oh, okay, go ahead and do your thing, I'll wait. Are you done yet? Oh, you are? Sorry, I didn't notice.* Um, I don't think me doing phone sex is a long-term, or even a short-term, solution to my financial problems."

"But if Nick called . . . ," she said in a teasing voice.

I glared. Of course she couldn't see me. "How come I don't say a thing, and you still know I've got a mad crush on him?"

"You asked him out, didn't you?"

"Well, yeah, but—"

"And have you asked anyone out? Ever?"

"Well, no, but—"

"Ergo, you have a mad crush."

"Hey, why didn't you become a lawyer? You probably would've done a lot better than Hugh."

"Hmph, no thanks. I'd rather show old movies than wear a suit and get litigious all day."

"Good point. What was playing tonight?"

"*Wuthering Heights.*"

"Which one?"

"The one with Laurence Olivier. Look, I know you have a mad crush on Timothy Dalton, but that version sucks ass."

"You're right, Miss Film Major. But damn, he's gorgeous."

"Does Nick look like *him*? Then I could understand all your fussing."

"Not really. Except maybe in the dark, dangerous way. Oh, and he has black hair."

"What color eyes?"

"Blue. Dark, stormy blue."

"Hold on, honey, you've got to check yourself. I hate to be the bearer of bad news, but he turned you down, right?"

I sighed. "Yeah. But, man, is he foxy."

"So now the bakery thing is done, what's next?"

"Oh, besides developing my love of scrapbooking?"

"Look, honey, I know you're white, you don't have to rub my face in it."

I cackled. "That's where you're wrong. Next to me? With dreads hanging down her back? A woman named Tamsin. Wearing kente cloth, no less."

"Ouch. Okay, I'm toast. I might as well be dating the Irish carpenter if my sisters are pasting photos into albums with some weird-ass confetti and shit."

"And next you'll be following NASCAR." She snorted. "Next up," I continued, "I think John has some more work for me. I really can't do much until I hear from the Teaching Fellows, which'll be in late May. Hugh sent me the rent money, and I canceled my cell phone. Mom's been doing some of the cooking—"

"God help you," Keisha muttered.

"—and she's kept the foreclosure folks at bay while she tries to figure out her finances. Nick gave her some advice on that, too." I continued speaking over her snort. "She's been picking up a few things here and there, which is nice. Not enough to live on, certainly, but I think I can make it until I hear."

"And then what?"

"Well, if I get in, I start training—and getting paid—a few weeks after that. If I don't? I have no frigging clue."

"It's sort of a plan."

I sighed, and looked out the window. "I don't know, Keish. I really don't. I know I have to do something, but I don't know what."

"What's up with the divorce proceedings?"

There I knew I was on solid ground. "Well, I was going to do it all amicably, back when Hugh had a job, but when he lost his job, and told me he couldn't pay that much, I lost it. He shouldn't be able to just tell me he can't support our child and have that be okay."

She cheered. "You go! I told you not to go down easy. Can I be blunt?"

"Um, like you never have been before?"

"Yeah, right. Well, Hugh is a lazy fuckhead. But, and this is the good part, he's also a pussy. See, he'll cave on the whole divorce agreement thing, and you can move forward knowing Aidan will always be okay."

"If Hugh doesn't pussy out and become a deadbeat dad."

"If he does, I *am* getting a law degree so I can sue his ass."

"Thanks, Keish. It's nice to know you have my back."

"Always, honey. Always."

"So?"

Dr. Lowell pushed her glasses back up on her nose. She was wearing her most intimidating therapist's outfit: a tasteful plaid suit with a double strand of pearls wrapped around her throat. If I saw her on the street, I would assume she was smarter than me, richer than me, and happier than me. All right, maybe I shouldn't be going there.

"Well, let's see. I did that big presentation, and I didn't fall on my face. Or have lettuce in my teeth. I went to somebody else's house to do scrapbooking—"

She raised her eyebrows in a question.

"—I'll explain in a minute. I made a lunch date with some new friends, I asked a man out, an absolutely stunning man wants me but I don't want him, my mother is *not* driving me crazy, Aidan is a sweetheart, Hugh is a jerk, and Keisha still lives three thousand miles away."

She leaned back, resting her hands on her knees. Her manicure was perfect. "Sounds like you've had a busy week."

I laughed. "Yeah, you could say that."

"You sound good." She sounded pleased.

"I am." Now I sounded pleased.

"Want to tell me about it?"

"Sure. I mean, besides the list?"

She nodded.

"I don't know if I can explain it." She wrinkled her nose at me. I held my hand up before she could speak. "Okay, I know, that's why I'm here. To explain. Okay. Well, with Simon, the thing is—he's gorgeous, but he knows it. And honestly, I'm not sure how much we have in common, besides both of us thinking he's beautiful. He doesn't read, he's a total go-getter business guy, and Aidan doesn't like him."

"Has Aidan told you so?"

I grimaced. "He asked me if foreign people—Simon's British, remember—were supposed to be here because we got our freedom from his country. And was there someone we should call to tell on him so he'd have to leave."

"Okay, then. So you'll dump him. That must feel—"

"Weird. Yeah, it is. I did dump him already, actually. And I mean, it's not like I've ever dumped anyone before. Not really. Especially not someone I'd usually be gnawing on my arm to get."

"But it's not right. And you know it. So you did the right thing and stopped it before either one of you gets hurt." She gave an approving nod.

"Mm."

"How's the financial situation?"

I heaved a sigh. "Bad. Not as bad as I'd first thought, but pretty bad. I'm checking into alternate insurance plans, and Mom and I are cooking, but—well, you know, I haven't paid you in a while." I knotted my fingers together and leaned forward on her couch. She waved her hand in dismissal.

"Don't worry about it. Let's worry about getting you on your feet first and then paying me. I'll survive." Good, because without her, I couldn't have survived myself this long.

"Do you really think I'll be able to make it?" I watched my hands clench each other.

"Look at me, Molly." I looked up and met her gaze. It was kind and warm. Immediately my insides relaxed a tiny bit. This was why she was worth every penny I didn't have. "I have confidence in you. *You* have to have confidence in you. And I know you can do this, and be happy."

"Funny, a lady at a bar told me the same thing," I said in a reflective tone. I flapped my hands. "But never mind. Really, that's all I've ever wanted. I mean, Hugh always talked about getting things, and buying stuff, and eating fancy meals—me, I just want enough to be able to give Aidan some of the toys he wants, have seafood once in a while, and buy new jeans in the fall. That's it. It doesn't take much."

"And you're more than capable of managing it. I know you are. Do you know you are?"

I exhaled. A big, life-affirming sigh that seemed as if it could sweep away all my doubts and insecurities. "Yes. I know I am."

She smiled and leaned back in her chair. "See? And once you know that, you can do anything."

"Now you sound like Helen Reddy."

She looked puzzled.

" 'I Am Woman?' Australian pop singer from the 1970s? Don't tell me you never heard that song."

She chuckled. "Yes, of course. And speaking of which, how are things going with Hugh?"

I stretched my legs out in front of me and clasped my hands behind my head. "He's going to regret my going all Helen Reddy on his ass. I've asked my lawyer to try to get sufficient child support, to put everything down in writing. Thank God I paid him in advance. Originally, we had a gentleman's agreement without official documentation, but since he's no gentleman, I'm not going to leave it up to chance. Of course, it could take longer this way, but that doesn't matter to me."

She beamed at me. "Roar away, Molly. You are Reddy for life." She emphasized the word so I'd know she was making a pun. A really, really bad pun.

• • •

It was a little later than usual when I finally left Dr. Lowell's office. I'd gotten stuck in the elevator with a messy kid who just had to press all the buttons on the way down. From the forty-third floor. His smile reminded me of Aidan's. His baby-sitter shot me a thankful look as I told him it had always been my dream to do the same thing. It was about fifteen minutes later when I emerged from the double glass doors onto the sidewalk. The subway was a few blocks away, and it was fairly balmy, for March, at least.

I was just reaching into my bag for my MetroCard when I slammed into him. The impact sent my purse flying out of my hands, and I stumbled a little.

"Molly?" A firm arm held me by the elbow. Nick's blue eyes held a look of concern. I guess they should, given my legs were akimbo and my purse was upside down on the ground. If I wasn't mistaken, a tampon was making its slow escape from the depths of my bag. I eased my foot around and stomped on it, then bent over and quickly stuck it back into the bag.

"Are you okay?" he asked, his voice all rumbly and gruff, as if he hadn't spoken in a while.

I nodded, zipping my bag closed. "Yeah, sorry, I wasn't watching where I was going." I looked up into his face. It was very close to mine. "What are you doing here, anyway?"

He loosened his grip on my arm a bit and stepped backward, looking down at the sidewalk as he did so. I did, too, hoping something else hadn't rolled out of my purse. Thank goodness, there was just some old gum and an empty Snapple bottle, neither of which was mine.

"Doing here?" He actually sounded—nervous.

"Yes. Doing here. You. What are?" I repeated.

"Um. I have an appointment." He gestured toward Dr. Lowell's building.

Interesting. As far as I knew, the only professional offices were therapists' offices. And if Nick—professional, smart, and all that—needed help, what hope was there for the rest of us?

But of course I didn't say any of that. Although I couldn't resist throwing out a line to see if he bit. "Really? What a coincidence. I'm just coming from my therapist's."

The expression on his face grew even more anxious, if possible. "Nice to see you, Molly, see you soon," he said, walking off with the stride of a man who did not want to explain anything else.

I wondered if his session was actually with Dr. Lowell. I chuckled as I walked away from the building. It was good to know even the most intently intimidating man needed help sometimes.

I pulled a Helen Reddy and roared as I headed toward the subway.

Pies-Fed Revisited

The day-old section at your local bakery has never been so . . . glamorous. Or so regally approachable. Take refuge here and reflect on yesterday's freshness. Still delicious, just slightly past their prime. Half price, too. An economic way to save an outdated baked good.

22

THE BUZZER RANG RIGHT AROUND TWELVE FORTY-FIVE. I'D
been glancing at the clock for the last hour, wondering just
when he'd arrive. Aidan was all packed and dressed, wearing
his special Justice League T-shirt, even though I told him
he'd have to wear a sweatshirt over it. He groaned but felt
better when I said he could wait until Nick saw his shirt to
put the rest of his clothes on.

I opened the door, smoothing my suddenly damp hands
on my thighs. I'd chosen my clothes carefully that morning
also—I wore my favorite pair of jeans, the slightly stretchy
bootcut Calvin Kleins, and a light pink top with a rose-
colored cardigan on top. The cardigan had little sparkles all
over it. I liked it because it looked so girly.

"Good afternoon," he said as he strode into the apartment. He must've just gotten his hair cut—again—since it
was shorter than a few days ago. A few specks of hair had
settled on his shoulders, and I reached up to brush them
away.

He reacted as if I'd tried to grab his ass or something. He
ducked, his cheeks got flushed, and he swallowed hard.

"Sorry. I mean, I just thought I'd help you get that hair—"
I flapped my hands in the air like a chicken.

He looked down at his shoulder and frowned. "Oh. Right. Sorry." He brushed the hairs off, and I watched them float to the ground. I quelled the impulse to pick them up and put them under my pillow or something.

"So. How are you?" I asked brightly, clasping my hands in front of me. He looked rumpled, newly shorn, and delicious.

"Good." He cleared his throat. "The shop's soft launch is coming up. Simon's coordinating for the opening event." A pause. "And nearly all of my work here is complete. Just tying some things up, and then . . ." His words trailed off.

Oh. He'd be leaving soon, then, I could figure that much out on my own.

Aidan bounded up, holding his Pokémon backpack. "Hi, Nick. Did you see my T-shirt?"

Nick squatted down and gave Aidan a piercing stare. "Pretty sharp, sport. Did you see *my* T-shirt?" He pulled open the button-down shirt he was wearing and showed his chest to Aidan. I'd never envied my son so much in my entire life. Nick wore a black Batman shirt with a yellow bat logo.

"Cool." Aidan exhaled, his eyes wide. Nick straightened and rebuttoned his shirt.

"Should we go?"

Aidan headed for the door, Nick looking back at me for one long moment. "I'll have him back in a few hours," he said, pulling the door closed behind him.

"Take your time," I said to the empty air. It was funny, I hadn't known Nick that long, but I trusted him implicitly. So much so that I let him take my son out alone. Heck, I'd always felt a moment of panic when Hugh took Aidan off for a boys' day out, and yet here I was, trusting someone with the most important thing in my life.

I wandered back to the kitchen and touched the coffeepot. Still warm. I opened the cupboard and took out my favorite mug, a wide, fat-bottomed cup with gay tulips painted all over it. Aidan had picked it out for me a few Mother's Days ago.

As I splashed in the milk, I wondered when Nick would be leaving. And if he'd be going straight back to England. It bothered me I knew so little about him—I knew he had a sister, but was he going to visit her first? Did he still have family in New York? It shouldn't bother me, but it did.

I wished things were different. I wished I could figure out why he didn't feel comfortable dating me. And even if the reason was because of work, the point was moot, because when the job was done, he'd be gone, it sounded like. Darn. Darn, darn, *damn*.

The coffee did a little bit to bolster my spirits, thank goodness. It was strange, not having anything pressing to do. My day was usually filled with tons of errands: work on copy, clean the house of stray Lego parts so no one would lose a limb, laundry, dishes, grocery shopping, Mom's finances, my worries.

Mom's off-key warblings reached me in the kitchen. How many times had I heard her singing Gilbert and Sullivan lyrics? And every time, she got them wrong. I walked down the hall, smiling to myself. She was gaining volume as I entered the living room. It looked like she was in the midst of organizing her finances. Had Nick actually persuaded her to take charge of them? If so, I was really going to miss him when he left.

"It's not 'sinful economy,' it's 'singular anomaly,' Mom."

She looked up and gave me a wry smile. "Oh, yes, it is sinful economy, Molly, my love." She took her reading glasses off and placed them on top of the biggest pile. "Where did all my money go?"

"To some guy on the trading-room floor?"

She wrinkled her nose. "No, I mean before that. I mean, yes, there, too, but even before that, I spent money so foolishly." She gestured toward the papers. "Spa visits, books, the expensive car, the trip to Morocco, the pool, for God's sake. I didn't need any of that. All I needed was to pay the mortgage, the taxes, and eat. Maybe buy a book once in a while. It all seems so . . . meaningless."

I patted her hand. "Why do you think you did it, then, Mom?" I asked softly. She shrugged, and I could see the tears beginning to form in her eyes.

"I thought I could make enough money from the stock market so I could stop worrying. So you could stop worrying about me."

I looked at her in surprise. "Worry about you? I didn't worry about you until you showed up on my doorstep wearing that old sweatshirt. Why, did I say something?"

"Not you. Hugh."

I felt myself stiffen. "What did he say?"

"One time when you were over, and you and Aidan were out by the pool, Hugh told me you guys weren't as solvent as he'd like."

My mouth dropped open in amazement. "What the—?" Then a nasty suspicion entered my mind. "When was this?"

"Last summer."

"The bastard." She raised her brows at me. I felt myself zoom from zero to sixty in 4.3 seconds. "He was already planning to leave. I was wondering where our savings had gone. I bet he squirreled it away before he told me, and now he's crying poverty." I stood up, shoving my chair behind me. "I'm going to call him now."

Mom held my arm. "Molly, are you really sure you want to talk to him now when you're so upset? I mean, what if you're wrong? Maybe he was genuinely concerned."

I sat back down again, shrugging her hand off my arm. "Mom, I know Hugh. And, forgive me for saying this about your favorite son-in-law—"

"My only son-in-law," she said drily.

"—but he's out for himself. And only himself. Even Aidan comes second to Hugh's desires. Bastard," I repeated, allowing her to take my hand again.

"Sweetie. You've got your lawyer working on this, right? And if you call and tell him you suspect Hugh's buried some assets, he should be able to find them, right?" For once she wasn't defending him—had someone challenged her to that "never in a million years" thing, too?

"Yeah. Although I'd love to give him a piece of my mind and find out if he really is that kind of lowlife. Grrr," I growled.

Her eyes widened. "I've never seen you so—aggressive, Molly. You're acting completely unlike yourself." Her tone implied she didn't like the change. "I mean, calling Hugh to yell at him is something you would never have done before. At least, before all this."

I felt my lips start to smile, despite my anger. "I wouldn't do it in a million years, would I? Sounds like a challenge."

I rose again and headed into the bedroom to call Hugh. "Stay here, I don't need an audience."

"But—"

The rest of her words were lost as I stomped down the hallway. Well, at least now I had something to do while Aidan was away: call his no-good, money-stealing, wussy-acting father.

"Hello?"

"Hi, Hugh, it's Molly. Nothing's wrong with Aidan, I called to talk to you."

"Oh, good, good, because I was hoping to talk to you, too."

I adopted a deceptively sweet tone. "Well. I was talking to Mom—you know she's staying here for a while—and she mentioned that you had said something to her last summer about us being in potential financial difficulty. Is that what you said?"

"Uh, I don't remember . . ."

"Oh, come on, Hugh, yes you do." I waited an extra beat to really give him time to sweat. "You told Mom we weren't as solvent as we'd like to be. Of course, you couldn't have predicted she'd take that information and become Michael Milken, but—"

"What?" Hugh sounded really confused.

"None of your business. Anyway, Hugh, what the fuck were you thinking? And what happened to all that money? I should've wondered why you were so interested in keeping track of our finances when you never had been before. Where's the money, Hugh?"

Now he sounded nervous. "Um, I don't know what you're talking about, Molly."

"Sure. Sure you don't. Remember this conversation when Aidan's getting teased because his clothes are out-of-date. Remember how important wearing the right thing is, Hugh? Remember how important it is to have health insurance, electricity, phone, Hugh? My lawyer will be talking to yours. You can bet on that."

I slammed the phone down, not even waiting for Hugh's reply. Asshole. I knew I didn't have any proof that he'd stolen from us, but I also knew he'd taken our money we'd agreed we'd save for the future.

And it was not something he was going to be able to get away with ever, much less in a million years.

I heard Aidan coming up the stairs, his voice as excited as I'd ever heard it. I couldn't make out what he was saying, but he sure sounded thrilled. I smiled that wistful smile I'd had on my face every time I thought about Nick's leaving. It's not as if I thought we'd fall madly in love and ride off into the sunset if he stayed; he'd made his intentions, if not his feelings, pretty clear. No, it was just that Aidan already adored Nick, and it would be amazing if my son had a grown-up male who was responsible, responsive to him, and actually liked him. That was a hard trifecta to find.

Aidan ran up the last few steps as I opened the door, his face lit up with excitement. "Mommy, Mommy, we got to go on the trampoline! And Nick said I was better than he was, do you believe that?"

I met Nick's eyes and gave him a grateful smile. His eyes crinkled at the corners as he tried to smother a grin.

"That sounds great, honey. Come on in and take your coat off and you can tell me all about it."

Aidan chattered nonstop while I removed his jacket, his sweatshirt, and his sneakers. "And then, Mommy, do you know what?"

"What, honey?"

"There was a boy there—an *older* boy, he said he was eight—and he couldn't even do what I could."

"Wow. That sounds amazing."

"Yeah, Aidan was great on the mats, too." Nick ruffled Aidan's hair, then stepped toward the door. "Well, I should get going."

Aidan sprang to his side, clutching his hand with all the gratitude of a well-fed puppy dog. His face looked like he'd been digging up bones in the dirt, too. "You can't go now. You promised to play dinosaur with me." Aidan screwed his face up into a pleading look. Nick shot me a questioning glance.

"Aidan, honey, Nick probably has something to do." Like leave New York City. "He'll be around another time." I licked my finger and tried to get the worst bit of the dirt off his face.

Aidan twisted away from my hand. "Nick?" It broke my heart to hear Aidan's anguished cry. He'd been almost stoic throughout the whole mess with Hugh, but I knew it had taken a toll somewhere. And I was seeing it played out as another grown-up male tried to leave.

"I can stay, as long as your mom makes me coffee," Nick said, winking at me.

"Coffee's what Mommy loves best," Aidan exclaimed. "Besides me, of course."

"Of course," Nick agreed.

I smiled at Nick over Aidan's head. "I'll go make it, then," I said and walked to the kitchen.

When I got back, bearing the best coffee I knew how to make, Aidan and Nick were sitting on the floor, about a hundred million Legos strewn around them. I put the cup down on the table next to Nick, who immediately picked it up and took a sip. His eyes closed in what I assumed was caffeine bliss. Yet another thing we had in common.

"Mommy, we're making robots!" Aidan exclaimed, gesturing toward at least half a dozen completed figures.

"I thought you said dinosaurs." I squatted down next to him and tousled his hair. He shook his head in clear exasperation. "Not dinosaurs, Mommy, robots. And when we're done, they're going to battle!" He got back to work, his little fingers painstakingly pushing the tiny plastic circles into the tiny plastic holes.

"Thanks for the coffee," Nick said.

I squatted down next to him. "Are you sure this is okay?" I asked in a low undertone.

He touched my arm in a reassuring gesture. "Of course. Don't worry so much."

Yeah, and while I'm at it, I'll try not to be brunette. Or whiter than a flake of snow. How about confident? Oh, shoot, I forgot. I am confident. Hear me roar.

"Well, thanks." Our eyes met and held for a moment. I gave him a half smile, then rose again. "Well, if you guys are okay, I'm going to go work on paying some bills. See you in a while."

I headed down the hall to my bedroom. I had to get out of there before I burst into tears. Why did Aidan have to bond with the one man who was leaving town? Why did I have to want him, too?

What was wrong with us that people kept leaving?

Remembrance of Things Yeast

We've done a good job summarizing works of literary fiction in these blurbs, haven't we?

Well, here we just have to throw our hands in the air and admit defeat. Proust is unwieldy, beyond long-winded, spinning out minutiae as if we had a lifetime to read his work. And sorry, Marcel, but we don't, even if you hand us a madeleine and some tea.

We'd rather eat this light, fluffy, and completely insubstantial bread. Yum.

23

THE NIGHT OF THE OPENING WAS A GORGEOUS SPRING EVENING:
A soft breeze drifted through the trees, it was mild, and most
of the tourists must have wandered over to Bubba Gump or
somewhere because the sidewalks weren't even that crowded.

I emerged from the subway and took a few deep breaths.
This was it. This was the moment I'd been working toward all
summer.

Plus, I tried not to remind myself, this'd be one of the last
times I'd see Nick.

I walked resolutely toward the brightly lit shop; most of
the other stores had closed for the night, so the store was a
beacon across Forty-second Street. I smelled the pastry aroma
half a block away, and my mouth started to water.

No matter what his other faults, Simon really was an incredible baker.

There was a camera crew at the shop's entrance, and a
tiny red carpet that made me smile as I stepped on it. This
was the closest to glamour I'd probably ever get, and I had to
admit it was pretty cool.

"Welcome, Molly." Simon, of course, met me at the door,
his expression showing none of the pissed-off-ness I'd come
to expect from him.

"Yes, welcome," a woman's voice chimed in behind him. Simon turned halfway around and put his arm around the shoulders of a stunning woman who gazed at him in adoration. He gave me that Cheshire Cat look.

No wonder he wasn't pissed off anymore. "This is Sarah," he said. "She does PR for the network." She had that thin, glassy-eyed look that came from not eating enough.

"Hello, Simon, nice to meet you, Sarah," I said. "The shop looks amazing."

It really did. The glass windows and clean steel lines of the tables were a complement for the wall décor, which featured old book covers, bookmarks, reading glasses, and other literary detritus. Behind the counter a large sign had pictures of Simon's offerings along with my descriptions, written in charming calligraphy. The people who were serving were garbed as the stereotypical absentminded authors, with pens tucked behind their ears, ink stains on their monogrammed shirts, and all wearing similarly geeky glasses.

"Thank you, Molly. Thank you for all of your hard work," he added almost as an afterthought. "I have to say, I had my concerns when Natalie was off the project." He frowned. "I heard about the stunt she pulled when her friend heard the plans. Thankfully we'd already booked the meeting with the network. Of course that's not the worst thing an ex has ever tried after we've broken up." He sounded as though heartbroken women pulled hijinks like this all the time. No wonder he was so aghast—and didn't believe me, in fact—when I dumped him.

Which was one of the best decisions I'd made. At least in the last few months, maybe ever. The guy didn't have an unselfish bone in his gorgeous body.

It was no wonder he'd chased after me so aggressively—once Natalie was out of the picture, he didn't have a woman on call. I doubted he'd ever been in that situation, not since he'd gone through puberty.

I snagged a glass of champagne from one of the author-waiters and eyed the tables piled with desserts of every shape and size. Tonight I was going to eat one of every single item, even if I burst at the end. I deserved it. What's more, I wanted it.

John came up from behind me as I was pondering which treat to eat next—the chocolate one or the other chocolate one. "Molly," he said, clasping my hand with both of his, "so glad you're here. The network is filming the event, they think they might be able to create some sort of special on it later on, especially if Simon's test goes well."

"Simon's testing for TV?" I said. I shouldn't have been surprised, I mean it wasn't as if there were that many—maybe not any—chefs as good-looking as Simon. He seemed born for TV, I shoulda been surprised he didn't already have a show.

"Yes, that was part of what Natalie was bringing to the table, actually. She has network connections, we almost lost the chance when she and Simon . . ." His words trailed off.

"It would just make so much sense for him to segue to TV, though. I'm glad your company gets the chance to see it through. You guys deserve it."

Speaking of deserving—I spotted Nick at the other end of the room. He had dressed up for the occasion, and was wearing a dark suit with a tie.

Holding a coffee cup in one hand and a huge flaky bear claw in the other.

As I watched him, he took a bite of the pastry, then grimaced as flakes drifted down and onto his suit.

Even without the baked flakes adorning him like tinsel on a Christmas tree, he was entirely lickable.

I told myself to settle down but still found myself making a beeline toward him. He gave me a guilty little-boy grin when I approached and wiped his face with a fancy linen napkin.

"Hey."

"Hey," he replied, keeping his gaze on me as he took a sip from his cup. "Want some?"

I shook my head. "No, thanks. I already downed a few at the door. Nervous habit." I tilted my glass toward him. "Have you had any champagne?"

"I wish I could. I have to make sure everything goes absolutely perfectly tonight. Make sure Simon impresses all the right people." His expression showed what he thought of that.

"Should I not—?" Suddenly I felt like I shouldn't be drinking or something.

He waved me off. "No, have fun. You deserve it."

"Hey, thanks for helping my mom out."

His face went blank, then his eyes widened in what looked like shock. "She told you?"

"Told me—what?" Now I was surprised. "She has voluntarily been going through her finances, whereas before you spoke to her, I had to threaten to destroy her glass figurines to even get her to open the files."

He looked relieved. "Right. Well, of course, no problem."

"What did you think she told me?"

There was that expression again. And silence.

"Well," he said, using what I recognized as his investor voice, "it's merely a matter of organizing the assets, she was just overwhelmed by the process."

What the hell did that even mean? Screw it. "What the hell does that even mean?" I said, downing the last bit of champagne and using the empty glass to make my point. "What did you do?"

"Nothing."

That was a lie. I knew it, he knew it, and I wasn't going to back down from it, not this time.

"What did you do?" I repeated. I kept my eyes on his face until his gaze faltered.

"Not much. I shouldn't have said anything—"

"You didn't!" I interrupted. "But you will now. What did you do?" I had years of practice with Aidan, repeating questions until I got the answer I wanted. I was betting Nick had never dealt with a Mother Intent on an Answer.

"I paid for her consultation with the money guy. My friend who owes me a favor?"

"How much money? We'll pay you back." My heart was racing.

He shook his head. "No. It's a gift. And I'm not going to tell you how much, Molly, you'll just worry." He really did know me, didn't he?

For once, I was silenced. It was clear from Nick's implacable expression that that information was all I was going to get.

"And, if you'll excuse me, I see one of those executives who were at the presentation heading for Simon." He darted away before I could find anything to say. Leaving me alone with my now empty glass.

Well, there was something I could have control over. I grabbed another glass from a passing waiter as I contemplated it, the reality of it settling in my stomach like I'd eaten too much chocolate. And I hadn't even come close yet.

Oh, hell, no. The perfect guy for me, perfect in every way except he had made it clear he wasn't interested in me, not to mention he lived in another country, had pulled a Mr. Darcy and saved my relative's ass?

Like I wasn't already ruined for any other guy. Ever. Damn.

"Wow," I muttered under my breath. I stood there, feeling the rush of competing emotions—relief, embarrassment, love, agony, heck almost anything I could feel—course through me. Nick. Nick had rescued my mother, and he hadn't done it for any other reason but me. Wow.

I took a sip. This was my secret to hold on to. My secret to hold on to, and cherish, every time I thought about the guy who got away. Who left. And not the rotten ex-husband who'd left, but the other guy. The smart, sexy, witty, Mr. Darcy–savvy one.

I promised myself as I stood there, watching the faux-authors drift around me with their champagne and pastry-laden trays, that I wouldn't be less than what he must think of me to do something like that.

It was a tall order, but I could do it.

I would do it. Just like Gloria Gaynor, I would survive.

I left the party after three truffles and an almond scone. Not to mention another glass of champagne.

And decided to do something so unlike me I knew I'd chicken out if I even thought about it for a second. I dug in my pocket and found the card—as I remembered, her office wasn't too far from here. I checked my watch: 7:00 P.M. I bet she'd still be there.

I buzzed the office number.

"Natalie Duran." She was there.

I took a deep breath. "Hi, Natalie, it's Molly Hagan. Can I come up?"

"Oh!" She sounded very surprised. Good. "Of course."

The front door clicked open, and I took the elevator up to her floor. She stood at the door, a puzzled expression on her face. "Hello, Molly, how . . . unexpected to see you."

"Mm, yes."

She stepped back so I could go into the office. Like John's office, it was in shades of business-edgy: maroon, olive, umber. She gestured toward the reception sofa.

"Please, sit." She was impeccably dressed, as usual, but there were circles under her eyes, and her hair was more disheveled than artfully disarranged.

"No, thank you. I prefer to stand." I paused. "Look, Natalie, I don't want to play coy with you. I know you know tonight was the shop's opening event, and I also know that you tried to sabotage it." She opened her mouth, and I held my hand up. "I don't know if you planned it, or your friend just called you up and you couldn't resist. I don't want to know. The fact is, it didn't work."

Her lips pinched together and I saw her swallow. "I didn't . . ." Her voice faltered. She sat down, suddenly.

I had to say the rest of it, everything I'd practiced on the walk over. "You tried to undermine my work and jeopardize the entire venture."

"That's not what I meant to do." Now she sounded entirely defensive—like when Aidan said there was no way he'd eaten the last cookie when the Oreo crumbs were decorating his face.

Her fingers were twisting together in her lap, and I felt a pang of guilt that I'd done that to her. And then a tiny blaze of triumph because *I* had done that to her.

"It doesn't matter what you *meant* to do." It really did feel as though I were speaking to Aidan. "The fact is, you did it. And I think you did it because of a man." I paused and let the words settle in. "And I wanted to tell you that's not okay. It's never okay to do anything just for a man." Especially one like Simon—good to look at on the outside, not enough filling on the inside. Kind of like an Oreo, come to think of it.

She looked up at me. I was startled to see the beginning of tears in her eyes. "You're right," she said in a whisper.

Wow. I was right? And she was admitting it? She continued, "And I'm really sorry." She rose from the couch and held her hand out. "I apologize, Molly. It was a rotten thing to do."

I took her hand and shook it. "Oh. Of course. Thank you. Well," I said, dropping my hand and sticking it in my pocket, "that's all I wanted to say. Thank you for hearing me out."

One lone tear tracked down her face, and I felt like a heel. A justified, finally-got-that-off-my-chest heel, but a heel nonetheless.

We didn't speak again as I left her office.

As I headed to the subway to return to Brooklyn, I thought of all the ways that could have gone, and that it went as well as it did astonished me.

Was there no limit to what I could do? Maybe I'd try to wear makeup every single day for a week, or read Proust, or

challenge my mom to a game of Scrabble that didn't allow us
to use the letter *e*.

On the other hand, there were limits. I was just happy I
was pushing them.

I was still in a Helen Reddy mood when I got home. I told my
mom the highlights of the evening—starting with the pastries, natch—and headed to my bedroom to peel off my fancy
clothes and put on my jammies.

The phone rang as I was kicking my shoes into the corner. "Hello?"

At first, all I heard was muffled crying, followed by a
wracking sob. I recognized that cry, I'd heard it when Alex-
ander McQueen died. "Lissa?"

"Oh, Molly." She wept. I sat down on the bed and un-
zipped my skirt. There were a few too many treats in there to
sit comfortably. "What's wrong, sweetie? Is it Tony?"

She gulped. "Yeeeesssssss."

I leaned back against the pillows. "What happened?"

The whole sordid story poured out, interspersed with loud
wails of anguish. Tony had insisted she accompany him the
night before to an art gallery opening, then belittled her in
front of his clients and told her she was fat. Then, when she
was still standing there, he introduced another woman to his
business partner and proceeded to flirt outrageously with her
in front of everyone, not even sparing a glance toward Lissa.

After a few minutes of gaping at him, Lissa slunk away
with the help of Tony's assistant, who made sure she got
home safely. She was humiliated, miserable, and worse, she
felt as if she deserved it.

"What the hell are you talking about, Lissa?" I demanded. "No one deserves to have someone treat you as badly as that. No one. Not even Hugh," I said, ignoring the memory of wanting to see him naked in Times Square while all the tourists pointed and laughed.

"I know. But if I had just tried harder to be like he wanted me to be—"

"—You'd be as much of an asshole as he is. Listen, do you want to come over?"

"No. Maybe we could just talk for a while. How's Aidan?"

"He's in the living room making a going-away present for Nick." I answered the silence at the other end of the phone. I sighed. "Nick's just someone I'm working with on this free-lance project. And he's leaving soon, obviously."

"And you're upset about that." If Lissa were any more empathic, she could sell readings for two dollars a palm.

"Yeah," I admitted. "He's nice. At first, I thought he was an arrogant prick, which he's not. I mean, he's arrogant, but he's also really nice. And incredibly good-looking."

"So what are you going to do about it?" She sure sounded better. She was like my mom in that way: Dangle an available man for Molly in front of her, and she'd perk right up.

"Nothing." I sounded as glum as I felt. "I asked him out, if you can believe it, and he said no. And he just told me he's leaving town."

"So make him not want to leave."

"What, seduce him? Lissa, remember who you're talking to."

"I didn't say tie him down and blow him."

"Lissa!" I was shocked; Lissa just didn't talk like that.

She giggled. It seemed the tragedy had worn off to be replaced with hysteria. "Well, I didn't say it. But you're charming, Molly, and if Aidan likes him, and he likes Aidan, that's more than half the battle. Remember, that British guy—"

"Simon," I interjected.

"Yeah, Simon, didn't even like Aidan. So you didn't like him, even though you said he was gorgeous."

"Well, this one is gorgeouser."

"That's not a word."

"Listen to you! When did you turn into the English grammar expert?"

She got sad again. I shouldn't have reminded her. "I'm not. Tony used to—"

My tone was sharp. "Fuck Tony. Tell me, how big was he?"

"You mean—?"

"Yeah. I'm guessing small. He was small, right?"

She giggled again. "Yup."

I sighed. "Happens all the time. Dr. Lowell calls it overcompensating."

"You talk to your therapist about penis size?" Her tone was incredulous.

"Well, not in so many words, but yes, we've discussed overcompensating."

"Does that mean Hugh . . . ?"

I let out an evil chuckle. "Yup."

"Thanks for listening, Molly." I heard her begin to laugh again. "Men have no idea we talk about this kind of stuff, do they? I mean, if they did, they'd be so freaked-out they'd probably undress in the dark. Instead of parading around like they're Brad Pitt in *Troy*."

"Or giving it a name." I waited for Lissa's squeal. It was louder than I thought.

"So what was it?" she said, after she finished howling.

"Ouch! You've got a set of lungs on you. I can tell you, but you have to promise to tell everyone he knows."

"Promise."

"Hef. As in Hugh Hefner."

I waited for her laughter to subside. "Did he dress it up in pajamas, too? Or have you put bunny ears on or anything?"

"No. Maybe that would've made it more fun. I wonder if his new girlfriend has any regrets about going out with the three-minute egg. At least she'll never miss one of her favorite shows—they can do it in the time it takes for a commercial break."

"Ouch back at you! That was one good thing about Tony—it might've been small, but he knew what to do with it."

"Honey, you'll find someone—"

She interrupted before I could continue. "I know I will. And I promise not to be so needy when I meet someone else." She paused. "As long as you promise, too."

She had me there. "Okay. I promise."

"Mommy!" The yell came from down the hall. Aidan did not believe in walking an extra few feet so he could get my attention without screaming.

"Speaking of needy . . ."

Lissa laughed. "Go take care of that boy of yours. Love you."

I hung up and yelled back. If he wasn't going to walk extra, neither would I.

"What do you want, honey?"

"I'm hungry!"

"Be right there."

If there was only going to be one man in my life, I was glad it was Aidan.

I fed Aidan the leftover pastries I'd snagged from the party to keep him from starving in front of my eyes while I made his second dinner. He was a growing boy, he liked to remind me.

Mom, thankfully, had gone out with her friend to see a movie—her friend's treat—and I didn't have to deal with her nosy questions.

I made us some chicken stir-fry, doubling up on the rice so we would be eating authentic Chinese entrée-to-rice pro-portions. I would've been proud of myself, only I'd had to do that in order to stretch the meager amount of chicken I'd bought. At least I didn't make rice and beans every *single* night.

Aidan started to get cranky around 9:00 P.M., so I marched him to bed.

Leaving me alone with my thoughts.

So I called Keisha to avoid my thoughts.

"That bastard did what?" Keisha was livid about what Tony had done to Lissa. "How's she doing?"

"She's really upset. She thinks it's her fault he dumped her like that. Can you imagine someone having so little self-esteem?"

"Hello, Ms. Pot? It's Mr. Kettle calling."

"Fine, be saucy. Only I don't think I was ever that pathetic—was I?"

Keisha's silence was deafening. How did she *do* that?

"Okay, well, thank goodness I'm over that." I rummaged in my bottom drawer for my pink sweatpants.

"You are, honey. Has John paid you?"

I wriggled out of my jeans and managed to put the sweatpants on without dropping the phone. Now how could I phrase *that* on my résumé?

"Yeah, one of the checks just came. I haven't been paid for the big project yet, so I called to ask about it." I couldn't help the note of pride in my voice.

"Go you! What are you going to do with all that money?"

I snorted. "Oh, maybe pick up a pair of whatshisname Blahniks, a PDA to keep track of Aidan's playdates, some caviar . . . what do you think? Rent, health insurance, maybe some cans of soup."

"How's your mother doing?"

"Oh, you will not believe this. Turns out the inspiration for her day-trading was Hugh saying we weren't as solvent as we should be. She panicked, tried to save our sinking financial ship, and ended up broke with the chance to lose everything." I didn't tell her about Nick. It just felt better as a secret between us.

"Asshole!" Keisha exclaimed. "Does Hugh know you know?"

"You bet. I called him right after Mom told me, and chewed him out."

"Good for you! What did he say?"

"Er, um, er."

"In other words, the usual. So next weekend Aidan's with Hugh, right?"

"Yeah, why? It's not like I'm going to say anything to Aidan about it."

"No, of course not. Just trying to keep your schedule in mind. When's your next scrapbooking extravaganza?"

My natural-born defensiveness surged forward. "Soon, why, do you think it's lame?" I sounded edgy and shrill.

"Calm down, woman. I was just wondering."

"With any luck, I'll have the Marriage Winding Sheet all sewn up by the end of it."

She gave an approving laugh. "All sewn up. Very clever."

I drew a deep breath. "And Nick told me he's leaving soon."

"How ya doin' with that?"

"Fine, I guess. Only Aidan spent about two hours asking me why Nick had to leave, just when he had met him."

"Out of the mouths of babes . . ."

"Yeah, and Nick is a babe. God, Keisha, I'm obsessed. Like, really and truly obsessed. And there's nothing I can do about it."

"I'm sorry, hon. Remember how I was about Denzel Washington?"

"I hate to break it to you, but he's an actor. Not someone you know. Not someone you asked out. Not someone who turned you down." Just saying it again hurt.

"Okay, you're right. So what are you going to do about it, Miss Uppity?" She was more likely than Lissa to suggest I seduce him; I was just glad she hadn't gone there already.

"What can I do? I've already asked him out, he's already said no. My *son* is already in love with him, for God's sake."

"Maybe you can ask him to come over for dinner? Like with you and Aidan, not like a date. Just before he goes."

"Yeah. Maybe." My tone was not encouraging.

"It's worth a try, right? Maybe not something you'd do in a—" She let her voice trail off.

"Million years. I know. Listen, I should go. My mom's coming back soon, I'd rather be asleep—or at least pretending to be—so I don't have to stay up with her and hear her rehash whatever geriatric thrill movie she and her ditzy friend just went to."

As I hung up, I wondered why I had allowed myself to get in such a state over Nick. Hm, I thought to myself, could it be because he was good-looking, smart, witty, sarcastic, honorable, confident, and had eyes bluer than the Aegean Sea? That is, if I knew how blue the Aegean Sea was.

Another thing to put on the "million years" list: Find out how blue the Aegean Sea is. Oh, and stop finding the wrong men to like in the first place.

Of Mousse and Men

You don't have to be a genius to understand this: chocolate, whipped cream, eggs, and sugar. Blended together, they can keep the simplest guy from doing wrong. Are they better than a farm full of bunny rabbits? That's your call, but we're thinking you might just succumb to this American Dream.

24

I'D AGREED TO SCRAPBOOKING AGAIN. I WAS LOOKING FOR-ward to doing something for just me, for once, even if it was something involving glue and cute phrases.

I picked up the bag of scrapbooking stuff and slung it over my shoulder. I'd worn my attempt at Saturday chic, a long black skirt, chunky black shoes, and a crazy-patterned vintage top. I put a rhinestone hairpin to hold my hair out of my face, then spent an extra five minutes making sure my eyebrows were even.

I checked my reflection one last time in the mirror. I was clean, my teeth were brushed, as was my hair, my makeup was good, and I was ready to scrapbook.

It was a good thing I didn't have a beret, I thought, or I'd pull a Mary Tyler Moore and fling it up into the air. Which, since I was in the bathroom, wasn't such a good idea.

I heard the hubbub of many women talking even before Caroline opened the door to the apartment. Instead of the usual feeling of anxiety, however, I felt a thrill of . . . antici-pation? Caroline swung the door open, giving me a sincerely warm smile when she saw me. I'd already checked; the woman who'd spilled the beans to Natalie wasn't going to be there, so I was just happy to be among people who might become friends. Granted, friends who thought scrapbooking was a good idea, but friends nonetheless.

"Molly, glad to see you." She waved me into the apartment, slipping the bag off my shoulder before I even knew she had touched me. I shrugged my coat off.

Caroline's eyes widened a little when she saw my shirt. I guess classic mom-style didn't usually include enormous hyacinths printed on fuchsia polyester.

I looked down also, chuckling a little. "It is loud, isn't it? Oh, and I was trying so hard to be invisible."

She gave me a disbelieving stare. "You? Invisible? I don't think so. Come on, most everyone is here already." Caroline led me into the dining room, the now familiar pieces of memorabilia piled on the table, even more faces than the first time looking up at me as I entered.

"This is Molly. Molly was here last time, for those of you who weren't able to make it. I think that was Sally"—a grayhaired woman nodded her head, her fingers never ceasing their movement—"Karla"—a fresh-faced twentysomething wiggled her fingers at me. "And Linda." A dark-skinned black woman about my age smiled at me, every one of her accessories screaming "money."

"Nice to meet you, Molly," she said, beckoning me to sit in the empty chair next to her. "Sit here, I want to hear all about you. I love your shirt—Pucci?"

"No idea," I replied. I sat, opened up my bag, and began laying out the photo album and the remaining items of my marriage on the table. Linda leaned over and cocked an eyebrow at me. "Let me guess. Divorce?"

I nodded, picking up a picture of Hugh from yet another company junket. I gazed over the table and located a Sharpie marker, then drew a mustache on him. I pondered bunny ears but decided the mustache was probably ridicule enough.

"There," I said in satisfaction. Linda had returned to working on her own project, something that seemed to feature a lot of pictures of shoes.

I found the first empty page and placed the photo right in the middle. I glued it down, then grabbed a piece of light pink paper and a hole punch that cut out hearts. I made four hearts, then put a heart in each of the four squares of the picture. A piece of pink plaid ribbon was lying nearby—probably one of Caroline's leftover hair ribbons—and I bordered the photo with it.

When I'd finished, Hugh looked ridiculous. It felt good to be vindictive, even if it was something only me and my friends would see. It felt good to be in charge.

I heard Linda laugh as she glanced over at my work. "You are sure putting the voodoo on him, chile," she said in an exaggeratedly Cajun accent.

"If only it really worked," I replied. "But it does make me feel better."

"And that's all that matters," Linda said, patting my hand. It felt as if she were my grandmother, although my grandmother would never have worn couture. Or have been black, but the couture thing was probably more of a reach. My grandmother may have been black Irish, but there's no way in hell she even knew who Coco Chanel was.

"Who's ready for snacks?" Caroline said, holding a huge silver platter and smiling broadly. I looked at my watch, surprised to see it had been an hour already. Malicious swipes at the ex took longer than I thought.

I rose and followed Linda through the doorway to Caroline's living room. Tamsin was already there, and she waved at me, patting the seat next to her on the couch. Linda turned to look at me and spread her hand out for me to precede her, dropping herself elegantly on the sofa beside me. She crossed her legs just so, and I wondered if the red patent-leather sandals winding their seductive way up her leg were Manolo Blahniks. I'd never seen any in person before. Did those shoes have the name printed on the sole like my fancy Kenneth Cole shoes did? I caught Linda's eye and leaned back, embarrassed, before I could find out.

"How you been, lady?" Tamsin asked, touching me briefly on the arm. Our lunch together had mostly been her murmuring sympathy while I poured out my tale of woe into her and Caroline's ears. Caroline had dreamt up some creative ways of getting back at Hugh, but unfortunately I wasn't brave enough to try any of them. I did admire her innovative uses for honey, mousetraps, and staplers, though.

"Pretty good, thanks. Do you know each other?" I asked, gesturing between the two women. They nodded, sharing a look I didn't understand.

"Linda's my mother-in-law," Tamsin explained. "I dragged her here today. This is only her second time."

"Yeah, and I'm still not sure I'm not wasting my time, Tammy," Linda said, drawling the words out a little.

Tamsin's voice got a bit sharp. "Because otherwise what—you'd be shopping? You wouldn't be spending time with your grandkids, that's for sure."

Ouch. I was stuck, literally, between the two of them. A rock and a hard place. And me the soft, squishy thing that hated conflict.

"Now, Tam, you know that's not true," Linda replied. "I was over there just last week. Is it my fault you don't invite me more?"

Tamsin blew a heavy breath out from her lips. "I've told you. You don't need an invitation to come see your grandchildren."

Make them stop, make them stop, I chanted in my head. And then *I* stopped. Why did conflict always have to bother me so much? Why couldn't I just let them snipe at each other the way they probably had dozens of times in the past?

Because I liked to make everything better. I liked it when people were happy, even if I wasn't.

And that was the problem with me and Hugh. I was so busy trying to make him happy that I didn't worry about my being happy. And since I wasn't happy, and very resentful, I took it out on him. And, being a weak-willed sonofabitch, he bolted.

It was ironic that he'd had the strength of will to do that, and that I was thankful for it. If he hadn't, we'd still be engaged in our dance of passive aggression: No, you lead. No, you lead. No, you.

It sucked. Our marriage sucked. It wasn't based on anything besides the shared need to make Hugh happy. And that just wasn't enough.

My thoughts must have shown on my face, because I realized suddenly that both women had stopped talking and were looking at me. I felt myself flush.

"Oh, sorry, did you say something?"

They both laughed. "Honey, you must've been thinking something pretty darn important to take your attention away from our bickering," Linda said. She swatted me on the arm. "What was it? A new beau?" She leaned in closer and whispered, "A new pair of shoes?"

I heard Tamsin snicker, but not in a mean way. It seemed the ladies had their own regular dance, and it probably was not nearly as nasty as it sounded from the outside.

Dr. Lowell had said something once about repeating patterns, and how people got caught up in trying to make the same set of events result in a different ending. A Sisyphean task, she'd said. Looking at Tamsin and Linda, and thinking about my own interaction with Hugh, I finally got it.

The only way things were going to change was if *I* changed.

And I *was* changing.

The only question was, could I change my situation enough so that Aidan and I could survive?

The only answer was, I had to.

"Ha! This is tremendous!" Dr. Lowell had the finished scrapbook on her lap and was flipping through the pages guffawing—actually guffawing!—at least every other page.

It was pretty neat. And funny. And clever. And rather nice to look at once you got past the black and the attitude and the goofy catchphrases.

Yeah, it was me. Entirely. Of course I knew that.

My mother had even chuckled a few times, although her mouth had pursed up when she'd seen what I'd done to a picture of me and Hugh on the beach. Who knew Wite-Out could be so effective?

Dr. Lowell closed the book and patted the cover. "I am so, so proud of you, Molly." She gestured to the book on her lap. "You could never have done something like this three months ago, much less six."

"Thanks." I cleared my throat. "It was fun to do, actually. And I made some friends, too. Not people who'll ever be as close as Keisha, but people I could call up to come over for coffee once in a while."

She smiled at me. "And your tasks?"

I rolled my eyes. "I've done all kinds of things I would never do in a million years, including that," I said, pointing to the scrapbook. "Not all of it was good, or worked out, but I did it."

"Great." She leaned back in her chair and crossed her legs at the ankles. "And how is your mother doing?"

Oh, Mr. Darcy. "She's fine. Aidan loves having her, and she's proven surprisingly helpful. Fingers crossed, though, that my lawyer will find enough of Hugh's money so I can help her. Neither one of us wants to live with the other any longer than necessary."

Her mouth tightened. "I hope you take him for everything he's got, Molly." I was surprised at the sharpness in her voice. "He deserves that, for jeopardizing your, and Aidan's, and your mother's livelihoods."

"He does, but I want him to be able to survive, too." And I did; I didn't think I could live with myself if I turned the tables on Hugh so thoroughly that he was the one pondering which type of bean to make for dinner. Aidan needed to have both parents relatively solvent; I just wanted some justice.

"And speaking of survival, I want to give you this." I opened my purse and drew out my checkbook. I tore the written check out of it and handed it to her.

She looked surprised. "Are you sure you can afford this? I can wait. I know things are hard."

I nodded and kept holding the check to her. "I can afford it. John paid me, and there are some more projects coming up. It's not nearly what I owe you, but it's a start."

"Well, thank you." She glanced at the clock. "Time's up. Until next week, then."

I got myself all put together without too much mishap and took the scrapbook from her, smiling to myself as I saw the cover. "Thank you. I couldn't have done this without your encouragement."

"You underestimate yourself, Molly."

I snorted. "Tell me something I don't know."

But I knew, as I walked out of her office and down the hall to the elevator, she was right.

Hugh picked up Aidan early Saturday morning. I was still so livid with him about Mom's finances I barely spoke, even though he was making all kinds of puppy eyes at me. Wasn't going to work, not anymore. Mom was acting all mysterious and headed out to visit a friend in the afternoon, leaving me alone in the house.

It was nice. I spent the day reading and drinking tea, not even changing out of my sweatpants. By the time I'd had dinner—a can of tomato soup and some stale Goldfish—I was ready for a bath. A good long soak followed by a glass of wine sounded perfect.

The phone rang just as I was about to get into the tub. I eyed the running water and the foaming bubbles for just a moment, then sighed and padded, naked, down the hallway to pick up the phone. Thank goodness there were no windows between the bathroom and the phone, or the neighbors would've been scarred for life.

"Hello?"

"Molly, I'm glad you're home." It was Lissa, her voice almost returned to its normal perky tone. I was so relieved to hear it I sat down. The hard wooden chair on my bare ass reminded me of my state of undress.

"What's up, hon?" I asked, rising gingerly from my seat. I eyed the other chairs, then shrugged and sat down on the rug. Promptly sitting on a Lego. Ouch, shows me for being a slovenly housekeeper.

"Well, um, I was wondering . . ." It sounded like she held her hand over the phone and mumbled something, then came back. "I want you to come into the city tonight. I need to see you. You're free, right? I mean, Aidan is with Hugh, right?"

"Yeah," I replied slowly, reluctant to give up on the idea of a Night at Home with Just Molly. "Why? Is there more stuff with Tony?"

She exhaled loudly. "Yes. Yes, there is. So come in, meet me in the East Village at the bookstore there. You know, the one that doesn't carry any of your sort of books?" She chuckled as she said the last part. I figured she must be recovering well. That, or she had gone insane.

"Okay. I was going to take a bath, but I can—"

"There's no time for that!" Now Lissa's tone was undeniably urgent. "Just come in. Now. I'll see you in an hour. And look nice." She hung up without letting me say anything. I glared at the phone for a minute, then retrieved my bathrobe from the bathroom. There were windows on the way to my bedroom.

Look nice? What the hell? Guess that meant the sweatpants were out.

I pulled on a pair of black pants, a black sweater, and wrapped a gauzy green scarf around my neck. "Look nice" might also mean "try not to look old and pale," so I threw some makeup on. I was out the door in twenty minutes, wondering what the hell was so important.

Once I got off the subway at Second Avenue, I strode up the street, smiling to myself as I passed the plethora of downtown chic stores. There was a time I would've oohed and aahed over the clothes in the window, and I probably would have bought a few of them. Time, circumstance, and Hugh's inability to hold a job had changed all that.

As long as Aidan and I were together, and we were both happy, it was okay. So what if I wasn't on the cutting edge of fashion? So what if all my nicest clothes dated from at least seven years ago? So what? It didn't matter. I felt good about myself. *That* was so what.

Lissa popped out of the bookstore doorway before I'd even spotted her. "There you are," she said in an accusing yelp. I jumped.

"What the hell are you doing lurking in the shadows like that, Lissa? Jeez, remember, I'm older than you, you could've scared me to death."

She grabbed my arm and yanked me. Hard. "Come with me, and nobody gets hurt."

"My arm already hurts." She loosened her grip a little but still kept a firm enough hold of me so I would know she wouldn't let me escape anytime soon.

"We're almost there." She was walking so quickly she was starting to gasp. I was too confused by what we were doing to worry about my own breathing.

She turned right on Tenth Street, her perfect little face screwed up in concentration. Then her eyes brightened and she pulled me down three steps to a dark doorway. There was a neon sign in the window for a liquor I didn't recognize. At least we had stopped speedwalking.

She pushed the door open and held it for me. I walked in, blinking a little as my eyes adjusted to the dark.

"Surprise!"

There they were. All of them, spread out before me like a class photo.

The cacophony of voices almost knocked me off my feet. And if Lissa hadn't been in back of me, I would have turned right around and run out.

John, my mom, some local college friends, neighbors, a few mom-friends, Simon, and . . .

"Hey, girl." Keisha walked up and gave me a big kiss on the cheek. "Surprised?"

I just looked at her with my mouth open. She laughed, then hugged me close. "Yeah, I thought you would be. Lissa and I decided you needed a coming-out party, sorta like those southern belles, only for fortysomething moms who've dropped the excess luggage. Think of it as your divorce party."

"But I'm not divorced yet." One of the moms swooped in and gave me a fierce hug. "You look great," she whispered in my ear.

"Okay, *freedom* party then," Keisha said in an exasperated tone. "You have that, right?"

"But—but . . ."

"This is for you, sweetie. Something Lissa and I figured you'd never do in a million years." Lissa walked from behind me and clasped me quickly around the shoulders. "It's a karaoke bar, and you are going to sing tonight, honey," Keisha continued. Her face was almost gleeful. No, it *was* gleeful. The bitch.

"Oh, no I won't," I said, beginning to edge backward almost without thinking. Lissa's hand shot out and placed itself firmly on my back.

"Oh yes you will," she said, poking me in the shoulder blade. Two bitches. "If I can read the great classics of literature without moving my mouth, you can perform karaoke."

I laughed, in spite of my anxiety. "This isn't something I would never do in a million years, though. This is something I would never do *ever*."

"Speaking of doing something you never ever thought you would—did you see what I got?" Keisha extended her left hand, which had a tiny, winking diamond on her ring finger.

"Oh my God!" I screamed, launching myself back into her arms. "When did he ask? How did it happen? What did your dad say? When can I meet him?"

She pulled back and put her hands on my upper arms. She had a sneaky grin on her face. "You can meet him tonight. Mike, come here!"

A tall man emerged from the shadowy figures near the bar. He was good-looking, classically Irish, with dark red hair and a smile I could already see was rogue-ish.

"Molly, this is Mike." I stuck my hand out and he took it, placing a light kiss on the back of my hand.

"Ooh, he is charming," I said in an audible aside. Mike's grin deepened.

"I've heard a lot about you, Molly," he said in a deep voice.

"All of it nice, so don't even think it," Keisha interjected. I nodded and smiled, unable, for once, even to think of anything to say.

I reached out and gave Keisha another hug. "You are the best friend in the world," I whispered into her ear. "I am so glad you came out."

Keisha put her hand on my back and rubbed my shoulder blades. I could tell by the way she was breathing that she was beginning to cry. "You're my best friend, too, Molly, and it's time for you to start loving yourself as much as I do," she whispered back.

I pulled away, grabbing Lissa by the arm and holding on tight so she could hear, too. "Keisha, I think I have. I really do. It's the craziest thing, even I can't believe it, but I do. I'm not in love yet, but I am quite fond of myself. And, with a few more dates, I should be well on the way to admiration. From there, who knows?"

The girls giggled, then we came together in another hug. Mike leaned into our group. "What can I get you to drink, Molly?"

I thought. What would I want at my Freedom Party?

"A sidecar, please."

"You go, girl, only don't make me pick you up off the sidewalk."

I turned to Mike and spoke in mock exasperation. "The worst part about having friends for a long time is that they remember what happened a long time ago. Keisha, we were in college. What was that, twenty years ago?"

She rolled her eyes and held up her hand. "Don't remind me. Okay, point taken. But make sure you drink water, too," she said, wagging her finger at me.

"My mom's right over there, Keish, I don't need another one." I slipped away from the group and walked over to where my mom was deep in conversation with Simon. What in heaven's name could they be talking about? I hoped it wasn't me.

"And she is an excellent mother, and so charming," I heard as I approached them. Next she'd be making him examine my teeth.

"Hi, Mom, Simon. This is such a surprise." Simon was wearing another ultrachic shirt, this time with the top three buttons undone so I could see a little patch of chest hair. I'd never liked chest hair anyway.

"Well, isn't this nice of your friends to do," Mom said, shooting Simon a sidelong glance. "It's because you're such a good person."

Simon smiled, that slow, lazy smile I'd lusted after the first time I met him. God, what kind of an idiot was I to want to pass this by?

"Or maybe no one was doing anything else tonight," he added in a matter-of-fact tone of voice. Oh, I was *that* kind of idiot.

Why did my friends even invite him, anyway? I'd have to corner Keisha later and find out.

I wondered exactly why he'd come. Did he still harbor visions of us getting together? Because as I recalled, I'd pretty much told him no. Or maybe he really didn't have anything to do.

Mike came up with my drink, nudging it into my hand. I took a bigger sip than I'd intended, wishing I could wash away my agony over my mom's blatant comments, Simon's pomposity, jealousy over Keisha's happiness—and, oh, hell, was that Nick I saw? I thought he'd left without saying good-bye. And here he was. At my Freedom Party.

I took another swallow, then pushed my glass back into Mike's hand.

"I don't want to give Keisha the satisfaction of being right, but I do think I have to watch it tonight," I muttered to him. "Can you grab me some water or something?"

Mike patted my arm and headed to the bar. I met Nick's gaze, and something in my stomach leapt.

"Who's that, dear?" Mom asked, a hopeful tone in her voice as she watched Mike at the bar. If she had her way, I'd be involved with all of the men in Manhattan, at least all of the ones with college degrees. I didn't want to tell her anything about Mike because I bet she'd get all intellectually snobby on him.

"Keisha's fiancé. He came with her from California."

"Oh," she said, her disappointment evident in her tone.

"Molly, dance with me," Simon commanded. Prince's "Cream" was playing. Dancing was probably my second favorite thing, right after hanging out with Aidan. It sure wasn't sex—Hugh had made sure that activity had gotten bumped down almost to double digits.

I wondered if Nick danced. I did not even allow myself to think about Nick having sex. Imagining him in rhythmic motion in public was risqué enough.

"Oh, of course." We headed toward the dance floor, Simon taking my hand and guiding me as if I were unable to handle it myself.

Simon was a good dancer, I had to give him that. He moved his hips as if he knew what to do with them and he kept gazing in my eyes as we moved.

I wondered, uncharitably, if the PR woman he'd been with at the opening night event had not met his mum's standards.

If I weren't so over him, I'd be halfway to bed with him on this one dance alone. Although I could tell he knew how good he was, and that he wasn't paying a speck of attention to me. Unless, maybe, it was to ask me what I thought of his dancing.

"Thanks, Simon, I want to go say hi to some other people." I walked off before he could try to persuade me otherwise.

"Molly!" John came up and enclosed me in a huge hug. He stepped back, eyeing my outfit. "You look amazing." He took my arm and steered me farther away from the music. "Thanks for everything, Mol. Your work saved my ass. I owe you."

"What are you talking about? You're the one who's saving me, hiring me even though I don't have experience."

He shrugged. "I knew you could do it, and probably do it better than anyone I could find with more degrees. Plus, you'll work for cheap."

I laughed. "That is true. So we're even."

My eyes wandered back over to where Nick had been. Now Lissa stood there alone, and I got a crazy idea. "Stay right here, John," I said, heading to where Lissa stood. I grabbed her and drew her back to where John was. "John, I'd like you to meet my friend. This is Lissa. Lissa, this is John."

John looked as though he'd seen an angel. Which, given how gorgeous Lissa was, was likely true.

Lissa just looked pleasant, as she always did. "Nice to meet you, John."

I couldn't quite figure out what they might have in common, besides breathing and both being available, but I knew John was enough of a salesman, and Lissa was empathic enough for them to figure it out themselves.

Sure enough, before I'd even left them, they were talking about men's fashion and where to find the best sushi.

Yay. I liked it when I could do nice things for my friends.

I came up to where Keisha was surveying the crowd. She spoke without looking at me. "In case you're wondering, Molly, the karaoke begins at nine P.M. And we've got the first half hour solidly booked." Then she glared at me, as if daring me to back out. I knew she'd never let me hear the end of it if I did, so I made sure to keep my mouth shut.

"Wonderful," I managed to say. I walked to the bar and leaned my elbow on it. Mike handed me a highball glass filled with something fizzy. I took a sip, relieved to find it was seltzer.

"Hi, Molly."

I nearly choked on my drink. Nick had somehow managed to get next to me without my noticing. I placed my drink down so I could wipe my sweaty palms on my pants.

"Hi, Nick. I didn't know you were still here, I thought you'd left already. I mean, we had the event, and all, and I thought work was done. But I'm glad you're here. I really appreciate it. Of course, I'm terrified for when the singing actually starts, but everyone knows I can barely carry a tune, even if I know the words to most of the popular songs from the past twenty years."

Dear God, I was babbling. And he was looking at me with that understanding glint in his eye, as if he knew just how uncomfortable I was. I only hoped he didn't know how much I wished he'd lean over and kiss me.

"You'll do fine. Your friends will make sure of it. They're quite fiercely protective of you, if you haven't noticed."

"Oh?" I replied as nonchalantly as I could, taking another sip from my drink. "Did they say anything?"

He chuckled. "They didn't have to. As soon as I said my name, your friend Keisha gave me this appraising stare, and the other one, the blond one, made sure I knew just how smart and funny you are, and how many people—that is, men—are just lying in wait for your divorce to be finalized."

Who knew Lissa was in training to be my mother?

"Oh. Well. Sorry about that."

He shrugged. "Don't be. Friends like that are precious. So what if they threaten someone's liver with a rusty butter knife? It just means they care about you."

I snorted into my drink, making the seltzer jump up my nose. His face got all concerned, like when someone accidentally ingests liquid into their nasal passages. Or just makes a complete and total ass of herself.

"You okay?" He reached out his arm and patted me on the back. I wiped my nose surreptitiously on my polyester sleeve. Hm. Not so absorbent.

"Fine. Great. Fine." Oh, God, I was babbling again. I checked my watch—at least seventeen minutes until the torture—that is, the karaoke—started.

"Want to dance?" At least it'd be better than trying to figure out how many ways I could find not to blurt, *I have the worst crush in the world on you, and I wish you were just the least bit interested in me.*

"Sure." So he did engage in rhythmic motion. Nick reached out and took my glass from my nerveless fingers, placing it on the bar. Then he grabbed my hand and led me toward the dance floor, like Simon had, only this time it was not so much proprietary as solicitous. Or so my biased brain said.

Stevie Wonder's "As" was starting to play. What cruel devil DJ was making me suffer so? It was long, well over five minutes, and it was one of my favorites, and it also usually made me cry. Not what you wanted to hear when with your unrequited crush.

I looked up into the tiny DJ booth and saw Keisha lodged up there, enormous headphones stuck on either side of her close-cut hair. I stuck my tongue out at her, then looked back at Nick.

"Ah, Keisha just . . . oh, never mind," I said, giving up on explanations. I looked down and stared at my feet.

A strong hand lifted my chin. I met Nick's eyes, and I could tell, even in the dark room, they were amused. "C'mon, Molly, I know you're not as shy as you pretend. I saw you dancing with Simon before and you didn't look at the ground with him."

That's because I don't care about him.

Had I said that out loud? His expression hadn't changed, I guessed I hadn't.

"Uh, sorry," I mumbled, not breaking eye contact.

"That's better," he said, reaching out and pulling me into his arms. I felt the solid warmth of him, even through the ancient polyester, and his smell—that very masculine scent that had sent me spinning even before I knew what kind of man he was.

"Thanks for coming," I muttered into his chest, only it came out sounding like "Nkf ffr krfing." He laughed, a deep rumble that echoed into my body.

After a while, his grip tightened, and I found my right leg moving in between his, his left leg between mine. A perfect fit.

We danced in silence. It felt so good, so comfortable to be there with him. Even though I was full of anxiety about how I felt. Glad to know I put the "moron" in *oxymoronic.*

I also couldn't avoid what seemed to be happening to Nick. Or, more specifically, to what was happening below Nick's belt. I'd just registered it when he pulled his body just far enough away so neither of us would be embarrassed. Hopefully.

It still felt comfortable, and now I knew he felt something, too.

When the song finally ended, he pulled away from me, giving my back a last, fleeting stroke. I wanted to lean into him, to pull his face down to mine, but I just stared at the ground. We stood there just a beat too long, and I felt as if there were an electric charge traveling between our bodies. My heart was beating just a little faster, and I almost looked up to say something, but then I felt somebody else bump into me, and the moment was gone.

" 'Kay, Mol, you're on!" Lissa poked me in the arm, forcing me to look up into her face. Cheery and cute, as usual. It was a shame she was so nice or I'd hate her.

"On?" I said stupidly, wishing my friend the floor would swallow me up. Nick smiled—was it an "I like you" smile, or just a friendly smile?—then turned and headed for the bar.

"Onstage? For karaoke?" Lissa said, as if explaining something to a very slow person. I acted the part, moving as slowly as I could toward the tiny stage.

All too soon, I was there. Keisha bounded up onto it, holding her hand out for me, grinning that grin I was beginning to despise.

I took her hand and clutched it, hard, allowing her to swing me up onto the stage. There was a wooden three-legged stool on one side, and a microphone on the other. I moved instinctively toward the stool, but Keisha positioned me directly in front of the microphone. The lights were in my face, but I could still see all too many faces peering up at me.

God, make this night stop.

"Don't I have to choose a song or something?" I asked.

"Nope. Already taken care of. Mr. DJ?"

Mike had replaced Keisha in the booth and nodded at me. Maybe I didn't like him so much after all.

The opening strains of Gloria Gaynor's "I Will Survive" came leaking out of the tinny speakers. Boy, did my friends know me. Despite my tension, I felt a smile creep over my face.

I took one step to the microphone, prepared to sing my version of the ultimate divorce song.

And froze.

My throat wouldn't let anything out.

I tried. I squeaked a little, squawked some, then took the step back and felt my face flame. I felt my eyes start to well up. I couldn't even sing in public, for goodness' sake, what made me arrogant enough to think I could survive on my own, and take care of Aidan, too?

I tried again, and this time, I managed a tiny little quaver. Triumph! I could do it! I opened my mouth wider this time.

And belted out the first few lines, just a little late.

I was just hitting the part about making him leave the keys when he moved into the spotlight.

Hugh.

All scruffy brown-haired no-good cheating sonofabitch of him. Who'd brought my mother close to financial ruin. Who was about to do the same to Aidan and me.

My mouth snapped closed.

Keisha, who'd been below me on the floor, looked behind her. When she swung her head back in my direction, there was a fearsome light in her eye. She darted back into the crowd—was she going to sock him?—and pulled Lissa up to the stage, hopping up next to me, holding a hand out for Lissa.

The music was still going, but no one was singing.

Keisha poked me in the ribs, then gestured for me to start moving. She poked Lissa in the ribs, too, and they both began shuffling in that backup singer lope.

"Sing, woman, sing!" she hissed into my ear. I shuffled toward the microphone. It was time for the chorus.

"Go on now, go," I sang, making a shooing motion with my hands. Hugh's eyes widened, and he blinked a few times, fast. I guess I wasn't too subtle. I knew I was loud.

Keisha and Lissa moved to either side of me, doing the bump, like the popular girls did in high school. I felt confident, exhilarated, pissed off.

What the fuck was Hugh doing at my Freedom Party?

When the song finally wound down, all three of us were giggling onstage, and most of the audience had thrown their arms in the air and were clapping.

I had actually done it! I was free! I *could* do it.

Except Hugh was headed toward me, a determined look on his face. Keisha stepped in front of me, blocking his view. He peered over her shoulder. "Molly, I need to talk to you."

"Not now, dickface," Keisha said. I winced at her bluntness. "Can't you see this is Molly's night? This isn't about you, or Ms. California, or how lame you are for getting fired. So go away and leave her alone." She planted herself in front of me.

Hugh blanched.

"And who the hell told you about it anyway?" she snarled.

We both turned and looked in my mom's direction. She looked guilty as she saw Hugh and the expression on our faces.

I pushed Keisha away and stepped forward to look into Hugh's eyes. "No, Keish, I can handle it. I can," I repeated, making sure she heard my confidence. She moved to the side, leaving me alone with Hugh.

"Is Aidan okay?" He nodded. "So. What's up?" I asked, placing my hands on my hips. At that moment, if Hugh had said anything I didn't like, I knew I was going to deck him. It felt good. Damn good.

"Um, well," he stammered, trying to take my arm, "I . . . I want you back."

An unbidden wave of relief washed over me. For a moment, I basked in being wanted.

Then I remembered it was Hugh, a man whom I'd realized was weak, shallow, selfish, and not so bright.

"Why?" I demanded. I shook his arm off like he was a pesky puppy begging for a treat.

He shoved his hands in his pockets. His pants, I noticed, were new since we'd broken up. They made his legs look short.

He pulled his hand out of his pocket holding a black velvet box. "Because I made a mistake." He flipped the box open, exposing his grandmother's ring and all its beautiful, shiny facets. The ring he'd given me already. But taken back.

I wanted to fall down on the ground and howl, but I knew what I had to do. "No kidding. Just one? I'd count at least each one of the dollars you siphoned from our savings account, the times you made Aidan feel bad for not being just like you, the way you got fired because you just couldn't cut it, maybe how you didn't even have the guts to tell me you were unhappy with our marriage. Not to mention how you never took your used water glasses to the kitchen sink."

He drew his fingers across his brow and rubbed it in that lame "I'm thinking so intently" way he'd innovated in college for especially hard oral exams.

He sighed. Heavily. "You're right, Molly." He shrugged his shoulders and spread his arms wide in a helpless gesture. "What can I say? You're right. But I miss you. I want you back."

"Why?" I asked again. "What about Sylvia?"

"We broke up," he said shortly.

"Oh, so you think you can come back and crook your little finger and I'll make it all better? She dumped you, didn't she?"

The expression on his face answered as clearly as his words could have.

"I knew it. You wouldn't be here if you weren't desperate. Geez, Hugh, how do you think that makes me feel?"

He stepped forward, as if to clasp me in his arms. The caress-instead-of-talk ploy had always worked on me before; I guess he thought he'd go for the sure thing.

"I love you, Molly."

Both of us stared at each other for a moment. In all our years together, he'd never said it. Never. Not when he'd proposed, not when I spent my paycheck on his law degree, not even when I'd given birth to Aidan.

I used to blame it on his upbringing and his heritage—his family just wasn't that demonstrative—but now I knew better. Bastard.

I stomped on his foot. He yelped, then gave me an accusing glare. "You *hurt* me, Molly."

"Yeah, well, join the club, Hugh. When you left, I was devastated. I didn't know what I had done. What was wrong with me. Well, I've since found out nothing is wrong with me. I'm a good mother, a good friend, and yes, Hugh, I was a good wife."

I poked him in the chest, hard. "But I'm not going to be a good wife anymore. I'm not letting you crawl back into my life and push me back into being that insecure person again. Go on now, go." I finished, pointing my finger toward the door. Gloria herself couldn't have done it better. I allowed myself a moment of satisfaction, then looked to see his reaction.

Apparently Hugh was as impressed with my dramatics as I was. His mouth dropped open, then he recovered, snapping it closed and taking a menacing step toward me.

"Let me tell you a few things, Molly, since we're being so open." He shoved his finger in my face, and I had to resist the temptation to bite it off. "You think you've been the long-suffering wife? Well, I suffered, too. Every time I stayed out just a minute later than I said, I heard about it. Not in words, no, you wouldn't ever go so far as to actually talk to me, but you said plenty in sighs and sad faces and silence. It got so I wished you'd just haul yourself up on the cross and be done with it."

He had me there. I *had* done those things. I wasn't proud of myself, but I knew I wasn't that martyr any longer. "Just go, Hugh," I said in a resigned tone. "I don't think there's anything more to say."

I turned away from him and walked up to the bar. "Seltzer and lime, please," I said to the bartender. He nodded, then passed the glass into my hand. "Cheers," I said, raising my glass to myself. I took a long swallow, then put the glass back on the bar and chanced a look behind me.

Fuck. Hugh was still there, glaring at me. What part of "just go" didn't he understand?

"Molly," he said, reaching a hand toward me. His voice

was meek, pleading. Did he actually still have hopes of reconciliation? And why would he want to in the first place, given everything we both thought of us when we were together?

"Molly, is this individual giving you trouble?" Simon sounded as snobby and British as he possibly could. I saw Hugh visibly stiffen.

Great. I bet even Gloria Gaynor never had nights like this.

The Ice Cream Man Cometh

Come on, you didn't think we'd miss something so obvious, did you? Yeah, well, he's done terrible things, he's tortured—and he's got pistachio, strawberry, and chocolate, and that's just for starters. So pull up a seat at the bar, grab a cone, and enjoy, because for this guy in white, life's failures are inevitable.

25

"SIMON, I'M FINE." I PUSHED HIS ARM BACK TOWARD HIS body. He'd lifted it, as if prepared to sock Hugh in the nose. Not a bad idea, but when it happened, I wanted it to be *my* arm that did the socking.

"Nobody talks to Molly like that." He cocked his fist again.

"Oh, for God's sake," I muttered, pushing his arm down again, more firmly this time. "I'm not yours to defend, Simon. Back off."

"Yeah, that's right, buddy, you heard her." Now Hugh was starting to get that caveman tone in his voice. "And she can't be yours, she's *my wife*."

What was next, chest-beating? Maybe one of them would decide to drag me by my hair to their cave. "Look guys, I'm flattered by this whole 'Me Tarzan' thing, but I'd like Hugh here to leave, and Simon to understand I can take care of myself. Is that too much to ask?"

They both looked at me dumbfounded. Apparently it was.

I glanced around at the others. They were looking at us all like we were the main attraction at a wrestling event.

Hugh's face got tight and twisted, like the night before he took the LSATs and realized he hadn't paid attention in his Kaplan prep course. Simon just shot me a condescending smirk.

"Don't pay attention to her, Hugh, good fellow, Molly needs taking care of from creeps like you."

And that's when Hugh hit him. Right in the arm. Hugh never could aim straight. Simon retaliated by punching Hugh square in the upper chest, making Hugh give this funny little squeak as he bent over. While there, however, he nailed Simon right in the belt. Simon's eyes got all wide before he kicked Hugh in the shins.

"Stop it," I yelped. "Stop it!" I tried to separate them and got an elbow in the mouth for my trouble. A strong arm reached in and grabbed me around the waist.

"Just leave them to it," Nick said in my ear. He pulled me away from the flailing limbs and tucked me snugly against his side. His warm, strong side.

Keep control of yourself, Molly, I said as I felt myself start to lean into him. He kept his arm around my waist and turned me toward the door. "Let's get out of here for a while," he said in a low voice. I nodded, hoping neither one of the guys in the Thunderdome would notice.

The air outside smelled great after being inside the karaoke bar. New York City had outlawed smoking in bars, thank goodness, but it hadn't figured out a way to ban the odor of old beer, ancient Naugahyde, and sweaty bodies rocking out to "Born to Run."

"You okay?" Nick still had his arm around me.

"Mm-hmm," I replied.

"I take it that was your husband?"

"Soon to be ex-husband. Yeah. A real winner, huh?"

"Well," he said, laughter in his voice as he walked me over to a nearby bench, "at least he can take a punch."

I giggled as I sat down and leaned back against the bench. He sat next to me, his leg right against mine. He draped his arm behind my head. If I leaned my head back, I'd rest it right on his arm.

I pulled my spine straighter.

"Thanks for getting me out of there. I hope they don't do any permanent damage to each other."

Nick chuckled. "Judging by what I saw, there's no chance. Unless bruised egos count as permanent damage."

"With those two, it probably does." I sighed. "Man, I have bad taste in men. Wimps, braggarts, and—" I stopped myself just in time.

"Men who say no," Nick finished. He pulled me tighter toward him with the arm that was around my shoulders. I held my breath, wondering what he was going to say.

"Molly, I—" I looked up into his face. The look in his eyes made me all quivery inside, and I didn't think that was just because I hadn't had enough oxygen lately.

He leaned down and kissed me.

At first, it was one of those romance-novel kisses, the kind that's just sweet in a getting-to-know-you kind of way. His lips were firm and soft and hard and wonderful and every other seemingly banal adjective I'd ever read. It was anything but banal.

And then he gripped my shoulder tighter, pulled me even closer, and went to work.

Man, could he kiss.

He did this swoopy thing with his tongue, gently easing it into my mouth and tasting me, then pulling it back so I was left wanting more. Which, no dummy, I did.

He pulled away completely, then moved back in and licked my lips with his tongue, outlining them in the gentlest, sexiest way imaginable.

Then he moved back in and dove into my mouth, taking possession of it until I felt as if I were going to melt into a little puddle at his feet.

At the same time, his hand was rubbing slowly up and down my arm. The feel of his strong fingers on me made my whole body react until all I wanted to do was to crawl inside of him and feel safe and at home.

It was the most sensual experience I'd ever had, with clothes or without. No one had ever kissed me like that, as if they were making love to me with their lips and tongue alone. It was delicious, it was heavenly, it was—

"Molly, I'm sorry."

Finished.

I pulled away, moving my fingers up to touch my mouth. My lips were warm from his, my body still tingling in reaction.

"Oh, no need to apologize." I kept my voice matter-of-fact, even though the effort made my jaw hurt. "Damsel in distress and everything, I know how it is."

I started to inch away from him on the bench, keeping my eyes locked on the ground. If I looked at him I'd probably burst into tears, and that was the last thing either one of us wanted.

"Molly, look at me." Did he want to *see* my final humiliation?

I raised my chin and stared him in the eyes. What I saw there made me lose my breath all over again.

His deep blue eyes had softened, somehow, the dark depths showing a level of emotion I'd never seen there before. He was smiling, a rueful smile that made his eyes crinkle at the corners in the most adorable way I'd ever seen. He looked sad, and happy, and bittersweet all at the same time.

I was guessing there wouldn't be a speedy resumption of the whole making-out-on-a-bench thing anytime soon. Rats.

"Nick, it's fine, really."

He placed his fingers—his long, knowing, sexy fingers—on my chin and held my face still. "No, it's not."

Just as suddenly as he had held me, he released me, and he dropped his head into his hands on his knees. I moved back over to him, putting my hand on his back and giving him a tentative rub.

"What is it?" It didn't seem to matter anymore that I had a mad crush on him and he wouldn't—or couldn't—reciprocate. What mattered was that he was my friend, and he was obviously in pain.

He lifted his head slightly and turned it to look at me. "It's you. It's me. It's us."

I increased the pressure on his back. "Now you sound like the hero in one of those trashy novels I read. Come on, Nick, it can't be *that* bad."

He rubbed his hands on his thighs, as if bracing himself for something.

I waited.

"I'm married, Molly."

"Oh. I guess it could be that bad." I pulled my hand off his back, as if it were poison. I even rubbed my hand against my pants as if to scrub him, scrub the proof of him, off of me.

Married. Oh, God, I hope he doesn't have kids. Why the hell wasn't he wearing a ring?

He got up and stepped away a few paces. I eyed his back nervously. "Um, so want to tell me about it?" Like who is she, where is she, and what were you doing kissing me if you're freaking *married*?

He turned back toward me. His face was set in resigned despair.

"She's Simon's cousin. Distant cousin."

"Oh." Was she as beautiful as Simon? As successful? Smarter?

He came and sat back on the bench. I noticed he kept his body carefully away from mine.

"We got involved when I was in England working for Simon's family's company. Her name's Emma, she's back in England. We separated a few months before I got here." He leaned his forearms on his knees and stared at the ground. "She was . . . she was cheating on me for years, almost as soon as we got married. I didn't know it, of course, I was too busy working. When I found out, it was too late to do anything."

"What would you have done?"

"Tried to work it out. I'm not a quitter, Molly, I married her believing it was till death do us part. I'm also not a cheater. We're still married, I still owe her the honor of treating her respectfully." He cleared his throat. "But since I've been here, I've been . . . dealing with a few things."

Ah, the therapist. No wonder. He went on, "And kissing you, getting involved with you, is not honorable, no matter what my personal feelings are."

Of all the men in the world, I had to fall for the one who most resembled a Japanese warrior. Great. Why couldn't he have been just a little more caddish?

Oh, but then he'd be just like Hugh.

"Okay. Thanks, I guess. But why didn't you tell me before? Why aren't you wearing a wedding ring, the universal 'stay away' signal?"

"Mol?" Keisha poked her head out the bar door. I heard the unmistakable sounds of "Like a Virgin" escaping from behind her. Was that *Lissa* singing?

Her face cleared when she spotted me, then she seemed to recognize the look on my face, because she started to scowl.

"It's fine, Keish, I'll be back in a minute." She nodded, threw a menacing glare at Nick, then withdrew her head back into the bar.

"I didn't tell you because I didn't find out who she was seeing until I got here." He blew out a deep breath. "It was Simon. And when I found out, I flung the ring somewhere, I don't know where it landed."

"Ouch. I thought you said he was her cousin?"

"Distant cousin."

"Not distant enough, I guess." My hand flew to my mouth. "Oh, sorry. Shouldn't have said that."

He laughed, then took my other hand in his and laid both our hands on his thigh. "No, you should have. That's what I lo—like about you, Molly, you say what you think. I don't think you could lie if your life depended on it."

"No. I stink at poker, did I ever tell you that?" And that my hand is on your thigh, did you know that, too?

"You didn't need to."

"So I'm still confused. Even if it was Simon——"

"Simon asked me not to say anything. It's over, it was over between them within a few weeks, apparently." I wondered how he could stand to continue to work with the guy. He must have heard my unspoken question. "I owe it to the company, if not to Simon, to keep working with him. A lot of the employees in Simon's company have invested their own money in opening this shop. They believe in Simon's talent. *I* believe in Simon's talent, for that matter. And if word got out that two of the principals were involved in such a messy drama, our company's future would be in jeopardy. I couldn't do that to my employees or to Simon's family."

I felt my mouth drop as I looked at him. "Wow, you really are honorable. Just warn me if you're going to do that falling-on-a-sword thing, okay, because I don't like blood. It's hard to get the stains out."

He chuckled, then gripped my hand more tightly. "There's more to it than that, too, or I would've told you. It's—it's complicated."

"I should be going back." Because if I stayed out here any longer with him, I would probably do something pathetic, like beg him to kiss me again. Or haul off and hit him. Or both.

"Molly, wait. I'd like to take you out to dinner before I head back to London. I leave in about a week. Is Tuesday night good with you?"

Tuesdays with Scary again. Only this time it'd be Tuesday with Soon-to-Be-Leaving-the-Country-and-Taking-My-Heart-with-Him.

"Tuesday night." I rose, somewhat shakily, and walked through the door without looking back.

• • •

"What've you been doing out there, girl?" Keisha asked with a leer as I staggered back inside.

"Nothing, unfortunately."

She cocked an eyebrow. "Really? Coulda fooled me. When I saw you guys before, he was looking at you like a starving Irishman eyeballing a pile of corned beef and cabbage."

"Keisha, for goodness' sake, can't you just use similes and metaphors like a good liberal arts graduate? Jeez, Louise, it's all that carpenter's fault."

She gave a satisfied smile. *"All* his fault, yes indeed."

"I bet you guys think you invented sex, too," I said in an undertone.

"What was that?" she said.

"Nothing," I replied with a smile. "So anyway, what did I miss? Did Hugh and Simon finally settle their differences?"

"Yeah, Simon jumped on Hugh and kneed him in the back. Lissa pulled him off, and she and Hugh left out the back door. Apparently Hugh didn't want to see you again."

"Yeah, well, the feeling is mutual. So Lissa is still out there with him? Should we call her?"

Keisha waved a hand. "Girlfriend can take care of herself. Besides, Hugh's no threat, right?"

I thought of Hugh's penchant for Waspy blondes. I thought of how he wasn't nearly as smart as he thought he was, and how Lissa wasn't nearly as dumb as she thought she was.

"No. No threat at all," I said with a smirk. Just to be safe, though—"Hey, John, you wanna go out and make sure Hugh and Lissa are okay?"

• • •

"You okay?"

Keisha pushed her head out from under Aidan's ancient Thomas the Tank Engine quilt. She'd left Mike at an old college friend's house after the Freedom Party so we could have some time to ourselves. We'd stayed up until 5:00 A.M., but a Lifetime on Aidan's Schedule meant I was up bright and early at eight. I'd given Keisha the courtesy of sleeping until nine. That's the kind of friend I am.

"Mmpshglk," she mumbled, rubbing her eyes.

"I brought you coffee," I chirped, handing her a cup.

"Thnkkkssshu," she replied, grasping it with unsteady hands. She took a big sip. "So you gonna call Nick today?"

She would not let up. "We went over this last night. No, I won't."

She shrugged. "Whatever you want to do, hon. It's your funeral."

I gave her a smirk. "No, it's my Freedom Party."

"A Freedom Party where your soon-to-be-ex got his butt kicked. That was pretty sweet. Too bad it was Simon, though. You were totally right about him."

"Yeah," I said slowly, "I thought he was interesting at first, but I realized it was just the British accent and the sleek clothing. Underneath it all, he's just a bubba."

"Whereas Nick . . ."

"Nick's a stone-cold fox, but I have to get over this silly crush. Besides, he's leaving the country, Keisha. I don't think there's a chance for us no matter what his 'complications' are."

"But you're seeing him on Tuesday, right? So you could have one night of passion." She put the back of her hand to her forehead and sighed dramatically.

I batted her hand away from her head. "Have you been reading my trashy romances again? Because it doesn't happen like that in real life. In real life, something like that is called a one-night stand, and it's usually sordid and you feel tacky and cheap afterward."

"Darn."

"Yeah, darn is right. I just hope I can handle Tuesday without freaking out. At least not too much."

My only question was, how much was too much? And what would I possibly say to him?

I only had a few days to figure it out.

Lord of the Pies

You won't need your glasses to view the delicious taste of these chocolate cream pies. They'll make grown, professional, too-gorgeous-for-words men cry. And you'll be elected ruler of the island without having to kill anyone. Unless you consider death by chocolate an actual mercy killing.

26

"WHAT THE FU— THAT IS, WHAT SHOULD I WEAR?"

Aidan, Keisha, Mike, and Lissa were all perched on my bed, trying to help me figure out the best outfit for the Not Quite a Date, but Not Quite Not Dinner with Nick. My bed hadn't seen so much action since—well, ever.

"Black. Black's a good choice," Keisha advised, a sassy grin on her face. I glared at her, then dove into my closet. I emerged with two pairs of black pants, a black dress, and a black and white skirt, just for variety's sake.

"So?" I laid everything out on the bed, trying not to notice Mike's and Aidan's complete lack of interest.

"The black pants. These," Lissa said, gesturing to the ones with the low waist. "You look sophisticated yet casual."

Keisha rolled her eyes. "Honestly, can't you drop the fashion oxymorons? Just wear whatever makes you look skinniest. That's what you want to wear, right?"

Mike leaned over and covered Aidan's ears. "Just wear whatever makes you look hot. Like, you know, with cleavage." He removed his hands from Aidan's ears. Aidan just smiled at him—he and Mike had already played about a thousand games of Justice League, so Mike could do no wrong.

My girlfriends nodded. "He's right. Give him some skin, baby," Keisha said, reaching over and yanking a slinky black tank top from the top of my bureau. She held it out for me to take.

"But it's March! I'll freeze!"

Keisha kept her hand out. "Would you rather be warm or *warm*?" she said, giving me a wink. Only Keisha could wink like that and not look like a perv.

"Warm." I sighed, taking the top from her hand. "And now, if you guys will get out of here, I'll get dressed."

When the bell finally rang, right around seven, I'd managed to screw up two applications of eyeliner and was thoroughly convinced my eyebrows were mismatched. In other words, a typical pre-evening out.

Keisha opened the door to let Nick in, but only after I admonished her about behaving herself. I still didn't trust her, but at the moment, I looked like the women from those old Tareyton cigarette ads from the 1970s where everyone was sporting a black eye and a cigarette. Yeah, I'd rather fight than switch, too.

I heard their voices drift through the hallway. Nick sounded smart, solid, gorgeous, and totally unattainable. All that from a few overheard words.

Oh, who was I kidding? I was so spoony over him I was surprised I hadn't sent him a Secret Admirer card like Bob Farrell did to me in third grade. I'd wound up with bubble gum in my hair and he'd gotten a split lip.

"Be right out," I called from the bathroom. I dropped my eyelash curler on the floor and immediately stepped on it.

Keisha came into the bathroom and fussed with my top, pulling it lower. I immediately hiked it back up.

We walked down the hall together, her trying to drag my top down, and me fighting valiantly to hitch it back up.

She won, but that's because I let her.

Nick was sitting on my sofa, surrounded by Mike and Aidan. Lissa was straightening up, bless her heart. Nick rose as soon as he saw me. "Ready?"

I nodded, struck dumb in his presence. I wondered if it had taken two women, one Irish carpenter, and a six-year-old Power Rangers fan to get *him* dressed. Probably not.

"Don't do anything I wouldn't do," Keisha sang as she locked the door behind us. Sometimes my friends could be *too* cute. I gave a nervous giggle as Nick offered me his arm.

"So where are we going?"

He opened the building door for me. I passed close enough to him to smell his scent, that totally masculine smell I'd adored even when I thought he was Mr. Forbidding.

"Actually, I was hoping you might want to take me to one of your favorite spots," he said, giving me this look that almost stopped me dead in my tracks. Or was it that he was actually soliciting my opinion? Hugh had always assumed he'd known best, and Simon had seemed to assume I'd known nothing.

"Um, I really like this Indian place down the street. Or maybe Italian? I mean, if you don't like Indian, some people can't eat coriander, they think it tastes like soap. Or Chinese, there's a good Chinese place just a few blocks away . . ."

"Indian's fine," he said, stopping my babbling.

We walked in silence for a block.

"Mol—"

"Nick—" We spoke in unison. "You first," I said.

"Look, we obviously have a lot to talk about. But I'm starving, and I can't think straight on an empty stomach. How about we talk after dinner?"

"Sure." A beat of silence, then I spoke again. "We can talk, right, just not *talk* talk."

"Right. Talking is fine. Talk talking is not." He sounded just as confused as any man who'd encountered the feminine use of the repeated word for emphasis. What good was an MBA against female double-speak?

Over poori, saag panir, and raita, I was reminded again why I just liked Nick so darn much. He asked me about Aidan, about the Teaching Fellows' program, my mother's debts, how I'd met Keisha and Lissa, and what made Jane Austen such an amazing author.

In short, he asked me about *me*.

When we finally pushed our saffron rice—strewn plates away, I felt satisfied. Oh, I was still anxious, because he hadn't told me about his marriage, or his feelings for me, or any of that, but he'd shown he cared.

He reached across the table and took my hand, which had been nervously playing with my water glass. "I suppose it's time we talked."

I gulped and nodded.

He took a deep breath and tightened his grip on my hand. "I told you Emma was Simon's cousin. She's also the daughter of Simon's primary investor. I got hired to work on the project because of her, and he's given me every opportunity. It's not that I didn't earn those chances, but I wouldn't have gotten past the front door without her. And for that, I owe her. We got married right after my first promotion, and she started cheating on me right after my third."

He took a sip from his beer. "I was too wrapped up in work to notice, at first. When I did, it was too late. And by that time, it was Simon."

"So what happened?"

"Naturally, Emma didn't want her father to know about it. She asked me to put off making any permanent decisions until after I returned from New York, after we both had time to think. I promised I would, even though I knew my feelings wouldn't change. I always keep my promises." He fixed me with an intense gaze. "No matter how hard that is."

I felt a little shiver run up my spine. "And you couldn't tell me you were married because—?"

"Because when we met, it was a completely professional relationship. And then when we did become friends, I just didn't want to bring it up. It's not anything I want to think about. I didn't think it'd be an issue. Until it happened, I had no intention of kissing you. You were just so—"

"So what?"

"So . . . you. Being with you makes me happy. Do you understand why I didn't tell you? I'm not sure I do. And now I can't stop thinking about you."

He swallowed. "And I'm going back home in two days."

We sat in silence for a moment. It was a comfortable silence, the kind of stillness that only happens when two people are in sync with each other.

But one of them was leaving to go home to his wife.

Man, my luck *sucked*.

I pulled my hands out of his grasp and placed them on my lap, knotting my fingers together. "Well, thanks for telling me. I mean, you did tell me before I fell madly in love with you"—*but not before I started lying*—"and you could have waited until after, that is, after things happened."

He lowered his gaze. "I was tempted."

"Look, things can't be different. We both know that. But we can stay in touch—can't we? You're not so honorable you can't e-mail me once in a while, are you? And Aidan would love to hear from you, too."

He gave me a sly smile. "That was a mean trick, bringing Aidan up. Of course I will. And, if you ever get to England—"

"I won't. Not anytime soon."

He drew a deep breath. "Well, then. E-mail it is." He handed me his business card. It looked like him: clean, neat, professional, totally in control. I tucked it into my purse and scribbled mine on an old receipt.

He checked his watch. "I have to get going back to the hotel. Simon's left some papers for me to go over before Thursday."

He walked me back home, holding my arm the way he'd done that first time. It was too soon when we arrived back at my apartment building. He walked me up the steps, then waited until I had my keys out.

"Good-bye."

I kissed him. Quick and hard on the mouth so he wouldn't have time to react. I stuck my key in the lock and flew upstairs, feeling my heart about to break.

• • •

"Mommy!"

I heard Aidan's feet scurrying down the hallway and he barreled into me just after I checked my watch: 10:07.

"What are you still doing up?"

"It's my fault. Aidan begged so he could—well, he can tell you." Mom beamed at him.

"Mommy, come here, I've got something to show you." Aidan took my arm and dragged me toward the living room. "Cover your eyes." I held my hands over my eyes, peeking out between my fingers just to make sure I wasn't going to trip.

Aidan ran ahead of me to his art table. "Sit down, Mommy."

I plopped down in the nearest chair. "Can I open my eyes yet?"

"Not yet." He grabbed something and dragged it over to me. "Now you can."

It was a huge cardboard box he'd decorated with markers, paint, and buttons from my button box. A large green animal was painted on the side with huge writing on top. Aidan hadn't quite mastered writing the English language, so I cleared my throat gingerly.

"Does it say 'Dragon Transportation'?"

Aidan scowled. Apparently not. "No, it's 'Dragon Transformation,'" he said. "Can't you read?" he added, obvious scorn dripping from his voice.

"Oh, of course. Dragon Transformation. And this box . . ."

"Transforms dragons!" He turned the box so I could see the other side, which featured a particularly gruesome dragon with blood dripping from its massive teeth. "See, the box goes on the dragon's head, and in just a few minutes, the nastiness is gone. See?" He flipped the box back around to show the same dragon, sans blood, wearing a beatific expression.

"That's great, Aidan. Really creative."

"And we can *charge* people for it so we can make money."

"Wow." I looked at Aidan's beaming face and smiled. "That's great. I bet all those mean-dragon-owning people will be thrilled."

"Mommy." Aidan's voice had that "you don't understand" tone to it. "We will make money, I know you're worried about it. I heard you and Grandma talking. And then we can get that Power Ranger, too."

"Oh." My heart leapt into my throat and I reached forward to enfold him in my arms. "Sweetie, we'll be okay. I promise." I kissed his head. "Thanks so much for doing something for our family. That's really thoughtful of you."

"I told him he could stay up to finish it," Mom said. "Such a sweet boy."

At least one good thing had come out of her problems: She'd gotten to spend time with Aidan, who adored her now more than he ever had.

I ruffled his hair. "Sure. But now it's *definitely* time for bed."

"Okay, but can I get that Power Ranger now?"

"Bed, Aidan."

"What about Beast?"

"Bed." He took one look at my face, then ran down the hall and threw himself under his comforter. Wise boy.

If only all the men in my life were so malleable.

Prunes and Prejudice

You don't like them—why? Because someone once told you something bad about them, and you're not even willing to give them the benefit of the doubt? You are, in fact, dead set against them, deciding to try raisins, figs, and, Lady Catherine help us, currants instead? Please. Our prune offering is a light, moist, utterly tasty prune bread, packed with walnuts worth at least £10,000 a year (okay, not really. But they're so crunchy!). Lavishly spread with cream cheese, this bread will make you realize everything you thought was true is not.

27

"I GOT THE LETTER YESTERDAY." I BOUNCED IN DR. LOWELL'S leather chair. "And I start the training in a month, and I start getting paid right away, during training, too."

"Very good, Molly. Congratulations!"

"And Mom said she'd stay until the fall—and I never thought I'd be glad to say that, actually, be happy my mother is living with me—but she's gonna take care of Aidan during the summer."

"And she'll move back home in September?" Her voice had a steely tone that reminded me just how much she knew about my mother.

"Yes. Finally." I exhaled. "She has enough to keep the house, and she got herself a part-time job at a Hallmark store. That and Social Security will pull her through until she sorts all the paperwork out."

I leaned back in the chair. "John and Lissa have been dating since my Freedom Party, and Lissa is so happy—John is head over heels. And Keisha gets married next summer, so I'm flying to California for it. I'm so happy for her."

"And what about *your* love life? Done anything you

wouldn't do in a million years lately?" Her eyes twinkled like she already knew the answer.

I laughed. "Yeah, well, Nick and I have been e-mailing."

"And?"

"And," I said slowly, "it looks as though he's gonna be coming back here for work."

"His wife?"

"They're getting divorced." The day he'd e-mailed me that, I'd dared to hope.

"And has he mentioned seeing you?" *If you mean seeing me writhing naked under him, yeah.*

"Mm-hm." She didn't need to know *everything* about my life. "We've both been pretty clear about wanting to explore a relationship."

She sat back and held her hands out, palms up. "There's nothing more I can do, then."

"What? You're dumping me?"

She chuckled. "Not exactly; I think you and I should see each other, just not as often."

"Is it a space issue?" I asked. "Am I crowding you?"

"I think," she said, meeting my eyes, "you are healthy. You have shown you can handle some pretty rough stuff, and you're doing great."

"Wow. I never thought I'd hear you say this." I shook my head. "I mean, remember the first time we met?"

"And you couldn't figure out how to tell your mother you were quitting your job to stay home with Aidan?"

"They just don't make telegrams the way they used to."

"You'll be fine, Molly. You've proven that."

"I guess so. I will survive," I said with a grin as I rose from the chair. "Thank you, Dr. Lowell."

"I didn't do anything you couldn't have done yourself, Molly."

And now I knew that, too.

The doorbell rang right around noon. The apartment was blessedly still—Aidan was with my mother for a week of preschool prep time in her newly rescued house. The hot, humid, fetid days of summer had ebbed a bit, and while fall hadn't exactly arrived, its smell was in the air.

I was so grateful that the summer—and the Teachers' Boot Camp—was over that I barely remembered that this time last year was around the time Hugh left.

I had just been making my lesson plans for my first month of school. I'd gotten lost in rereading *Pride and Prejudice*— gee, wonder why?—so was startled to hear the bell. Beast leapt from my lap and tore off into Aidan's room.

"Coming," I said, scooting down the hall. Who would be dropping by on a Saturday? "Hello?" I said through the intercom.

"It's me."

My breath whooshed out of me and I felt my knees weaken a little. I buzzed the front door, then opened up my apartment door and waited on the landing. I shouted down the stairwell, not even waiting for him to get up to the landing.

"You're here."

He loped up the last couple of steps and pulled me up against his chest, his scent immediately surrounding me. I sniffed it all in while my arms crept around his waist. Still holding me, he walked into my apartment and kicked the door closed.

"Finally."

I pulled away from him for a moment. Except for a little five o'clock shadow, he looked about the same as he had five months ago: thick black hair, devilish blue eyes, that chest, those lips . . . I spoke before I started drooling.

"But . . . *why* are you here?"

He cocked an eyebrow at me. "After the way you burned up my ISP with your sexy talk? Molly, I'm surprised you didn't see the smoke from London."

Okay, Mr. Deliberately Obtuse. "But you didn't tell me you were coming!"

He pulled me even tighter, if that was possible. "I didn't want to make any promises to you and Aidan I couldn't keep. I wanted to make sure Emma's father understood when I told him I was leaving, and then I needed to wrap stuff up there."

"So now *you're* the unemployed one? Does this mean you'll be a kept man?"

"If you'll keep me," he said, sweeping me into his arms for a kiss.

Yow. No deposit, no return, baby.

Hey, those romance novels do a pretty good job of describing passion, but not so good when it comes to all-encompassing lip and tongue concentration. Of course, it sounds really weird to say you feel as if your entire being is centered in your mouth, but that's how it felt.

The memory of Nick's kiss—the only one we'd ever had—

had grown in my brain so it had reached mythic proportions. Keisha had yelled at me to shut up when I repeatedly insisted on titling it "The Best Kiss Ever."

It wasn't. *This* one was. One arm held me around the waist and was already beginning a descent onto my hips. The other arm grasped me behind the head, his fingers slowly massaging the sensitive area behind my ear. His lips were soft, yet hard, in perfect romance novel opposition, while his tongue was slowly removing every single one of my inhibitions.

I was a living noodle.

When we finally emerged from our five-month libido release, it was sometime in the afternoon, and I was starving. Nick walked to the kitchen in his boxer briefs, and I watched him walk. A little sigh of satisfaction escaped my lips. I knew I was going to be eyeing that view a lot in the future. Heck, I'd only been waiting my whole life for someone like him.

He brought back a bag of animal crackers and two Diet Cokes. I put on his shirt and my underwear, and we went to the bedroom, where we perched on the bedspread and munched cookies and drank caffeine. Bliss.

"I know you really wanted a houseboy/sex slave, Molly, but I already have some leads. I'll be going on interviews for most of next week. You start school next Thursday, right?"

I nodded, chomping a lion's head off. "Yes. I'm nervous as hell, but I think it'll be okay. Lissa promised she'd come over Thursday night with some Junior's cheesecake, and Aidan is really excited he doesn't have to go to after-school after all. Thanks for the Power Ranger, by the way."

"No problem. He mentioned it in his last e-mail, remember?"

"And the one before that, and the one before that, and the one before that. I got tired of typing it."

He laughed as he leaned over to kiss me. "You and your son share the same ineffable sense of subtlety."

I whacked him on the arm. "What do you mean? I am totally discreet."

"Yeah, you only sniffed me all the time during our meetings and gave me these hungry doe-eyes—"

"Hungry doe-eyes? Does that mean I looked at you as if you were a salt lick or something?"

"Did someone say lick?" he asked, drawing his tongue over my throat.

"Nick's staying here?" Aidan's voice squeaked in excitement. He'd just gotten home, laden with books unearthed from my mother's attic. Now he only had to learn how to read.

"Yes, he'll be here for, for a while." It was sudden, but we'd come to know each other over e-mail, and he'd look for his own place when he landed a job.

"Wow." And then, "Does Dad know?"

"Yes." He wasn't happy about it, but he was in no position to say anything. My lawyer had done everything but nail him to the wall, and he owed me. Big time. Plus ever since Sylvia dumped him, he'd been chasing after anything with blond hair, including Lissa. And no, she *wasn't* that dumb. Besides, she and John were seeing each other. She was teaching him about literature, of all things.

"Can he stay in my room?"

"Um . . . well—"

Aidan frowned. "Nah, maybe not, because Smoochy

won't like it." Smoochy was the stuffed lizard he'd bought at the Museum of Natural History. Thank goodness for Smoochy's idiosyncratic desires, or I'd have to explain the concept of "cohabitation" to my son. Not a pretty sight.

"And he'll eat dinner with us, and hang out, and play games?"

"Yup."

"Cool, Mom." He looked at me with dawning admiration in his eyes. I had to say, that admiration was in my own eyes when I gazed at my reflection.

After Aidan had eaten dinner and he'd gone to bed surprisingly obligingly—probably so he could explain his new roommate to Smoochy—I started to try to clean up the mess I'd made when making up my curriculum. It was hard to work when the Smartest, Handsomest Guy in the World kept wanting you to stop working so he could make love to you.

As I was straightening, I found my scrapbook project. Banded in black lace, with black construction paper and written in silver ink, it was as glaringly self-absorbed as I'd intended. I leafed through the pages, laughing as I saw my work.

It felt good to laugh. Heck, *I* felt good. I shoved the book into my overcrowded bookshelf and finished putting stuff into piles. Then I walked to the kitchen and pulled out a bottle of white wine from the fridge. It was supposed to be "lemony with a strong finish," whatever that meant. It sounded like we'd be drinking furniture polish.

I grabbed two wineglasses from the cabinet and went back to the living room. After turning off a few lights, I lit some candles, fluffed a pillow or two, and waited.

He got home around nine. He'd been out with a few business associates, people who were now eager to hire him, and I knew he'd be tired. After all, he'd been working nights for me. Heh, heh.

"Honey?"

"In here."

He came in, dropped his briefcase, and pulled me up into his arms. "God, I missed you."

"You've only been here a few days, how can you miss me already?" I said, smiling up at him. His only response was to kiss me.

"Oh. That's how," I said when I could breathe again.

"How was your talk with Aidan?" Nick's concern for my son's happiness moved me even more than his feelings for me.

"Fine. Great, actually. You were spared having to share Aidan's room because Smoochy wouldn't like it."

"Thank God for Smoochy," he said in a tone of heartfelt relief.

We sat down on the sofa and drank wine. I talked over my curriculum plans with him, and he told me about his meetings. The conversation was boring, routine, and ridiculously wonderful.

As I glanced over at him, I felt a thrum of happiness beat in my chest. It wasn't that Nick and I were together—although that was pretty nice—it was that I had survived the past year, and done it all by myself. Well, with a lot of help.

I was stronger, more confident, and happy.

I *did* survive. What's more, I'd grown as a person, discovered what was really important to me, and realized I was smarter than I thought.

I'd suffered Self-Esteem Lows, and Mothering Heights.

And no matter what life threw at me from here on in, I vowed
as I sipped my wine, I will survive.

> *How do I love pastries? Let me count the ways.*
> *I love cream for the depth and breadth and height*
> *The dairy can reach, when feeling out of sorts,*
> *For the return of calm Being and ideal Grace.*
> *I love chocolate to invoke the level of every day's*
> *Most quiet need, by sugar and cocoa bean.*
> *I love cake freely, as chefs strive for the light,*
> *I love crème brûlée purely, and want to graze*
>   *its crust of glaze.*
> *I love donuts with the passion put to use*
> *In my old memories, and with my childhood's faith.*
> *I love cookies with a love I seemed to lose*
> *With my lost carbohydrates!—I love thee with the bread,*
> *Muffins, éclairs, of all my life!—and, if I choose,*
> *I shall but love pastries better than shoes.*

RECIPES FROM

Vanity Fare

Recipes courtesy of
Emily Isaac
of Trois Pommes Patisserie
(troispommespatisserie.com).

Much Ado About Muffins

MAKES A DOZEN MUFFINS.

    1 stick unsalted butter (room temperature)
    1 cup granulated sugar
    2 whole eggs
    ½ teaspoon vanilla extract
    2 cups all-purpose flour
    2 teaspoons baking powder
    ¼ teaspoon salt
    ½ cup milk
    ¼ cup dried cranberries
    ¼ cup chocolate chips
    ¼ cups chopped walnuts

For the crumb topping:
    1 cup flour
    ⅓ cup dark brown sugar
    ¼ cup granulated sugar
    1 teaspoon cinnamon
    ¼ teaspoon salt
    2 ounces (one half stick) melted unsalted butter
    2 tablespoons chopped pecans

Are the chocolate chips paired with the flour here? Or maybe they're with the dried cranberries? And what about the walnuts? They seem to have an eye toward overthrowing the pecans. There's a superfluity of ingredients here, all changing partners as quickly as you change your mind.

But once you taste this muffin, you'll never switch again.

1. Preheat the oven to 350°F. Prepare a 12-cup muffin pan with paper liners.

2. In the bowl of a standing mixer using a paddle attachment, cream together the butter and sugar until light in color and fluffy in texture.

3. Slowly add the eggs one at a time, scraping down the bowl after each addition. Add the vanilla extract.

4. Sift together the flour, baking powder, and salt. Add one cup of the dry ingredients and ¼ cup of the milk to the sugar mixture. Then add the rest of the dry ingredients followed by the other ¼ cup of milk, being careful to scrape down the bowl once again to ensure that all of the ingredients are well combined.

5. Add the cranberries, chocolate chips, and walnuts and mix.

6. Spoon the muffin mixture into the prepared muffin pan and top with the crumb topping. Bake about half an hour, until the muffins start to brown, are firm to the touch, and a knife comes out clean when you insert it. Allow the muffins to cool for 10 to 15 minutes before serving.

7. Crumb Topping: Combine all the dry ingredients in a mixing bowl. Slowly add the melted butter while mixing with a wooden spoon or your hands. Add the pecans at the end.

Tart of Darkness

MAKES 6 TO 8 SERVINGS.

For the chocolate tart dough:
- 1 stick unsalted butter
- ½ cup powdered sugar
- 2 eggs
- 1 teaspoon vanilla extract
- 1 ¼ cups flour
- ¼ cup cocoa powder
- ½ cup salted peanuts or other groundnuts

For the chocolate ganache:
- ¾ cup heavy cream
- 1 tablespoon unsalted butter
- 1 tablespoon sugar
- 8 ounces high-quality bittersweet chocolate
- 1 tablespoon white rum

Obscure, faintly dangerous ingredients—Belgian chocolate, white rum, African groundnuts—combine in a swirl of flavor, topped off with a heady adventure of whipped cream. Delicious, delectable, and almost completely inscrutable, this tart reveals your most secret desires. And if Kurtz had been able to savor this, who knows how the story would have ended?

1. In the bowl of a standing mixer, cream the butter and sugar until light in color and fluffy in texture.

2. Add the eggs and the vanilla extract.

3. Sift together the flour and the cocoa powder and add to the bowl.

4. Form the dough into a ball, wrap in plastic wrap, and allow to chill in the refrigerator for one hour.

5. Spray a 7-inch tart pan that has a removable bottom.

6. Place the chilled dough between two pieces of wax or parchment paper and using a rolling pin roll into a 10-inch disk. Peel off the top layer of paper and drop the dough inside the prepared tart ring. Press down on the dough, removing the other layer of paper. Using your fingers, press the dough into the tart pan, removing any excess dough. Place the tart pan in the freezer for at least 30 minutes.

7. Bake the tart shell in 325°F oven for about 20 minutes, until firm. Allow to cool for half an hour.

8. Sprinkle half of the salted peanuts on the bottom of the tart shell. Pour the ganache into the shell and sprinkle the other half of the peanuts on the top. Allow to chill for about half an hour. Serve with whipped cream.

9. Chocolate Ganache: Combine the cream, butter, and sugar in a pot and bring to a boil. Break apart the chocolate in a bowl. Slowly pour the cream mixture over the chocolate and allow to sit for 5 minutes. Whisk together, adding the rum, until creamy and well combined.

Gravity's Rainbow Cookies

MAKES 32 COOKIES.

4 ounces almond paste
1 stick (4 ounces) soft butter
1 cup sugar
3 eggs
3 teaspoons almond extract
1 cup flour
¼ teaspoon baking powder
pinch of salt
green and red food coloring
¼ cup raspberry jam
¼ cup apricot jam

For the chocolate glaze:
4 ounces chocolate
1 stick butter
1 tablespoon light corn syrup
2 tablespoons water

Is it possible for a cookie, a mere dessert, to achieve an altered state of consciousness? Pynch yourself. It is. Marzipan, food coloring, almond extract, raspberry jam, and chocolate chips blend into a splendid mishmash of flavors, very confusing but ultimately completely satisfying. Rainbow nonpareils top the cookie, which is a nonpareil in itself.

1. Preheat the oven to 325°F. Prepare three 11-by-7 brownie pans by spraying with vegetable spray and lining with parchment paper.

2. In a standing mixer, cream together the almond paste, butter, and sugar until fluffy and light in color. Add the eggs, one at a time, scraping down the bowl after each egg is added. Add the vanilla extract.

3. Sift together the dry ingredients and add to the sugar mixture. Mix until well combined.

4. Divide the batter into three bowls. Add a few drops of green food coloring to one bowl and a few drops of red food coloring to the other. Leave one bowl of batter white.

5. Pour the batter into the prepared pans. Bake until firm, about 5 minutes.

6. Allow to cool completely before continuing.

7. Place the red layer on a plate and cover with raspberry jam. Place the white layer on top and cover with the apricot jam, and then place the green layer on top. Freeze for at least one hour.

8. Remove the cake from the freezer and cut into four equal strips. Pour the chocolate glaze over each strip, being careful to cover the sides. Put back in the freezer for another half hour until the glaze sets. Cut into 2-inch slices and serve.

9. Chocolate Glaze: Combine the chocolate, butter, corn syrup, and water. Whisk together over hot water bath until smooth. Remove from heat and allow to cool for about half an hour before glazing the cake strips.

Lord of the Tea Rings

MAKES ONE 6-INCH CAKE. SERVES 4 TO 6.

2 sticks unsalted butter

½ cup sugar

scrapings of ½ vanilla bean

4 eggs

2 cups flour

2 teaspoons baking powder

½ teaspoon salt

powdered sugar

It's a world far removed from ours. A world where magical creatures hunt for the ultimate dessert ring, the dessert that will bestow power on whoever eats it. Our hunt has culminated in this rich, vanilla-scented cake, perfect for long days and nights on the road to Middle Earth.

1. Preheat the oven to 325°F.

2. Prepare a 6-inch cake pan by spraying it with vegetable spray and then placing a circle of parchment paper on the bottom and spraying it again.

3. In a standing mixer, combine the butter, sugar, and vanilla bean and, using the paddle attachment, beat until light in color and fluffy in texture.

4. Add the eggs one at a time, scraping the bottom of the bowl after each addition.

5. Sift together the flour, baking powder, and salt and add to the bowl. Pour the batter into the prepared cake pan.

6. Bake until browned and a knife comes out clean when inserted, about 20 minutes. Allow the cake to cool for about half an hour. Unmold and sprinkle with powdered sugar. Serve at room temperature with a cup of tea.

Dorothy Parker House Rolls

MAKES 12 ROLLS.

3 cups cottage cheese

1 tablespoon sugar

3 tablespoons onion, chopped and sauteed

1 tablespoon soft butter

⅛ teaspoon baking soda

2 whole eggs

1 package dry yeast

4 cups flour

1 teaspoon salt

1 tablespoon chopped fresh sage

1 egg, for brushing

You'd bet this has got a bite to it—and you'd be right. Tangy, dry, and ever so slightly bitter, this by-no-means meek breadstuff is something to eat when you're ready to take a chomp out of the Big Apple. It's better in short (story) bites, but one taste of this sage-and-onion roll and you'll be ready to take your place at the Algonquin Table. (We'd say the head of the table, but the table is round, dear, *round*!)

1. Preheat the oven to 350°F.

2. In a mixing bowl, whisk together the cottage cheese, sugar, onion, butter, baking soda, and eggs.

3. In a separate bowl, mix together the yeast and 3 tablespoons water.

4. Place the flour and salt in the bowl of a standing mixer, using the dough hook. Slowly add the yeast mixture and then the cottage cheese mixture. Add the chopped sage. Knead the dough until it is smooth and forms a ball. You may need to add a bit more flour.

5. Place the dough in a bowl covered with plastic wrap and let sit in a warm area until it rises about 50 percent. Punch it down and form into 12 balls. Brush with the egg and allow to rise again.

6. Bake until very brown and puffy, about 20 minutes. Allow to cool for at least 20 minutes before eating.

HERO OF MY HEART
Megan Frampton

In this emotional and powerfully erotic tale of love and redemption, a tender vicar's daughter and a tortured war hero discover that sin may be their only salvation.

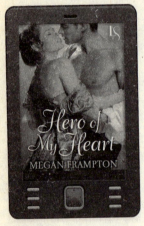

When Mary Smith's corrupt, debt-ridden brother drags her to a seedy pub to sell her virtue to the highest bidder, Alasdair Thornham leaps to the rescue. Of course the marquess is far from perfect husband material: Alasdair is too fond of opium, and prefers delirium to reality. Still, Alasdair has come to her aid, and now she intends to return the favor. She will show him that he is not evil, just troubled—and exceedingly handsome, with his perfect, strong body, chiseled jaw, and piercing green eyes.

Mary was a damsel in need of a hero, but Alasdair's plan is shortsighted. He never foresaw her desire to save him from himself. Alasdair is quite at home in his private torment, until this angel proves that a heart still beats in his broken soul. The devil may have kept her from hell, but will Mary's good intentions lead them back to the brink—or to heaven in each other's arms?

MEGAN FRAMPTON majored in English literature at Barnard College with a double minor in political science and religion. She worked in the music industry for fifteen years, editing and writing music reviews for a music industry trade magazine, eventually becoming the editor in chief. Megan married one of her former interns and lives in Brooklyn, New York, with him and her son. When she's not writing, she's the Community Manager for the romance novel website Heroes and Heartbreakers.

LOVE **LS** SWEPT

Love stories you'll never forget by authors you'll always remember.

www.RandomHouse.com